NO COMMITMENTS

A NOVEL

VAL SHARP

www.TheLaValleCollection.com.

ISBN: 0615634524
ISBN 13: 9780615634524

CONTENTS

PROLOGUE

Clay got up a little unsteadily. He ambled over to the edge of the terrace and looked out over the valley. The air was shimmering from the dry, furnace-hot heat of the sirocco. "It's hot, he said. "Fires are breaking out in the pines again. If we don't get some rain soon, this whole mountain may go up in smoke. I'm not even sure I'll be able to get down the road to the airport in the morning."

"That would be fantastic!" Marianna said, as she walked over beside him, slipped under his arm, and gave him a little squeeze around his waist. "We could spend the whole day in bed, just like we used to in Cagnes. Remember?" He looked down at her with a smile that told her that he loved her. "You do remember those days in Cagnes, don't you Clay; our squalid little flat; you tending bar and hustling your ass off for a lousy couple a hundred francs a week? We were happy then. Everything was so simple. Life was fun. I don't know how we let ourselves get so messed up. Or why things have to be so complicated. It seems so much has happened these past few years I can hardly remember how it all began."

He looked out over the valley again. Out ahead of him, as far as he could see, the grain fields were scorched and yellow. Below him the pine trees were smoldering and burning their way toward the range of mountains far off to his left. He looked toward the jutting peninsula of Antibes, only faintly visible in the haze, and he pointed beyond, toward Nice and the sea. "It began right out there," he said quietly. "Remember…I was low on gas and had to land? It'll be five years ago tomorrow – Bastille Day."

PART ONE

Love really has nothing to do with wisdom or experience or logic. It is the prevailing breeze in the land of youth.

---Bruno Lessing

I

❀

NICE

Lieutenant Junior Grade Clay Stoner was committing one of flying's many, sometimes fatal, errors; letting his mind wander. His F-4 Phantom jet fighter was slicing through feathery cirrus clouds, wings banked in a gentle turn that imitated to near perfection the lone, lazy grace of a gull. He was circling in a holding pattern twenty thousand feet above the misty sun-drenched Mediterranean, somewhere off the south coast of France. But his mind was five thousand miles away, nestled in the wooded hills of the Ozarks - the virgin lakes; the cypress swamp; the winding, gurgling creeks that once had formed the boundary of his universe.

A glint of sun off his visor triggered a sixth sense that alerted him. He scanned his instruments. "Hey, Victor! How far are we from Nice?" he barked over the intercom.

"About a hundred miles," came an instant response from Vic Powers, the radar officer in the back seat.

"Give Control another call. Tell 'em fuel's down to twenty minutes. If the deck's not clear in three, tell 'em we're gonna bingo for the beach."

The F-4 made one more turn around the holding pattern while Vic radioed the aircraft carrier steaming four miles directly below them. Clay monitored the reply. "Bad Dog Two, this is Champion. Emergency still in progress. Deck is still fouled. Expected time before you can be recovered is fifteen minutes. I repeat! Fifteen minutes. Control requests that you continue to hold. Acknowledge. Over."

Clay flipped the F-4 out of its thirty-degree banked turn and set it on a course in the general direction of Nice. "Give me a heading to Cote d'Azur and tell Control we're diverting for fuel."

"The Commander won't like it," Vic cautioned.

Clay cut him off. "I know. But it won't be his ass down there swimming with us in the drink if we run out of gas. Call Control and tell 'em we're on our way to Nice."

They were in sight of the coast within minutes. Vic radioed the tower at Cote d'Azur, requested a straight-in approach, and they came skimming in over the beach and palm trees and touched down with less than four minutes of fuel remaining. The landing was fast, and when Clay tapped the foot pedals, they sank all the way to the floor. "Holy shit! No brakes!" he shouted. He banked the nose of the F-4 in the air, letting the resistance of the wind against its belly slow them to sixty knots before he eased the nose wheel back to the pavement and gently applied the parking brake. They rolled to a stop a scant two hundred feet from the end of the long runway, climbed out of the aircraft and were examining its smoldering brakes when the crash trucks arrived.

The F-4 was towed to a maintenance hangar. Half an hour later the chief mechanic explained the problem to them. "The hydraulic line must be replaced, Messieurs," the old French mechanic said, shrugging in a lackadaisical way. "It will take at least two days."

The two aviators looked at each other, eyes crinkling, each restraining an impulse to laugh. Words did not need to pass between them. A team since flight training, they had learned to read each other's eyes. Clay's were pale blue, steady, almost unfathomable; but Vic had learned to detect the tiniest flicks that reflected the oft-changing moods. By contrast, Vic's eyes were dark, framed with black, bushy eyebrows that conveyed his every feeling: blazing when he was angry, glossing over when he was sad, sparkling when he was happy. They sparkled most of the time because Vic was an open and happy person - except for a time during his early days at Pensacola when his eyes caused him to fail the depth perception test, and he learned he could never be a navy pilot. The two of them went out drinking that night, and their friendship was formed as Clay watched him sobbing over a beer at a bar.

They had been classmates at Annapolis, but other than that had little in common. Vic was the son of a three-star admiral and had prepped to go to the Academy all his life. He arrived already well known to many of his classmates and attacked the Annapolis regimen with the eagerness and intensity inherent in his character. Short, but tough, he wrestled welterweight and was a star of the Academy team. And because of his wholesome goodness, he was elected president of the class. The eye test at Pensacola was the first and only time he had failed in life at anything.

By contrast, Clay had never anticipated going to the Academy. His mother had bull-dozed him into applying, even though knowing that no one from their rural Ozark county had ever been appointed - and neither was he through the normal congressional process. But he was fast and could catch a pass, and unbeknownst to him that fact wasn't lost on the navy. So it came as a complete surprise when, two weeks after graduating from high school, he received a telegram from the Secretary of the Navy informing him that the alumni association had arranged a third alternate appointment from a congressman he had never heard of in Pennsylvania, a step that technically enabled the Secretary to offer him an appointment to fill out the class. Two weeks later he was a Midshipman.

In less than two years he managed to overcome his Ozark accent, no longer saying "cain't" instead of "can't", "fark" instead of "fork", or "ruff' instead of "roof". After that he had taken Annapolis in stride, earning his varsity letter as a flanker back on passing downs and managing through the academics with reasonable ease. But he had never taken the navy or the program seriously, like Vic. So it was odd they had become such close friends. After the night in Pensacola, Vic went on to become a radar intercept officer, or RIO as they were called, and Clay to earn his aviator's wings. They requested the same squadron, which was granted, and they stopped off in Washington just long enough for Vic to marry Darcy Ashton, the socialite daughter of a prominent United States Senator from Maryland horse country, before reporting to their first duty assignment at NAS Oceana, in Virginia Beach, Virginia. Now they were five months into their first cruise, and Clay knew that Darcy had been following Vic around the Mediterranean, meeting him for a few days whenever the ship put into port. He also knew the ship had been at sea for more than a month now, and that in between ports Darcy was staying in a tiny hilltop village, an artist's colony called Haut-de-Cagnes, less than a half-hour's drive from the Cote d' Azur aerodrome in Nice.

Clay slapped Vic on the shoulder and winked. "So what are you waiting for ole buddy? Get going and hit the road. I can take care of things here."

Vic needed no further encouragement. He started jogging across the tarmac toward the pilots' lounge. Halfway across, he slowed momentarily and shouted over his shoulder. "Hey! Meet us tonight at the Gorilla Club. About twelve o'clock!" Clay waved a hand in acknowledgment. Then, alone, he strode across the apron and climbed the steps to the control tower. He drafted a message to send to the ship describing the aircraft's status. As he drafted it, he could picture the Commander's reaction. The old man would be pissed, no doubt. Then he noticed the date on the radiogram, and a thin smile formed at the corner of his mouth. The date was July 13, 1965. He was going to be ashore in Nice on Bastille Day.

Clay walked into the Gorilla Club right at midnight. He and Vic had been there once before when their ship had put into Ville-franche for a few days, and they had enjoyed it. At street level the Gorilla looked like any ordinary French café and bar. Upstairs, though, were rooms housing prostitutes, and downstairs in the cellar was a club with a dance floor, piped-in stereo music and a bongo player. Clay was greeted at the cellar door by a French Alge-rian hostess, a dark-looking pied noir draped in a flowing orange robe of thin mesh, slit on one side up to her waist that gave fleeting glimpses of her flanks as she guided him down to the club and a table near the back wall. He sat down, ordered a scotch, and sur-veyed the room: noisy; smoky; tables made of brass and aleppo pine only two feet high; no chairs, just cushions scattered around on the floor. He saw quickly that Vic had not arrived. Then his eyes were drawn to a fascinating girl at the adjacent table.

She was dressed in the typical attire of the French girls who came to Nice on holiday - white hip-huggers cut below the navel, a blue denim shirt stretched across her bosom fastened by only two buttons, its tails knotted around her rib cage. She was slender, of medium height, and her hair was dark blonde and streaked the color of straw by the sun - and it was curly, with hundreds of tiny ringlets that bounced each time she laughed; she seemed to laugh constantly. She kept brushing the ringlets from her face as if it were a nervous habit, and in the dim light one could not tell her age - only that she had an aura of class that singled her out as differ-ent. Clay studied her as she sat perched on a pillow, barefoot, legs tucked under, her head erect and tossed back with an air of amused detachment as she moved to the beat of the bongos. He observed her fine hands, her high cheekbones, her perfectly straight pointed nose that tilted slightly upward at the end, and her arched eye-brows, plucked with an expertise that accentuated the mahogany-like darkness of her eyes. He caught her eye and smiled. She turned her head away and started twittering in French with her escort, tall and slender, wearing jeans and a long-sleeved buttoned down white shirt, black hair down almost to his shoulders but tanned and handsome with an aquiline nose that was difficult to distinguish between Gallic and Greek, youngish-looking, almost too young to be in a place like the Gorilla. Clay drained his scotch, ordered another and scanned the room again. The next time he looked at her table, she was alone. He hesitated a moment, then leaned over toward her with an unlighted cigarette in his hand. "Pardon, Mademoiselle. Avez vous du feu?" he said in stumbling French, as he made the motion of striking an imaginary match and holding it to the tip of the cigarette. Expressionless, she offered him a lighter. He set it on the table and smiled at her, gesturing awkwardly toward the dance floor. "Dansez vous avec moi?"

"Pourquoi pas," she replied with a curt nod.

They danced one dance, a slow one, long enough for her to make him believe she did not speak a word of English. When the number ended, she turned quickly and returned to the table. Her young companion had reappeared and was sprawled on his back across a cushion, smoking intensely and exhaling giant wide rings that wafted slowly toward the ceiling. He sat upright as they approached and quipped in very plain English. "Some sister! I leave for two minutes, come back, and you've already hooked up."

Clay turned toward the girl, surprised. "You're not French?"

"Mais oui," she said, and she flashed a mischievous smile. "But I'm also Swiss - and also an American. And you looked so American I just could not resist stringing you along."

"Oh, really!" Clay stared at her, his eyes turning cold. Another young tease who was full of herself. He had met them before and felt stupid for not recognizing this one, for allowing her to make a dupe of him on the dance floor. He had sized her up all wrong. At first glance she had not looked like that kind of girl.

The harshness in his eyes jolted her and she looked at him for the first time with more than a smattering of interest. What she saw was a lithe, athletic looking, dishwater blond with close cropped hair, about six feet tall, who would be attractive to most women. He's probably not a bad Joe, she thought. She reached out and touched his hand. "I'm sorry," she said gently. "Why don't you join us. My name's Marianna and this is my brother Robert. We just came down to Nice for the weekend to see one of my old room-mates from boarding school."

They sat down on the cushions together. He started asking her about herself, then, and before long she was talking freely. She told him as much as she dared. She and Robert were attending summer school at the University of Grenoble, in the Alps, about six hours north of Nice. Their parents lived in Greenwich, Connecticut, and they were both going back to New York in the fall, she to finish her Masters at the Juilliard School, Robert to start his freshman year at Columbia.

A shout railed across the club just then, piercing the noisy clat-ter. "Marianna!" Marianna's head whipped around, and Clay fol-lowed her eyes toward the entrance. Vic and Darcy were standing in the doorway on their tiptoes, waving at them across the throng of heads bobbing on the dance floor. "Marianna!" Darcy shouted again.

"Darcy!" Marianna cried out, and she leaped from the table and started pushing her way through the crowd. The two girls hugged each other, kissing cheeks all the way back to the table.

As Clay stood, Darcy turned to Marianna. "Well, I see you've already met Clay Stoner."

Marianna was bewildered. "You know this guy?"

"Sure. Clay was Vic's best man at our wedding."

Minutes later the five of them were crowded around two tables pushed together, lounging on pillows and guzzling orange juice and vodka out of tall glasses. Darcy and Marianna began chatter-ing like two excited chinchillas about their boarding school days in Switzerland. Left ignored, Vic and Clay turned to their usual topic of conversation - flying. And with a young, avid Robert as their enraptured listener, they started describing to him the differences between loops, immelmanns, and half-cuban eights, and what g-forces were like on a cat-shot or when hitting afterburner to blast through mach one. But Clay could not help overhearing the girls' conversation; their giggling about their old girl friends, playing tag and leapfrog, climbing trees; an Austrian prince they had kissed in the cornfield that separated the boys' part of the school from that of the girls'.

Vic interrupted. "What's this bull about making out in a corn field." he yelped, feigning indignation.

"Oh, come off it, Vic," Darcy scolded him. "You know it was all perfectly innocent. And that was Marianna's first kiss ever. She was so naive and sheltered she thought she was in love with her cousin. The prep school boys at Le Rosey used to call her Pollyanna instead of Marianna."

Clay winked. "I'll bet no one calls you that now," he said teasingly.

"I don't know, do they?" she said and shrugged. And then she turned away from all of them, and an icy stillness settled over her. *Damn Darcy!* Did she have to bring Jean Pierre up in front of him, she thought, as she started remembering again all the summers she and Jean Pierre had spent together in Tregastel, the little fishing village on the tip of Brittany where his parents had a summer house and she and her mother would spend six weeks vacationing with the French part of the family. Tregastel - the rugged little village overlooking a harbor carved into rocky cliffs along the English Channel. It was windy there, even in summer; the water was cold, and the sky overcast most of the time. But for her, between the ages of ten and sixteen, Tregastel had been Mecca, a perfectly natural, unspoiled place that she would dream about for ten months each year while she was waiting for her summer rendezvous with Jean Pierre - the lazy days they would spend sailing in the harbor, building sand castles on the beach, hiking the cliffs along the coast in their rope-soled espadrilles. Jean Pierre was her general, commanding her to follow as he leaped from rock to rock, offering his hand when she needed it, telling her when she could stop and rest. Invariably he would discover some new place to spread a blanket, a spot with an awesome view of the sea where they would sit and talk for hours about art, music, virtue, ideals, integrity, values, self-respect. She had accepted all his opinions and made them her own, and each summer when they parted they had vowed to each other that they would never allow themselves to become mediocre.

Marianna's mind wanderings were interrupted by the sound of Darcy pounding her glass on the table, commanding everyone's attention. Clay raised himself from his prone position on the cushions, and Vic and Robert cut off the talk about flying. They all waited for what Darcy had to say, but she just sat there for awhile, looking calm and serene, her wavy black curls hanging down over her warm, kind face, green eyes twinkling, as she let the suspense mount. "Okay - I've been waiting all day to let all of you in on my secret. I am going to have a *baby!*" she stated finally, staring at Vic and waiting for his reaction.

Vic was too stunned to say much. He just sat there, grinning proudly, leaving it up to Clay to order champagne and keep it flowing. Four o'clock and closing time came sooner than they realized. Robert had long since departed, and outside the club, Vic and Darcy offered Marianna a ride to her hotel.

"I'd just as soon walk," she said quickly. "I can use the fresh air."

"I think I'll walk too," Clay said.

After a flurry of hugs and kisses they split up, and Marianna and Clay started walking slowly up the Avenue Victor Hugo. Another couple passed, their arms around each other's waists, walking up the street in a hurry. The couple turned at the corner, and then the street was empty. "I guess you haven't seen Darcy in quite awhile," Clay said after they had gone two blocks.

"No. We sort of lost touch after boarding school. I went to college out in the mid-west for two years. She went to Georgetown. The last time I saw her was in New York during Christmas, my second year in college. We had our coming out together at the International Debutantes Ball at the Waldorf. Her parents had just divorced, and her mother didn't come. She was off in the Caribbean someplace with a big-shot new husband whom Darcy had never even met, so Darcy and her father came and stayed at my parents' house out in Greenwich for a few days. Then junior year I transferred to Juilliard, and she moved to Paris to study art at the Sorbonne. Somehow our paths haven't crossed since. Have you known her long?"

"Just since her wedding. Too bad you couldn't make it. It was a ball too."

"I...I heard," she said, a strange shakiness in her voice. "She asked me to be maid of honor, but...but I just couldn't...that's why I was so happy to see her tonight, see that she was still the same old Darse, and meet Vic. He seems to be a fantastic person, so straight and clean cut and everything."

"Yes, Vic is special all right. I trust him with my life almost every day."

"Tell me about flying. Isn't it terribly dangerous?"

"Sometimes, maybe," he said, and his eyes flickered. "But let's not talk about flying. I'm much more interested in you and what it was like being a debutante? I guess I should be impressed?"

She laughed. "I would think you should be," she said with a quick, practiced shrug of her shoulders. "Not just anyone can be a debutante, you know." She reached over and grabbed his arm and leaned against him and laughed again to show him she was making light of her answer. "Actually it was kind of fun," she said seriously. "Especially the Ball at the Waldorf. It was a heck of a party." They reached a corner, and turned, and started walking down a side street.

Actually the ball was a goddamn bore, she thought. I wouldn't remember it at all if it weren't for the fact that was the night I first met Douglas Franklin Threadgill the Third. Good old Douglas. Pompous and pedigreed enough to suit even my father.

They had walked three blocks down the side street, none of it too soberly. They were away from the major avenues now, and it was soon apparent that Marianna was lost. Complicating matters, she had even forgotten the name of her hotel. They started walking faster, and the more streets they wandered down the more she became flustered. They ended up an hour later back on the Avenue Victor Hugo just as the sky was starting to turn grey. They stopped to rest on one of the green benches lining the curb of the broad, tree-lined avenue and watched as two water trucks rolled by, spraying the pavement. Trailing behind them was a gang of silent men in tatters, toting palm fronds that they were using to sweep away the dampened grime. As they passed, one of the men stepped over to the curb and offered Marianna a rose. The man was old and dingy, and the rose was wilted, one he had obviously found in the street. Marianna accepted it graciously and weaved it slowly into her hair. She smiled and blew the old man a kiss, and he burst into a grin, a broad toothless one that showed his gums. Then, as if the incident had never occurred, he and the other sweepers who had stopped to watch all started swishing their brooms back and forth and shuffled off humbly down the Avenue in pursuit of the water trucks. After the men had gone, Marianna and Clay set out looking for her hotel again. At daybreak they turned down an alley they had bypassed several times before, and at the other end they found themselves in front of the Hotel Locarno. Marianna recognized it instantly, and pressed the outside buzzer to rouse the night clerk. In the lobby, Clay clasped his arms around her waist. "You know, I don't even know your last name," he sort of mumbled.

"It's Haizet," she said, dreading the proposition that she was sure was going to follow.

"A-zay...Mar-i-awna A-zay. That's a beautiful name," he said drowsily. "In the Ozarks they'd pronounce it like Mary Ann. But you pronounce it Mar - like in car. I like that...So tell me. Are you going to invite me up? Or do I have to invite myself?"

So there it was, the proposition she knew was coming. Her response was barb-like. "Sorry Mr. Navy Pilot," she said, wriggling from his grasp. "You have a lot to learn about debutantes. It's been fun, but not that much fun!" And with that, she whirled and rushed into the elevator before he could utter a word.

The night clerk muffled a chuckle as the elevator ascended out of sight toward an upper floor. Clay gave him a disgusted look. He turned and walked briskly out the door, and by the time he reached the street the encounter was over as far as he was concerned. She sure as hell isn't worth any more of my effort, he thought. She's just another stuck-up coed who doesn't know her ass about life. Might even be a goddamn virgin. He started walking in the direction of the Trocadero, the tiny cheap hotel near the train station where he had taken a room, and he thought instead about Cindy Sue, the darling, sweet first love of his youth. There had been a time when he considered her worth all the effort in the world.

Bastille Day dawned warm and sunny, and by early morning the beach was crowded. Not that this was unusual. Nice's soul is the beach, a gentle half moon arc that stretches for five miles, from Mont Boron, a three-hundred meter jagged promontory overlooking the old seaport at the eastern edge of the city, to the Cote d'Azur aerodrome situated on a flat spit of land jutting out into the sea at its western boundary. Rimming the beach the entire five miles is a white-washed, twelve-foot high seawall, along the top of which runs the Promenade des Anglais, a broad avenue lined with palm trees that buzzes from morning to night with mopeds and motorcycles darting in and out among honking automobiles and the throngs of pedestrians swarming back and forth across it from the promenade on one side to the majestic resort hotels on the other. It is an unusual beach, because it has no sand. It's piled high, instead, with millions of silver stones and pebbles honed silky smooth by the perpetual ebb and flow of the tides - and it's also unusual in the way wealth and poverty coexist side by side. Interspersed about every three hundred yards are private beaches - plages with names like Lido and Riviera and Tahiti that supply mattresses and lounge chairs on a sundeck, tables and umbrellas, and bars and cafes with waiters who scurry about at the beck and call of every oil-drenched sunbather who can afford the price of admission. In between each of these mini-resorts are the public beaches, and it is there that the local Nicois congregate. The mothers stop off in the morning en route home from the market on their mopeds. They leave their bikes parked at the top of the seawall with their saddlebags and knapsacks bulging with groceries and baguettes of bread while they stride down to the beach, strip off their peasant skirts, swim, and stretch out on a slab of flat rock for an hour or so, invariably topless and oblivious to everything and everyone around them. They are gone by noon, usually, and in the early afternoon their children come. And just like their mothers, they too shed their clothes deftly under the cover of a beach towel and slip on their bikinis with a natural grace that is admirable to behold. They come and shake hands all around very formally, lie on simple towels on the rocks, play some cards or volleyball or boules, then kiss each other good-bye and are gone in less than two hours. To them, the beach is so much a part of their lives that it is just a minor everyday diversion.

Clay had risen early and walked the entire length of the beach during the morning. About noon, as he was on his way back, he spotted Marianna. She was sitting with her back propped up against the seawall, reading a book and wearing a chartreuse bikini. He sauntered over and flopped down on her towel. "Hi fella'! Have a good night's sleep?" he said grinning.

She peered at him over the edge of the book. "It was fine, thank you, what little there was of it," she said icily, and she buried her face in the book again.

"No hard feelings about last night I hope."

"No. Why should there be?" she said without a glance.

"May I share your towel?"

"Be my guest," she said, and she moved to the far side and turned her back toward him.

He studied her body as she read. Its lushness captivated him gradually. Her stomach was flat and taut, hips lean and cola bottle shaped, thighs slender, ankles narrow. What infatuated him most, though, was the way she moved so naturally in the scanty bikini held together around her hips by two thin strings...and the two large dimples above her ass...and the tawny wisps of golden hair dangling from the crevices under her arms.

An hour passed, and then he asked her, "Is your book really that interesting?"

"It would be if someone would let me concentrate," Marianna said as she closed it and rolled over to meet him face to face.

Clay smiled. "That's better. Now, why don't you tell me about yourself? I'm curious."

"There's really not much to tell," she said blithely. "My father is from an old Swiss banking family, Banque Haizet, founded in Geneva before the turn of the century. You've probably never heard of it, but it's quite well known in private banking circles. Father and his brother worked there until they were in their late thirties. Then just before World War II, Grandfather sent them to open some branches abroad, the brother to London, father to New York. He met my mother there. She was from Paris, working as a sales representative for a French perfume company. To make a long story short, they married, and soon after I came along, then Robert. I was born in New York, which makes me an American citizen. As the daughter of a Swiss father, I'm Swiss; dual nationality; two passports. But I feel more French, because of my mother. Our family always spoke French at home. Is that enough to satisfy your curiosity?"

"Not really. What about you?"

"Well, I was raised in Manhattan until I was twelve. Then Grandfather died and Father was chosen to move back to Geneva to take over headquarters until his brother's son was deemed old enough to handle it. That took five years. During that time Robert and I were sent to boarding school not far from Geneva. I studied piano there and was told I had a talent, but other than French I didn't learn much else, except maybe how to do makeup and host an afternoon tea. By the time I finished boarding school Father had already moved back to New York and bought the house in Greenwich. Robert stayed to finish school at Le Rosey. Not knowing what I wanted to do, I enrolled in a small junior college out in Missouri, a girl's school called Stephens, because it had a very good music program. I was the solo pianist for the orchestra."

Clay burst out laughing. "Are you serious? You're a Susie? I didn't think you girls were allowed out in public without the proper hat, hose and high heels outfit."

She looked surprised. She had not met anyone familiar with that local reference to Stephens' coeds in a long time. "I see you've heard of Stephens," she said dryly.

"Oh, sure. I'm from Creekwood."

She gave him a blank stare. "I'm afraid I've never heard of it."

"You must have. Creekwood, Missouri! About two hundred miles south down near the Arkansas line. State high school football champs for five straight years back in the fifties. Slim Sparks' home town!"

"Slim Sparks?" she said, as if the name meant nothing.

"Surely you've heard of him - one of the greatest country honky tonk singers who ever lived."

"Sorry. I don't follow country music. Or football either," she snipped, and she turned her head away. *God, what a dolt, she thought. I've had this conversation before...when I was at Stephens, and nothing turned me off more. The boys I used to date there were just like him, boasting all the time about their home town and their athletic prowess, thinking I should be impressed. They were too dense to realize that I didn't give a damn about any of that - or their mid-western cultural wasteland.*

"Are you serious that you never heard about Creekwood? Or are you just stringing me along again?"

"What makes you think Creekwood's so special?" she lashed out at him. "Is it any different than any other small town? What do people do there anyway, besides watch television and grow old?

"They farm mostly."

"Oh...how quaint! I suppose your father's a farmer?"

"No. He owns a body shop."

"A what?"

"A body shop. You know, the kind where they fix dents in cars."

"You can't be serious!" she said, and she erupted with a short, shrill laugh.

"Yes. I am," he said. His eyes paled, and she was jolted down to her toenails by their intensity. She realized, then, that she had underestimated him. She wanted to kick herself. He wasn't a dolt, and she knew she should have realized that sooner. The quiet way he had been observing her body all afternoon and the way it had excited her should have been signal enough. For the first time she looked at him seriously: the blond hair, angular face, light golden tan, slim waist - boyish looking, but with chest and shoulders rippling with young muscles that looked as if they would twitch to the touch. It was his eyes that really got to her though. So clear blue - wrinkled at the corners. She saw in them an intelligence she hadn't noticed before, smoldering at her, and all of a sudden she felt ashamed.

"I'm sorry," she said as gently as she knew how.

"That's what you debutantes always say, isn't it?" he said, his voice stinging. "You think all you have to do is bat your eyes and say you're sorry and then all is forgiven. You've pulled that stunt on your daddies so many times, it just comes naturally!"

She grabbed his wrist and held on to it tightly. "I'm not that way. A lot of my friends may be, but I'm not. I don't want you to think I'm like that."

"Why shouldn't I? That's the way you've acted ever since I met you."

"It was just a pretense. I...I didn't really mean anything by it," she stammered. "I wish there were some way I could prove it to you."

"Do you really mean that?"

"Yes," she nodded fervently.

He stared at her for a long time. "If that's the case, how about going to the Bastille celebration with me tonight?"

She didn't answer right away. As much as she wanted to go out with him, she wasn't sure she was ready yet for even a casual relationship - especially one that could only lead to nowhere. She was still mulling it over when he attacked her again.

"Listen, goddamnit! Do you want to go out with me tonight or not?"

His anger subdued her. "Sure. Why not?" she shrugged. "I'll meet you at the Gorilla - upstairs in the bar about eight o'clock."

"I can pick you up at your hotel."

"Don't be so conventional. A rendezvous is quite continental, you know. Besides, I have to meet Robert at the bar."

"And if I don't find you there?"

"Oh, I'm sure you'll figure out a way to find me," she said impishly. And with that, she gathered up her towel and beach things and scampered up the stairs to the promenade before he could argue any further.

Clay heard the music blaring from the Gorilla when he was still two blocks away. It grew louder with every step he took, and when he walked into the place he was blasted by a cacophonous sound that was deafening. The juke box had been turned all the way up. Throngs of revelers were crowded around tables with confetti spattered in their hair, and the Bastille celebration was well underway. Confetti blanketed the tables and was two inches deep on the floor. The ceiling was covered with balloons, and a crowd was standing in the center of the bar, arm in arm, singing the *Marseillaise*. Clay saw Marianna and Robert sitting at a corner table engaged in a conversation with a monstrosity of a woman, grossly overweight and caked with make-up. She looked like an old Montparnasse whore. He started elbowing his way through the crowd, and as he approached the table the woman stood up suddenly, clutched his arm, and jerked him toward her. "Sit down babee!" she said in a husky French accent. "For a man like you, I fix up with my best girl...I make a good price."

"I'm sorry, chérie, but I'm with them," Clay said as he laughed and gestured toward Marianna and Robert. The old woman pouted a second. Then she broke open a sack of confetti and poured it over his head and laughed until she shook.

"Meet Beatrice!" Robert shouted over the noise. "She owns the place."

Clay sat down, and Marianna gave him a part of her beer. Then she leaned over the table, looking at Clay, and she said for all three of them to hear. "Robert and Beatrice are having a little squabble. Beatrice wants to fix him up with one of her girls. Robert thinks sixty francs is too high a price - almost twelve dollars. What do you think?"

Clay was startled. The question did not fit his schoolgirl image of her. He looked around the table and saw that they were all waiting for him to say something. "Sixty francs certainly sounds like a fair price to me," he said quickly, as if he were very experienced in these kinds of matters.

"For only thirty minutes?" Robert squawked.

Beatrice rolled her head sideways and flashed a knowledgeable smile. "I guarantee you it won't take that long my son," she said, as she clapped her hands to summon a slender, fresh looking young girl who had been standing next to the bar. The girl came over and introduced herself shyly, and then Beatrice hoisted herself out of her chair and guided the two of them swiftly to the staircase that led to the second floor. Clay looked at Marianna after they had gone. She was leaning on her elbows with her head on the table. She didn't move for more than a minute, but then, as a new song started playing on the juke box, she leaped up and grabbed his arm and started dragging him through the crowd to the tiny dance floor in the middle of the bar. "This is my favorite song," she said. "Non, Je Ne Regrette Rien."

"What does it mean?"

"It means, 'I don't regret nothin'! Edith Piaf. It's very sad."
She rested her head on his shoulder, closed her eyes, and began
swaying to the music with perfect rhythm. She clung to him tightly,
and after awhile she began humming softly, and from time to time
roughly translating some of the words into English.

> *"No nothing...not a thing...*
> *No, I don't regret anything.*
> *Not the good things I have done, nor the ba-a-ad...*
> *They are all the same to me.*
> *No, I regret nothing.*
> *My sorrows...my pleasures...I don't need them anymore.*
> *They've all been paid for, swept away for always.*
> *I don't care about the past.*
> *No nothing...not a thing...I don't regret anything.*
> *I start again from ze-ro*
> *Because my life, my hap-piness...*
> *They begin again with you today."*

The song ended, but Marianna kept on moving as if she did not
notice. Another one began. She buried her head into his shoulder
and clung to him even tighter. People were starting to look at them
strangely, and Clay tried to nudge her out of her trance. "Aren't
you at all worried about your brother becoming corrupted?" he
murmured in her ear.

She raised her head and looked at him for all of two seconds.
"The poor kid's been locked away in prep school all his life. It's
about time he got laid," she said, and then she flopped her head
back down on his shoulder.

For the second time in just a few minutes she had said something that surprised him - not something he imagined a naive,
young debutante would normally say. "You shouldn't be so cava-
lier about your brother," he said very seriously. "The first time for
anyone's important."

She kept dancing with her eyes closed. "Everyone has to get
laid sometime. There's no reason the first time should be any big
deal," she whispered in his ear.

The song ended. They went back to their table and Clay paid
for the drinks. The parade had begun, and the Gorilla was empty-

ing. They hurried with the crowd to the Promenade and watched floats roll by for an hour, exquisite floats made from thousands of carnations and roses stitched together in painstaking fashion. A half-dozen of Provence's most beautiful young women perched daintily on top of each one, smiling and waving and tossing flowers into the crowd. The quietness was eerie. There were no bands; no whistles or clapping by the spectators in ninety degree heat and humidity like at the Cotton Carnival parade in Creekwood. A cool night breeze began drifting in from the sea, and the people in the street started donning sweaters.

As the last float passed, a showering of roman candles and sky rockets launched from the top of Mont Boron lit up the sky and then dissipated in a rain of multi-colored sparks over the eastern half of the harbor. The parade was over. The crowd started breaking up and migrating toward the Place Massena, a huge square near the casino where a street dance had already begun. Marianna and Clay drifted with them, and at the square, they danced. Sometimes they danced together. But other times they danced in a circle with all kinds of people - young couples, old couples, children - all of them just having a good time. The band stopped playing at three in the morning, and the crowd started filtering out of the square and filling the cafes. Marianna and Clay found a table along the sidewalk and stayed, drinking coffee and eating sugar-coated crepes until the street was empty and they saw the sweepers and water trucks come passing by. They looked for the old man with the rose, but he was not there. It was dawn when they walked into the lobby of the Locarno, and this time she was too sleepy to be very alert. He grasped her shoulders before she could scurry away and kissed her once lightly on each eyelid. "Vic and Darcy and I are going motorbike riding tomorrow. I'll pick you up about ten," he said smiling. Then he turned and walked away without giving her a chance to answer.

Vic and Darcy were already at the motor bike shop the next morning when Clay arrived. They rented two Vespas and puttered four blocks over to the Hotel Locarno. Marianna was waiting for them, and they set out at once to explore the countryside. Vic and Clay were unfamiliar with the bulky scooters and they started off driving very unsteadily through the teeming streets, narrowly missing several pedestrians as they dodged between fruit laden push carts and honking cars. Darcy and Marianna seemed mindless of the danger as they balanced precariously on the rears of the scooters laughing at the irate motorists as they passed them by. Amazingly, they managed to weave their way out of the city without mishap and up a dusty road into the mountains behind Nice. They stopped after half an hour and parked their bikes at a place where there was an opening in the acacia hedges that lined the road. No one spoke for several minutes as they looked down at the city of Nice and mentally recorded the majesty of the scene. They saw orchards of olive and orange trees terracing neatly down the slopes of the mountain, merging at the bottom into finely cultivated vineyards and fields of lavender bushes and the wild, yellow-flowered agave. The fields stretched out across a narrow flat land to the edge of the city, with its yellow limestone buildings and russet-tiled roofs looming out of a soft golden haze. And on the far side of the city, way off, they could see the silver-stoned beach, a thin strip dotted with umbrellas of every shade and hue blending into the backdrop of the grey-green Mediterranean, all streaked with whitecaps and spattered with gaily colored sails bobbing in the wind. The view inspired them to go higher. They cranked up the Vespas and proceeded onward, and Vic and Clay started becoming more skillful at handling the machines the higher they went. They crossed an old Roman archtype bridge spanning the Var River Valley and drove up a windy mountain road into the Alpes Maritime. They reached the tiny hilltop village of Haut-de-Cagnes in early afternoon and stopped for lunch at the Cafe St. Jacques on the center square. They stayed for an hour, seated outside under the shade of a towering evergreen oak, letting their bodies cool as they quenched their thirst with carafes of Provencal rose. Afterwards, Darcy took them on a short guided tour, escorting them through the steep and narrow, winding cobblestone streets, past the house where Chagall had painted and on upward to the old sandstone brick apartment that housed her flat. Proudly, she showed them two of her own paintings, views of the countryside and the coast from which they had just come. They stayed just long enough to wash their faces and go to the bathroom, and then walked back to their scooters and sped down the mountain road to the highway junction at Cagnes-sur-Mer. Nice was fifteen kilometers to the east. They decided to go in the opposite direction, toward Cannes. Cruising side by side along the freeway at ninety kilometers an hour, they reached the resort in less than thirty minutes and drove straight to the beach, deftly changed into swimsuits under cover of a large green and yellow striped beach towel, and swam for an hour.

They set out again in the late afternoon, taking the beach road instead of the freeway back to Nice. They stopped one more time, at a sidewalk café in Juan-les-Pins, and they consumed another liter of wine and talked and laughed insanely at nothing until Vic noticed the time: six o'clock. The aircraft was to be repaired by now, and he and Clay had been ordered to be back aboard ship before nightfall. They left the cafe in a hurry and whipped the scooters through the heavy traffic along the narrow beach highway, leaning into each turn so hard that their shoulders almost grazed the whitewashed stone walls lining the road. They arrived at Cote d'Azur just before sundown, sunburned and exhausted, lips chapped, cheeks raw from the sun and the wind. Vic and Clay changed quickly into their flying gear and emerged from the locker room corseted in g-suits with knives strapped to their ankles, forty-five caliber revolvers slung in holsters under their armpits, and parachutes bouncing off their butts. They were each carrying an oxygen mask and a white helmet with their name stenciled in large red letters on the back. They look like modern day Don Quixotes, Marianna thought, as she and Darcy walked them out to the aircraft.

As Clay started to climb up into the cockpit, he leaned over, put his two fingers on Marianna's eyelids, closed them and kissed them gently. "Well, it's been tense, fella'," he said huskily.

"What's this tense *fella'* bit?" she said with a quizzed look.

"Just a way of saying goodbye...without any commitments."

She laughed. "Well, you'll never have to worry about that with me, fella! I'm strictly a *no commitment* kind of girl." Her eyes crinkled. "There is one thing I'll admit though."

"What's that?"

"You're right. It has been tense, Clay Stoner."

He scrambled into the cockpit, started engines, and was taxiing in thirty seconds. Taking off into the fast sinking sun, he thought he would never see her again. Another brief encounter - one that he would forget quickly. There had been no sex. They had never even really kissed. Still, for the first time since Cindy Sue, he had met a woman who intrigued him.

Marianna gazed sadly at the F-4 as it shot upward from the end of the runway, victory-rolled once and climbed southward out over the Mediterranean. "They remind me of when I was a kid," she said to Darcy, sounding nostalgic, "like my favorite teevee heart throb, Flash Gordon, blasting off into space"

"They live in another world, Marianna," Darcy said in the voice of a thoughtful mother.

"Clay seems really nice."

"He is. There's a lot more to him than he lets on. It's too bad you didn't meet him before you got tangled up with Douglas."

"Hey, old buddy. You forgot something back there," Vic piped over the intercom.

"Yeah, what's that?" Clay replied as he dropped a speed brake and slowed the aircraft to enter into the landing pattern.

"Marianna's address in Grenoble." Darcy gave it to me while you were checking the weather."

They were not exactly welcomed when they were safely back aboard ship. The Commander of the Air Group, Admiral Martin, was outraged at first by what he considered to be nothing more than an unauthorized, forty-eight hour boondoggle to Nice. He was very old navy and that generally meant punishment of some kind. But he soon calmed and relented. He did, however, relay to them two items of bad news. Duke Dawson, their handsome down-to-earth squadron mate and classmate from Annapolis had been involved in a mid-air turning on a final approach two nights before, and he was lost. The ship had searched for him for two days and had given up hope of recovering the body. The squadron had also received news of its next scheduled deployment. It was leaving in February for a ten-month cruise to Vietnam where another nasty little Asian war was starting to boil!

II

≈

SUMMERS ALWAYS HAVE TO END

Even in August the air in Grenoble is fresh and tangy. The nights are cool. Dew is on the grass in the early morning and a thin haze shrouds the mountains. But by the time the sun beams full over the highest peaks the haze and dew are gone, and the air is clear enough to make one feel he could see all the way to Switzerland if the mountains were not in the way. The days warm up. By noon the sweaters worn to work in the morning are doffed, and the luncheon crowds in the cafes around the city square are in shirt sleeves, sweaters draped loosely over their shoulders as they bask in the soothing cool warmth of another glorious day. If a single word could describe Grenoble in August, it would have to be serene. And much too serene for Marianna. The mountain peaks cut the sun off from the valley in the late afternoon, and the nights came early. Five miles out in the country at the manor house where she and Robert were staying, dinner was over by nine o'clock and the entire house in bed before ten.

Marianna had just retired and was in bed reading when there was a frantic knock at the door. "Mademoiselle Haizet! Mademoiselle Haizet! Venez vite! *Come! Come!*" It was the illiterate maid, too excited to explain anything. Marianna threw on her bathrobe and followed the maid downstairs to the kitchen, and there, peering through the bars covering an open window, she saw him.

"*Clay?* Clay Stoner!" she exclaimed in amazement.

He had not thought about what he would say or do if and when he found her. He uttered the first thing that came to his mind. "You shouldn't lock your gate so early. I had to climb over the wall."

"I don't believe it! What are you doing here? How did you find me?"

"It's a long story. Call it fate, if you want. I left the carrier in Barcelona as it was leaving the Med and heading home to Norfolk. Took some leave and been bumming around Europe for awhile. I was in the American Express office in Paris yesterday to buy a train ticket to Amsterdam when I overheard two English ladies in line inquiring about a road map to Nice, and, quite brazenly I might say, I asked them if they could use a driver. They seemed delighted to have my company. What they didn't tell me was that they were going to stop off to see a friend in Grenoble along the way. We arrived here about dusk and their friend insisted the ladies stay the night with her and all day tomorrow to see the city. No room for me, though. Then I remembered I had your address and decided to try to look you up. The ladies were kind enough to drive me out here. Took us a good hour to find this place."

"You're crazy, you know that?"

"What's so crazy about going back to Nice? Why don't you come along?"

She thought about the surf and warm beach of stones for all of five seconds. "Do you mean it? I'd love to!" she gushed. "But there might be a problem. Let me see." She left the kitchen, leaving him standing outside in the dark. He waited, and soon he heard the rapid twittering of French voices coming from an upstairs window. He could tell from the tones that an argument was in progress. It ended abruptly, and Marianna barged out through the kitchen door looking happy. "Well, that's settled," she said. Madame Silvey, the widow who owns this place, is a close friend of my Mother's and doesn't like the idea. But she's willing to acquiesce if Robert comes along too. Okay?"

"Sure."

"Then it looks like you've made yourself a sale Mr. Navy Pilot. So how do we get to Nice?"

"Why don't we just walk out to the road in the morning and stick out our thumbs."

They left early in the morning before the rest of the house was awake and hiked out to the highway where they hitched a ride within minutes with two young and hefty Norwegian school teachers driving a tiny Citroen 2CV. They were squished in the backseat with the luggage like a truckload of cattle The Norwegians rolled their own

cigarettes and chain smoked as the 2CV rattled through the countryside, but Marianna didn't mind. She was going back to Nice one
more time before summer was over, and that was all that mattered.
They drove southeast through the mountains for the remainder of
the morning. But about noon, just as they reached the intersection of
the highway to Marseilles, the Norwegians' destination, it started to
rain. Dumped out by the side of the road, Clay and Robert and Marianna took turns trying to thumb another ride. After thirty minutes
and still no luck, the rain was coming down hard. Clay pulled a flight
jacket out of his bag, and they all sat huddled under it, jumping up
every now and then and waving their arms whenever a car passed.
Clay looked at Marianna, drenched through to the skin. "You sure
know how to travel first class," she said, smiling bravely.

They hitched five rides before reaching Nice. The rain stopped,
and only one more unusual event occurred along the way. Robert
casually asked Marianna what she thought of the time she spent in
Geneva the past fall. Clay picked up on it. "What were you doing in
Geneva last fall?" he asked, puzzled. "I thought you said you were
at Juilliard."

"That's right," she answered too quickly, and then she stammered. "I...I was just in Geneva for a short time, attending a special
Master Class."

If she had not been so panicky and nervous and he had not seen
the look of surprise on Robert's face at her answer, he would probably not have thought any more about it. But he knew she wasn't
telling the truth. He didn't question her again. He was intrigued,
though, about why she was being evasive. After the incident she
did not want to talk anymore. She curled up beside him in the back
seat of the Peugeot they were riding in at the time and dropped off
to sleep. Her face soon acquired the washed look of a child, a look
of innocence that an hour before he would have thought incapable
of deceit.

It was late by the time they reached Nice. They checked into the
Hotel Trocadero and took the two cheapest rooms on the top floor
underneath the eaves, ones in which the ceilings sloped from a
height of about seven feet at the doors to four feet next to the walls.
The floors were bare hardwood. The plaster walls were cracked.
Each room contained only a dresser and a single, iron-posted bed
with a very thin mattress. The nearest bathroom was one floor
down. The rooms cost only fifteen francs a day, though, including
breakfast.

For Marianna the next two days and nights sped by in a whirl. She met Clay and Robert about nine-thirty each morning for a small continental breakfast in a nook off the Trocadero lobby. From there, it was an eight block walk to the beach, their daily adventure. They would stop at a market and buy a bottle of limonade and some bread and cheese for their lunch, and stop a block further at a Tabac, Robert for his filtered Old Gold cigarettes and Clay for his *Herald Tribune*; and at least two or three times a day Marianna would see some little trinket in a store window and rush in and buy it on impulse. Their destination was always the Lido Plage where for thirty francs they were supplied with an umbrella and mattresses on a burnished wooden sundeck. They stretched out for the rest of the day, letting their bodies luxuriate in the sun. Then, about six o'clock, they would take one last short swim, towel off, change clothes, and walk over to the Gorilla Bar to meet Beatrice and slake away their thirst with a couple of beers. Robert would stay to flirt with Beatrice's girls, and Marianna and Clay would go to a sidewalk cafe nearby for an early, cheap three course prix fixe meal. Afterwards, they walked back to the Trocadero, making one more stop along the way at a small grocery owned by Madame Benoit, a lonely old woman who would sell them a bottle of sparkling white wine for six francs and toss in a bag of ice for free in exchange for a few minutes of their conversation. From Madame Benoit's it was only a block to the Trocadero. They would go to Clay's room, chill down the wine and sit out on the balcony taking in the sights and sounds of the city until the wine was polished off. The sun, the beers, the dinner and the wine would have them in a mellow, drowsy state by then. She would go to her room, leaving Clay in his, and they would sleep it off until midnight and then wake up fresh and ready for another night of dancing at the Gorilla.

By Sunday, the day before they were supposed to leave, Marianna and Robert were down to their last thirty francs. Mortified, she had to ask Clay for a loan to pay for their bus tickets back to Grenoble, and to economize, she checked out of her room and moved in with Clay and her brother. They spent the day on the beach and a last night at the Gorilla. They danced until they were exhausted, and they were still drenched with sweat when they arrived back at the Trocadero at four in the morning. Robert helped Clay tug the mattress off their bed and lay it out on the floor, and then the two of them collapsed in a heap on the bedsprings. Marianna flicked off the light and crawled under a sheet on the mattress. Robert started snoring right away. Clay waited a few minutes, and then eased off the bedsprings and onto the mattress.

"What do you think you're doing?" Marianna started to protest.

"Shh!" he whispered as he cradled her and kissed her on the mouth for the first time. She kissed him back, a long deep kiss, and then she snuggled against his chest and fell asleep as he lay there running his hand over her back and shoulders, admiring how soft and supple she was.

They were still lying together at eight o'clock in the morning when Robert opened the curtains and the sun filled the room. "Wake up sleepyheads! The bus leaves in an hour!" he bellowed cheerfully.

Clay nuzzled Marianna as she stirred awake. "Stay another day," he said quietly. She lay in his arms for a moment, expressionless while she let the day wash the sleep from her eyes. She sat up then and looked at her brother.

"I'm going to stay," she said calmly, firmly.

They dressed in a hurry and walked Robert to the bus station. Clay gave him twenty francs to purchase a ticket. Marianna gave him her last five francs - just enough to buy a snack along the road. The bus departed a few minutes later, and Robert poked his head out the window, waving, laughing, and shouting. "I won't tell! But I hope no one back at the Silvey's finds out that I left my sister shacked up with a sailor down in Nice!" Marianna saw many faces in the crowd on the curb turn and stare. She leaned against Clay. He draped an arm around her shoulders. She kept waving until the bus was out of sight. They started walking back to the Trocadero then, and as they walked she started wondering what her father's reaction would be if he found out. A year ago the thought would have terrified her. By the time they reached the Trocadero, she had decided that she didn't really care.

She opened up to him a little that afternoon on the beach.

"Why don't you tell me a little more about yourself," he said, "what was it like to be a young girl growing up in New York?"

"New York," she said, and her eyes dimmed...Manhattan. The first place she remembered. Long ago, but still a vivid memory. They had lived in a cavernous two story apartment on Park Avenue, eleven rooms with marble floors and high ceilings and an oval staircase leading up to the second floor. She could still remember the giant playroom on the second floor, all the toys, the fireplace in the corner, the long dreary days of winter that she and Robert had spent in the playroom with their dear, sweet nanny, an old Irish woman named Rose. Her father's banking business necessitated a very active social life, and she and Robert had seldom been allowed downstairs in the evenings because of the endless succession of dinners and cocktail parties her parents were always hosting. "I...I was kept so sheltered that I saw very little of New York," she said haltingly. I went to one of those private girls' academies. It was only about six blocks from our apartment, but even so, my father had me chauffeured back and forth every day...Crazy father. He thought it was too dangerous for me to walk the streets alone. I know he meant well, but the other kids all walked to school by themselves."

"Your father sounds like a very protective man. He must love you very much."

"Oh yes. He was protective all right," she laughed softly. *In fact, she thought, if it hadn't been for Rose, she and Robert would never have seen much of the city. Rose took them places; Central Park in the spring-time, Radio City and the skating rink in Rockefeller Center at Christmas, the circuses at the Garden, puppet shows in the village. She had loved Rose, and she cried hard when she had to say goodbye to her. Robert had cried too. And Rose had cried.*

Clay saw her eyes looking watery. "Why so sad?" he asked her. "That must have been a fantastic time in your life - a young girl growing up in Manhattan."

She waved her head and smiled. "No. I left before I really got to know it. I was in boarding school in Switzerland by the time I was twelve. Most of the kids were older, and I was lonely at first, which is maybe why I escaped into my own little world of music." She looked away and closed her eyes for a moment. "The piano was my whole life for a while. The teachers encouraged my parents to push me, which they did. Father hired some of the finest private tutors money could buy. It seemed like all I did was practice or listen to recordings of symphonies until Darcy came. I was fourteen when she arrived, and we quickly became best friends. Especially ski buddies. Our boarding school, the coed part of Le Rosey, had its own private ski chalets in Gstaad. School shut down every February and we all went to Gstaad and did nothing but ski for the entire month. That was a fun time, but other than that we led a very Swiss, sheltered life."

"What about your cousin - the one Darcy said you were in love with? What happened to him?" She looked into his eyes and saw the faint trace of a smirk. *Goddamn him, she thought...he thinks it's funny.*

"I'd just as soon not talk about my cousin." she said abruptly.

"Oh come on." he prodded her. "That was years ago."

"Do you really want to know? Do you really want to know?" she said shrilly. "If you do, my cousin's name is Jean Pierre. He's from Paris. And you may think it's weird, but I was in love with him once."

She gazed out to sea at the horizon for a long time, thinking about her fifteenth summer, the summer Jean Pierre had failed the entrance examination for the Ecole Polytechnique. He had become consumed with bitterness. He spent most of the summer in Tregastel brooding alone and avoiding her. The morning she left to go back to Switzerland he had gotten up before she awakened and gone horseback riding along the cliffs. He had let her leave without even saying goodbye.

Clay looked at her. She was staring at her feet, fiddling with some beach pebbles with her toes. She looked very sad. "What happened?" he said.

"What do you mean?" she said.

"You speak of him in the past tense."

"He changed," she said in a distant voice. "When I was fifteen he entered St. Cyr, the French 'West Point'. I didn't see him again for years."

"And when you did?"

"And when I did he made me realize how foolish I'd been pining over him for all those years. My parents had since moved back to the States and I had just graduated from Stephens. My mother and I went to Brittany that summer. I knew Jean Pierre was on leave from the army and was going to be there. I couldn't wait for him to see that I was no longer the little girl he remembered. I wanted to make him fall in love with me...and then I found him changed so drastically. It seemed as if the army had erased every trace of the sensitive idealism that had been the root of his hold on me. His head was shaved. He could only talk about war and how glorious it was. He wanted to go fight in Viet Nam, even though the French had already lost, which upset him very much. I refused to believe the change in him at first, and on one of our long hikes along the cliffs I poured out the feelings I had kept inside me all those years. He was kind. He said he had known about them, but that the church would never approve a marriage between cousins. And he told me that his first duty assignment was going to be with the Foreign Legion in Africa; he would not be allowed to take a wife. So that was it. I haven't seen him since."

"It sounds like you're still not over him." Clay said, covering up his amazement over the way she had just bared her soul to him.

"No. I'm over him," she said as she nervously brushed back a curl.

Sharing the same room, something had to happen eventually. It occurred the second night after Robert left. They had finished their bottle of champagne and were lying next to each other on the bed, sun-weary and inebriated, and Clay kissed her and then unfastened her blouse and touched her. She responded by kissing him harder, holding her breath as he grappled with the zipper on her yellow shorts and pulled them down to her ankles.. He began caressing her hips and running his hands over her, and then he bent down and kissed her naval. She lay there quietly for a few seconds - and then she stiffened, shoved him away and sprang from the bed toward the doorway that opened onto the balcony. She zipped up her shorts and turned facing him, hands on her hips, eyes smoldering. Her words dripped with venom. "When I said I'd stay, we agreed - just as friends! No sex! I meant it Mr. Stoner, so if that's all you're after, you're wasting your time!"

"Don't be an asshole."

"You're the asshole!"

The words stung and he lashed back. "And you're a snob! Too high class for anyone to get in your pants, aren't you? Oh, no. Not yours!"

She stared at him a moment, trembling and stunned by his anger. "I'm sorry, Clay. Let's just forget it. Okay?"

"Like hell I'll forget it! You're right. You are just a waste of my time. Here's fifty francs!" he shouted as he slapped a roll of bills on the bureau. "That should be enough to get your ass back to Grenoble first thing in the morning!"

She turned and strode angrily into the lavatory and slammed the door. He put on a shirt and walked onto the balcony to smoke and to think. He looked down at the city that had been theirs for the past five days. He stared at the evening traffic in the streets and at the shops where they had stopped every day on their treks to the beach. The shops were closed now. Their brightly colored awnings were rolled up and black shutters and bars covered their windows and doors. He spied Madame Benoit leaving her store late. They had stopped by to see her for five straight nights now. She had referred to them as lovers once. She's too old to understand, he thought, that when you're having fun and living just for the moment you can appear that way. He wondered if she would miss them dropping by each evening; whether she would care about what had happened to them.

Marianna appeared suddenly on the balcony. "Don't be so mad at me, Clay," she stammered. "I just said it because I thought it was the proper thing to say at the moment."

"You mean you don't still think I'm interested in only one thing!"

"No. I don't feel that way about you, Clay. It's just that I would never go to bed with you unless I thought we were both in love. You know that's not the case with us. It's just Nice...the beach... the end of summer. The only reason we're together is to have a good time."

"Is anything wrong with that?"

"There needs to be more."

"Listen. I'm sorry too," he said as the frost went out of his voice and he started to smile. "I was wrong to try to put the make on you. What do you say we forget the love and sex bullshit and just go out and have some haps. Okay?"

Her face exploded with a smile of relief and she nodded, and then tiny tears that she could no longer hold back started trickling down her cheeks. Five minutes later they were in the street skipping along arm in arm as if nothing had happened. "You know, it really impressed me when you got so mad," she said, and she hugged him. "I thought you were going to walk out on me. Most men would have just whined and apologized and tried to get me back in bed again."

"How do you know I'm just not being devious and that those are exactly my motives?" he chided her.

"Because I know you now," she said with a coquettish jerk of her head, "and you're not that way." They headed for the Gorilla and another night of drinking and partying with their friends.

"What was it like, growing up in Creekwood?" she asked him the next afternoon on the beach. It was the first time she had probed into his past, and it caused him to rouse from his after-lunch catnap. He sat up, muffled a yawn, and stared at her curiously.

"Do you really want to know?" he asked.

"Yes, I really do," she insisted. "You make it sound like such a wonderful place. You must have been very happy there."

"Yes, I was," he said, and his face started to brighten. "Creekwood's the greatest place in the world for a kid to grow up. People have roots there. They're friendly. Everyone knows each other."

"I don't think I would like that."

"Yes, you would. There was something to do all the time. Good fishing. You could even shoot rabbits off your back porch."

"What did you do...like in the summers?"

"I'd go up to my grandfather's cabin. It's on a beautiful little lake about twenty miles up in the hills. It's got the finest bass and crappie fishing in the state."

"It sounds wonderful."

"Yeah, it is. And the fall's great too. Cotton Carnival, late September. Friday night high school football games. Weekend coon hunts."

"What in the world is a coon hunt?

"A coon hunt is when friends go out into the woods in the early evening, build a bonfire and start barbecuing ribs and chickens. A jug gets passed around in a circle while the meat is cooking and everyone tells stories and gets high. The food is served about dark, and then the dogs are let loose. The jug keeps getting passed around, and everyone just sits in the circle and listens to hear which dog is leading the chase. The dogs howl like crazy, and everyone can tell which one's ahead just by listening to the yelps. One guy will beam and say, 'that's my old Sport in the lead.' Then, when another dog takes the lead, he'll start frowning and rooting for old Sport to catch up. The chase goes on like that sometimes for more than an hour before the coon is treed."

"What happens then?"

"Why then, the owner of the dog that treed the coon has the honor of goin' out and shootin' the critter."

"That's the most despicable thing I've ever heard!" Marianna said angrily. "What kind of horrible people live there who would kill a poor helpless animal like that?"

"Hey listen, fella', coon huntin's as old as the hills. They aren't horrible people. They're basic, good, down-to-earth American people."

"Yeah, sure...I know. The backbone of the country and all that, with their basic American down-to-earth football mentality."

"What's so wrong with liking football?"

"Oh, nothing. I suppose you played?"

"Yeah. As a matter of fact I did."

"And I suppose you were the big Creekwood hero?" she said disgustedly.

"I was good enough. But a guy by the name of Terry Malone was the real star. One of the greatest athletes Creekwood ever had."

"Oh, really!" she sniffed. "And what's he doing now? Still playing football? Or farming?"

"I don't know," Clay said as he dropped his eyes. "Terry was my best friend once. But he left town years ago and just disappeared."

They started trying to save money to make the days last. They each had only one drink at the Gorilla Club that night, and the next day they skipped the Lido and went to the free public beach. They spread their things out on the rocks and read until noon. For lunch they had croissants that were left over from the hotel breakfast. As they ate, Clay noticed the wind picking up. "About the other night," he said all of a sudden, "for awhile there I thought you were enjoying it."

"Maybe I was," she said with a shrug, "but I told you, that's as far as it goes."

"Oh come on. You've been further than that."

"I thought I explained to you. I've led a very sheltered life."

"Sure. And the next thing you'll tell me is that was the first time you've been with a man with your clothes off."

"I didn't say that."

"Ah! Now we get to the truth. So...when did it happen? The first time."

She looked at him peevishly. "Do you really want to know?"

He looked straight into her eyes and they didn't waver. The wind was kicking up a spray and moistening her hair, making it look even more curly and frizzy and electric than usual. "Yeah. I do," he said with a short laugh. "I'm a very inquisitive person."

"Well...it was the summer after I graduated from boarding school," she said slowly, and then her voice started gaining confidence. "I spent a month vacationing with my parents on Capri. I met an Italian naval officer. Southern Italian. I was still naive as hell, but, somehow, my father let me go out with him. On our first date he parked his little Fiat on a cliff overlooking the sea, and we kissed, and I let him take off my blouse and touch me. That was the first time - and I must admit it excited me. I didn't try to stop him until he started reaching under my dress. He played it cool - just like you. He stopped and took me home. The next night we took a blanket and a jug of wine and went to the beach. I guess I trusted him by then. We went skinny dipping in the moonlight, and we drank wine and smoked cigarettes and I thought it was so deliciously romantic until he all of a sudden jerked me into his arms and pushed my head down in his lap. I swear I didn't know what he wanted at first. When I realized, finally, I went berserk and started kicking and screaming. After awhile he gave up trying to convince me what a great act of love it was he wanted me to per- form, and he took me home. I never saw him again."

"You make it sound like a shattering experience."

"No. It served me well," she said very analytically. "I was a little more prepared for college that fall. Stephens was the first time I'd ever been thrust into everyday contact with men, and the experi- ence taught me how to handle them. It taught me one other thing too."

"What's that?"

"To be forever wary of fast talking naval officers and Mediter- ranean summer romances!" she squealed, and she dived on top of him and pushed him over on the rocks. He grabbed the string on her bikini.

"Do you want me to tear it off?"

They laughed and rolled over and sat up. She leaned against his back and started kneading and squeezing his shoulder muscles. "Whatever made you go to Annapolis?" she said after awhile.

"You know, I really don't know. What's strange, I still don't know."

"You sure don't seem like the Annapolis type."

"What type is that?"

"I went to a dance at West Point once. The cadets there were all stereotypes; talked alike; looked alike; all wearing the same uni- forms with crew cuts and all."

"Now wait a minute," Clay said, becoming irritated. "I assure you we were not all alike. Annapolis had its share of rebels."

"How could anyone there be considered a rebel?" she scoffed. "You had to do exactly as you were told, didn't you?"

"Pretty much. But there are other ways to rebel."

"Yeah. Like how?"

"Well...I could tell you a story about my plebe year. One of the seniors had been hazing me for weeks. Every night he made me run up and down six flights of stairs and fetch him a coke from the vending machine in the basement. Then, while he drank it, he would make me stand at attention up against a wall in his room holding a rifle straight out until my arms started shaking."

"How did you ever put up with that stuff? I would have refused."

"And you would have just kept getting demerits until you were kicked out...or until you gave up and let the system break you. I fought back in a different way. Every night when I went to the basement I stuck my dick in that senior's coke cup and stirred it before I delivered it up to his room. He never did understand why I was always laughing as I stood there sweating and shaking and watching him drink it. And even though I had to obey his orders, in my own way I knew I'd beaten him.

Marianna laughed until, tears came. "No shit!" she exclaimed.

"No shit. Some of us fought back in many ways like that."

She stroked her chin and looked at him in a different light. "Tell me. Have you ever been in love?"

"Once. A girl I grew up with in Creekwood."

"What happened to her?"

He sighed and stared out to sea, and tiny crow's feet indented the corners of his eyes. "Nothing. I left. She stayed."

"Well, I won't pry in your past." She rolled over, turning her back, and asked him to cover it with lotion. He rummaged through her large beach bag looking for the bottle, and as he rummaged, he removed a handful of envelopes wrapped in a rubber band. He flipped through them, frowning.

"That's funny. You told me you went to Juilliard last year."

"That's right," she said, her back still to him.

"Then how come all these letters are addressed to you in Geneva; in Switzerland?" And as she rolled over to face him, he slowly and deliberately flipped each envelope on the beach towel. "This one's postmarked in November...this one in January...this one in March...this one..."

It was her turn to stare out to sea now. The wind was picking up again, and the sky was darkening rapidly. Whitecaps were starting to froth on top of the waves and black clouds whipping in from the south were starting to overtake the sun. "I guess I have some explaining to do," she said quietly after a moment. "That first night at the Gorilla Club, when I thought I would never see you again, I just left out a year of my life that I didn't feel like explaining. I did go to Juilliard, and I'm going back in the fall. But I dropped out a year ago. I've been in Europe ever since last September."

"So why lie about it?"

"Because I've been in a sanitorium. I had a nervous breakdown."

Her answer shocked him. It was one of the few he had not considered. "Do you want to talk about it?" he said gently.

"I never have. I will if you want me to."

"Why don't you try?"

She hesitated and her body tensed. "I...I don't know where to start," she said meekly. Then, in a voice crackling with strain, she began. "I guess I should go all the way back to the time I made my debut at the Waldorf. Father had arranged my escort, his name was Douglas Threadgill, a law student from Yale. He was smart. Sophisticated, I thought. And he was a devotee of classical music. We dated off and on for the next year and a half or so. He would drive over from New Haven and take me places: the opera, the symphony, Twenty One for lunch, the Plaza for cocktails. His family was very well-to-do, and he adored me. But I was never serious because - again to correct a lie- I was still in love with Jean Pierre and waiting for him to get back from Africa. Then...a year ago last June, I received an announcement that Jean Pierre was engaged. It destroyed me. I cried for three days. His wedding was in mid-August. My parents were away at a convention, and I invited the Yalie out to Greenwich that weekend and...and quite frankly I seduced him. It was my first time, and I don't remember it very much. It was over swiftly. I was troubled afterwards because I didn't know what I felt for him. I invited him out to Greenwich a week later to find out, and we did it again. I didn't like it any better than the first..." She paused and covered her eyes with her hand. He could see her lids trembling as she rushed to get the words out. "My...my parents came home a day early and caught us in bed together. There was a horrible scene, and my father decided he wanted me out of the house. I had been living at home and commuting to Juilliard before that, but I was so devastated I knew I couldn't stay in New York. I left for Geneva the week before Labor Day. That's why I wasn't at Darcy's wedding. I...I enrolled in the music conservatory in Geneva. I was living in a one room apartment, all alone, and I became depressed. I telephoned my father and told him I wanted to come home and...and he called me a whore and said he never wanted me to set foot in his house again." She was gasping to get the words out now. "I...I was twenty years old and I'd done it twice in my life, with one guy, and my father called me that. I sort of went crazy, I guess. I tried to kill myself. I slashed the veins in my wrist and behind my knees." She extended her palms, face upward, and he saw the scars. "I was unconscious when the landlady found me and was in a hospital five days. My mother flew over and put me in a rest home in Switzerland...up in the mountains. I stayed there seven months. Then Robert graduated from Le Rosey, and we started summer school together in Grenoble. So that's the story, and now I'm completely honest with you...what do you think?"

"I don't know. I think I'll take a nap," he said coldly, and he rolled over on his side with his back to her. He rested his head on his arm and stared at the beach pebbles for awhile, his mind flicking back and forth. Why did learning about the loss of her virginity upset him so much? It was something he would have normally assumed had happened as a matter of course. He closed his eyes to try to forget about it, but instead of forgetting, he kept thinking about the sequence of events in his life that had brought them together. Why was he lying next to this strange, complicated girl on the beach in Nice right now instead of being back home in Creekwood, married to Cindy Sue and farming, or working in his dad's garage? Every time he thought about it, the reason kept tracing back to the Homecoming Dance his senior year in high school, the night he and Cindy Sue first met the man who became their metaphysical savant: Slim Sparks.

Slim was a blind man, a Creekwood native and a legend, and although he spent most of his life barnstorming on the road, he came home religiously to play a few gigs a year, such as during the Cotton Carnival and at the Country Club dance on New Year's Eve. He was home that year, though, recuperating from an illness out at his brother's farm. Slim was a big man, with a bulbous nose and weather beaten face that made him look older than his fifty years. But when it came to performing, he had the endurance of a mule. He could go on for hours without a break, which he did often if the crowd was with him, slouched behind his piano sporting a silly grin that caused his nose to squinch up like a chipmunk as he sang through clenched teeth with his trademark, a black Meerschaum pipe, jutting out from his lips. And to see him sweating profusely, his beefy hulk rolling with a country rock rhythm and unruly gray hair dangling in his face, no doubt was left in anyone's mind that he loved what he was doing. And when he sang ballads in that gravelly voice of his about unfaithful women and no-account men and his eyeballs disappeared behind his lids leaving only two glistening white orbs staring blankly into space, as if trying urgently to communicate but being unable to do so except through the medium of his music, he could hold an audience spellbound.

Cindy Sue was Homecoming Queen that year. Slim's band was playing at the high school gymnasium and at his first break he came over to the table she and Clay were sharing to congratulate her. He sat down, sipping a beer, and all of a sudden asked the two of them what they were planning to do when they were older.

"Clay's going to college next year, and I'm going the year after!" Cindy Sue had bubbled.

Slim packed his pipe and begun puffing thoughtfully. "Goin' to school ain't *doin'* sumpthin'," he said suddenly. "Seems like ever'body thinks it's so goddamn important that they never think beyond. It's what yuh do that matters, what yuh learn in life, not school, that counts. Don't y'all have any plans besides goin' to school?"

They looked at each other for a moment, startled. "We're planning to get married!" Clay said.

"Little young to be thinkin' 'bout that already, ain't yuh?" Slim grumbled.

"We're not so young!" Cindy Sue said almost pugnaciously.

Slim paused for a long while, as if he was calling upon his other senses to size up what he thought the feeling was they had for each other. "So y'all think you're grown up, huh?" he said then. "Yuh know, ah felt the same way when ah was yore age. Ah could still see some then. Got married when ah was seventeen. She was the prettiest thing..." He began to mumble.

"What happened to her?" Clay asked.

"Aw, she dumped me for a drummer down in Birmin'ham. Couldn't put up with a man goin' blind, or the life on the road, the drinkin' and stayin' up all night. And ah couldn't give that up!" His eyeballs rolled and seemed to twinkle as he said it.

"That's sad," Cindy Sue said. "I guess you've really experienced a lot, haven't you Slim?"

"More'n most, I reckon. Music bizness teaches yuh a lot. Yuh learn it's a big world out there. Lots of diff'rent people with diff'rent ideas 'bout things. You kids oughtta see some of it 'fore yuh settle down."

"There's nothing to stop us from seeing it after we're married," Cindy Sue said.

"Aw, but yuh won't. Yuh'll have kids 'a yore own, and Clay'll have'ta think of providin' fore 'em. He won't be free, and neither will you. Y'all wind up just like ever'one else, right back here in Creekwood."

"And what's so wrong with that?" Cindy Sue asked defiantly.

"Oh...ever'body thinks the same here. Most of 'em never even been beyond Memphis or Saint Looie, if they ever went that far. Most of the ones who *do* find life's not so simple as here. They don't last long 'fore they're back."

"Creekwood's not so bad," Cindy Sue argued. "Clay and I are happy here."

"Ah know yuh think y'are, honey. And listen. Ah can tell yuh love each other. Yuh really do for now. But don't get married just to prove it to ever'body. Yore young enuff to go see all the things ah never could. Someday yuh'll wish yuh had. Life is short. Don't waste it. Go to Europe. Have a summer romance. Have two! Then, if yuh still feel the same 'bout each other, fine! But stay free so that if yuh don't, yuh don't end up hatin' each other when it's over."

"What made you come back here if you feel that way?" Cindy Sue asked curtly.

"Ah really came back to die, sweetheart. Ah had a heart attack, and emphysema real bad. Ah don't know if you kids know what that is, but it's from smokin' too much. The doctors said ah'd be dead in six months if ah didn't quit the drinkin' and life on the road. So ah came back to Creekwood just to wait. Been here six months now, stayin' at my brother's farm. Feelin' better all the time."

"It must have been terribly frightening, being told that you were going to die?" Clay said.

"Yep. It was. Makes yuh stop'n think 'bout things. But ah've made peace with the thought of dyin'. Yuh see, when yore dead, yuh don't know nothin'. Cain't feel nothin'. So what's to be scared of? It happens to ever'body. Yuh know, what's really scary, though - gittin' old and findin' out there ain't much left to live for. Like me not bein' able to go on the road no more. Ah'm doin' sumpthin' 'bout that, though. Bought a roadhouse up in Hays Ridge. Gonna call it Slim's Place. And ah'm gonna play up there on weekends and around here at dances, and at the Cotton Carnival, and the Country

Club on New Year's Eve. Ah'm just gonna sing and drink and raise cain 'til ah'm so old that nobody'll come listen to me anymore!"

"That will never happen around here, Slim," Clay said. "Everyone around here thinks you're the greatest."

"Maybe so," Slim said, his eyes narrowing into a steady, bleary-eyed gaze that made them uncomfortable. "But it'll happen sure as ah'm sittin' here. Happens to all of us. And when it does, ah'll know it's over. Ah'll be as good as dead then. You kids should think 'bout that. You only take this trip once. Get outta Creekwood and go see what it's all about while you can. Try'n make yore mark. Shoot for a star. If yuh don't make it, least yuh'll know yuh tried."

Clay was awakened by a gentle splash of raindrops, large intermittent ones like the kind that signal a coming storm. He rolled over to find an empty blanket beside him. Marianna and all her things were gone. He looked at the sky and the sea and saw rain torrents moving swiftly across the water toward shore. He slipped into his jeans, rolled up the blanket, grabbed his shirt and ran toward the steps leading up to the Promenade, propelled by claps of thunder. He scanned the wide boulevard, searching for the familiar yellow shorts and curly hair, but Marianna was nowhere in sight. Nor was she in any of the sidewalk cafes where the other beachgoers had fled seeking shelter under the awnings. He tried the Gorilla, but no one there had seen her either.

He was jogging toward the pier in the Old Port when he spied her across the street in the garden in the Place Massena square, sitting alone on a bench in the rain amidst the lilac bushes and palm trees. She was holding her bikini limply between her legs and staring at the ground, shoulders hunched over in an arch of anguish. She didn't notice as he approached, nor protest as he sat down beside her and took her arms and placed them around his neck. He tilted her chin upward and gazed into her eyes - the desolate, woeful eyes of a little girl looking lost. She forced a brief, strained smile, but said nothing. He kissed her with the rain beating down. She offered no resistance - and as if by a silent fiat, their need became established then, with their clothes soaked, her head on his shoulder and kinky drenched hair in his face, clinging to each other on the bench in the park in the rain in the heart of downtown Nice.

They strolled in silence back to the Trocadero, holding hands and leaning against each other. In the room they moved about quietly. She hung up their wet clothes to dry. He closed the shutters leading out to the balcony. The room became one large, grey shadow. And for a moment they stared at each other, hesitating. And then they moved together. He wrapped his arms around her, under her buttocks, and laid her gently on the bed. And then all that was heard were soft groans and sighs and gentle murmurings - and then clawed backs, bitten shoulders and bruised lips as the world turned upside down. They fell asleep with a cool, rain-freshened breeze wafting gently across the sheets.

Another two days passed and their habits remained the same, except they now made love each morning before they set out for the beach, and again in the evening during the pleasurable two hours they napped between dinner and their nightly sojourn to the Gorilla. One afternoon on the beach they talked about values.

"Do you remember the other night when you called me a snob?" she asked.

"I was angry. You know I didn't mean it," he said.

"Yes you did. And you were right. I was raised that way. But I want you to know I'm not impressed by material things. It nauseates me to hear people talking about their new clothes, new cars... their house."

"Don't knock money, fella'. That's what buys the freedom to do what you want."

"Freedom, maybe. But not happiness. Take you and me. We're staying in a room that's eight blocks from the beach and only costs three dollars a day. But I'm happier there than I would be staying in a suite at the Negresco."

"Listen, I'm sorry about the hotel," he started to apologize.

"Oh, don't be! I'm having a marvelous time learning what it's like to be poor. I know you're hurting for money – and spending half of it on me. I intend to pay you back for that, every penny of it. But I don't feel you're doing it just to sleep with me. It's more like... friendship, actually."

"It's easy to think feeling poor and bumming around can be fun if you can just quit and go home and rejoin the Greenwich Country Club set anytime you want."

"That has nothing to do with it."

"It has everything to do with it! Don't you think most people would like to take off to Nice for the summer? The only difference is, they're trapped. They can't afford it. They have a wife or a husband, kids, mortgages, furniture and things, a fuckin' job. Responsibilities you've never had to worry about."

"And they're stupid for letting themselves get committed like that. It means they didn't plan things out very well. Life should never stop being intense."

"That's a nice dream."

"You have to have dreams, Clay! I mean...don't you have some ambitions?"

"It's a little hard for me to have many right now. I haven't told you, but my squadron is shipping out for Nam in February. We're going be gone almost a year."

"Oh my God!" Her eyes dimmed to a glaze and she stared at him pitifully. "Does that mean you'll have to *bomb?*"

"Yeah, probably - if the war's still going on then."

"Doesn't it bother you?"

"Sure. I've never been asked to bomb people before. It was something I never thought about when I decided to go to Pensacola and become a pilot. Neither did Vic. None of us did. We just thought flying jets would be fun."

"I don't see how you can do it," she said dazedly. "Isn't there some way you can refuse? Say that you're a conscientious objector, or something?"

"I could turn in my wings anytime I want. Flying is strictly a voluntary duty. But I couldn't look Vic and the other guys in the squadron in the face if I did that. Besides, the Navy would put the screws to me if I did. I'd probably end up on a garbage scow in the Indian Ocean."

"That's better than having to bomb *innocent human beings!*"

"I know. I can't stand the thought of it either. I just keep hoping that the war will be over before we have to go."

Her mood sobered and she retreated in silence. She tried to read her book, but the words were a blur. She gave up in a short while and closed it. "What do you think you'll do after the Navy...with your life I mean?"

"That's too far away to think about now."

"But if you had to choose now, what would you want to do?" she persisted.

"Who knows? Maybe be a beach bum. Just lying here with you is sort of nice."

"Can't you ever get serious about anything?"

"Maybe I am serious. Maybe that's exactly what I'd like to do... go find an island someplace...white powdery sand...just collect seashells for the rest of my life."

"You're ridiculous, you know that?" she chided him fondly.

He turned away from her, not laughing anymore and wondering if she was right; wondering if he was really being ridiculous...he had lived on an island off the west coast of Florida once, one with palm trees and coconuts, white sand, and tangy, salty sea breezes. He and his mother had spent a winter on the island the year he was five and his dad was still away in the war, and it was there that he had learned the joy of being alone. It was six miles around that island, and he explored it every day - searching for seashells. He collected only the most unique ones, shells that were larger, smoother, more colorful or different in some respect. He'd also collected seahorses and starfish and glued the most perfect of each species onto framed slabs of fiberboard and sold them to tourists who came to the beach on weekends. There had only been two tiny restaurants and a single eight-room boarding house on the island then. He had gone back once, when he was much older, and found the island mostly concrete, overrun with motels side by side and fast food diners. And he had walked the beach early in the morning without finding a single seashell worthy of collecting.

She broached a different subject to him later in the afternoon. "You've never told me whether you like having sex with me or not?"

"You've never told me either," he said.

"Am I supposed to?"

"Sometimes it helps."

"I'll bet you've had lots of affairs?"

"You dignify them by calling them affairs."

"What about the girl in Creekwood you were in love with?"

"I told you. I left. She stayed."

"But you were really in love with her?"

"Yes."

"Why didn't you marry her then?"

"I did," he said, looking straight into her eyes.

Her mouth slumped open. "You're joking!"

"No. I'm not." He told her about Cindy Sue then, about how shortly before their high school graduation they had secretly eloped to Hernando, Mississippi, a little town just across the state line from Memphis that specialized in quickie marriages. Cindy Sue had been pregnant. Three weeks later she miscarried, and the next day he received a telegram notifying him of his appointment to Annapolis. "I told her that I wouldn't accept the appointment," he said in a quavering voice. "But she insisted that I go. 'It's God's will,' she said. 'That's why I lost the baby.' And then she reminded me of some advice an old blind singer named Slim Sparks had given us once. She said she wasn't going to stop me from going places and seeing things. She promised to wait for me. We spent a week at the cabin at the lake... and then I left for Annapolis."

"What happened?" Marianna asked anxiously when he paused for a moment.

"Two years later a classmate of mine told her about me shacking up with a girl on cruise. She turned to me, expecting me to deny it, but with one look she knew it was true. I'll never forget the look of hurt on her face. From that night on, it was all over. She filed for divorce two months later."

"It doesn't sound like much of a marriage if that's all it took to end it."

"You're wrong," he said with a faraway look. "I loved her. She loved me. It was just that it was one of those young first loves, the fragile kind where absolute faithfulness is demanded. She expected too much. But we did love each other."

In the late afternoon, he apprised her of their finances. "I've stayed longer in Europe than I planned and spent more than I expected," he said matter-of-factly. "I'm down to my last twelve dollars. This has to be our last day."

"That's all!" she exclaimed. "What are you going to do? How will you get home?"

"I had a military flight reserved out of Germany three days ago, but I've missed that now. I'll hitch my way down to Spain. There's an air force base there where I can probably catch a ride to the States."

"It's such a shame this all has to end because of money, don't you think?"

"Those are the breaks of naval air, as we often say. So how about one last swim?"

"Go ahead. I don't feel like it," she said abruptly.

He dived into the surf and swam a quarter mile out to sea where a deserted sailboat lay at anchor. He climbed aboard and stretched out on its deck for half an hour before swimming back again. She was gone when he returned. She had left a note pinned to the blanket: *'be back at five,'* it said.

At five-thirty he heard a beep above him on the seawall and someone shouting, "hey, asshole!" He glanced back over his head to see Marianna beckoning to him from the seat of a shiny new Vespa.

"Where did you get it?" he asked, astonished, after climbing the steps to meet her.

"I hocked my necklace!" she answered proudly. "Come on. Let's go check out of the hotel."

She kept him in suspense as they packed and checked out of the Trocadero. After pausing for only a brief moment to stare backward at the tiny, dimly lit room under the eaves that they had shared since Robert had left, she instructed him to drive westward, out of Nice, refusing to tell him their destination. "Turn here!" she commanded at the intersection where the road to Cagnes joined the highway. They turned north on the narrow road leading through the pine forests up into the Alpes-Maritime, bypassing Haut-de-Cagnes and proceeding another eight miles up into the mountains on a rutted dirt road until they reached a tiny village fortified by a red dust-encrusted wall. It was perched on the highest peak around.

"All right," Clay muttered at last. "You can end the suspense. Where are we?"

"It's called La Gaude!" she announced with an ecstatic smile. "You can drive the scooter inside, through the gate there."

The Vespa strained and jolted up the cobblestone streets on a nearly perpendicular hill until they reached a bakery and Marianna instructed Clay to halt. She went inside, emerged in less than two minutes with a long key on a large round hoop, hopped onto the back of the scooter and pointed toward the top of the hill. They stopped at its peak where the street dead-ended in front of two giant red cedar doors. She unlocked them, and they stepped inside into a courtyard in the center of which was a long, slender shallow pool surrounded on all sides by bougainvillea in blossom. Beyond the courtyard stood a house on the very edge of the cliff, three stories of Spanish tile, covered patios and walkways extending between its sprawling wings.

"It belongs to Jean Pierre's mother. Isn't it fantastic?" Marianna said, her face animated in excitement.

"It's the most beautiful place I've ever seen," Clay said in awe.

"It's ours for the rest of the week! And do you know what else? There's a boat in Antibes that we can use anytime we want."

And so – just as it nearly ended – they salvaged a few more days together. Marianna put together a bounteous breakfast each morning and they dined on a balcony off their bedroom that jutted out over the edge of the cliff into a bristling wind. From their roost they could see all the way to Nice, and to the peak of Cap d'Antibes, and across a parched, pine-covered valley to their sister peak, upon which nestled the village of St. Jeannet.

They were on their way most mornings before noon, gliding and bouncing down the mountain on the Vespa to the yacht club in Antibes where the boat was docked. The boat was a twenty-one foot wood-paneled inboard, and they used it to explore the small, isolated coves east of Nice between Villefranche and Menton. They would anchor in one of the coves in the afternoon and sunbathe in the nude, out of sight on cushions on the deck well flooring; and make love - sweaty and salty - and, afterwards, dive over the side for a swim to wash away the traces.

They felt strange and out of place at the yacht club. Each day after they docked, they had to walk by the patio to reach the Vespa in the parking lot, and past the club members socializing there, dressed impeccably, sipping their Bloody Mary's and reeking with opulence. On the second day Clay remarked as to how wonderful it must be to be rich, and to be able to just hang around a yacht club all day. Marianna brought him quickly to his senses. "Didn't you notice how pompous and old they are?" she said. "I wouldn't trade my youth for their yachts for anything!"

He thought about it and agreed with her completely. No yacht club member in Antibes would have tolerated the jolting, hot, dusty thirty minute Vespa ride they took back to La Gaude each day, an event that thrilled them immensely because it made the pleasures that they knew were awaiting them seem all the more meaningful. As soon as they arrived they stripped off their soiled clothes and plunged into a large, sunken marble tub in the master bedroom, a luxury they didn't know how they had been able to do without when they compared it with all the days they had spent at the Trocadero, and their only bath had been the sea. They learned about each other's bodies there, making love each evening on the giant oversized bed until they dozed off in each other's arms. But no matter how wasted or exhausted they were, they managed to awaken by eleven each night and dress and challenge the mountain road two more times, all the way to Nice and back in pitch black darkness in order to make their obligatory pilgrimage to the Gorilla.

The fourth night they skipped going to bed after their bath. Jean Pierre's mother was arriving the next day with friends from Paris, and they had to vacate the house. They packed, stopped by the bakery to drop off the key, and drove one last time down the mountain into Nice. They checked their bags at the bus station and returned the Vespa to its garage, after which they walked to the Gorilla to spend one last night with Beatrice and her friends. Beatrice fed francs into the juke box all night, playing "*Non, Je Ne Regrette Rien*" over and over again, and they drank vodka and orange juice and danced until closing time. As they left, Beatrice hugged and kissed them and extracted a promise - they agreed to return some day. They ambled down to the beach and sat on the seawall overlooking the Lido Plage, staring at the moon starting to fade with the approach of dawn.

"Do you know what's amazing?" Marianna said after a long period of silence. "This is the fourteenth night we've been together. I've counted them. Do you know we've stayed out past four o'clock every single one."

"I know," he smiled. "It's been tense, though, don't you think?"

"Oh, it's been more than that. It's been fantastic, Clay. I know it's just the summer...the beach...Nice. I know that. But someday I'm going to think back and wonder how it all happened...the meaning of it all."

"There is no meaning to it, Marianna," he said and his voice grew low pitched. "Don't you see, that's the beauty of it! It just happened. At this time, in this place...it was actual. That's all that matters because what is actual can only be actual but once."

"I know... And summers always have to end."

The street sweepers and water trucks came passing by and lorries began appearing with the break of day, hauling produce and flowers in from the country to the market. Clay and Marianna watched them for awhile and listened to the sounds as the city yawned and started to awaken.

"Do you think we'll ever see each other again?" she asked somberly, as they sat on the seawall tossing rocks at the surf.

"I'd like to if you would."

"I'm going to be in Washington for a wedding Labor Day weekend. That's not too far from your base in Virginia Beach."

"I'll meet you there."

"No commitments?"

"Touche'! No commitments," he said, and they both laughed.

She looked up and saw a glow flickering over the top of Mont Boron. "Oh, look! The sun!" she shouted excitedly. "That makes us friends forever, you know, the sharing of a sunrise together."

At eight o'clock he walked her to the bus station. The money she had received for the necklace was gone, and after paying for her bus ticket, Clay had exactly seven dollars worth of francs remaining. She leaned up and kissed him briefly on his eyelids, then backed away, offering a simple handshake. "One thing for certain, Mr. Stoner," she said with a nymph like grin, "when you think about it, you'll have to admit: it has been tense, fella!" And with that she turned and bolted aboard the bus.

He stood there recalling the many similar partings with Cindy Sue; all the times they had embraced and kissed passionately at airports and train stations. Cindy Sue had always cried whenever he left. Marianna did not look back or wave or do anything as the bus pulled away.

An hour later he hitched a ride. He was fortunate and reached Madrid in two days and only had to lay over there two more before catching a C-130 heading for New Jersey. He had to ride in the cargo hold, wrapped in a blanket amidst the crates for sixteen hours, half-frozen and hungry, and he had some problems clearing customs because he had lost his passport. But with a little persuasion and a great deal of luck, within three hours after he touched down in the States he caught another flight that took him to Scott Air Force Base in Illinois. From there he started hitchhiking toward Creekwood, two hundred miles away, with exactly thirty five cents in his pocket.

III

CREEKWOOD

Seventy miles north of Creekwood, Clay thumbed his fourth and last ride. A jolly, grizzly and grey headed black man driving a Ford pick-up truck stopped to give him a lift. The old man was an Uncle Remus sort of character. He wore bib overalls and a tattered straw hat. He smoked a corncob pipe. Clay told him about his Mediterranean cruise, and the old man asked hundreds of questions about what flying was like as they bumped along a rutted blacktop road, winding deeper into the hills. The road crossed a number of one-lane bridges and crispy cool creeks gurgling into the woods. They passed three or four cabins and saw some mules and cows. But those were the only signs of civilization for the next hour and a half. As the landmarks started becoming familiar, Clay grew quieter, and a nervous excitement began simmering within him. His impatience to cover the last few miles was almost uncontrollable. It had always been that way when he returned home.

Before leaving for Annapolis he had known of little beyond Creekwood, a farming community of about four thousand people located at the eastern fringe of the Ozarks in the southern part of Missouri - an isolated region almost impossible to reach by any commercial means of transportation. Until Petey Monroe built his airstrip, the only access to the outside world had been the rutted blacktop road. But only one bus a day travelled it, a local between St. Louis and Memphis that stopped at every small town along the way to drop off a package or pick up a passenger or two, causing the one hundred and sixty mile trip to either of those cities to take a minimum of six hours if the bus didn't break down along the way.

Twenty miles north of Creekwood the road passed through Hays Ridge, a tiny hamlet on the banks of the White Rock River and the gathering place on Sunday afternoons for one of the region's favorite pastimes - floating down the river in a canoe or flat-bottom johnboat, drinking beer and casting for bass. Winding out of Hays Ridge, the road ran on top of a levee that cut through a cypress swamp for a half-dozen miles. It was when the road entered the swamp that Clay's excitement started to bubble over, for he knew that when it emerged he would be at Creekwood's North 'Y'. The road divided there into a bypass and a business route straight down Main Street before merging again two miles south at the other end of town. Main Street led into the town square, around which were gathered the stores and shops that provided the basic necessities of life: Kroger's, the A&P, a Walgreen's and a Rexall, Woolworth's, two barbershops, a beer joint, a movie, and the bank - owned by the Collins family, the richest in the county. The town hall occupied the center of the square. It was surrounded by a small park where the farmers who came to town on Saturdays sat on green wooden benches while their wives shopped, some of them whittling, others talking in their Ozark twang about the weather. Farmers lived and breathed the weather. It was their main topic of conversation. Sometimes they complained of too much rain; other times of not enough or too much sun; Clay had never tried to understand it much, except to realize that it was very important to farmers to have the right mix of each.

The terrain to the south and east was very much different than it was to the north and west. The road east passed the shoe factory, owned by a large company in St. Louis; the John Deere and International Harvest dealers; the A&W Drive-In - and just before reaching the town limits, the Creekwood Country Club with its weedy, hilly nine hole golf course where for dues of ninety-six dollars a year almost anyone who was white and could pay was welcomed as a member. Beyond the country club the road was straight and flat, traversing rich delta farmland for sixty miles until it reached the Mississippi River. The road was lined the entire way with fields of cotton, soybeans and wheat, and sharecroppers' tarpaper shanties, most of which were painted brown, signifying that they were on Baker family land - the only other rich family in the county.

On the south side of town was the County Milling and Grain Company, owned jointly by the Collins and the Bakers. It ginned the cotton, processed the soybeans into oil, and ground the wheat into flour where it was then stored in tall cylindrical shaped concrete elevators until it was ready for the market. The road to the south was similar to the one to the east, straight and flat for twenty miles until it reached Junction City at the Arkansas state line. The shanties in that direction were painted mostly green, the trademark of Collins' family land.

West of town, in a swampy bottom on the far side of a hill that concealed it from view, was an area called Sunset. There in their squalid shacks, the town's thousand or so blacks lived, keeping to themselves and seldom venturing out except to work in the fields or as daytime domestics in white family homes.

West of Sunset the road disappeared very quickly into the Ozark woods - but not before it passed Stoner's Auto Body Shop, Clay's dad's place of business. Bill Stoner had been a mechanic before the war. When he returned home after being away three years, he started his own business, worked hard, and over the years built a reputation as the best and most honest mechanic and body repairman in the county. And during the process he aged. He added thirty pounds, lost most of his hair, and always looked older than he was. He became chairman of the Chamber of Commerce; owner of two wreckers; employer of a full-time bookkeeper, a parts man, three mechanics, two body work men and two young black helpers. He had faults, but they were not evil ones. He didn't like to talk about politics or ideas or heavy things. He loathed the few vacations he allowed himself whenever Lara Stoner tore him away from his work. She was a doer who made things happen, always wanting to go and see something new. He was the opposite, always anxious whenever he was away to get back To the garage in Creekwood where he was in charge and sheltered from the fast pace and pushiness of the outside world.

The old man went out of his way to drive Clay all the way home to the modest white frame, two bedroom house on Williams Street where he had lived for sixteen of his seventeen years before going to Annapolis. He unloaded his duffel bag from the back of the truck and asked the old man to come inside and meet his parents. But with the typical polite, embarrassed shyness ingrained in the southern black of his era, the old man declined. They shook hands, and Clay stood in his front yard watching as the pick-up truck drove down the street and out of his life forever.

He knocked on the door of his house for the first time in his life instead of just barging inside. It was opened, momentarily, by his mother. "It's about time you got home!" Lara Stoner shrieked, as she hugged him in the doorway before he had a chance to set down his duffel. "We've been expecting you for a week." Her eyes flashed with a crinkly smile. "I was at the lake yesterday. Fish are bitin' if you wantta go while you're here." There had always been a special chemistry between them, a resemblance in looks and character that caused everyone in Creekwood to look upon him as his mother's son much more than his father's. And a large part of that relationship had centered around the lake. While his dad was busy working, his mom had taught him how to fish, make doughballs, set trotlines, skin catfish, thread a worm on a hook and hook a minnow through its gills. They had spent every spring vacation and most summer weekends together at the cabin on the lake, arising by five most mornings in order to have time to stop by the lodge for bait and be on the water by sunrise in their johnboat with its five horsepower motor, putting toward their chosen fishing spot for the day. In the spring they fished among the cattails and lily pads in the shallow coves where the crappie and bass came to spawn. On hot summer days they worked the bottom of the river channel that ran through the middle of the lake where the catfish congregated seeking refuge from the heat. Other times they explored the dozens of little coves that branched off the lake. Their favorite was a secluded cove called Possum Hollow. It was on the far side of the lake from the cabin, deserted, usually, because it could only be reached by paddling down a winding creek cluttered with logs that would shear a motor's pin for certain if anyone attempted to navigate it with an outboard running. "Last one in is a rotten egg!" his mom would shout as soon as they reached Possum Hollow. And then she would strip and dive gracefully over the side of the boat, challenging him to a race before sprint-crawling fifty yards across the cove and back again with her two white buttocks bobbing porpoise-like through the water. It wasn't until he was fifteen that he could beat her. She imbued in him her narcissistic devotion to the sun. They would lie in the boat after the race, naked and sunbathing for hours, while she read a book and he monitored the fishing lines. She was a self educated woman. Often, she discussed what she was reading with him. "I don't understand this book," she might say. "It's about rats and a plague in North Africa. But that's just the surface, I know. The author is trying to say something more." Her favorite was *Grapes of Wrath*. "You have to read it when you get older," she said. "It's about a poor family without a home that always has to move around, and a world that treats them most unjustly." The story was not unlike her own life. She had been raised deep in the hills a hundred miles southwest of Creekwood in a house with a backyard privy, hand pumped well water, woodstove heat and kerosene lamps for lighting. She left home when she was fifteen to find work during the Depression. She moved into a rooming house in Creekwood and took a job working all night as a switchboard operator for the telephone company and going to school during the day. She had met Bill Stoner then, and married him when she was seventeen. A year later she had the honor of being named Queen of the Cotton Carnival. At forty-two, she was still the most stunning woman in Creekwood: tall, with slim legs and wavy brown hair, a sculptor's finely chiseled neck and chin, eyes that radiated a penetrating intelligence, a face that always looked as if it had just been scrubbed with cold creek water. Her poise belied her upbringing, and because of it she was always invited to the best social affairs, all the parties at the Collins and Bakers, and she more than held her own. But Creekwood throttled her at times. The PTA, the weekly card games and potluck dinners with the same people, the occasional trip to St. Louis or Memphis to shop or see a ball game - they were not enough. Somehow, though, by turning her energies and attention to the raising of her only son, she had managed to stay with Bill Stoner in Creekwood and find happiness.

Lara Stoner served a rabbit stew for dinner, and they caught up with each other's lives, laughing and joking until Clay told them he would be deploying to Vietnam on his next cruise. That caused a few moments of somber reflection until dessert was finished and coffee served, and Bill Stoner broke the good news. "I got a car down at the body shop I think you might like. Sixty-two corvette. Maroon convertible. Saw it at an auction down in Memphis Sort of banged up, but I checked it out. Only twenty thousand miles, so I bought it. Got it fixed up as good as new now. You want it?"

"Are you kidding! Just tell me what I have to do."

"Well...I got the paycheck you had the navy forward here. Why don't I keep half of it as a down payment and you can pay me the rest of what it cost over three years. No interest. Fair enough?"

"Dad, you're the greatest," Clay said admiringly.

After the meal, Clay helped his mother clear the dishes. "You know, we have a list of friends a mile long who've called to ask when you'd be home," she said as they walked into the kitchen.

"What about Terry Malone?"

"Nope. He's never been back since he ran off after that Flat River game. His father says he's still in the army someplace. Vietnam, I think."

Clay shook his head. It would have been great to see Malone again. The guy had been his best friend in high school. They double dated, got drunk and in trouble together, and senior year they were the cornerstone of the Creekwood football team, the team that broke the famous streak - the fifty-nine game streak - all victories.

* * *

It was the last game of the season and the game was played up in Flat River in the rain on a field of muddy gumbo. Creekwood was up against a bunch of lead miners' kids and were outweighed forty pounds to a man. And because of the rain and the mud, Terry, the first team all-state quarterback, was not able to pass. Still, with ninety seconds left in the game, Creekwood was trailing by only five points and had a first down on Flat River's two yard line. Then Terry tried a quarterback sneak - and fumbled. The Flat River crowd went into a frenzy. The Creekwood crowd, only a moment before being confident and expecting to pull off a sixtieth straight win, was stunned beyond belief. On the last play of the game they were still on their feet screaming desperately for some miracle, even though the ball was at the middle of the field and in Flat River's possession. When the game ended they slumped to their seats, devastated, and they sat there for a long two minutes until a lone trumpet player in the band mustered enough strength to start playing the school song. Another trumpet took up the refrain, and then several clarinets, and the Creekwood crowd began to sing:

> *"There's a school in south Missouri*
> *That is known throughout the state,*
> *It's a school of highest credit,*
> *None other half so great..."*

At that point they could go no further. First the girls in the stands started to cry; then the members of the band; finally the mothers and fathers. The song was never finished - and around the town square for the rest of the month the normal smiling chatter was conspicuous by its absence.

That was the second to last time that Clay had seen Terry Malone, who was absent from school the following Monday. No one had seen him since the night of the game. Clay went searching for him, and found him two days later in a seedy motel down in Junction City, across from one of their hangouts, the Driftwood Tavern, which had a reputation that anyone tall enough to reach the top of the bar with a quarter was old enough to buy a beer. Terry's steady girl friend, her name was Kay, was with him. He was lying in bed, one eye black, swollen shut. His nose was broken. His head was half shaved, sutured with at least twenty ugly stitches where it had been split open. Clay asked Kay what had happened. "A bunch of drunks followed us out of the Driftwood Saturday night and jumped Terry in the parking lot," she said, and she threw her arms around Clay, sobbing and trembling. "I...I ran inside and begged for help. Terry was laying out in the lot, unconscious, and I couldn't get anyone to come. And...and you know what they all said, Clay? They...they all said, 'that'll teach him not to fumble...'"

Clay helped them pack and drive back to Creekwood, but Terry never came back to school. Three weeks later Clay received a letter.

Stoner, old buddy:

Sorry I didn't say goodbye. I guess you'll have to make it through basketball season without me. Kay and I got married in Hernando about two weeks ago. I enlisted in the army, and we're on our way to Texas. Tell everyone in Creekwood to stick it up their ass for me. Okay?

Good luck,
Malone

That was all. Seven years ago. No one in town had seen him since.

Clay looked up at his mother, shaking his head sadly. "So Terry's never been back?"

"No. But Chuck Stanback's home and wants to see you! He's driving down from Flat River tonight. There's a dance at the country club. Slim Sparks is playin'.""

Clay brightened. It would be great to see the Chucker again. Clay still remembered vividly how they first met. It had been that same infamous Flat River football game. Creekwood had been run into the ground physically by Flat River's all-state fullback, Chuck Stanback, a raw-boned, six foot-three, two hundred and twenty pound lumberjack type of guy who lived in the hills and ran six miles to school and back every day. Clay tackled him fifteen times that night. Stanback kept coming around the right side through a hole that opened between Creekwood's left tackle and linebacker, and Clay was the only one left to stop the big runner. Outweighed by sixty pounds, he had to keep coming up each time from his deep safety position and hit Stanback head on. Near the end of the game he scored the winning touchdown over Clay, running the ball four straight times, same play, Clay tackling him each time. Clay slammed into him on the one yard line on the last run and had been carried tumbling into the end zone so groggy that it was a struggle to get back on his feet. Stanback was also slow getting up.

They met in the showers after the game. Chuck's nose was smashed up between his eyes, caked with blood and mucous. "Where is that fucker who hit me on the goal line!" he bellowed.

Clay walked over to him slowly and said, "I'm the one."

Chuck squinted at him menacingly. Then he stuck out his giant paw. "Great fuckin' game, pal! Put her there. Great fuckin' game." He laughed uproariously, then squinted again and looked at Clay up close in his face. "You're Clay Stoner, aren't you? I hear you applied to Annapolis?"

"That's right. Don't have any appointment though," Clay said bluntly.

"Well I do. Hope to see you there." And that was the beginning of their precious friendship. The guy had been his roommate for five years - four at Annapolis and one in the apartment they shared at Pensacola. They had played ball, partied like hell, chased women, and travelled home on leave together. They had even graduated from flight training and received their wings on the same day. But then they had been split up. Chuck received orders to a different squadron and shipped out almost immediately on a cruise to the

NO COMMITMENTS
57

Pacific. He had been off Vietnam when the shooting started. He and Clay had much catching up to do because Chuck had been gone almost a year.

Clay and Chuck met in the bar at the country club at nine o'clock. The first thing they did was order double scotches on the rocks, toss them down, and quickly order refills. Hard drinking was part of a navy pilot ritual - one of their common bonds. They could always be seen at officers' clubs, grouped around the bar and laughing and drinking as if tomorrow would never come. They communicated in a language that was all their own, a strange kind of sign language that required frequent wild waving hand gestures as they talked about complicated acrobatic flying maneuvers that no one but they could understand. They stood out from the rest of the crowd. They were lean and gaunt, usually, hardened by their daily bouts with the forces of gravity, g-forces that sometimes placed inhuman stresses on their bodies. And their eyes had a distant look, often tinged with streaks of jagged red blood vessels strained from the g-forces and the intense scanning of instruments and hundreds of hours spent squinting into the sun. They were known for getting roaring drunk as a matter of course. They had a saying: "you can't trust a pilot to fly on your wing unless you've gotten drunk together." So they got drunk together often. To the casual, uninformed observer, they could appear callous and obnoxious. But the casual observer had never experienced those cold, early mornings in the locker room when the chaplain and the personnel officer came in with bolt cutters to snip off the lock of one of their squadron mates and box up his belongings for shipment home. Many of the nights the pilots were seen drinking at the clubs, nights they were usually their rowdiest, they were drinking just so they could forget those kinds of mornings. They could care less about what anyone else thought. They knew there was no way anyone else could ever understand.

"What was it like in Nam?" Clay said halfway through their second double.

"It was a real milk run for the first six months," Chuck said with a strange eerie quietness in his voice. "We were flying the South, and no one shot back. But the last two months we moved the bombing up North, and it became one big clusterfuck. I've gotta tell you, Clay, it was bad. Real bad. Our targets had to be pre-approved all the way to Washington. Without that approval, which took days, not hours, we couldn't attack MIG airbases or missile sites, fly closer than thirty miles from Hanoi or ten miles from Haiphong harbor where ships were just sitting at the docks unloading incoming weapons and supplies. Through it all the air group commander seemed to be much more concerned with how many sorties we could launch a day just so he could beat the record of the air group commander before him. It didn't seem to matter how many times we had to take-off without any real targets or armed with only one bomb. We lost sixteen out of the air group. Fourteen in just the last six weeks. Our C.O. bought the farm. Smoky got it too."

"Oh my God! Not Smoky!" Clay moaned. "You guys flew wing on each other, didn't you?"

"Yeah. I was with him when he got hit. He tried to make it out over open water, but his plane caught fire. He had to punch out. I saw his chute open. He landed just fine. I radioed for a chopper and flew cover overhead 'til it got there. It only took twenty minutes. Smoky made it to the chopper and...and it was just lifting off the ground when the dinks blasted it. It caught fire and blew up." Chuck's voice cracked and his eyes reddened. "Those...those fuckers knew Smoky was there all the time. They were just waitin' to get the chopper..." Chuck shook his head. "And do you know," he said then slowly, "the navy classified everyone on board that chopper as an MIA. That's because I saw one guy get out and run into the woods before it exploded. But it wasn't Smoky. I'm positive of that. I made a pass at fifty feet and saw him plain as day. He was wearing a green flight suit. Smoky's was orange. I told the navy that, but it made no difference...When I came home I went to see Smoky's wife. I tried to tell her that he's not just missing...that he's never coming back. I...I tried as gently as I knew how, Clay, but she won't accept it."

"God, that's gotta be tough on her," Clay said hollowly. "I'm sure deep down she knows you're right. She'll have to learn to accept it eventually." They stared at their drinks for more than a minute, not looking at each other until Clay broke the silence. "That goddamn Smoky! They would've had to shoot him down twice to get him. He was the toughest bastard I ever knew. Oklahoma. Remember when I boxed him at the Academy? He damn near knocked my head off."

"Yeah," Chuck said as he looked up with a faint smile. He looked at Clay. "I didn't tell you, but I had to punch out over there myself?"

Clay slapped him on the shoulder and leaned back on the bar stool laughing, Smoky forgotten for the moment until another time. "No kidding, you big oaf! What happened? Get lost and run out of gas like a dumb shit?"

"It wasn't funny. I caught some shrapnel that knocked out my hydraulics. By the time I got back to the boat my controls were starting to freeze up and I couldn't get the gear down."

"How did it go?"

"A piece of cake. I climbed up to five thousand feet just like they taught us in flight school, tilted the nose up ten degrees, set the autopilot, and pulled the curtain. The chopper was there by the time I hit the water. I was on the boat in ten minutes."

"I guess flying the North was really an experience, huh?"

"You better believe it. My last six missions were way inland, near the China border. The goddamn flak and missiles were flying everywhere. I never even saw a target. I just rocked in following my flight leader, pulling five g's the whole run, and when he said 'pickle' I dumped my load, reversed course with a half-cuban eight, and hauled ass. I could have been blasting holes in the sand for all I knew. For all I cared too...I'll tell you one thing, Stoner, my squadron has to go back in another six months, and there ain't none of us looking forward to it."

"I'm going in February," Clay said quietly.

"No kidding. I guess they're gonna get us all sooner or later." Chuck draped his beefy arm around Clay's shoulder and gave him a warm, woozy and affectionate look. They ordered another round of doubles and started getting soused.

"I don't like the way we're getting into this war, Chucker," Clay said after awhile. "Take the President's new plan to raise the troop level from twelve thousand by sending in another hundred and twenty five. We're not calling up the reserves, or the guard, so we're going to be drafting kids off the street who've never even been on a camping trip and sending them over there. It's stupid."

"It sure won't be any picnic," Chuck said, nodding. "But what would you have us do? Let the whole country go communist?"

"Who cares? They've been fighting each other for centuries, long before they ever heard of communism. This is basically a civil war, you know. I don't see how it's any of our business."

"You don't mean that."

"Yes I do. Does it really make any difference to us whether they're communists or not?"

Chuck exploded. "It sure as *hell* made a difference to guys like Smoky, I can tell you that!" he raged. People in the lounge started to turn and stare. "You're not gonna tell me they were all killed for *nothin'!* I know guys who would punch your lights out for saying something like that Stoner. Try it in an Officer's Club sometime and see what happens!"

"Did you ever think that maybe those guys can't face the truth? That maybe this is a no win war?"-

"Bullshit! We've lost too many guys to stop now. We have no choice except to go in there and win the war."

"Win it for whom, Chucker? The South Vietnamese? Or Smoky? Let me ask you a question. Can you even define what you mean by 'winning the war'?"

"Sure. That's easy. We whip their ass until they surrender. You know."

"No, I don't know," Clay hammered at him. "How do you go about it?"

"How about leveling the North? Just blow it right off the fuckin' map!"

"We can do that," Clay said calmly. "But is it worth it? That doesn't stop the Cong in the South. Does it make sense to level another country - to wipe out all its dumb innocent peasants; women and children? Our bombs don't discriminate, you know. Did you ever dream you'd have to do something like that when you signed up to go to Pensacola?"

"No, of course not," Chuck muttered, starting to became confused now. "We're obviously not going to do that. That's why the President is sending in all those army troops. We'll have to invade the North on the ground and occupy it. That's how we'll win the war. It should be over in a few months."

"Hanoi is only thirty miles from the China border, Chucker. What happens when the army gets there if a million Chinese jump on them from out of nowhere, just like in Korea? Do you want to take that risk? Then the only way to win the war is to H-bomb China. Nuke fifty million Chinese or so. Is Vietnam worth that?"

A drunken look of despair spread across Chuck's face. "No," he said, and he covered his eyes with his hands.

"That's why we're never going to win this war, Chucker. Mark my words. It's going to be the first war in the history of America that we lose. And you know what else? All the kids we send over there, well...the ones who make it back, who survive, are going to come home feeling betrayed. It's going to wreck us for years, Chucker. Mark my words."

"You're telling me Smoky was wasted?"

"Yeah. That's exactly what I'm saying."

They ordered another round of doubles, and as they started to savor their taste, a tall, lanky man wearing a leather jacket, jeans and cowboy boots tottered up to the bar and plopped down on a stool beside them. "Hey Stoner! When in the hell did you get in town?" the man cried out. He was red-eyed and weather beaten looking. He turned to Chuck and extended his hand. "Petey Monroe's the name. Flyin's my game. What's your bag, man?"

Chuck accepted the handshake hesitantly, too drunk and startled to reply. "This is Chuck Stanback," Clay said to Petey. "Chuck and I went to the Academy together."

"No shit, man! Are you an airplane driver too?" Petey said, still pumping Chuck's hand.

Chuck drew his hand away frowning, and gave a *harrumph*. "I don't know. Am I?" he said sarcasticly.

"Chuck flies F-4's," Clay said. "He just got back from Nam"

"Hey, all right!" Petey roared, and he reached out and grabbed Chuck's hand and started pumping it again.

Petey was Creekwood's resident pilot. He lived in a house trailer next to a small grass airstrip off Dog Trot Road that he owned and had built himself. He also owned two Stearmans that he used for crop dusting and a six passenger, twin engine Piper for flying charters. He was about eight years older than Clay, but he looked much older. Too much booze and too many hours in the open cockpit of the Stearman had taken their toll. He had been a mechanic in the air force and learned his trade in a flying club. After his discharge he knocked around crop dusting in Texas for awhile until he saved enough money to move back to Creekwood and start his own business. Most people in Creekwood thought Petey was an irresponsible cad, but he was the kind of cad that most people liked.

"Did you get in on any of the bombin'?" Petey asked Chuck, now trying to reflect a reverent tone of respect.

"Yes. As a matter of fact I did," Chuck uttered in a low growl.

"He got seven air medals," Clay chimed in.

"Jesus Christ!" Petey exclaimed in awe. "You must be a goddamn hero!"

Chuck shrugged. "Naw. We all got them," he growled again. To anyone but Petey it was obvious he wanted to change the subject.

"Chuck lost his wingman over there," Clay interjected.

"Wow! It must have been wild over there," Petey went on as if he hadn't heard. "I really envy you guys being able to get in on that action."

Chuck gave Petey a look furious enough to stop a wild boar in its tracks. "Listen asshole," he said. "Didn't you just hear my friend here tell you I lost my wingman over there? So why don't you go piss off somewhere else before you make me really mad."

Petey backed off. "Hey, sorry, man. No hard feelings. Okay? I understand." He turned to Clay. "Say, I forgot to mention it. Cindy Sue's here. She's in the ballroom. By herself, too. Tim's out of town."

Petey's remark caught him off guard. The prospect of Cindy Sue being at the club tonight was not one he had considered. He had not seen her since their divorce. She had married again and done all right for herself. She had married Tim Collins, the only male heir to the Collins' family fortune.

Clay left Chuck and Petey at the bar and walked down the hallway and into the ballroom, more like a dance hall at an Elk's Club than a ballroom actually, card tables with white paper table cloths and chair legs that folded. He had a sense of déjà vu. On stage was the legend, Slim Sparks, crooning an old, sentimental favorite, *Too Young*. The thought of seeing Cindy Sue sent a tingle fluttering down his spine. The stirring he felt caused him to remember another time, the day they each surrendered their virginity to one another, as if it were yesterday.

* * *

It was spring of his sophomore year and Cindy Sue was absent from school. During first hour her brother, Bobby Joe, told Clay that she was home sick. Clay knew that her parents worked and that she was home alone. They had been exploring sex for several weeks. She had let him put her arms around her at the movies and feel her boobs, and twice he had his hand in her pants and fondled her to an orgasm. But they had never gone all the way. After first hour he skipped class and started hiking, hurriedly, the two miles out across cotton fields to her house, a ramshackle, four room sharecropper's shack propped up at the corners on concrete blocks.

She met him at the door wearing pink, shorty pajamas. She was the most beautiful girl he had ever imagined - olive skin, shiny black hair, long legs, high hips, a large sensual mouth that had teeth so white they seemed to sparkle. Even at fourteen she was fully developed; her breasts jutted out liked two footballs sculptured in marble. She invited him inside, and very calmly, as if she sensed what was going to happen next, she removed her robe and crawled back into her rumpled bed. He lay down beside her, and when they kissed she opened her lips and darted her tongue inside his mouth. He had never been so in love. He took off his clothes and started caressing her. And when he did she opened her legs. He reached down and touched her and warm juices flowed over his hand. She started shuddering and she clung to him, moaning and mumbling soft words of love. He wrapped his arms around her, overcome with a feeling of power and tenderness that he never before had dreamed possible.

They showered afterwards and changed the sheets. Two tiny bloodstains were the only evidence of how things had changed between them. They had lunch and talked about how someday they would get married. When he left that afternoon he knew their love was something special, that very first young love that can be so intense that adults seldom comprehend.

By the time they were sixteen they had done it seven times, and each time caused an inner struggle. Cindy Sue was Catholic, and after each time she insisted on going to church to confess her sin - always out of town where the sin could be confessed discretely. By the end of that year he had driven her to every Catholic Church within seventy miles, and after each visit he would ask her, "what did the priest say?" And she would always answer, "that if you really loved me, we wouldn't do it anymore until we were married." And each time he would hold her gently and make a vow to stop, even though he knew that was impossible.

* * *

Clay picked Cindy Sue out of the crowd right away, sitting at a table on the far side of the dance floor talking to a massive, oafish-looking young man with heavy hanging jowls who was dressed proudly in his deputy sheriff's uniform - Howard Hawkins, or Hogjaw, as everyone called him, the nickname by which he was far more proud to be called than by his given name. He was Clay's high school classmate, the linebacker who kept missing all the tackles in the Flat River game. Clay started walking across the dance floor, up to Cindy Sue from behind, and tapped her on the shoulder. "Hi! Wantta dance?" he said simply, just as if nothing had changed. She turned and looked at him, a flicker of bittersweet memory there, and got up, and he led her out onto the floor. She rested her head against his shoulder, and they started dancing. Slim was still crooning *Too Young*.

"Long time," he said, after a few quiet moments.

"Three years."

"Do you remember the last time we danced to Slim singing this song?

"Yeah - your senior year in high school - the Homecoming Dance. And he came over to us and told us we were too young to get married...not to do it just to prove we loved each other...he said get out of Creekwood and go see the world first."

"But we didn't listen, did we?"

"We wouldn't have listened to anyone at the time, Clay. But at least you got out."

"So, how've you been?"

"Fine," she said. "I don't know if you heard, but I'm a mother now, a little girl this past spring named Sue Ellen."

"No, I hadn't. But that's great, Cindy Sue," he said warmly. "I hope you're happy."

"I'm learning to be. I know Tim is ten years older and that you hardly knew him, but he treats me well. And we just built us a beautiful new house out off Dog Trot Road."

"Which is one thing he could give you that I never could."

"That's not why I married him."

"I hope not. So where is Tim tonight anyway?"

"Down in Florida at a bankers' convention with his dad."

"And meanwhile, Hogjaw's the old reliable escort."

She shrugged. "Hogjaw's harmless. You know that."

He swirled her around and pulled her close against him. "It's been a long time. I was still in love with you when you got the divorce. I hope you know that," he said, and he kissed the side of her neck. He felt her cling to him for a second, and then she backed away.

"Don't blame me, Clay," she said, looking straight into his eyes. "I know we had something physical. But getting married at seventeen was dumb - and then you went away to Annapolis. We never had a chance to have a real marriage."

"We could have made it work if you'd tried."

"No we couldn't. I just wanted to settle down, have kids, a home, some roots. You were gone all the time. And whenever you did come home all we did was fight."

"I suppose you and Tim never fight."

"No...we don't. Second loves are different, Clay. Not as intense, maybe, but still okay. With you it was always all or nothing. You wouldn't let me be my own person. I couldn't take that for the rest of my life."

"I'm sorry."

"Oh, don't be. It wasn't your fault. I did love you. I loved you so much," she said, and she squeezed the back of his neck. The dance ended, and he started walking her back to her table. She clung to his arm. "I hope you'll find what you want and be happy," she said. "I know it wasn't me."

"I will," he said. "And I'll be happy just knowing that you're happy, Cindy Sue. I mean that."

He left her with Hogjaw and walked out of the club feeling that a great ponderous weight had been lifted. It was all over between them now. He had not been sure before.

IV

PASSING THROUGH

She was admiring her friend's bridal gown in the upstairs bedroom of an old three story colonial estate in Chevy Chase when the maid walked in and said, "telephone Miss Haizet."

She walked to a stand in the hallway and lifted the receiver. "Hi fella'!" She heard a cheerful voice come on the other end of the line.

"*Clay!* Is that you? Where are you?" Marianna said, surprised.

"Georgetown. I'm just a mile or two away."

"Oh..." she said quietly. "That's great. I hope we get a chance to see each other."

"What do you mean a *chance?* I busted my ass to get here for the weekend. Drove straight through from Creekwood - eleven hundred miles without stopping, just to see you."

"But...but I never heard from you after Nice. You never called. I didn't think you were coming."

"I told you I'd be here, didn't I?"

"Yes...I know," she said hesitantly. "There's a problem though. The wedding starts in two hours. I'm a bridesmaid and I have to go to the reception afterwards. And my ride back to New York is leaving at noon tomorrow. I don't know when we'll have time."

"Can't you stay here tomorrow? I don't have to be back to Oceana until Monday."

"No. I'm sorry, Clay. I have to go home tomorrow. You should have come yesterday."

"Then I'll pick you up after the reception."

"That's sort of touchy. It's a dinner dance and I'm expected to go with the bride's brother. It won't be over until very late."

"Since when did you care how late it was? We never went out in Nice before midnight."

"That's...that's true, she said, nervous now. "But we're not in Nice anymore, Clay. Things are a little more complicated here."

"It's sure starting to sound that way. Listen, Vic and Darcy are having a party at his dad's house in Arlington tonight. Half my squadron's going to be there, and I'd like you to meet the guys."

"I don't see how it's possible."

"Then *make* it possible," Clay fumed.

"Okay. Okay. There's a bar about two blocks from here called the Zebra Lounge. I'll try to slip away and meet you there about midnight."

"You'll *try?*"

"I'll *try*. Now I have to go," she said, and she hung up and walked into the bathroom and stared at her reflection in the mirror, wondering what she was going to do now.

Vic and Darcy's party began calmly enough. A dozen aviators were already there when Clay arrived; six from his own squadron, a half-dozen from Chuck's, just back from Vietnam. All of them were bachelors except Vic. Chuck's group was the center of attention, busy describing what it was like to fly in real combat. The stereo was turned low and the girlfriends were all standing around listening, mesmerized by the stories. Admiral Powers was there, too, lapping it up. It had been a long time since the navy had had any young, decorated war heroes to bolster its image. Clay went to the bar in the adjoining room to mix himself a drink. He had no sooner mixed it when he was pounced upon by Darcy's stepsister, Katrina Asquith, known as Cat to her friends. She was in one of her more frisky moods. "I'm bored. You wanna take me home?" she suggested brazenly.

Clay and Chuck were staying the weekend at her apartment in Georgetown. Chuck had made the seventeen hour drive east with him, and this weekend was to be Chuck's celebrated reunion with Cat after his ten month cruise. They had dated only a few times, but she slept with him once the night before he left, wrote to him while he was gone, and Chuck had fallen hard. Now, the dumb cluck thought he was in love with her. But a number of other guys thought they were in love with Cat, and she had slept with more than a few while Chuck was away. She was a stunner, early twenties like many of the other young party girls around Washington, a wiry, five foot six, frizzy red-haired, green-eyed tease who thought she was exciting and impressive. She did have a father - also

Darcy's stepfather now - who *was* impressive. Clay had seen his name in the news many times: David Asquith, the senior partner and heavyweight lobbyist in Washington's most prominent firm. Through him and Darcy's father-in-law, Admiral Powers, Cat kept herself quite busy on the social circuit.

"I thought you were with Chuck?" Clay said disapprovingly.

"Just because I came with Chuck doesn't mean I have to leave with Chuck. Besides, he's all wrapped up telling his war stories."

"Sorry. I have a late date," Clay said.

"Bet she can't give you as much action as I can," Cat squealed, as she reached down and quickly unzipped his fly.

Clay tried to pacify her. "Easy girl. I've seen you in action before – Vic and Darcy's wedding. I don't think I can handle it."

She cooed as she zipped his fly up and down two more times. "What's the matter big, tough navy pilot? Can't get it on when you drink?"

Clay pushed her away. "Sorry, Cat. I'm not in the foolin' around mood tonight. Especially with someone who's supposed to be my best friend's girl."

"You're just afraid to take me on, big tough navy pilot," she smiled, pouting. "I bet you can't even chug your drink as fast as I can chug mine."

She foxed him. He had seldom been goaded into drinking more than he could handle, but he accepted her challenge and she handed him a water glass filled to the brim with straight warm bourbon. She was drinking a weak Tom Collins. He bested her in about thirty seconds, patted her on the fanny, and stumbled off to find Vic and Darcy. He wandered into the den and instead found Admiral Powers, seated by the fireplace all alone and watching the late evening news on television. The Admiral motioned for him to sit down. A film on the war in Vietnam was showing. When the commercial bleeped on, the Admiral took out his pipe, packed and lit it, and took three strong puffs.

"In a few months you and Vic will be over there. Looking forward to it?"

"No sir."

"No?" The Admiral looked surprised. "I hope you realize this war is a great opportunity for you boys. You'll be the first pilots since Korea to get any combat experience."

Perhaps it was the bourbon. Perhaps it had been building up for a time, but what Clay said next surprised even him. "Admiral, I don't mean any disrespect, sir, but quite a few of us think this war is just plain stupid. We'd feel different if our country was at stake. But that's not the case here."

The Admiral studied him carefully, puffed on his pipe for a moment, and then said, "I don't blame you for feeling that way, son. There were times during the Korean War that I felt the same way. But that's not your decision to make. When the time comes, you'll do what's asked of you. I'd bet on that. Vic says you're good."

"So is Vic, sir."

"You think so? It pleases me to hear you say that son. I wanted him to be a pilot. You can't imagine how grieved I was when I heard he failed his eye test."

"He would have been a great pilot, sir. He's the best RIO in the squadron."

"That makes me proud."

"You should be. But what if he gets killed over there, Admiral? How would you feel about the war then?"

It was as if a button had been pressed. A moment before the Admiral had been puffed up and affable. The question jolted him, and his response was brusque. "How do you think I would feel? I'd feel rotten, just like any father! But I'll tell you one thing, Lieutenant, I'd still be more proud of him for having gone than if he hadn't. Now if you will excuse me, I'm going to bed."

The Admiral left, and Clay wandered into the next room and rejoined the party. Chuck approached him, looking exasperated.

"Cat's sick. She wants to go home. I don't suppose you could drive us?"

Clay checked his watch. "I've got to meet my date in half an hour. I can take you if you're ready to go now. Where is Cat?"

"She's already out in your car. Passed out."

They walked outside to Clay's Corvette. Cat was slumped against the door. Chuck opened it, lifted her up and plopped her in his lap. He thought they were going to Cat's apartment but as soon as Clay started driving and the wind started blowing, she woke up and insisted on going to her father's house out in McLean. Chuck was furious. Clay pulled off onto a side street and let them argue for ten minutes. Cat won out. He drove them out to McLean, up a long winding driveway to a circle in front of an impressive country estate, and watched Cat leap out of the car and run inside without so much as giving Chuck a kiss on the cheek.

They were both quiet as they sped back toward the bridge across the Potomac to Chevy Chase. Clay could think of nothing to say. He had tried to warn Chuck about Cat before, but there was no way he was going to volunteer the brutal truth - that she was a manipulator of men. *So welcome home Chuck. I've got my own problems.* It was already twelve-thirty, and the trip to McLean was going to make him late at the Zebra Lounge. He had to wonder if Marianna would be there. .

Marianna was standing on a street corner in front of a neon sign flashing the silhouette of a zebra as Chuck and Clay drove up. She was smoking a cigarette and pacing back and forth. She jumped into the Corvette as soon as it pulled up to the curb. "Say, I like your car," she said with a bouncy exuberance as she wedged herself in next to Chuck. Clay introduced them as they sped toward the bridge that would take them to Arlington.

They arrived at the Powers' at one-thirty, and Darcy greeted them at the door. "You'd better watch yourself," she apologized to Marianna. "The girls have all left, and it's getting raunchy inside. Sammy Powell's been dropping his pants and mooning everybody."

Marianna was horrified by the spectacle. Six of the pilots were still there; six drunken louts. One was beating a bongo aimlessly off in a corner, another passed out, his legs over the back of the sofa. Clay started introducing her around, and she made an effort to be a good sport. She met "Swinging Sammy" Powell, as he was called, Clay's wingman; then "Stinger" Thornton, who came up to her, grinning, singing a little ditty: *"well, it's Saturday night and I just got paid, so why don't you and me go get laid."* At the same time, Sammy pinched her on the ass. She slapped him and stormed off in a huff. Sammy was indignant.

"Hey, Stoner! Where in the hell'd you get such an uptight broad?" he bleated.

"She's a debutante," Clay joshed. "They're all like that."

Marianna went into the kitchen with Darcy. "Are they always like this?" she asked, shocked and still incensed. "Look at them! Who would think anybody would trust them to fly airplanes. Why... why they're just a bunch of animals!"

"You've just got to learn to understand them," Darcy said.

"Understand them! Are you serious, Darse? Look at that slob in the corner. Are you going to tell me he needs some understanding?" A loose, limp form of a body was slumped in the corner, leaning against the wall, too drunk to move. His legs were spread in a semicircle around a puddle of vomit.

"That's Jimmer Jones," Darcy said in a sympathetic tone. "I'll have to clean his mess up later. He's the one who had the mid-air with Duke on cruise."

Marianna had no idea what she was talking about. "What are you talking about?" she asked. "Who's Duke? What's a mid-air?"

"Duke Dawson. He was a squadron mate. Jimmer and Duke's planes ran into each other one night over in the Med. Jimmer was able to eject. But Duke and his RIO never got out. They never found them. BNR, it's called. Body not recovered. Jimmer blames himself for it, so you shouldn't be too harsh on him."

Marianna stared at the pitiful creature in the corner, and her anger softened a bit. "How do you stand it, Darse?"

"Stand what?"

"The fact that Vic will be gone for almost a year - that he won't even be home for the baby - that...who knows what might happen to him." She looked at Darcy, staring back at her, clear eyed.

"Why don't you just say it...that he might never come back? We all know that," Darcy said, showing no emotion. "We just try not to think about it, that's all. I keep hoping something will happen and Vic won't have to go. But I know he will. So will Clay and all the rest of the guys out there. We learn to accept it."

"Accept it! Why?" Marianna said, shaking her head in disbelief.

"None of us can tell you why, Marianna. We just do. We're part of a family. If you were part of it, you'd understand."

Marianna and Clay were the last to leave. By then the chugging contest with Cat had taken its toll. Clay was so drunk that he tripped off the front steps and fell into the yard, landing on his back in the grass. "I think I'd better drive," Marianna said, staring down at him with her hands on her hips. "You're not sober enough to make it two blocks."

"Shure I can," Clay slurred, staring up at her with a silly grin. "Ah've been drivin' drunk all my life. Don't you worry none." He got up and staggered to the car and managed to steer it passably across the bridge into Georgetown. But at an intersection on M Street he bumped over a curb and across the median into the oncoming lane, missing a tree and a lamp pole in the process by inches. He braked to a stop and shook his head. Marianna insisted on driving. He pushed her away and started weaving the car down M Street again, fighting a swimming feeling going round and round in his head. As they neared Columbus Circle the spinning overcame him. He swerved into an alley, stopped, and tumbled out of the car. He leaned against a brick wall behind a delicatessen for a few moments, gulping in the night air. Then he slid down the wall and crumpled face down onto the pavement.

Marianna let him lie there for a half-hour before she got out of the car. She knelt down beside him, rolled him over, and whispered in his ear. He heard a soft voice saying, "hey asshole. It's time to get up."

She helped him to his feet and into the car. This time she drove. She stopped at an all night diner and watched as Clay fiddled with an order of toast and coffee for nearly an hour. He managed to down it and light a cigarette, finally. "Feel better now?" she asked.

"I couldn't feel any worse," he said, smiling wearily.

"I'm glad you didn't know me when I first started drinking. I passed out all the time."

She paid the bill, and they wandered out of the diner into the dawn. She stopped at the curb all of a sudden and pointed toward the eastern sky. "Look, Clay. The sun - our third sunrise together!"

"Yeah. But do you think you'll still be my friend after tonight?" he said, flipping his cigarette into the street.

"Forever," she said, smiling at him impishly.

"Ever and ever?" he asked and she nodded. "Then why don't we go try to find a motel," he said as they climbed into the Corvette.

Marianna moved away from him, leaning against the door. "Clay, I can't stay with you," she said in no uncertain terms. "I skipped out of the wedding party tonight by telling everyone I had a headache. They all think I'm upstairs asleep. They'll be expecting me down for breakfast this morning. It would be just too embarrassing if I didn't show up."

Clay switched on the ignition and drove her up to Chevy Chase without saying a word. He walked her to the door of the bride's stately mansion and they sat down on the porch steps. She put her arm around his neck and studied him for awhile. "You look horrible," she said finally.

"You don't look so hot yourself," he said.

"Do you know...going out with you has been crazy, Clay. We've stayed out past four every night we've known each other."

"Anything wrong with that?"

"No. It's been fun. *Haps*, I think you called it."

"Do you ever want to have any more haps?"

"I'd like to," she said, looking serious all of a sudden. "I have to go back to New York tomorrow, but I hope you call me sometime." She kissed him on the eyelids and went inside.

Clay's squadron flew out of the Oceana base near Virginia Beach in mid-September to meet the aircraft carrier coming out from Norfolk for a three week shakedown cruise, a short training exercise designed to simulate the toughest of combat conditions. Three launches a day were routine, and sometimes four, a test of the endurance that might someday be required for maximum round-the-clock operations. Four launches a day was an unsustainable pace, one that allows a pilot no time to do anything except eat, sleep, and fly. The routine was precise and repetitive. Up at four in the morning. In the ready room by four-thirty, sipping coffee, smoking cigarettes, being briefed on the things a pilot has to know - radio frequencies, rendezvous positions, the prescribed maneuvers for the mission. On deck in the chilling wind at five-fifteen. Ten minutes to preflight the aircraft. Then start engines and taxi into line for launching. Tune radios, set instrument gages, lower the folded wings and check them locked. Taxi onto the catapult. Watch the yellow shirted CAT officer, mufflers over his ears, twirling his hand to signal when to rev engines. Final check list: visor down, radar caged, a firm grip on the throttle, one hundred percent power on both engines. Then a fast salute to the CAT officer and head and body are jolted back against the seat and vision blurs as the aircraft is shot into the sky in less than two hundred feet. Climb to altitude. Rendezvous with the rest of the flight and practice for an hour - dogfights, bombing runs, rocket attacks. Regroup and return to the ship, wingtip to wingtip at four hundred knots, ten feet apart, eyes riveted on the aircraft ahead, jockeying throttles constantly to maintain position. Over the ship. Slap the stick over, chop throttles and peel off one by one. Speedbrake down, flaps down, gear down, tail hook down. Descend in tightly spaced intervals until downwind abeam the carrier. Bank into a gentle descending turn and maintain the prescribed airspeed and angle of attack until the meatball - a tiny orange dot on a mirror on the deck - pops into view. Keep the meatball in the middle of the mirror and listen to the LSO. Smash aboard at one hundred fifty miles an hour, add full power and brace for the jolt of the tail hook snagging a wire. Stop in less than a hundred feet. Back to the ready room for a debriefing of the mission. More coffee.

More cigarettes. In bed at eight o'clock. Two hours to sleep before the routine starts again. And so it goes. Twenty four hours around the clock with no time to do anything - except eat, sleep and fly.

The carrier deck is a dangerous place, even in peacetime when no one is shooting to kill. Catastrophes strike without warning. Tires blow, landing gears collapse, jet fuel gets sloshed around causing fires and explosions. And there are freakier accidents. A catapult malfunctions, and the dreaded "cold cat shot" dribbles an aircraft off the bow into the sea. An arresting wire snaps on impact sending a chain of cable flying through the air and slicing through anything or anyone in its path like a scythe. A pilot on the catapult raises his finger to scratch his nose instead of salute and is blasted off into the night with his wings still folded. An arresting wire with its tension set for a fifty thousand pound A-3 catches a nine thousand pound A-4 by mistake, stopping it as if it had run into a brick wall and breaking the pilot's neck. The greatest danger of all is the landing, trying to plunk a jet at high speed onto a three hundred foot spot on the deck without overshooting or plowing into the stern of the ship, not an easy feat in the best of times. But in rough seas with the deck rising and falling more than forty feet, or on foggy nights low on gas when the pilot knows he only has one chance to make it aboard or he'll have to eject, a carrier landing can be stark terror.

Clay had already seen or experienced a number of flying's mercurial thrills, when on the tenth night out at sea, he and Vic launched in a fog. They were climbing out to rendezvous when the next plane off the catapult drove straight into the sea, its' pilot a victim of vertigo and unable to adapt to his instruments as he was shot off into the dark blanket of mist. There was mass confusion on the ship, and all the planes in the air were instructed to return and land, creating even more confusion. A night radar controlled approach was required, the most difficult of all. Clay's aircraft was the second down. He turned the base leg at one thousand feet, still in the fog, and was turned over to the guidance of an air controller on the ship. He lowered his flaps and gear, slowed to one hundred and forty knots, and following the calm instructions of the controller, he commenced his descent down the glide slope.

"Right two degrees," the controller instructed. "You're fifty feet above glide slope, easing further above. Bring it down. Now, left one degree. You're coming down. Coming down. Thatta baby. You're on glide slope. On heading. Looking good now. You're passing through five hundred feet...*What the hell!*"

Clay felt a crunch and knew instinctively what it was. In one swift motion, he reached his arms over his head and pulled the curtain. The next thing he knew it was pitch black and he was in icy water being dragged by his parachute in the wind. He struggled for almost a minute before freeing himself, and then methodically, just as trained, he inflated his life raft and climbed aboard. He was cold and shivering, but other than that, he wasn't hurt. He called out to Vic, who he was sure would be close by since they had both ejected at such low altitude. "Over here," came a feeble cry. He saw a tiny light flickering about fifty yards away and paddled toward it. Vic was floating motionless in the water, supported only by his Mae West.

"Get in your raft!" Clay shouted. "You'll freeze in this water."

"It's gone, Clay," Vic moaned. "My chute tangled and was holding me under. I slashed everything loose. Worse yet, I think I busted my tail bone. It hurts real bad." The situation was grim. Clay tied a lanyard to his waist, rolled into the sea, and with great effort, helped Vic crawl aboard. Vic's pain was so severe that he promptly passed out. Clay climbed on top of him, unable to get his entire body into the tiny one-man raft. He was forced to spend the remainder of the night hanging on the side of the raft, half-in, half-out and freezing, as he watched Vic drift from one delirium to another.

A helicopter discovered them about seven o'clock in the morning. They were hauled out of the water semi-conscious, flown to the ship, and confined in its hospital for the last four days of the cruise. Clay had recovered fully by the time the ship reached Norfolk, and Vic's injury was not too serious. He was able to walk with a cane and a back brace. After sixty days of convalescence leave, he was expected to be as good as new. It had been a disastrous cruise for the squadron, though. In less than half an hour it had lost three F-4's and three crewmembers, including Jimmer Jones, who had been flying the plane that crashed into Vic and Clay. A quick investigation concluded that for some inexplicable reason Jimmer had started descending for his approach before getting final clearance. He was not supposed to be below one thousand feet.

A message was waiting for Clay in Virginia Beach. 'Marianna called,' it said. He telephoned her at once. "I'd like to see you again," she said simply.

They met on a Friday night in mid-October at the Rathskellar, a local restaurant hangout in Georgetown. Marianna arrived late. "Hi! Been waiting long?" she bubbled with her best preppy smile.

"Long enough to go through a couple of martinis and a half-dozen cigarettes. I made it up here in less than three hours," Clay grumbled.

"Sorry. Friday afternoon traffic out of New York, you know," she shrugged.

They splurged and had a fancy dinner: escargots, prosciutto and melon, duckling in an orange sauce, cherries jubilee, a bottle of Pouilly Fuisse, Irish coffee. The meal cost more than the entire last week of their stay in Nice. Afterwards, they drove to Arlington. Vic and Darcy were hosting another party, and Marianna and Clay were the last to arrive. Vic, trussed in his back brace, was seated on a stool at a piano surrounded by Chuck and Cat and a half dozen other couples. He was playing, and everyone was singing old Navy songs. Marianna and Clay joined them, but the first time Darcy went to the kitchen, Marianna trailed after her. "What happened to Vic?" she asked.

"Clay didn't tell you?" Darcy blinked in surprise.

"No."

"He and Vic were in a mid-air two weeks ago. They had to eject. Vic cracked his tail bone."

"Are you serious?" Marianna gasped. "Is he going to be all right?"

"He'll be okay in another month. I'm surprised Clay didn't tell you. They were in the water eight hours. They were lucky. I don't know if you remember them from the last party, but Stinger Thornton and Jimmer Jones were both killed."

"Jimmer...do you mean the poor boy who was so sick?"

"Yeah. He was flying the plane that crashed into Vic and Clay. Stinger just splashed his in off the cat."

"And they're both dead?" Marianna leaned against the wall, stunned. In all her life she had never known anyone who had been killed. She started to cry. Darcy walked over with a kitchen towel, placed an arm around her and dabbed at her eyes. "I'm...I'm sorry, Darse," she sobbed. "It's just that I said such horrible things about them the last time I was here. I...I didn't know!"

"You have to forget about it," Darcy consoled her. "Come on, let's go join the party."

"Fix me a drink first, Darse. A strong one."

Everyone was laughing and singing in the other room. Marianna drank compulsively and soon was laughing at the jokes and wisecracks as loudly as anyone. When Sammy Powell pinched her and cringed, waiting to be slapped, she turned around and tweaked him on the nose, smiling. All the aviators and their girlfriends cheered and applauded, and Sammy preened like a peacock, boasting, "See! I knew she wasn't an uptight broad."

Vic started to play *Anchors Aweigh*. Darcy interrupted him before he could get started. "Let Marianna play. She's forgotten more about the piano than you'll ever know."

As Vic relinquished his stool, Sammy called out. "Can you play *Battle Hymn of the Republic?*" Marianna nodded as she sat down and started playing the tune. Sammy took up the verse, singing loudly, and making up his own words:"

> *"I was turning at the ninety, a little low and slow,*
> *And then I felt a shudder and heard the engine blow.*
> *The earth rushed up to greet me as I sang the pilot's hymn.*
> *Bye mom...ain't never flying home again."*

Then everyone joined in on the chorus and sang with gusto:

> *"Glory, glory, what a helluva way to go,*
> *Glory, glory, what a helluva way to fly,*
> *Glory, glory, what a helluva way to go,*
> *As you stall - spin - crash, burn, and die!"*

The last line was their favorite. They all stood and stomped their feet on the floor and yelled out the words: *STALL! SPIN! CRASH! BURN! DIE!*

Marianna stood up. "Okay. It's my turn now!" she exclaimed, and she sat back down and started attacking the keyboard, swinging and swaying atop her stool, singing a verse of her own:

> *"You catapult off the deck in the middle of the night,*
> *Winging away in clouds looking for a fight,*
> *If your fate is to never come back, I'll sing the pilot's hymn,*
> *Remembering you as little boys once, way back when."*

The entire room erupted on the chorus. They composed another twenty verses, taking turns, and kept singing the song until three o'clock in the morning...*She's becoming one of the family*, Darcy thought to herself as the party ended.

"Where are we going now?" Marianna asked after the party broke up, and they were in the Corvette, driving.

"Cat's apartment. She and Chuck left for Annapolis for the weekend," Clay said.

After they had gone about five miles she snuggled up to him and asked, "Why didn't you tell me about the accident?"

"Maybe for the same reason you didn't tell me what a hell of a singer you are. You're damn good, you know."

"I told you I played the piano," she blushed. "Lessons for years. All classical. I also studied voice. One thing I learned is that I can't sing opera. When I went back to Juilliard after Labor Day, I quit all that. I've been studying combining voice and piano, doing my own compositions, experimenting with melody, harmony, rhythms, ballads, even rhythm and blues and country rock; just hacking around. I've never hacked around like tonight though."

"If you asked me, I think you missed your calling. You should've been hacking around all along," he said fondly.

"You know, I've never known people like tonight. They're so wonderful and different from anything I've ever known."

They were stone tired when they reached the apartment. Cat's spare bedroom had two twin beds. They each chose one and collapsed on it, and in minutes they were fast asleep.

The next morning they went to Baltimore to see the Navy-Maryland football game. Marianna had brought a wardrobe down from New York especially for the occasion. She wore a bulky beaver coat, leather boots, a six foot long Princeton blue and gold scarf, and an Australian kangaroo skin hat. Her appearance notwithstanding, by the middle of the first quarter it was apparent to Clay that she knew nothing about the game. When she stood and cheered, it was always at the wrong time or for the wrong team. After a while she admitted she had never been to a game before, and he spent the rest of the afternoon trying to explain the rules to her. But terms as simple as touchdowns, first and tens, and goal line stands were too complicated for her to understand. Midway through the fourth quarter he decided she was hopeless and gave up trying to educate her.

"I have a suggestion," she said, as they drove back to Washington after the game. "Let's not go out tonight. I'll fix us a little dinner at Cat's."

It was dark when they arrived at Cat's apartment. Marianna skipped out of the car and across the street to a neighborhood store on the corner. Clay went inside and built a fire. He had it blazing by the time she returned with an armful of groceries, a frozen pizza, an assortment of cheeses, two bottles of wine. They ate in front of the television. Time passed. They uncorked the second bottle of wine. The fire died down, and they both got high.

"What do you think is going to happen to us?" she asked suddenly out of the blue.

"I don't try to think. I'm just passing through. We both are. You know I'm shipping out soon."

"And between now and then all it is with us is *haps*, isn't it?" she said, becoming agitated.

"That's right. No commitments. Remember? Besides, I'm not your type. We don't really fit, you know."

Her head sagged. She rested her elbows on the coffee table and clutched and fidgeted with her glass, tilting and staring at it as if she were trying to analyze the movements of the wine sloshing back and forth.

"What's wrong?" he asked gently. "I've never seen you look so glum."

"So many things are wrong, Clay. Things I would like to tell you that you don't know...that you would never understand."

"So...tell me."

"I can't. I'm too depressed right now. I'll get over it." She wipes a tear from her eye, but as others start trickling down her cheeks, she slumps over on the sofa. He grabs her by the shoulders. "You're hurting me!" she cries, wrenching away and burying her face in a pillow.

Clay shakes her. "What the hell's your problem?"

"Everything," she mumbles between sobs. "People. Friends changing. The way money is such a big deal. Young boys being sent off to war... Parents you love who just tear you to pieces."

"That just sounds like you can't take life, fella."

She sat up and managed a feeble laugh. "That's what they said when I did such a lousy job trying to kill myself. Then I met you and learned what it was like to have fun. I came down here this weekend to see if you could cheer me up. But you've only made me more depressed."

"What did I do?"

"Remember in Nice, when we didn't have any money and it was just you and me, all alone and having fun...and we said that summers always have to end. Well, we were right. I realize that summer is finally over now, fella'. We're back in the complex world, and it's not fun anymore. I don't want us to end up hating each other. That's why I'm going back to New York tomorrow and forget you ever existed."

"You sound like you mean it."

"I do. I *guarantee* you I do."

He gazed at her eyes for a moment, studying the defiant look there, and then burst into a short laugh. "Well, if this is it forever, at least I hope you won't deny me one last dance." He placed a Frank Sinatra record on the stereo, and they began to dance to the slow, rhythmic tempo of a song called *Nice and Easy*. She pressed her face into his shoulder and kept it there so that he could not see her weeping, or the way she bit her lip to keep from sobbing out loud. The record repeated three times before she pulled away and announced that she was going to bed. He stayed and sipped the last of the wine while she showered. After she finished he took his own shower, a long one. He lathered slowly, letting the pelting jets of water wash away his weariness as he pondered her behavior. He was puzzled by it. She wanted to tell him something, but she wouldn't unless he made her. He decided he was not going to do that. He toweled himself dry, wrapped the towel around his waist, and knotted it before emerging from the bathroom. She was standing in the hallway in a pair of purple, shorty pajamas, her hair mussed and curly from what looked like had been a fitful attempt to sleep

"This is the last time," she said as she leaned against his chest and unknotted the towel, allowing it to drop to the floor. He rubbed his face in her hair and nibbled at her ears and shoulders as he helped her undress, led her to the bedroom, and lay down beside her, holding her gently. She trembled when he touched her, then lunged at him, pulled him inside, and began thrusting, moaning, arching her back, clenching the sheets with her fists, begging him to do it harder - and it happened. She collapsed and did not move. He fell asleep in a stupor.

He heard the faint ringing of church bells in the distance and felt someone shaking him. "Wake up asshole," she said. "I'll have breakfast ready in five minutes." He lay on his back and stretched and smiled contentedly before opening his eyes. Marianna was standing over him, wearing high heels and her beaver coat. The coat was unbuttoned, and he could see that she had nothing on underneath. "I've been out shopping," she replied to his stare.

Throughout breakfast she babbled about inane things - the weather, how the eggs tasted, a movie she had seen the prior week, the decorations in Cat's apartment. Not once did she mention the night before. She was being uncharacteristically phony, and it rankled him. After coffee, he lit a cigarette, smoked it down in five puffs, and ground the cigarette out in his plate. "Come here!" he growled, lifting her up. He carried her into the bedroom, laid her on the rumpled sheets, and began removing his shirt. She stood up, placing her hands against his shoulders.

"Please don't," she pleaded.

He shoved her down and climbed on top of her. She kicked and scratched his face and sprang from the bed, screaming, "Don't touch me you bastard! I told you last night was the last time. I meant it!"

"I'm sorry...I'm sorry," he said, blinking.

"Go to hell!"

"Listen, fella',I apologize. What can I say to make it up to you?"

"There's nothing to say. They would only be nebulous, meaningless words anyway."

There was no mistaking the contempt in her voice or the burning resentment that flashed in her eyes. Hastily, she began to dress and pack. He shuffled into the living room and paced back and forth in a miserable silence. In ten minutes she emerged, ready to leave. He walked her to the car. "At least you can't say it hasn't been tense," he said, managing a weak grin.

"Yes, we have had some *haps*," she said coldly. She started up her little Triumph and then rolled down the window. "At least we were honest about one thing. We never said we loved each other!" she yelled as she gunned the engine and accelerated down P Street.

One week after Clay returned to Oceana, his squadron shipped out on another shakedown cruise. They were at sea three weeks, and the squadron survived it without a mishap. The first thing he did when they arrived back in port was telephone Marianna. He called her three days, in succession, but each time she refused to speak to him. The last time her mother asked him not to call again, and he gave up trying. He became depressed. The deployment was only ten weeks away. He began hitting the bottle more heavily, and popping benzedrine pills. He had taken his first benny when he was a senior at Annapolis. He met a corpsman in the hospital ward on the carrier after his accident who sold him a bottle that contained a hundred. The bennies stimulated his mind and he liked that. And he thought he knew how to handle them. He would take a pill or two in the early evening and then go out and hit the bars. The pills made him not the least bit hungry and enabled him to drink for hours without noticing any effects. They also kept him awake all night, and he would drive around aimlessly in his Corvette until dawn, listening to music until his brain fuzzed before returning to his room at the BOQ and collapsing in a drunken heap. After a while he had to take three pills, and then four, to reach the same satisfying high.

The pills began to affect his flying. Often he would miscalculate their impact and still be sleeping them off when the alarm clock rang on a morning he was scheduled to fly. When that happened he had to take another one to get pepped up enough to be able to perform. Under their influence, he was convinced that he was the greatest pilot in the world, blessed with an inherent God-given talent that made him incapable of making a mistake. He began flying into the landing pattern at speeds far in excess of normal procedures and flipping into vicious seventy degree banks just to see if he could crack his RIO's helmet off the canopy glass. He would pull an extra two g's in his loops and chuckle if he could make the RIO groan and black out. He persisted an extra second on every practice bombing run, pulling out of his power dives at less than a hundred feet above the ground. And once, on a solo flight, he buzzed right underneath an airliner, hit afterburner, and swooshed upward in front of its nose, spiraling in successive victory rolls to prevent anyone from reading his number. Vic would have noticed the change in behavior, but he was still grounded because of his back and a rookie was in the backseat who had no benchmark for comparison.

Buoyed by the bennies, Clay began openly questioning the war. He asked everyone in the squadron: "define winning it?" Few had very good answers. "Our reputation is on the line," they said. Or, "too many guys had already died there." The more Clay agitated them, the more he became intrigued by their answers and continued to badger them.

One day in mid-December, shortly after he returned from his convalescent leave, Vic drew Clay aside. "The guys all say you've been acting weird lately. They're starting to talk about it."

"Is that a fact," Clay sniggered. He slipped a pill box out of his pocket, popped two of the capsules into his mouth, and offered the box to Vic. "Wantta try a benny? They make your motor run faster, man!"

Vic took a step backward, shocked. "So that's your problem. That stuff will burn up your brain, Clay."

"It's not my problem," Clay mumbled. "It may be yours, but it's not mine."

"Maybe so," Vic said, staring him right in the eye. "But you better get hold of yourself, Clay. I don't like the thought of riding shotgun with a speed freak."

Vic's admonishment brought him down to earth. He said what was really on his mind. "You wouldn't have to if I quit...turned in my wings."

"Get serious."

"I am. The only thing stopping me is the squadron...the thought that I'd be copping out on you guys."

"None of us want to go to Nam either, Clay."

"Then why are we if nobody wants to?"

"Because the President has decided. It's our duty."

"The President is just a man."

"And you think you know better than he does?"

Clay winked and laughed. "That's the beauty of the pills, babe! They make you omnipotent."

Clay locked himself in his room after Vic left. He called in sick and remained there for three days, lying in bed in a cold, damp sweat, popping pills, and staring at the ceiling. His mind raced as hours passed by in flashes - and he talked to himself: *I love my Mom and Dad. I wish I'd been a better son. Especially if I get killed over there... Why did Cindy Sue's baby die? Fate...Thank God I didn't lose Vic... God didn't have a fucking thing to do with it...Marianna was a beautiful thing... I wish I could go live on an island...I don't want to blow people up....I've got to see Marianna one last time before I go over there.*

Clay sobered up on the twenty-second of December. He went to Vic and Darcy's rental apartment and coerced her into telephoning

Marianna. He took the receiver as soon as Marianna came on the line. "Don't hang up on me."

"Who's this?" she breathed quietly.

"Come on. You know who."

"No I don't. I said I was going to forget you ever existed. Re-member?"

"I have ten days leave coming up, starting tomorrow, my last, and I'm going home for Christmas. I'd like to see you."

"It's impossible, Clay."

"You can't be so cruel not to see a guy one last time before he ships off to war."

She hesitated for a moment, and then she said, "I'll think about it. Let me call you back."

She telephoned an hour later.

"I'll be in St. Louis on the twenty-sixth at three-thirty. TWA flight 894," she said, and she hung up without any further explanation.

V

⟨≈⟩⟩

ALL OR NOTHING

Clay watched Marianna from the cocktail lounge window as she darted down the steps from the Astrojet that had whisked her from New York to St. Louis. She was bundled in her beaver coat and kangaroo skin hat. Within minutes she met him in the lounge.

"Merry Christmas," he said.

"Same to you fella. How've you been? No more mid-airs lately, I hope," she said, tilting her head flippantly.

"No. Nothing that exciting. How was your trip?"

"Boring. So what are our plans?"

"I thought maybe you'd like to drive over to Columbia and see Stephens again."

"Oh, let's do!" she exclaimed, clapping her hands excitedly.

The decision made, they set out for Columbia, a drive of a hundred miles, riding in the four-speed, four barrel 1965 Ford Mustang convertible Clay had borrowed from his dad after flying home for the holidays. They stopped once to purchase Seven-Ups and spiked them with gin, and it was dusk when they arrived. The town was blanketed in snow, a proud ten inches originally that now was a dirty looking, charcoal speckled slush. They drove by Stephens, but there was not a sign of life on the campus. The students had all left for the holidays. The trees were barren, bent in the bitter wind, and the old, red brick buildings were deserted. Clay began to wonder why they had come.

"Oh, look, the stables!" Marianna burst out all of a sudden. "I used to ride horses there. And look over there! My old music hall. There's a pond behind it where we used to sit and gossip between classes." She pressed her face against the window glass as they drove slowly by the campus. In a minute it was behind them, and she turned and said, "You know, I was happy when I was here, Clay... just a young silly girl, doing young silly things. I wish it could be like that again. If I had it to do over, I'd like to come back here and just be a little innocent college freshman for the rest of my life."

Clay continued driving toward the outskirts of town. It began to mist. Snow fell lightly, blotting out the streetlights and plunging the road into darkness. Icicles started forming on the radio antenna. "Where are we going?" Marianna asked when they reached the edge of town.

"I don't know. You tell me. Where are we going?" Clay muttered as he drove around in a residential neighborhood trying to make out the addresses. After a while he swerved into a driveway and turned off the ignition.

"Whose place is this?" Marianna asked.

"Judy Collins. She teaches at the University. She's also the best looking woman in Creekwood and home for the holidays tonight. She's always been to me like the big sister I never had." They went inside. The house was cold and damp, empty, the furnace turned down to fifty degrees. Clay built a fire while Marianna scouted out the bar and mixed a half-quart jar full of martinis. They started drinking, huddled on a rug in front of the fireplace. In the middle of his second martini, Clay took out two bennies and washed them down with a gulp.

"What are those?" Marianna asked curiously.

"Happiness pills."

"What are they for?"

"They turn you on when you're down and make the world seem beautiful."

"Let me try one."

He opened up his pillbox and offered her one, and she gobbled it down. "I have to take a whiz," he said as he got up and stumbled off in search of the bathroom. It took him a while to find it. It had a deep sunken tile tub. When he returned, Marianna was lying on her back on the rug in front of the fire, gazing dully at the ceiling. "Let's go get something to eat," he said.

She looked at him and smiled mischievously. "If you take three pills does that make you three times as happy?"

"You didn't take three?" She nodded and closed her eyes. "You shouldn't have done that," he scolded her. "Not the first time. You're gonna get stoned."

"I *want* to get stoned! Don't you realize that! We both do, Clay. Isn't that what it's all about with us - getting stoned, having some *haps*. Isn't that why we're here tonight, in Columbia, Missouri in the middle of winter - running away?"

"I'm not running away from anything."

"Yes, you are. You're running away from the thought of killing people...away from Vietnam and dropping bombs. I've seen it in your eyes. It's eating away at you."

"What are you running away from?" he said quietly.

"I have my own problems."

"Well, problems I don't want to hear about. Let's go get something to eat."

A sudden rage came over her. "Goddamnit! I don't want anything to eat! And you are going to hear about it! There's something I have to tell you."

"So, tell me."

"I'm getting *married!* I'm getting married on *New Year's Eve!*" He stared at her and his cheek twitched.

"I guess I should ask who the lucky guy is," he said, stunned.

"Douglas Threadgill. He's the one I had the bad experience with in Greenwich."

"Then I guess I should offer my congratulations. When did this all happen?" He looked at her like a stranger. He was not smiling.

"Just before I first met you in Nice. I met my mother and father in Paris for a weekend. Douglas was with them. We all went to dinner and Douglas gave me a ring. It was a *done deal!* My father and Douglas' father had talked and it was all arranged. Douglas was with me at the wedding in Washington Labor Day. That's why I had to sneak out to meet you. The wedding invitations were mailed out about six weeks ago. That's why I didn't answer any of your phone calls."

"And you've been screwing him ever since you got back from France!" He resisted the impulse to tell her to go fuck herself.

"That's not true, Clay. I swear! He hasn't touched me since I met you."

"You don't expect me to believe that?"

"I swear it's true." She fell into his arms blubbering like a baby. "And I don't want to marry him! That's why I want to get stoned!" Clenching her martini glass, she began smashing her fist against the wall. The glass shattered, slashing her hand, and blood spurted from the cut.

Clay grabbed her wrists and shook her. "You're bombed out of your mind."

"That's right. It's the happiness pills. They're making me realize that I'm a fool for marrying him. We'll probably be divorced in a year." She started blubbering again.

He drew her more tightly against him. His hands became bloodied too. He lifted her head. "So why do it?"

"It's too late. Douglas' family is having a big party in Chicago day after tomorrow for me to meet all their friends - at the Onwentsia Club in Lake Forest. The governor and a senator are coming. I have to be there. Then it's straight to New York for the wedding. Father's doing his thing. He has three hundred people coming to the Greenwich Country Club for the reception. Bankers. The Swiss ambassador..." She wrenched away from his grasp and flung herself face down on the rug, quivering and crying. *"Too many people have made too many plans!"*

Clay walked away. He went to the bar and fixed another drink, lit a cigarette, and swallowed another benny. He grabbed a towel and walked back, leaned over and stroked her hair. She sat up and wiped her eyes. He wrapped the towel around the cut. "You could marry me instead," he said softly.

She didn't say anything right away. Then she smiled at him and shook her head slowly from side to side. The emotion was gone from her voice. "Don't be absurd. I have to marry Douglas, and there's not a thing either of us can do about it."

He did not want it to end. "Okay, then let's play a game," he said. For the next thirty-six hours let's pretend it's not going to happen. Come down to Creekwood with me tomorrow. Chuck Stanback is going to be there. I've fixed him up with a date. You can meet Judy Collins. See my hometown. I'll drive you back to St. Louis early the next morning so you can catch a plane to Chicago in time for your party...Deal?"

She smiled and looked relieved. "Deal," she said weakly. He leaned forward to kiss her, but thought better of it. After awhile she tottered off to the bedroom, leaving him alone. He drank and smoked for an hour. Then he went to the bedroom, crawled in the bed and draped his arm across her, and lay beside her until dawn, stoned on pills, his mind racing.

They made the two hundred mile drive to Creekwood the next day in less than three hours. "What's that?" Marianna asked, pointing across the road as they pulled into the driveway at his house..

"A cotton field."

"Oh, I've never seen real cotton before! Can we go see it?" she bubbled excitedly.

They strode across Williams Street to the field on the other side and walked among the cotton rows. The field was stripped bare except for an occasional boll that had been missed in the fall picking. He stopped to open one and show her the seedy tuft inside, all matted and hardened by the winter rains. He handed it to her. "Put it under your pillow," he said. "Let it be a wedding present from me to you."

Lara Stoner fixed a hearty dinner that night and served it in the seldom used dining room instead of the kitchen. They had roast beef, brown potatoes and gravy, green beans, corn on the cob, all topped off with a pumpkin pie. Marianna was the center of attention and Lara Stoner quizzed her. "Tell me about Europe, Marianna. I understand you've lived there. I've always wanted to go. I ask Clay about it, but he never seems to have seen anything except beaches. Or bars and cafes. What about the museums and the cathedrals?"

"Oh, but the bars and cafes *are* Europe, Mrs. Stoner. That's where you get to know the people. In fact, if I hadn't met Clay in one of those bars, I never would have had the privilege of being here and meeting you tonight."

"Well, I suppose that's true," Lara Stoner said. "I hope you can stay with us awhile. It's not often we have a girl around the house, especially one who can tell me about things." And as she rose, cleared dishes, and Marianna followed her into the kitchen, she said, "by the way, call me Lara. If we get to know each other better, you might even be able to tell me a few things I don't know about my son." She gave Marianna a warm, perceptive look, one that let her know she was sympathetic with the delicate affair taking place between Marianna and her son and did not intend to pry.

As soon as the women disappeared, Bill Stoner gave Clay a sly look and said, "I can see now why you're not looking forward to February's deployment."

"She's not the reason, Dad. It's how asinine this war is!"

"You shouldn't be so upset, son. The government knows what it's doin'. Just like when I fought the Japs. It took us a while to get started then, too. But as soon as we put our minds to it, we showed 'em. You boys'll do the same with those communists."

Clay let himself go. "That was goddamn twenty years ago, Dad! Another era! Nobody understands what the hell is going on today. Certainly not the *government!* It just wants everyone to think everything is hunky dory. Well, I'll tell you, it's *not!* The guys in my squadron are just among the few who are being shipped ten thousand miles away to lay our asses on the line while a bunch of old-fart politicians sit up in Washington and twiddle their thumbs talking about it!"

"Now, now," Lara Stoner interrupted them, drawn back into the dining room by Clay's shouting. "We have a guest present, so no more arguing between you men."

"I'm sorry, Mom," Clay said, calming. "I was just trying to make Dad understand."

Marianna and Clay said goodnight to his parents about nine o'clock and left and drove up to Hay's Ridge. They pulled into a parking lot in front of an old wooden structure that looked like it had once been a barn and stable, except it now had a bright neon sign on top spelling out *Slim's Place.* As soon as they stepped out of the car they heard shouts and saw a body come flying backwards out the front door pursued by two strapping farmers in overalls who jumped on it and pummeled it four or five times before dragging it over to the side of the lot, dusting off their hands, and going back inside. "What kind of place is this?" Marianna asked incredulously.

"Just a country, roadhouse honky tonk. Don't worry. They don't let them fight inside," Clay said as he hustled her toward the door.

Slim's Place was typical of so many Ozark road houses, with a long bar to the right of the entranceway, ten barstools with room for a crowd to stand three deep. Across from the bar, and separated by a gate that swung through a chest high partition, were tables and a dance floor. The band was on its break and a juke box was playing *Hey Good Lookin'*. Marianna and Clay paid four dollars at the gate, got the back of their hands stamped purple, and ushered themselves inside. Clay's quick eyes surveyed the room and saw Chuck Stanback standing up and giving out a shout: "Hey Stoner! Over Here!" He edged Marianna through the crowd and toward a long table near the stage. As they approached the table, the young girl sitting next to Chuck, a sweet flower of the Ozarks, a slender brunette with a pixie cut and warm laughing eyes, the blind date Clay had arranged with hopes that she would make Chuck forget about Cat, stood up to greet them. "Hi, I'm Patsy Foster," she said to Marianna. "Welcome to Slim's Place. We've all been waiting for you." Marianna was interrupted before she could answer. A tall, striking woman, late twenties, good looking enough to be a Ford model, arose from her chair, gave Clay a hug and confidently took charge of introductions.

"I'm Judy Collins," she said, tilting out her hand to Marianna. "I think you stayed at my place last night." She winked at Clay. "And you've brought home a New Yorker, I hear." She put her arm around Marianna. "Come meet everyone."

A massive, affable southern gentlemanly type, ruggedly handsome but a little slow on the uptake, rose and clasped Marianna's hand.. "Pleased to make yore 'quaintance ma'am," he said gallantly. His drawl was as thick as southern fried gravy.

"This is my date, Donald Joe Baker," Judy chimed in. "Works at the County Mill with his dad. Chuck Stanback I think you already know. And over here is Cindy Sue Collins. She's married to my big brother Tim. He's in the bar right now."

Marianna was startled at the unexpected meeting. She tensed and felt that everyone was staring at her. "How do you do," she said as politely as she knew how.

"Pleased to meet'cha," Cindy Sue said as her wide red lips parted and her gleaming white teeth flashed a warm open smile.

"And this is Bobby Lee Crawford, Cindy Sue's brother," Judy continued. "He's just home on leave from the army."

Bobby Lee gave Marianna a friendly nod and then switched his attention to Clay, shaking his hand vigorously. "It's great to see you again, Clay. I never dreamed I'd get to see you while I was home. It's been a long time."

"About four years. So you're a ground pounder now," Clay said, teasing his former brother-in-law.

"Platoon commander," Bobby Lee said proudly. "Big Red One. I know it's not as exciting as flying, but it sure beats sharecroppin' with my dad. We're shippin' out for Nam next month."

"Seems like everybody is," Marianna said before Judy interrupted again and introduced Marianna to an overly inebriated couple draped over each other at the end of the table, Petey Monroe and Mona Faye Hinkle, an off duty barmaid who was always good for a lay.

Donald Joe fetched two chairs from another table and brought them over. Marianna and Clay sat down. "Y'all gonna be heah vur-rah long?" Donald Joe mumbled to Marianna. "Lak 'ta haf yuh ovah if yuh ahr." She did not understand a word he said.

"Marianna has to leave first thing in the morning," Clay inter-jected.

"You can't be serious – leaving so soon!" Judy Collins looked wounded.

Marianna was made nervous by the attention. She had never known people like this. Clay poured her a beer and slipped her a benny. He stood up and proposed a toast. "To Creekwood, and the best friends in the world." They all clinked glasses and drank, and Marianna drank the benny down. Patsy and Cindy Sue wanted to talk to her. She moved around to the other side of the table in be-tween them, and in a minute they were all engaged in a squirrel-like chatter.

A tall, lean man with an arrogant Ivy League look walked up and sat down in the seat Marianna had just vacated. "Mr. Stoner! I don't think I've seen you since you were nine years old. How's it going my young man?"

Clay had never really known Tim Collins. He was the same age as Donald Joe, thirty-three, but had gone to prep school and college in the east and was in law school when Clay left for the Academy. Long before Tim even knew Cindy Sue, though, Clay had consid-ered him to be a conceited ass. He low-keyed it and said, "Things are fine, Tim. How about with you?"

"Farming's only so-so right now. Other than that, I can't com-plain," he said smugly. "I don't know if you heard, my dad died a couple of months ago, so I'm pretty much running things for the Collins family now, all our farmland and the bank. If you ever decide to come back home and need a job, you should look me up."

"Farmin's a lot worse than so-so, Tim," Donald Joe interjected. "If it don't get better real soon there *ain't gonna* be any jobs."

Before Clay could ask how bad farming really was, Slim Sparks and his band came back on stage and started playing some honky tonk interspersed with Slim singing a ballad or two. Clay asked Marianna to dance. On the floor he whispered in her ear. ""What were you girls talking about?"

"Just our lives. A little bit about you. You know, that Patsy's simply adorable. She's already invited me to come out here and stay at the lake with her next summer while you and Chuck are in Vietnam. She likes him."

At the next break Clay guided Marianna over toward Slim at the piano to make a request. "Hey Slim, how about next set playing a little *Wild Side?*"

Slim's head bobbed around. His nose squinted up like a pekinese, and he broke into a silly grin. "Clay Stoner!" he bellowed. "I know that's you. Where yuh sitttin'? Ah'll come right ovah." They led Slim over to the table. Sweating like a walrus, he sat down and began firing questions. "What's it like flyin' them planes, Clay? Landin' on a boat must be tuff, huh? Say, whatta yuh think 'bout this war? Don't make much sense to me. Been seein' any of the world like ah told yuh?"

He paused just long enough for Clay to get in a response. "Doing my best. Just got back from a Med cruise. Spent some time in Europe."

"Europe! I was in Europe once. Met the prettiest little thing..."

"So did I Slim. She's sitting beside you. Her name's Marianna. She's half-French, half-Swiss and from New York, and she sings and plays the piano pretty good too."

Slim reached out and touched Marianna's face. She took his hand and held it against her cheek. "Ah can tell yore pretty just by touchin' yuh," Slim said as his eyeballs rolled up and disappeared. He took out his tobacco pouch and lit his pipe. "Now tell be about New York," he said. "I used to play there. A place called Jimmie's. Evah heard of it?" They started talking and Clay left them alone. They ignored everyone and talked for twenty minutes. When Slim's break was over, he went back to the stage and sang one song, *The Wild Side of Life*. Then he stood up and made an announcement. "Folks, we have a young lady here tonight all the way from Noo Yark City. Ah've been told she can play and sing pretty good, so if we all give her a hand, she just might come up here and do us a little ole song. Whatta' yuh say, Marianna?"

Marianna gasped. "Tell him no," she whispered to Clay."

Clay laughed, and he and Chuck lifted her up from her chair and out to the stage. She shook her head and protested until Slim placed a microphone in her hand and the crowd began to applaud. Resigned, she sat down at the piano and spoke into the mike. "Well, here goes nothin'. I think Slim's going to be surprised to find out that a girl from New York knows a pretty good comeback to that song he just sang."

She began with the old Kitty Wells tune, *It Wasn't God Who Made Honky Tonk Angels*. She sang the song up tempo, her voice strong and earthy, no trace of any east coast accent. Her nervousness showed at first, but by the time she was half way through, the crowd was lulled into a peaceful, swaying mood. At the end of the song she burst into a rendition of Fats Domino's *I'm in Love Again*. Slim's band knew the song and picked up the rhythm. The lead guitar riffed some chords and the sax jammed in at just the right moments. Marianna's style was unique. She slurred the melodies and bent the notes a full tone instead of just a half. By the time she finished, Slim's Place was jumping. In a flash she exploded into *What'd I Say*. Her fingers pounded the keyboards, the band joined in, and soon the crowd was stomping and shouting to the beat. When it was over she stood up and bowed and tried to leave, but everyone was yelling, *"one more time!"*

She picked up the mike and raised her hand to quiet them. "I'll sing one more song," she announced softly. It's called 'Non, Je Ne Regrette Rien'. It's in French, so you may not understand the words, so I'll repeat some of them in English, but it's for someone who's very special to me. It means 'No, I don't regret nothin'." She started singing with her eyes closed, vibrant, cool and crisp without accompaniment, and the crowd hushed. They listened in awe, not understanding a word, but sensing the feeling as every few seconds they saw a tiny tear trickle down her cheek. When the song was over, she ran quickly to the table, and everyone in the place began to whistle and cheer.

"You were fantastic, fella'!" Clay exclaimed over the din.

She was excited, and she snuggled up to him, nearly out of breath. "I've been practicing country and rock ever since the party in Washington," she gasped, "but I never could have done it without that happiness pill!"

Marianna was the center of attention until the party broke up about two o'clock. Everyone said their "good nights" in the parking lot, none too soberly, and then Donald Joe and Judy headed off for Creekwood with Cindy Sue and Tim driving his big as a boat, *look at me*, Cadillac Coupe de Ville. Chuck was going to drive Patsy home in her blue and white Pontiac Bonneville convertible. Clay warned him to watch some of the curves; it was starting to get foggy out. Chuck waved him off and peeled out of the parking lot, spinning gravel. Marianna and Clay watched them disappear before saying goodbye to Bobby Lee, Mona Faye and Petey, who went back inside to procure some go-cups of beer.

Eight miles south of Slim's, leaning hard coming around a curve in the Mustang, Clay glimpsed the wispy silhouette of a pickup truck broadside in the middle of the road. He blinked momentarily, shouted *sonuvabitch,* downshifted, braked, swerved, and skidded sideways past the truck, narrowly missing it before he came to a stop on the shoulder. He scrambled out of the car. It was a cold, still night, too dark to see. He grabbed a flashlight out of the glove compartment and told Marianna to drive back around the curve and flash lights to flag down anyone coming before they plowed into the truck. He approached the pickup, shining the light on it, seeing that it was smashed in like an accordion. Inside, arched backward over the seat with his mouth open was the sprawling figure of a man who was obviously dead. Clay tried to open the doors, but they were jammed. It was then that he heard a whimpering, a sound like a baby crying coming from the other side of the road. He flashed his light and saw a car in the ditch. *Patsy's Bonneville!* He ran, stumbled, half slid down the shoulder into the ditch and waded knee deep through icy water to the car. Chuck was slumped behind the wheel, moaning and mumbling, "a mule...I hit a fuckin' mule."

The flurry of events that followed were a blur. Clay screamed at Chuck to talk to him, to say that he was all right. Chuck just sat there, his eyes glazed, moaning. The Bonneville's doors were jammed. Clay tore through the convertible top and climbed inside. Patsy was wedged between the seats, breathing raspishly as blood gurgled out her nose and mouth. Marianna flagged down a car - Petey and Mona Faye - and sent them to Creekwood for help. Shortly, she stopped Bobby Lee, who took over her watchout duty, and she walked back to join Clay at Patsy's car. There was nothing much either of them could do, then, except stand there and urge Chuck and Patsy to keep on living. They didn't dare try to haul them out over the side of the car. Clay started to steel himself to the idea that Patsy might be dying. Chuck sat up after awhile, though, rubbing his leg and staring at him with eyes wide open. Clay was confident he would make it, even though the stare was dull and Chuck did not know where he was, or know that Patsy was probably dying right there beside him.

Half an hour elapsed before county deputy sheriff Hogjaw Hawkins arrived. There was another twenty minute wait for an ambulance and a wrecker to move the truck off the road. Still impossible to open the shattered doors, Chuck and Patsy were finally hoisted over the side of the Bonneville onto stretchers. Patsy's breathing was faint and fading when she was placed in the ambulance, and her face had acquired a strange, yellow, sick-looking pallor. Two cars, Clay's and Bobby Lee's, followed the ambulance's wailing siren as it sped through the night, forty miles to the hospital in Mountain Springs. Chuck's stretcher was the first wheeled out of the ambulance. Two corpsmen were pushing it, and Chuck's eyes were closed. Clay grabbed them, and asked in a frenzy, "He's all right? He'll be all right, won't he?"

"He's alive...barely," the corpsmen said as they hurriedly wheeled Chuck into the emergency room.

When Patsy was removed from the ambulance, her face was covered with a sheet. Marianna dropped to her knees and started to cry.

Patsy's mother and father arrived about five in the morning, and learned the finality of the devastating news. As if in a trance, they made arrangements for Patsy's body to be transported to a funeral parlor in Creeekwood. They were grieving. "She was only nineteen," they said as they wandered out of the hospital.

Chuck was still on the operating table an hour later when Hogjaw Hawkins strolled into the waiting room. "Looks like the poor soul in the Bonneville hit a mule," Hogjaw said. "They're chunks of mule splattered on the front of his car and all over the road leading into the curve down there just before you see skid marks. Looks like he hit a mule and lost control just as that other guy in the truck was comin' around the curve and they hit head on. We ain't found out whose mule it was yet."

Chuck died at ten-thirty in the morning without regaining consciousness. Clay refused to believe it. "He was sitting up and talking," Clay pleaded with the doctor. "I thought he would be all right."

"Internal hemorrhaging," said the doctor. "There was no way we could stop it. I'm sorry."

Clay didn't move off his bench for half an hour. The waiting room was deserted when Marianna sat down beside him and suggested that they leave. They didn't speak again until they were half way to Creekwood. "We'll have to pack and leave as soon as we get back," Clay said. "It'll be at least three o'clock before I can get you to St. Louis. You'll miss the earlier plane."

Marianna was emotionally drained. "I don't have to leave to-day," she said quietly. "I was supposed to be in Chicago this afternoon, but the party's really not until tomorrow night. I fibbed about that." He didn't say anything, and after awhile she said, "It's ironic. I thought we would be saying goodbye forever this morning. Now there's one more day. Fate has a crazy way of working, don't you think? Chuck flew a hundred combat missions, and ejected, without a scratch. Then he comes home for Christmas, goes out on a date with a most darling girl, runs into a mule, and gets killed. It doesn't make sense."

"It could have happened his next time up."

"*I know that!*" she said, her voice becoming tense and high pitched. "And don't you see the absurdity in it all, Clay? How can we afford to waste our lives, to sacrifice so much, when we know that at any time we may step out into a street - and wham - we get run down by a bus or something. It's all over in a second and you don't even know what hit you! Life's too precious for that. I don't know if it's the pills, or Chuck and Patsy, or what, but I'm not going to marry Douglas, Clay! I'm not going to punish myself anymore just to make everyone else happy."

He pulled abruptly off to the side of the road, leaned over, and stared her in the eye. "I thought you said the plans were made - that it was too late to back out?"

"That was before last night. To hell with everyone's plans!" she said, staring back at him defiantly.

"Are you sure?"

"More than anything in my life."

"Listen, if you think I meant it the other night when I suggested getting married, I didn't. I was stoned."

"Don't be such an egotistical asshole. I didn't decide this because of you...I just don't love Douglas. And I still have to go to Chicago and tell him that before the party tomorrow."

"Why don't you just send him a telegram? That's simple enough."

"I can't do that, Clay. I don't hate him. Besides, I have to return this." She reached into her purse and pulled out a ring with a diamond on it large enough to clog a cannon. All of a sudden he felt that if he let her go he would never see her again.

"Okay, if that's the way you want it," he said quickly. "I can get Petey Monroe to fly us up to Chicago in the morning. He can have us back in time for the funeral."

Petey Monroe landed at two o'clock the next afternoon at the airport in Waukegan, Illinois, a north shore suburb of Chicago. Marianna and Clay rented a car and drove the ten miles to Lake Forest, looking for a bar. Not finding one, they drove south along the Lake Michigan shoreline for another five miles until they reached a much less affluent suburb and spotted a beer joint with a sign picturing a reindeer out front, named appropriately: the Rudolph Tavern. They stopped and went inside, and Marianna placed a call to the Threadgill residence.

"Douglas wasn't at home. The maid is going to try to locate him," she said as she slid into a worn, wooden booth next to Clay. He had already ordered them each a double manhattan on the rocks. There were only five other customers in the tavern, three men at the bar drinking beer and two throwing darts at a board in the corner, all Italians who gave them stares like they weren't used to seeing women in beer joints in the middle of the afternoon. During the next hour Marianna and Clay had two more manhattans, along with a couple of bennies. They were on their fourth round when a distinguished middle-aged gentleman poked his head in the door. He was a wearing a homburg and a cashmere coat, a Hickey Freeman suit, Hermes tie. "My God!" Marianna gasped. It's Douglas's father!" She slid down into the booth and tried to make herself invisible; but the gentleman spotted her and came walking over.

"Marianna, I wasn't sure this was the right place," he said, a bit unnerved. "Douglas is still in Chicago, so I came instead. Why didn't you call us from the airport?"

Marianna was feeling the drinks now, and Clay intervened. "I'm Clay Stoner. Would you care to join us for a drink, sir?" he said quickly.

"No thank you. It looks like you've had enough," Threadgill snipped without looking at Clay, and in the next breath he said, "may I get your things Marianna?"

Marianna's head nodded back and forth and then flopped against the wall. She managed to mumble, "I want to talk to Douglas first."

Threadgill was shaken. "On second thought, maybe I will join you in that drink."

"Three manhattans!" Clay shouted across the tavern.

Threadgill cringed as the Italians turned and stared, but by the time the drinks arrived he had composed himself and said pointedly to Marianna, "We expected you yesterday, you know.

I telephoned your father, and he thought you were already here. We were worried about you."

Marianna closed her eyes and plopped her face down on the table, and Clay intervened again. "I understand you're in the investment business, Mr. Threadgill," he said politely.

Threadgill looked at Clay for the first time. "Well...uh...yes, that's right. What about you, Mr. Stoner? What do you do?"

"I'm a mechanic." He did not know why he said it. It was spontaneous and just slipped out. Acting dumb to throw a person off guard was one of his mother's ruses.

Threadgill smiled for the first time, but it was not a friendly smile. "Oh really!" he said. "And where is it that you perform this line of work?"

"Down in the Ozarks," Clay said humbly, shifting his accent into the Ozark twang. "My pa owns a little g'rage down there. It's hard work, but we manage."

"That's too bad." Threadgill smirked. "Fortunately my son has been more fortunate. He graduated from Princeton summa cum laude and was Law Review at Yale." He smiled haughtily and glanced to see if Marianna was listening. Her face was still pressed against the table, and she hadn't moved.

"What's sooma koom loudy?" Clay asked, as if bewildered by a new term.

Threadgill looked at him as if he were an idiot and stood up. "I think we should leave now, Marianna. You should get some rest before the party."

Marianna lifted her head and gazed dully at him, one eye half open, the other squeezed closed, as if she were trying to peer through a fog. "I can't go until I talk to Douglas," she muttered before dropping her head back on the table.

Threadgill was non-plussed, and before he could answer the telephone rang. The call was for him and he took it at the bar. "That was Douglas," he said when he rejoined them at the booth. "He just got home. He should be here in a few minutes."

Clay stood up. "Well, in that case, I should probably be leavin' then," he said, donning his navy blue parka. "It shore was nice meetin' yuh, Mr. Threadgill." Threadgill looked relieved as Clay ambled out the door, taking his half-finished manhattan with him. He drove about aimlessly for more than an hour and popped a benny. It began to sleet, and a glaze of thin ice started coating the roads. By the time he got back to the Rudolph Tavern he was starting to feel a rush, and with it, the slight cold sweat that always accompanied the feeling. This is the ultimate test, he thought. Would she be there, or would she have been talked into leaving with Douglas and his father?

He went inside and saw her still in the booth, just as immobile as when he left her. She was sitting with a tall, well-dressed, straight and serious looking type who was talking rapidly, obviously perplexed. Clay staked out a stool at the bar between two Italians and ordered a beer. He was half way through it when Marianna's fiancé stood up, angrily donned his cashmere overcoat, silk scarf and gloves, and sauntered over to Clay's stool.

Douglas Franklin Threadgill's upper lip quivered as he said, "Congratulations ace! You must certainly be proud of yourself."

Clay swung around on his stool, his beer still in his hand. "I didn't have anything to do with it, man. She just doesn't want to marry you."

"She doesn't know what she's doing!" Douglas said shrilly. "She just keeps saying she wants you to give her another happiness pill. My father could have you arrested."

"Friend," Clay said, his eyes turning steely blue, "If you want to sit down and have a drink and discuss it, fine. If not, watch the accusations." The Italians moved away.

"I wouldn't drink with riff-raff like you in a million years!" Douglas sputtered. He turned toward the booth. "All right, Marianna, I'm leaving! Are you coming, or not?" Marianna shook her head and looked away as Douglas towered over her, trembling in a rage. He whirled, knocking over a chair, and stormed out of the tavern.

The sleet had changed to snow, and it was slow driving back to the airport. They had to wait an hour while the ice on Petey's plane was being washed off with glycol. During the wait Marianna spread herself out on a couch in the tiny terminal building, and Clay plied her with coffee. It helped very little. As soon as they were airborne she threw up, and then fell asleep in the backseat under a blanket.

The funerals the next day for Chuck and Patsy were long, and Clay was relieved when they were over. He didn't like funerals. He also didn't like the scene he had to have with his mother. She had been very hurt when he told her that he and Marianna were leaving right after the funeral, and she had let him know it. She had wanted them to stay a few more days.

Petey flew them to St. Louis, and by mid-afternoon they were on a flight to New York. Robert met them at LaGuardia and rushed up to greet them as soon as they stepped off the plane. He started pumping Clay's hand. "I couldn't believe it when I heard it was you!" he exclaimed. "I nearly laughed my ass off." He turned to Marianna. "Boy, are you in trouble, sister. Father's gone crazy. He's cussing and hitting things. I was afraid he was going to have a heart attack." On the drive to Greenwich, Robert explained what had happened. "Old Threadgill telephoned Father the day before yesterday and told him that his chauffeur had waited all afternoon for you at O'Hare, but that you never showed up. Of course Father thought you'd already been there for two days. He called the police; even the FBI. Then last night old Threadgill phoned again. He said the wedding was off - that he and Douglas had left you in a beer joint with some bum named Clay Stoner. Father had apoplexy. He's been tied up all day cancelling wedding arrangements. The club is going to bill him for three hundred dinners and is delivering fifteen cases of champagne to the house and charging him for them. Boy, is he pissed!"

Forewarned, they exited the freeway and drove through Greenwich and up Round Hill Road until they reached a turnoff into a drive blocked by a huge wrought iron gate. Robert opened it automatically with a signal from an electronic gadget in the car and then drove another two hundred yards along a winding drive through giant oak trees until they reached the house. A butler was waiting in front to meet them and fetch their luggage. Clay whistled. "It's a far cry from the top floor of the Trocadero, isn't it?" Marianna said smiling.

Marianna's mother met them at the door, flapping her arms and screeching like a goose. "Are you crazy?" How could you do this to us? Your father worked so hard to have a wedding you could be proud of! And not only that, you're late for dinner," she said furiously, as if that was the greatest insult of all. "Hurry up. You can come to the table as you are." They were dressed identically in jeans, white sweaters and navy blue parkas.

Clay and Robert trailed behind the two women into the dining room, and one of the maid servants showed Clay his seat. Marianna's father was already seated, glaring ominously. He started eating without saying a word, but in two minutes his wrath overflowed and he launched into an attack on Marianna. "Do you realize the trouble Mr. Threadgill and I went through for this wedding? The

Swiss ambassador in Washington postponed his trip home for the holidays just to be here. I had to call him today to tell him it's all off. You've made me look like a fool." Marianna fidgeted with her food and kept her head down and did not say anything. "Where have you been for four days?" She did not answer. "You're an ingrate, do you know that? You should be thankful Douglas still wanted to marry you after your cheap little affair last year."

She still did not answer, and Robert interrupted. "She doesn't love Douglas," he tried to explain.

"You shut up!" Mr. Haizet bellowed, turning his venom on Robert.

Clay seethed. He had not touched the meal. He held his tongue, sipping wine and watching the spectacle taking place before him as if he were at a tennis match, the ball going back and forth, back and forth.

It was her mother's turn to scold her. "Douglas is from a very fine family. That's very important to us. Don't you care how we feel?"

"What about how I feel?" Marianna said, softly, without lifting her head

Mrs. Haizet kept on talking as if she hadn't heard. "We only wanted the best for you - someone from your own class."

"I said what about how I feel! Doesn't that count for anything?" Marianna said much louder. She raised her eyes and looked at them coldly.

"You keep your mouth shut when your mother's talking to you!" her father pointed at her, shouting in a threatening tone.

Marianna lunged out of her chair, knocking over the candelabra on the table, and threw her wine glass against the wall, splashing all of them. "If you want to know," she said trembling, "I can't stand living in this house anymore. I'm leaving, and for good! And you, and the ambassador, and all your friends at the club, and the proper young men you would like me marry...*you can all go to hell!*" She burst from the table crying and ran up the stairs. Her mother sat there for a moment, startled, and then trailed after her.

"Another pleasant family dinner at the Haizet household, eh, Dad?" Robert said hollowly.

"I suppose you think she's right and I'm wrong, as usual," Mr. Haizet fumed.

"No. You're always right, Dad," Robert said. He excused himself and walked quickly out of the dining room.

"What about you, Mr. Stoner?" Mr. Haizet continued ranting, only the two of them left at the table, now. "You, the interloper who just sits at the table and says nothing while he drinks my wine. Do you think I'm being ridiculous for being upset when my daughter pulls a stunt like this the day before her wedding? On second thought, I guess you think it's pretty funny."

"No sir. I think it's pretty sad."

"Oh you do, do you. And what would you propose to do about it?"

"I'd like to spare you my presence. If someone would call me a taxi, I would like to say goodbye to Marianna and leave as soon as possible."

"Now that's the first intelligent thing anyone has said all evening. I'll have my chauffeur waiting for you at the door. Just tell him where you want to go. He'll drive you all the way back to Missouri if you want."

Clay excused himself and went upstairs to look for Marianna. The door to her room was open. She was packing, and she and her mother were arguing. Clay walked in and was drawn into it. "Tomorrow is Sunday, the day Marianna was supposed to be married. I want her to go to church with me. Please ask her to stay," Marianna's mother pleaded. "I'll prepare a room for you." Clay looked at the old woman and saw that her grief was sincere. He agreed to stay.

Marianna had already left for church by the time Clay awakened. He went downstairs and was invited to join Mr. Haizet on the sun porch for breakfast. Mr. Haizet did not waste any time with small talk. He poured some coffee and got right to the point. "Marianna says she's leaving with you as soon as she gets back from church. I'd like you gone before then. I don't know what you think your relationship is with her, but I assure you you're not the first."

"I know that," Clay said, as he buttered a toast.

"Good. Then you know that she doesn't know what she is doing. I don't want to see her make some asinine mistake, and I don't want to see her mother hurt. That's why I've made out a check to you for a thousand dollars. If you make yourself scarce before she gets back from church, it's yours." He slid a check across the table next to Clay's plate. Clay pushed it back. "You don't seem to understand that I want you to leave, young man. Take that check and never come back here. If you don't, I promise you'll never get a dime out of Marianna. I'll cut her off without a cent if I have to."

"You should thank me. I won't tell her about this," Clay said, his tone defiant. "But you, sir, may take your check and stuff it!" He was gone in an instant, grabbing his coat and bag by the front door, down the porch steps, and outside waiting in Marianna's Triumph when she returned from church. Five minutes later she was next to him, her bags packed, and they were on the road to Washington.

As they passed through downtown Greenwich, they stopped at a store, and Clay went in and bought a quart of orange juice, some cups, and a bag of ice. When he came out, Marianna had the top on the Triumph rolled down. It was thirty degrees, and there was six inches of snow on the ground. He suggested they put the top back up, but she refused. Half an hour later they were on the New Jersey Turnpike weaving in and out of traffic at eighty miles an hour with the radio turned all the way up and a cold, wet wind biting at their faces, drinking vodka and orange juice. Clay popped four or five bennies; Marianna a couple. They honked and waved and held their cups up high each time they zoomed by a car. People looked at them like they were crazy. They stopped at Howard Johnson's for gas. Marianna handed the gas pump attendant a twenty dollar bill, asked him to close his eyes, kissed him flush on the mouth, and told him to keep the fifteen dollars of change. He stood there open-mouthed as they sped away.

It was after dark when they arrived at Cat's apartment on P Street. It was empty, but Clay had a key. It was Sunday and the liquor store on the corner was closed, but it was New Year's Eve and they knew there had to be a party going on someplace. They called Vic at his father's house, and sure enough, Vic and Darcy were having a party.

Marianna and Clay showered and changed, and about ten o'clock they drove over to Arlington to another drunken navy pilot bash at the Powers' residence. Marianna was commandeered by Vic and Sammy Powell as soon as she walked in the door. They escorted her to the piano and insisted that she play *Battle*. And play she did as twenty rowdy people gathered around singing. Clay took another benny and started to get drunk. It wasn't long before Cat cornered him at the bar. He started to thank her for use of her apartment for the weekend, but she wanted to talk about Chuck. His death had hurt her badly. Clay described at length what had happened: Slim's Place, the mule, the eerie stillness and sense of helplessness on the road, the sheriff, the ambulance, the doctor's simple pronouncement. Cat cried a little. Clay got high and lost track of the time. They were still talking when a very pregnant Darcy started blowing a horn and shouting out the countdown to midnight. As if all thoughts of Chuck had been erased, Cat draped her arms around Clay's neck, thrust her pelvic bone against him, and gave him a deep French kiss. He swallowed her tongue for a moment before disentangling himself and looking around for Marianna. Sammy Powell ambled past, wearing a pointed hat and guzzling from a bottle of champagne. Sammy told him that he had just seen Marianna run upstairs.

He found her in the first room off the hall, spread across a bed on a pile of coats tossed there by the guests. He knelt down beside her and stroked her hair. She was sobbing. "Hey fella', cheer up," he said. "It's New Year's Eve. How about another happiness pill?"

"They don't make me happy," she mumbled as she buried her face deeper in the pile of coats. "In fact, they make me miserable. Why don't you go fuck Cat?"

"Don't be such a drag," he said as he stroked her. "Cat doesn't mean anything. She just likes to have a good time."

Marianna was sitting up now. "That's all you ever think about, isn't it? Just having a good time." She was looking into his eyes with a way she had of looking. She looked as if she were afraid of so many things.

"You used to like to have a good time."

"Maybe I think certain things are more important now - things like responsibility."

"Oh hell!" he laughed. "Don't get serious on me. That's never been our attraction."

"I know...and that's why I hate your guts!"

"What's the matter with you?"

"It's none of your goddamn business."

He grabbed her shoulders and shook her until her head snapped back and forth. "You're not telling me something, Marianna. What are you hiding?"

She fought and wrenched away and yelled at him. "It has to be *all or nothing* with you, doesn't it, Clay Stoner? But you don't own me!"

He could see the little tremblies around her lips as they quivered and prepared to cry some more. His arm went around her and she leaned back against him, and all of a sudden she became quite calm. "Please tell me...why do you hate my guts?" he said in a wounded tone of voice. He could see her mind leaping about.

"Because...," she said very softly. "Because of you I gave up the most important thing in the world to me."

"Listen, if you're blaming me because of your father..."

"I'm not talking about my father, you *fool!* I'm talking about *our baby!*" She stared at him with a sadistic smile, and the words tumbled out. "Do you know what I did after that weekend we went to the football game in Baltimore? I went to a doctor on Park Avenue and had an abortion. Guess who the father was fella'? If you can't, I'll give you a hint. It happened in Nice when we were having such a *good time!* Haps, I think you called it." She hesitated and struggled to catch her breath.

"Go on," he said, looking at her as a stranger.

"There's not much to tell," she said. "You don't have to look so shocked. It's no big deal, you know. They just take a little scalpel and scrape you out inside and you go on your way."

His first impulse was to strangle her. "Why didn't you tell me?" he screamed at her.

"I tried to!"

"You did not! Why didn't you?"

"I didn't want to be a bother!" She burst into tears.

As if it were a reflex, he slapped her hard in the face and knocked her down, splitting her lip. Darcy witnessed the blow from the hallway and came rushing in. "Are you crazy, Clay? You hit her!" Darcy railed, and she started pounding away at him.

"Get the hell out of here, Darcy!" Clay ranted. "This is just between us." He grabbed Marianna's hair and dragged her into a closet and slammed the door. "You *bitch!*" he shouted as he slapped her back and forth across the face. "Why didn't you tell me?"

"Because I didn't want to know what you'd do if I did!" she cried out loud.

He rammed her body against the closet wall. She clawed his face, broke free and burst out of the closet. When she came out a half dozen guests were in the room, having been drawn by the commotion. Marianna pushed through them, crying, and ran wildly down the stairs. Clay ran after her. She crashed into the bar and knocked two of Admiral Powers' best bottles of scotch shattering against the floor. She ran out the front door into the yard, and Clay chased after her. He tackled her from behind and pushed her face down into the snow. He rolled her over and straddled her and grinded more snow in her face. And then, in the very next moment, he was lying on her and kissing her and babbling over and over, "I love you. I love you. I love you."

Sammy Powell helped Admiral Powers grab him roughly from behind and jerk him to his feet. The Admiral was incensed and ordered Clay to leave. Clay thought about arguing, then shrugged, and walked away up the street toward the Triumph. Marianna trailed after him. He was too stoned to drive, so she drove back to P Street. "Did you really mean it when you said you loved me?" she asked when they were safely ensconced in Cat's apartment.

"Yes," he said.

"Are you sure, after what I did?"

"I'm sure."

"Then I love you too," she said, as she leaned forward and kissed him on the eyelids.

It was all out, finally, and there were no more secrets between them. She led him into the bedroom, but when they tried to make love, he was unable. The booze and the pills had been too much. She was gentle and patient and they tried, but each time it was the same. He wilted. She fell asleep, finally, and he lay against her, perplexed and confused. He tried to doze.

His beating pulse awakened him. He was wide awake, suddenly, sitting on the edge of the bed, feeling chilled. He got up and staggered into the kitchen. He started shaking. He found his sweater and put it on. He tried to boil some water to make coffee, but his trembling hand dropped the pot. The crash brought Marianna wandering in from the bedroom. "I felt you get up," she said unsteadily. "I thought maybe you were leaving." His teeth were chattering too much to answer. She sat in the kitchen with him for four hours and held his head in her lap, stroking it while he sweated and shook and stared fixedly at the rosy terracotta floor. He had been on a ten pill a day high for more than a week, and he was coming down now. About ten o'clock in the morning he collapsed in the bed and slept fitfully until late afternoon. He was hungry when he awakened. Marianna fixed some coffee and toast. The coffee was good, and they drank a whole pot.

They went out to the Rathskellar for dinner. They drank beer and were serenaded by two old Germans in leather knee pants playing an accordion and a violin. They brought a bottle of Moselle back to the apartment with them, drank it, showered, and went to bed and made love. For the first time, it was completely honest. The next morning they woke up sober. Still in bed, she snuggled up to him and asked, "what's going to happen to us now?"

He lay there looking at the ceiling. "I don't know," he said after awhile. I'm going back to Virginia Beach this afternoon. You're going back to Juilliard. You'll probably go home and make peace with your parents."

"No way," she said, shaking her head slowly from side to side. "My tuition is paid for, and I have a little money. I'm going to find my own apartment in the City. I can take care of myself. I'm much more concerned about you."

He laughed. "Why me?"

"Because I've figured out why you've been the way you are, Clay. It's Vietnam. You don't want to go."

"So? Does that make me any different from anyone else?"

"Yes, because it's tearing you to pieces. You were a different person those first two days I met you in Nice. Happy. Carefree. You didn't know you were going to Vietnam then. The next time I saw you, you had already started to change. I saw an anguish in you. I haven't seen you really sober since, and I think I understand it now. How can you go fight in a war and drop bombs on people if you think it's wrong? Or worse than wrong: immoral."

He lit a cigarette, inhaled deeply, and spit out a flume of smoke over his shoulder. "Marianna, except for the bombing of innocents, I don't necessarily think this war is morally wrong. That's where you and I differ. But I know it's a stupid war, and innocent people should not be killed because of that.

She raised up on one elbow and looked at him inquisitively. "I said I loved you, Clay. I couldn't bear it if something happened to you over something stupid. If you feel that way, how can you be a part of it?"

"Who in the hell has a choice?"

"Someone has to say no. You could be the first."

"I wouldn't be the first."

"You'd be the first pilot. That would mean something."

He rolled over and nipped playfully at her boobs. "Why don't you get the hell up and fix us some breakfast?" he groused. She sat up and pulled on her tee shirt and panties. A half hour later she called him into the kitchen. She had fixed toast and eggs and sausage. The toast and eggs were burned to a crisp. They ate them anyway, and when they finished he told her what he had decided.

"No more bennies, ever," he announced solemnly. "And I'm going to turn in my wings."

Marianna washed and put away the dishes and tidied up the apartment while Clay sat down at Cat's typewriter and pecked out a letter. It was short and succinct, through the chain of command up to the Chief of Naval Personnel. In two terse sentences he stated that he was resigning from his status as a naval aviator in order to express his dissent against the country's policies in Vietnam. "What do you think the Chief of Naval Personnel will say?" Marianna asked after she read it over.

He'll probably never see it. Some low level officer in the Pentagon will just process the papers. It's my fleet air wing commander, Admiral Martin, who I worry about. The letter has to be routed through him, and he'll blow a cork when he sees it. He'll probably try to make sure I get transferred to only god knows where, and it won't be a pleasant place."

She walked into his arms, rested her head on his shoulder and hugged him. "I feel partly responsible for this, and I won't let you get away from me that easily, you know. I'll follow you wherever you go." They parted an hour later. Vic and Darcy came by to pick Clay up for the drive down to Virginia Beach, and Marianna left for New York in her Triumph, exactly one long week from the day she had met him at the airport in St. Louis.

VI

❧

THE REALITY OF REBELLION

Clay was summoned to Admiral Martin's office on January eighth and ordered to stand at attention in front of the Admiral's desk. The Admiral commenced sputtering and bellowing like a wounded rhinoceros. "In thirty years in the navy I've never seen such a goddamn insubordinate letter! I wanted to court martial you on the spot. Fortunately for you, my staff says I can't!" The Admiral stood up from his desk and stalked over to Clay and glowered at him in an attempt to stare him down. He reached out and tore the wings off Clay's uniform. "You don't deserve to wear these, Stoner! You're a coward - a yellow belly! I'll approve your letter if that's what you want. But not until you resubmit it and leave out all that bullshit about turning in your wings because you're against our policy in Vietnam. Just admit you're too gutless to fly in combat, and I'll have you transferred out of here so fast you'll think you're on a rocket ship to the moon!"

"I can't do that, sir," Clay said as calmly as he could, still standing at rigid attention. "My whole purpose of turning in my wings is to let the navy know through official channels that I'm against what we are doing in Vietnam. A lot of pilots feel the same way but are afraid to speak out."

The Admiral tore the letter in half and tossed it in a wastebasket. His tone became threatening. "Stoner, when you signed up you lost all right to pick and choose your wars. Don't make waves. If you don't want to find yourself in more trouble than you ever dreamed, you'd better get your butt out of here and go rewrite that letter the way I told you...or *else!*"

Clay resubmitted an identical letter the next morning. By noon he had been informed that Admiral Martin was reopening the investigation of his mid-air with Jimmer Jones, which had cleared Clay completely and found Jimmer to be the one at fault. The forwarding of his letter was to be delayed until the investigation was completed. Clay knew the military mind well enough to recognize a set up when he saw one. This new investigation would be to try to assign some blame to him as justification for stripping him of his wings instead of allowing him to turn them in voluntarily as a protest against the war. That night he mailed a copy of his letter to the head of the Senate Armed Services Committee, attached to another letter explaining how his official correspondence was being improperly blocked and the ruse that was being implemented to censure and disgrace him. A week later Martin's aide called him in and informed him that the investigation had been halted as a result of a congressional inquiry and that his letter had been forwarded directly to the Secretary of the Navy. He was ordered to restrict himself to the base until further notice while he awaited orders from Washington detailing his next assignment.

The squadron deployed on the first Friday in February, and Clay obtained a three day pass to take Darcy to the pier in Norfolk the morning the carrier pulled out, and then escort her home. They stood in a drizzle as a band played and hundreds of wives and girl friends cried and waved and blew kisses to the men lined upon the carrier deck. After two hours the majestic ship pulled away escorted by eight tugboats and chugged out the channel toward Chesapeake Bay and the sea.

Afterwards, Clay drove Darcy home in his Corvette to the estate in McLean where her mother now lived with Cat's father. Her baby was due almost anytime, and for most of the trip she was subdued. But when they arrived finally at her stepfather's, she shared her anguish. "Do you know what Vic did last night?" she said dazedly. "He went over his will with me! He's twenty five years old, and he has a *will!* We spent our whole last evening together with him explaining what I should do if he doesn't come back...how I should manage things...raise the baby. It was unreal, Clay." She leaned on his shoulder and started to weep.

"I know it's tough, but don't worry, Darse. Vic'll be home before you know it."

"I wish he were flying with you."

"He's flying with Sammy. You may think he's a goof-ball, but Sammy's a great pilot. They'll come home safe. I promise you."

She stopped crying and dabbed at her eyes. "Ten months is such a long time, though. And I don't want to wait here all that time. As soon as the baby can travel, I'm going back to Haut-de-Cagnes and stay until Vic comes home. I intend to find out once and for all whether I can paint or not. Cat's going to come with me for awhile. She says she needs a change of scenery."

Clay left Darcy at the Asquith front door about four o'clock and drove on up to New York to visit Marianna for the weekend. It was after eight when he arrived at her apartment, six steps down from the sidewalk level in an old brownstone off Amsterdam Avenue in the west eighties. There were garbage cans out front. She threw her arms around him at the door and dragged him inside to show off her new home. The apartment was a one room studio with a tiny kitchenette in the corner, a couch that converted into a bed, a cheap cocktail table and a second hand chair. The only decoration was a black fish net with orange corks in it hanging down from the ceiling. "What do you think?" she said excitedly. "I know it's not much, but it's mine. I've got a job in a piano bar, and I'm paying for it myself." She looked at him. "God, it's been almost five weeks. I'm so glad you're finally off restriction."

"That's because I just got my orders. I leave in ten days."

"Where?"

"Iceland"

"You're not serious!"

"Yeah. I hear it's not bad."

She shook her head. "Iceland. Unbelievable!"

She was scheduled to perform in fifteen minutes, so they had to leave right away before having a chance to talk. She took him to The Cellar, a dim pub near Columbia where she worked. Robert was there waiting for them, drinking a beer. Marianna had to play until midnight. She sang quiet songs, mostly ballads, and Clay and Robert had a long time to talk. Robert's hair was even longer now, and it was soon evident that he was consumed by the subject of the war. "On the record," he said up front. "I'm a journalism major and a reporter for the Spectator, Columbia's school paper. Many of the students here are starting to panic over the thought they may be draft bait real soon. I think they would be extremely interested in the story about you turning in your wings. Marianna said it got a little nasty."

Clay shrugged. "A little. I guess I was the first to turn them in to protest the war. The navy was just trying to nip it in the bud."

"You're not the first."

"I'm not?" Clay was surprised.

"No. I've been doing some research. There's a lieutenant in San Diego. He flew a hundred missions, came back two months ago all fed up and turned in his wings as a protest. The navy stuck him in a hospital psycho ward. No reporter visits allowed. I called his wife last week. She told me it was all part of a scheme so that as soon as the news of his protest blows over he can be discharged from the service for being mentally unfit."

Clay was a little drunk. Not too drunk in any disabling sense, but just enough to be careless. He launched into a discussion of what he really thought about the war and the bombings. Sometime during the conversation he and Robert switched to rusty nails and the conversation became hazy. They ended up agreeing that Vietnam was going to be a calamity for the country, and they probably would have gone on discussing the subject all night if Marianna had not interrupted them when her three hour stint was finished. Robert departed for his dorm, and Clay and Marianna went back to the apartment with one thought in mind - to cram as much pleasure into their lives as a short weekend would allow. They made love for the rest of the night, caressing and kissing each other until the grey of dawn poked through the apartment window.

They slept until early afternoon, and when they awakened, they took a subway to mid-town and went ice skating at Rockefeller Center. At dusk they walked over to Park Avenue and twelve blocks up it to a cocktail party at a swank apartment belonging to the parents of one of Marianna's schoolmates. The party bored them quickly. It was too full of too cool people; a late twenties, early thirties crowd all trying to outshine. The conversation centered around bloody mary's and backgammon, spring vacations in Bermuda or the British Virgins, summers in Southampton or the Vineyard; how difficult it was to find good help anymore. Clay and Marianna tossed down one champagne cocktail, took a second with them into the powder room, locked the door and commenced having sex, half standing, half seated, entwined together. Twenty minutes later they left without saying goodbye, taxiing over to the west side to The Cellar, arriving in time to wolf down a hamburger before Marianna started her shift at the piano. Her voice was soft and smoky, as if she were singing each song to him, and during her two ten minute breaks she joined him at the table. The way he held her hand and looked at her made her know that she had not been wrong in casting her stone with him.

They hailed another taxi at midnight and drove back over to the east side to the Hippopotamus, a chic discotheque that was one of the gathering places for New York's late night party goers. The dance floor was mobbed, packed with bodies in outlandish attire bumping and frugging underneath flashing kleig lights to a stereophonic sound that was deafening. Miraculously, they found an empty booth and claimed it. Marianna took off her heels, and they wandered into the crowd and started to dance. Clay held her close, nibbling at her shoulders. She unbuttoned his shirt. He felt her boobs, and realizing she was braless, he pulled the top of her dress down, letting them both flip out, and they danced, pressing their chests together for nearly an hour. They returned to the booth, drenched with perspiration, and ordered white wine spritzers. She cuddled up against him, covering him with her raincoat. He pressed an ice cube down the front of her pants, and as they kissed, she fluttered with little spasms, and started biting his neck.

They left at three-thirty. At her apartment, she stepped out of her damp dress, collapsed on the bed, and motioned. He did what she wanted. They had one giant orgasm together and fell asleep.

He woke up, and she was stroking his back. "Did I pass the test?" she said as, she snuggled up to him and caressed his shoulders.

"What test?" he said drowsily, as he smiled and sat up and cradled her under his wing.

"The night Chuck was killed - at Slim's Place. Cindy Sue told me how much you demanded of a woman...that you'd always be testing me. I just wanted to show you that I can pass the test. You can do whatever you want with me, and I will always love you."

Clay left at noon on Sunday to make the four hundred mile drive back to Virginia Beach. On Thursday afternoon he was summoned to Admiral Martin's office. He walked into an inquisition. The Admiral's staff were all lining the walls and looking at him accusingly as the Admiral ordered him to stand at attention and then recited carefully as if he had memorized what he was going to say. "Mister Stoner, your transfer is cancelled. You are now hereby considered to be under house arrest and restricted to your quarters. I have ordered an Article 32 Board of Investigation to be held within

two weeks to determine if there is sufficient evidence for me to convene general court martial proceedings against you for violations
of Articles 133 and 134 of the Uniform Code of Military Justice. You
have the right to be represented by a counsel of your choice. If you
choose not to exercise that right, the navy will make one available
for you. Do you have any questions?"

Clay was staggered and could not believe what was happening.
"Yeah, a lot," he said in a daze. "What's this all about, sir?"

The Admiral walked over and shoved a newspaper article in
his face. It was a copy from the *New York Times*. "Your big mouth,
for starters. This article is enough for me to hang you, Stoner!"

Clay pawed it away. "I don't know what that says, but I've never done anything that I know of to deserve a court martial, sir."

The Admiral stared at him defiantly for a moment, and then
changed his tone. "You know Stoner," he said in a fatherly way, "I'd
hate to see even you face a court martial for something like this. I
must advise you this is considered a serious offense, but if you were
willing to cooperate, there's probably a way out of it for you."

Clay was wary now. "How is that sir?"

"My staff thinks you should have a psychiatric evaluation. It's
strictly voluntary, I assure you, but if the doctors concluded you
had a problem - maybe a case of nerves because of your mid-air - I
could sympathize with that. And if that were the case, I'm sure the
navy wouldn't want to see you tried. After a few weeks rest someplace, you might even get a medical discharge. I'd think you might
like that."

Clay rebelled instinctively. "No sir!"

"What do you mean, no?"

"Just that! We both know the outcome if I talk to your shrinks,
don't we Admiral? Anyone who makes waves and bucks the system must be crazy, right? It's much tidier to lock me up in a loony
bin instead of having a messy court martial that might go public
and show how screwed up the system really is. Well, it won't wash
with me, Admiral."

Admiral Martin's oily smile was gone and his face was purple
now. Only the presence of his staff enabled him to control his rage.
"You're taking a big risk, Stoner. You could end up in Portsmouth
for this. You'd better think it over."

"I don't need to think it over," Clay said, calming down now. "I
haven't done anything wrong. You're just pissed because I turned
in my wings. But that's my right. I'm willing to fulfill my service

obligation any other way - even if that means building igloos in Iceland. But I'm not going to incinerate a bunch of village peasants for the sake of Vietnam."

"You're a disgrace to the navy!" the Admiral shouted, his jaw jutting six inches from Clay's face. "You're dismissed." Clay executed a sharp about-face, and marched toward the door. "You'll hang for this, Stoner! I'm going to have your *ass!*" the Admiral shouted at him as he walked out of the room.

There was a knock on Clay's door at the BOQ late the next morning. He opened it and met the counsel assigned to defend him, Randolph Stewart Whitney, a lieutenant from the Judge Advocate General's office in Washington. Whitney was twenty eight years old, medium height, sandy haired, a Yale law graduate and a blue blood, but the seriousness and sincerity of his smile was infectious and Clay's first instinct was to trust him. They discussed the case and Whitney described the charges. The most serious was the accusation of violating Article 134 by making disloyal statements that were prejudicial to good order and discipline and brought discredit upon the armed forces of the United States. Under Article 133, he was accused of the catchall charge of conduct unbecoming an officer and a gentleman. Attached as an exhibit to the charges was a copy of an article from Wednesday's *New York Times*, the bulk of which was a reprint of one published by Robert in the *Columbia Spectator* the day before. Whitney explained that two of Clay's quotes could be very damaging. One said, "God is not sufficiently on our side for us to destroy Vietnam." The other said, "I've turned in my wings because it's the only honorable way to show how I feel. If every pilot who felt the same way did the same thing, there wouldn't be enough of us left to blow up a foot bridge."

"As I see it, the navy's case boils down to those two statements. It would help matters if I could claim you were misquoted," Whitney said hopefully.

Clay gave him a hard, stubborn look. "I have nothing to hide. That's what I said. I can't deny it."

"I don't think you appreciate the seriousness of the charges," Whitney advised him.

"No, I guess I don't. Quite frankly, I think they're a goddamn joke."

"That kind of attitude makes it very difficult for me to defend you. We have less than two weeks. The best I can probably do is try to convince the investigating board that the statements you made were because you *are* a loyal officer, not the other way around - throw the first amendment in their faces - freedom of speech. I'll let them know that the publicity of a court martial is going to make the navy look bad."

Clay warmed more to the Lieutenant. "That sounds like the right tack. What do you think of your chances for success?"

Whitney shook his head. "I don't know. The Board members are all part of Martin's staff. If he's told them to ram through a court martial, then it doesn't make any difference what we do at the hearing. Otherwise, we have a reasonable chance."

The Board of Investigation was all Admiral Martin's show. The proceedings were a mere formality. They were over in less than an hour. Whitney fought eloquently, but his effort was as futile as that of a high school team up against the pros. The Board concluded that sufficient evidence existed for Clay to be tried by general court martial on all charges. Martin agreed, and as the convening authority, he placed Clay under house arrest, restricted to the BOQ, and set the trial date for the middle of April. Whitney was shaken afterwards. "I'm sorry, Clay," he said. "I tried and failed. Martin means business. Perhaps you should get a more senior officer to defend you. Maybe even consider hiring a civilian lawyer, the best you can find."

It was odd, but Clay felt almost as bad for Whitney as he did for himself. "Have you ever defended anyone in a general court before?" he said. Whitney shook his head. "Well...my mother always said to leave the dance with the same girl I brought. Let's go back to my room at the BOQ and have a drink and talk about it."

Whitney stayed in Clay's room until one in the morning, and they had more than a few drinks. Whitney began attacking the court martial system; little better than a kangaroo court, he said. A commanding officer could convene a proceeding almost anytime he wanted. The members of the court - the jury - would probably all be officers under his command. And he wrote their fitness reports, hardly a system conducive to the jury bringing in an unpopular decision. It was a tough system to beat, and Whitney wanted Clay to know it.

Clay and Whitney had five weeks to plan for the trial. Whitney asked Clay if he would be willing to plead guilty if Martin would enter into a pre-trial agreement to suspend whatever sentence might be rendered by the Court. Clay said no. Their next strategy was going to be to ask for a pre-trial hearing up-front and request a change of venue, the move of the trial to another base outside of Martin's purview of command. Whitney thought that if such a request were denied by Martin, it would be great grounds for an acquittal upon appellate review. Next was the matter of the jury. Court martial rules required only a two-thirds vote to find Clay guilty. Martin had appointed a panel of nine members for starters. The panel could be reduced to a minimum of five through challenges. Whitney would be allowed one peremptory challenge without cause; so would the prosecuting trial counsel. Any more challenges would require convincing the law officer of the court - the judge - that reason for prejudice existed. The members that Martin had assigned to the panel included his chief of staff, a captain; three of his aides, a commander and two lieutenant commanders; the executive officers of two squadrons under his command, also commanders; a forty year old lieutenant, a mustang who had come up through the ranks, and two young lieutenant junior grades. If none were challenged, four votes in Clay's favor would be needed for acquittal. Any number of successful challenges up to three would still require three not guilty votes. If the panel could be reduced to five, however, Whitney would only need to win over two members of the panel for success. He convinced Clay that was the route to go. Keep the young junior officers whose careers had less at stake; get rid of the most senior officers, and the mustang; mustangs were notoriously tough disciplinarians. The objective was to reduce the jury members to a panel of five.

The pending trial was mentioned very little in the press. Two days before it commenced, however, the Virginia Beach papers gave it a front page spread. The next day visitors started to arrive. Still under house arrest, Clay was allowed to meet with two of them at a time for a maximum of half an hour. His parents were first. Lara Stoner was incredulous. She was so incensed that Bill Stoner could hardly control her. She raged. "What are these people trying to do, son? You didn't do anything wrong!" Her eyes started watering. Bill wrapped one of his hairy arms around her and hugged her. He smiled weakly at Clay.

"We support you all the way, son. No matter what happens, we want you to know that." He did not sound optimistic. He had been in the army and knew the way the system worked.

The next visitor was Robert, and with him was a jaunty, cocky looking man impeccably dressed in a herringbone suit with a neatly pressed grey and white handkerchief jutting out of his breast pocket. Of medium height, his wavy black hair was meticulously groomed, his Italian shoes spit shined. Clay guessed him to be about forty and intelligent. "Hi, I'm Larry Smith, CBS News!" the man said

Robert explained why they were there together. The *New York Times* had asked him to cover the story on a free lance basis. He'd met Smith while they were each sitting in the BOQ lobby waiting for a chance to interview Clay. Robert's face was ash white. "I...I would have come anyway," he stammered. "I had no idea my article could lead to this. I'm sorry, Clay."

Larry Smith was businesslike, and he said what was on his mind. "After my broadcast tonight, there's going to be a crowd here tomorrow that will surprise you. This war is starting to lose its popularity real fast. It's not going to sit too well with the American people when they see you being marched into the courthouse under arrest for speaking out against it. Most Americans still believe in the right of free speech." In the short time they had together Smith asked him a number of questions about his background and the events that occurred since he turned in his wings. Robert took notes. When they left, Marianna came in to see him. They spent the allotted half hour talking quietly, each trying to reassure the other that everything was going to turn out all right.

A crowd of newsmen and protesters carrying signs were in front of the courthouse building the next morning when Whitney and Clay drove up. Photographers swarmed their car, flashbulbs popping. A marine guard forged a path through the crowd and led them into the court. Lara and Bill were already in the gallery, sitting next to Marianna. Clay nodded to them as he walked down the aisle.

The court was gaveled to order by a gray-haired navy captain, a trained law officer who had been appointed by the Judge Advocate General to preside over the trial. Within ten minutes he had sworn in the panel of nine members and charged them with their responsibilities. It was then Whitney's turn to question them.

The first thing Whitney did was go to work on Martin's chief of staff, a navy captain who had been present in Martin's office when Clay was first accused. "Who do you report to?" Whitney questioned him.

"Admiral Martin," replied the Captain.

"And he writes your fitness report, does he not?"

"Yes."

"Were you present at a meeting in the Admiral's office when Lieutenant Stoner was first informed of the possible charges against him?"

"Yes."

"Did you hear the Admiral say words to the effect that he was going to hang Mr. Stoner; that he was going to have Mr. Stoner's ass?"

"I don't recall exactly. He may have said something like that," the Captain replied nervously.

Whitney turned to the law officer. "I challenge for cause. The Captain was there. No way can he be expected to render an impartial verdict." The law officer deliberated for a minute and then agreed and dismissed the Captain. *Round one: Whitney.*

Whitney next went to work on one of Martin's aides, a Commander. The line of questioning was similar, except this officer had not been present in Martin's office when the Admiral threatened Clay, but he had heard about it. Whitney challenged him for cause. The law officer's response was abrupt. "Be advised counsel that it is your client who is on trial here, not the other way around. Challenge is denied."

Whitney was incredulous. He protested the ruling vociferously, and then used his one free challenge to get rid of the commander. Next he proceeded to challenge every remaining member of the panel except the junior grades, but the law officer denied each request almost before the words were out of his mouth. The trial counsel used his free challenge to get rid of the youngest junior grade, who appeared to be showing the most empathy, and when Whitney returned to his seat, he was fuming. "That law officer screwed us. We have to get 'three votes out of six for acquittal now, instead of two out of five."

The trial counsel started introducing evidence. His first exhibit was a copy of the *New York Times* article accompanied by the Board of Investigation transcript in which Clay admitted to making the statements contained in the article. Next was a deposition from Clay's squadron commander attesting that the *Times* article had been read aboard the carrier while it was en route to Vietnam and that Clay's statements in it had undermined squadron morale. It was another nail to add to the Article 134 charge, and since the commander was on a carrier eight thousand miles away, there was no way Whitney could cross-examine him. The next deposition was from the rookie radar officer who had flown with Clay during the time Vic had been injured, and in it he attested that he thought Clay had been on drugs. The trial counsel was quick to connect this allegation to the mid-air collision that had killed two fellow aviators. Whitney objected immediately and was sustained by the law officer. Still, the court had heard it. The damage was done and could not be erased.

The next move to cement the "conduct unbecoming an officer and a gentleman" charge came as a complete surprise. The trial counsel called Admiral Powers to the stand. An old friend of Martin's and resplendent in his highly decorated uniform, Vic's father strode down the aisle and stood easily as he swore to tell the truth. He described the events in his home on New Year's Eve, how Clay had been drunk and disorderly, had battered a girl around upstairs in the bedroom and then made a spectacle by chasing her through his house; how he was on top of her outside in the snow, battering her, until the Admiral pulled him off. Whitney asked the Admiral just one question. "Your son flew with Lieutenant Stoner for more than a year, and Lieutenant Stoner helped save his life, did he not? What do you think your son thinks of him?"

The Admiral did not even blink. "My son did not desert his squadron mates. He's with them right now on a carrier in the South China Sea - doing his duty! I believe that shows what he thinks." Marianna looked at the Court members and saw them all nodding sympathetically. She glanced over her shoulder at Lara Stoner and shook her head.

The trial counsel rested his case, and Whitney started his defense. He cited Clay's record: top of his flight class at Pensacola; the conclusions from the midair investigation that had exonerated him; the letter of commendation he received for helping save Vic's life. "Let me read to you what Clay's commanding officer had to say about him in his last fitness report," Whitney continued. "Quote: Lieutenant Stoner is the finest first tour officer and pilot in my squadron. He has shown leadership qualities far beyond his age and performs his duties with the deepest sense of dedication and personal honor. Close quote. He gave Clay a perfect fitness rating. Now isn't it strange...just two months after the C.O. wrote that fitness report he signed the deposition that was introduced here today, and now Clay finds himself undergoing a court martial just because he turned in his wings."

"Objection!" complained the trial counsel.

"Sustained," said the law officer, and he reprimanded Whitney. "Your client is not on trial here for turning in his wings. You are well aware of that, so stick to the case."

Whitney called Admiral Martin next. The Admiral strutted forward, and with a look of deep satisfaction, he took his seat on the witness stand. He was a hostile witness, and Whitney grilled him. "Admiral, do you think Lieutenant Stoner is really guilty of the charges against him?"

"Objection!" the trial counsel yelped.

"Sustained."

"No, I want to answer that question," the Admiral said brusquely. "Obviously I do, or I would not have convened this court."

The trial counsel cringed, and Whitney moved for a mistrial. The law officer ordered a fifteen minute recess. When court reconvened, he ruled that the trial could continue and cautioned Whitney against using any more devious tactics to disrupt it. Whitney continued the questioning. "Admiral, didn't you try to make a deal with Lieutenant Stoner and agree not to press charges if he would submit to a psychiatric examination and it found him mentally unfit for duty?"

"Absolutely not," the Admiral huffed. "I may have suggested that he might need some help. Quite frankly, I think he does - just like all those other pseudo-intellectual young punks running around protesting out there. I think they're all whack jobs!" Whitney smiled and waited for the Admiral to calm down. Marianna was not smiling though. She saw the members of the Court nodding their heads in agreement again. The military mind is a wondrous thing to behold, she thought despairingly.

It was late in the afternoon, and the law officer dismissed the Court until the next morning. Clay was hustled out through the crowd by his marine guard and off to the BOQ. Whitney came by to see him that night brimming with optimism. If they lost in court, he said, he was certain they would win on appeal. He also said that he wanted Marianna to testify. Clay was against the idea, and they discussed it. Over a couple of drinks, Whitney convinced him that her testimony was needed to refute the Article 133 charge, and in the end, Clay consented. Whitney had stood up and fought for him. He decided to trust him all the way.

Marianna was the first witness the next morning. She looked calm and beautiful. Whitney asked her, "what was Clay doing when Admiral Powers pulled him off of you on New Year's Eve?"

"He was kissing me."

"He was kissing you?"

"Yes. And I was kissing him back."

"Then he wasn't battering you?"

"No. We were just rolling in the snow because we were happy and in love."

"No further questions."

"I have a question," the trial counsel said as he rose and walked slowly over to the stand and eyed Marianna defiantly. "Tell me, Miss Haizet, have you ever seen Mister Stoner take drugs – especially the night in question?"

"Objection! Immaterial!" Whitney shouted.

The law officer gave him a chilling look. "Overruled. The witness is directed to answer the question." Marianna shook her head. "Young lady," the law officer said, "you must answer the question or I will hold you in contempt."

"Yes, she said blankly, "but..." The trial counsel interrupted and cut her off in mid-sentence. The law officer excused her quickly. She burst into tears as she was escorted from the stand.

Marianna's testimony was still hanging over the courtroom like a heavy blanket of smoke when Whitney called Clay to the stand to make a closing statement. Whitney stepped back to let him talk. "As part of my education at Annapolis," Clay began slowly, "I was required to memorize a quote made by another young Lieutenant. His name was Stephen Decatur, and he achieved some degree of fame in the war against the Barbary pirates in the early nineteenth century. His quote was, 'my country, may she always be right, but right - *or wrong* - my country.' I never questioned the logic of that statement. After all, it was patriotic. It wasn't until Vietnam came along that I thought about it again. And if you really think about it, ever since all of us started school we've been taught that being patriotic is good, that Christianity, democracy, baseball, mom's apple pie...yes, the American way of life, is superior to that of the rest of the world. And when we went to war, God was always on our side because we were the good fighting evil. Think about it. All you have to do is substitute the Nazi's definition of superiority - the Aryan race - for ours...the American way of life - and you become fearful of what might happen. If you recall, the Nazis on trial at Nuremburg were convicted because an American judge ruled they had an *obligation to dissent* - to refuse to obey orders they should have known were immoral. This is the real issue before this Court today. Whether you agree with me or not, I believe it is morally wrong for us to bomb innocent people in Vietnam. I turned in my wings so I would not have to participate in that act. And when asked about it, I said what I thought, not with any intent of being disloyal, but because I believe it is my *obligation and right* as an American to say what I think is the truth. I did say, 'God is not sufficiently on our side to destroy Vietnam.' I don't retract it. And if this country is not strong enough to face up to a single, simple voice of dissent... without trying to persecute the dissenter...then God help us all."

There was a smattering of hand clapping in the civilian gallery until the law officer gaveled for silence and stated that the proceedings were adjourned until such time that the Court reached its verdict. Clay and Whitney stayed behind in the courtroom and talked until it emptied. As they walked out into the crowded hallway, Marianna rushed up and flung her arms around Clay and started crying uncontrollably. "Hey, chin up fella'," he said. "They haven't found me guilty yet."

"They will. They will," she sobbed. "They weren't even listening." She leaned on him with all her weight, and he helped her over to a bench and sat her down. Her chest was heaving. "Vic's dead, Clay! Vic and Sammy. Shot down. No parachutes. It's definite. I was just outside and heard them tell Vic's father."

Clay slumped against the wall. *Two more. For what?* He could have cared less about the outcome of the trial when he was escorted back into the courtroom an hour later. He vaguely heard an officer stand up and say; "as President of this Court it is my duty to inform you that in closed session, by a vote of four to two, the Court has found you guilty of all charges. Your sentence is to be to be dismissed as an officer from the United States Navy and confined in prison for one year."

And so it was over. The law officer ordered him to be taken immediately to the BOQ, held there under guard overnight, and then to be transferred the next day to the Portsmouth naval prison, the Alcatrez of the East it was called, on an island between the coast of Maine and New Hampshire. During its more than fifty year history no one had ever escaped alive. A marine major walked over and handcuffed him and, along with two corporals escorted him up the corridor and out of the court house. The steps were swarming with reporters, including Larry Smith and his cameraman. Smith walked beside him holding a microphone. "How does it feel to be the first officer court martialed for protesting the Vietnam War?" he asked. The major stepped over and brushed the microphone away, and amidst an outburst of jeers and catcalls, he herded Clay through the crowd to a car, and they sped away.

Whitney came to Clay's room that night after his parents left. "I told your parents not to give up," he said. "This case will be reviewed by the Court of Military Appeals. Any judge in his right mind is going to rule that Martin prejudiced the Court. You should have heard what Larry Smith had to say about it on the news tonight."

"How long will the review take?"

"I just finished meeting with Martin. I tried to get him to suspend your confinement until after the appellate review is complete. As the convening authority, he's the only person who can do that. He refused."

"How long, I asked?"

"If Martin doesn't stall it, probably three or four months."

"And in the meantime I go to Portsmouth."

Whitney nodded. "I'm afraid that's right. He has the final decision. You don't have the right to bail in the navy."

As soon as Whitney left, Marianna came in. "I can't believe this is happening!" she cried. "That trial was *not fair!* It was a mockery!"

"I know," he said bitterly. "And I'm not going to take it."

"What do you mean?"

"I'm not walking out of here in the morning in handcuffs in front of television cameras and let them haul me away in a paddy wagon like any other con. I'm going to need your help." She listened quietly as he explained his plan.

After she left Clay took his tape recorder into the bathroom, switched it on, stepped into the shower and started singing as loudly as he could. The sounds in the shower stall reverberated as if he were in an echo chamber: *"Ninety nine bottles of beer on the wall, ninety nine bottles of beer. Take one down and pass it around - ninety eight bottles of beer on the wall. Ninety eight bottles of beer on the wall, ninety eight bottles of beer..."* He showered and sang for more than twenty minutes before stepping out of the shower, and rewinding and turning off the tape recorder.

The marine guard outside his room changed at midnight, and when the new guard poked his head in to check on him, Clay was wearing only a towel. "My last shower as a free man," he grinned at the guard. "Hope you don't mind if it's a long one." His grin vanished as soon as the young marine closed the door. He tossed away the towel, went into the bathroom and dressed quickly in a pair of jeans, black turtleneck sweater and his leather flying jacket. Then he turned on the shower, and after a moment, he switched on the tape recorder and it started playing: "*ninety nine bottles of beer on the wall, ninety nine bottles of beer...*" He winced at the sound from the recorder. His ability to carry a tune was nil. It should fool the guard though, he thought, and play long enough to give him a good head start. He lifted his body up to the tiny bathroom window, wriggled through it, and dropped silently to the ground behind the BOQ. It was a dark, cloud-covered night; drizzly; cold. Still, he was perspiring by the time he had run across the base grounds to a wall behind the married officers' quarters. He scaled the wall quickly. On the other side was Marianna's Triumph, parked in the shadows with the keys in the ignition just as they had planned.

Clay arrived at Cat's apartment in Georgetown at three-thirty in the morning. Marianna was waiting in the kitchen with a pot of coffee. She had been smoking. "Cat's not here," she said. "The landlady said Cat left six days ago for France with Darcy and her baby. I parked your Corvette in the garage. I think it was smart that I drove your car and left you mine. You might have been tracked down before you got here otherwise."

They stayed up the rest of the night and talked. Clay's plan was to get out of the country and go back to Nice. Marianna wanted to go with him. "No," he said. "If I'm caught you could be arrested for helping me. Besides, you only have about six weeks of school left to get your Masters."

"I don't care about any degree right now," she argued stubbornly.

"You say that now. But I may be on the run a long time. We both need time to think about this. I've signed over the title of the Vette to you. I want you to sell it and send the money to my dad. I'll contact you when I get situated."

"Okay," she said, looking disappointed. "But as soon as I get that diploma I'm coming to join you. You can count on it."

"No commitments?"

"Yes," she said, smiling sadly. "No commitments."

They slept for three hours. At nine o'clock Marianna drove to two different travel agencies and purchased two airline tickets under assumed names, one to New York, and the other from New York to Paris. By the time she returned to the apartment, Clay was ready to leave. They called a taxi and rode together to the airport. She snuggled up to him in the back seat. "Don't worry about me. I'm a big girl now. You're the one who's going to need help. My cousin, Jean Pierre, is stationed not too far from Nice. Go back to the Trocadero. I'll call him and tell him to contact you there. You can trust him. I know he will be willing to help you."

They had time for one long kiss in the back of the taxi, and then he was gone. He sweated out the layover at Kennedy, and again the next morning clearing customs at Orly. The customs officers barely glanced at his passport before stamping it. If they had scrutinized it more carefully, they would have determined that it did not match any names on the airline manifest. In a matter of minutes he was cleared and disappeared into the crowd, safe on the continent.

VII

EXILE

Clay boarded the Mistral in the late afternoon, the sixteen hour express train from Paris to Nice named after the strong cold winds that form over the English Channel between November and May and blow southeastward down across the south of France, bringing with them clouds and rain that invariably hang over the Cote for a week or more. He curled up in a second class compartment that he was sharing with a peasant family from Provence. There were six in the family; frail husband, sturdy wife and four squirmy children, aged eight to twelve. They had brought enough food with them for a week's journey, and they started eating before the train left the station. First out of the peasant woman's bag came four baguettes of bread; then ham, salami, cheese, onions, tomatoes, lettuce, wine. The woman grinned at Clay. She was missing a front tooth. She nodded and motioned for him to join them in their feast, but he declined. He was too exhausted to eat, and in less than hour he drifted off to sleep. He was roused occasionally by the sound of a munching apple, burps and snores, or a kid climbing over him to go to the bath room. But each time he was lulled back to sleep quickly by the jostling of the train as it lurched and roared southward through the night toward the Mediterranean and his chosen place of exile.

He woke up as the train slowed down coming into Marseille. It was grey and cold, and in the compartment he could see his breath. He shivered and looked out and saw factory smoke, and then the train started passing close by windows of houses until it reached the switch yard and weaved its way through many tracks to the station. The train stopped for half an hour at Marseille. People got on and off. The French family got off there. Clay got off, too, and went for a walk through the station and found a little cafe. It had red and white striped table cloths and was light and warm and comfortable. He had a cafe au lait and a croissant. They were hot and good and warmed him. He went back to the train and the compartment was empty, the family from Provence having left behind only their reeking odor of garlic for him to remember them by.

It was another four hours to Nice. Clay watched from the window as the train passed through the seaport of Toulon and into the Maures, a low mountain range covered with scrubby evergreen oak and olive trees and aleppo pine that stretched from St. Tropez to St. Raphael. The train passed swiftly by a yellow stone house with a garden and tables in the shade under three thick palm trees. Beyond the house he could see the sea. Then the train was cutting through red clay and limestone and across the Esterel, a cliff of red porphyry rock that plunged as if drenched in blood straight down to the shoreline and along the little blue coves that had been worn over time between the rocky promontories. He thought about his situation and how ironic it was. He had been broke when he left Nice eight months ago. Now he was coming back in almost the same condition. He had three hundred dollars; not much to start a new life. He had brought with him one small suitcase. It contained his shaving gear and underwear, two sweaters, three shirts, two pairs of jeans, a pair of slacks and a sport coat. That was all. He was going to have to find a job as soon as possible. He was still looking out the window and meditating as the train rolled out of the hills and into Nice's Gare Centrale. He walked the two blocks to his old familiar habitat, the Hotel Trocadero, splurged and forked over an extra dollar a day to take a room with a bath.

He was aroused the next morning at nine o'clock by a loud knock at the door. He opened it sleepily and stood facing a tall young Frenchman with a Gallic nose, short-cropped sandy brown hair, and pale grey eyes that were penetrating and alert. Jean Pierre Girard introduced himself and stepped into the room. "Marianna telephoned and asked me to come here," he said very formally. "She said you were in trouble and might need my help."

Jean Pierre's English was good, but they talked uneasily for half an hour before Clay gained enough confidence to open up to him.

"I was court martialed for protesting against the war in Vietnam. I chose to flee the country instead of serving my sentence."

"Marianna told me," Jean Pierre said with a touch of aloofness. "And you should know where I stand. I'm professional army. I would give almost anything to be in Vietnam leading my men in battle, so I cannot sympathize with any of your actions. Nevertheless, I will help because Marianna said she was in love with you and asked. That is enough for me." Jean Pierre sat down, and his stiffness flew out the window. "You will need a fake passport and driver's license," he said as effortlessly as if he were ordering lunch. "I will make the arrangements. They will cost a thousand francs."

"I don't have that much money."

"Then I will loan it to you."

"I can't let you do that."

"It's only a loan. I expect you to repay it as soon as you can." Jean Pierre smiled, and Clay suddenly warmed to him because of the non-humiliating way he had made the offer. "As for a place to stay," Jean Pierre said then, "Marianna told me that her friend, Darcy, has rented an apartment in Haut-de-Cagnes. I called her. She says there is a small flat available. She is expecting us for lunch."

"You know Darcy?"

"I met her once in Paris when she was studying art at the Sorbonne. Charming girl. Shall we go?"

They drove in Jean Pierre's kelly-green Porsche westward along the beach highway, and then upwards into the hills to Haut-de-Cagnes. Jean Pierre parked his Porsche in the lot at the base of the last peak and they started walking quickly, through the town entrance and up the street to the square. Clay spied Darcy sitting at a table outdoors under an oak tree at the Café St. Jacques. She was wearing a white turtleneck sweater and one of Vic's old leather flying jackets. Cat was with her. Darcy saw Clay as he crossed the square. Her eyes widened and her mouth opened, and then she rushed from the table and threw her arms around him with a desperate lunge and clung to him. "Darse, I'm sorry about Vic," he said as he held her tightly and rubbed her hair.

"I knew it was going to happen," she said as she stepped back, wiped away tears, and stared at him blankly. "We've only been here a week and I just heard about it two days ago. They're having a ceremony in Arlington for him next Sunday. I'm not going back for it, Clay. Do you think that's horrible?"

"No, of course not."

"I couldn't bear it," she continued in short little gasps. "There's really nothing to go back for, Clay...there's no body to be buried or anything. He's just gone...it's like he never was."

"I understand," he said as he watched her struggling to convince herself not to feel guilty. He understood because he was struggling too...*Why didn't he go with his squadron?*

Darcy turned to Jean Pierre, who had been standing by quietly. "Bon jour, Jean Pierre," she said, as she wiped away the last trace of a tear. "It's been a long time. I'm sorry you have to see me this way."

Jean Pierre leaned over, reached out and kissed her hand gallantly. "Please accept my deepest sympathies madam." They walked over and sat down with Cat under the oak tree.

"Where's your baby?"Clay asked.

"She's sleeping. She's with the landlady at our apartment. You'll see her later...So tell me," she said, shaking her head and looking puzzled. "What are you doing here anyway? I thought the navy was trying to court martial you on some crazy charge or something." He told them everything. Darcy and Cat thought he was joking at first, but when they realized he was serious, they were both astounded. They ordered nicoise salads and stayed at the café for three hours, and about every half hour Jean Pierre ordered another bottle of wine. They finished four. There was not much else to do off-season in Cagnes in the middle of the day, Cat explained. During their conversation they helped Clay choose a name as an alias: Clay Anderson, they all thought would be fitting.

Jean Pierre paid the check at the end of the meal, arose very dignified and addressed the three of them. "Your company has been delightful. If you can please come, I would like to invite all of you to a dinner party at my mother's villa in La Gaude tomorrow night. Eight o'clock. I think Clay knows the way."

After lunch Cat and Darcy took Clay back to their apartment, a two bedroom on the second floor. The flat for rent was a garret on the third floor, a one room studio with two chairs, a carved wooden table, a wrought iron single bed, tiny kitchenette, and a bath tub and bidet and lavatory in the corner. Across the hall under the eaves was a water closet containing a toilette. It suited his liking. He sought out the landlady. She was a slim, attractive fifty year old Provencal woman with a body that looked half her age, He paid her one month's rent in advance: two hundred twenty francs, or forty five dollars American. "It's been quite a week for me," she said kindly, graciously. "Two new tenants and a new job as a part time baby sitter." He had a new home.

At eight o'clock the next evening Clay drove the three of them on up in the hills to La Gaude in Darcy's rented Peugeot. Clay felt strange driving up the winding road he and Marianna had navigated so many times on their Vespa together. They rounded the last turn and stopped to take in the view. The snug, fortified little village was just as he remembered it, perched like an eagle's nest atop the highest peak around. It was cooler. The sky was less blue and the walls of the town were not as encrusted with the orange colored dust as they had been in August, but other than that, little had changed. It was still a three hundred year old Shangri-La unsullied by modern civilization.

The party was a sit-down dinner for eighteen people. The three of them and Jean Pierre were the only guests under forty. The rest were all wealthy French friends of Jean Pierre's mother - with one exception. The guest of honor was Howard Nussbaum, a short, rotund, and jocular balding American in his late forties, distinguished by a neatly trimmed, grayish goatee, diamond ring on his left pinky finger, navy blazer, shirt opened in a deep vee where a turquoise locket dangled from a golden chain around his neck. He was the founder and president of Utopia International, a well known money management and mutual fund organization headquartered thirty miles away in the tiny principality of Monaco. Jean Pierre's mother and Nussbaum were seated at the two ends of the long table. Cat was seated to Nussbaum's left, and she started flirting with him right away. Darcy was placed between Jean Pierre and Clay, along the opposite side of the table. The meal was authentic provencal and lasted three hours, starting off with a lentil soup; then prosciutto and melon; bouillabaisse, a stew consisting of clams, sole, shrimp and lobster flavored with onions, garlic, wine, olive oil, tomato sauce, and served with a sprinkling of flour, basil and parsley. The salad came afterwards, and for dessert there were peach tarts and custards and cheeses. As they finished dessert, Darcy asked Jean Pierre innocently, "Where is your wife tonight?"

"In Paris," he said. "She's grown tired of being an army officer's wife. We're in the process of getting a divorce. In France, that takes a long time."

"Oh...I'm sorry. I didn't know," Darcy stammered. She smiled and looked at Jean Pierre in a new and different way.

The meal was a strain for Clay. His two years of French at Annapolis enabled him to grasp the subjects of the dinner table conversation but not their details or subtleties. As a result, he was relieved when the dinner ended and Nussbaum, an unlighted cigar in one hand, a flute of champagne in the other, glib as a gigolo, stood and made a toast. "To our gracious hostess, Madame Girard, I would like to thank you for giving me the privilege of meeting all your charming friends here tonight. And before the night is over I hope I have convinced at least some of them that Utopia International is the most advantageous place to invest their assets." Jean Pierre's mother thanked him for his kind remarks and announced that café and liqueurs were now going to be served in the courtyard.

Outside, Jean Pierre asked Clay to bring a cognac and come walk with him over by the trees. Once alone, Jean Pierre told him of the arrangements he has made for a license and a passport. "On Monday at ten o'clock go to the old port in Nice where the ferry from Corsica lands," Jean Pierre said. "Ask for a young boat handler named Antonio. You can recognize him because he walks with a limp. He will be expecting you. You must also bring two photographs. I paid him two hundred francs in advance. Here is another eight hundred to give him on delivery."

Jean Pierre slipped four bills into his hand and hurried to join Darcy, who was sipping her champagne alone. Nussbaum walked up with Cat hanging on his arm. "Hi!" he bubbled as he grabbed Clay's hand and started pumping it. "If I recall, you're Clay Anderson, the American, aren't you? I'm Howie Nussbaum, from the Bronx."

Clay was flattered that the famous businessman had remembered his name. "I know. I've heard a lot about you tonight, Mr. Nussbaum," he said in as sophisticated a manner as he knew how.

"Oh, they're lies, all lies," Howie winked slyly. He still had not let go of Clay's hand. "And call me Howie. Cat, here, was telling me that you just moved into her apartment house in Haut-de-Cagnes. I'm intrigued. How did a guy like you end up in the South of France?"

"I used to be a navy pilot. I was over here on cruise and fell in love with the place. That's all."

Howie slapped him on the back. "You know that's how I ended up here. I was in the navy, on a carrier home ported in Villefranche, and I fell in love with it here too. When my enlistment was up, I just stayed. Started selling mutual funds, mostly to sailors around the Med. Mutual funds were a brand were new item in Europe then. Before I knew it, I had my own company and began recruiting agents to sell to the soldiers in Germany. That's when sales really took off – and the rest is history." Howie let go of his hand, finally. "I always admired you carrier pilots. Here, take one of my cards. If you're ever interested in becoming a mutual fund salesman, let me know." Howie draped his arm around Cat's shoulders, squeezed her boobs, and said, "come on kitten. Let's go mix with the customers."

Cat did not come back to the apartment that weekend. Clay motor biked into Nice on Monday to the port in the old section of the city where the daily steamer from Corsica tied up. He found the boat handler waiting for him on the pier and gave him the photographs. Antonio told him to come back at noon and then limped up the gangplank aboard the ferry. Clay walked around the port and stopped at a bar and sipped a pernod for an hour. At noon he went back to the ferry, met Antonio, and picked up his passport and driver's license. The documents looked authentic, and he paid Antonio the eight hundred francs. That task completed, his next concern was to get a job and repay Jean Pierre.

Darcy and Clay were having lunch at the Café St. Jacques the next day when Cat joined them with two eclectic looking young men, early thirties, each wearing an earring and dressed identically in ankle boots, jeans, thin black turtlenecks and denim jackets. "We've missed you the last couple of days," Darcy said to Cat, more a question than a statement.

"I've been at Howie's in Monaco. It was *absolutely unreal!* His place is a castle. It looks right out over the harbor and has its own yacht basin - and a helicopter pad! And he has a three bedroom guesthouse. That's where I slept and met these two guys. They live right here in Haut-de-Cagnes, but have a little band and were playing at Howie's party on Sunday. They say his Sunday parties are an every other weekend event, all day from early afternoon to late, late night. A real blast!" She paused for a breath and introduced her companions: Malcolm O'Reilly Watson, who everyone called Riley: Scottish father, Irish mother, tall and lanky, unruly dark hair, mottled skin, ears that stuck out like daisy cups, a caterpillar for a mustache. His partner's name was Chauncey

Elliot: medium height, moppish blond hair, dimples and fair skin, love handles that made him look like a pear. They were both from London's East End and had been playing guitars in bands together for a decade; Riley lead, Chauncey bass. They lived together, and like so many of the artists in Cagnes, they were easily and understandably gay. "Riley and Chauncey have a trio that plays at a club in Cannes called the *She-She*," Cat continued excitedly. "Howie owns it. He offered me a job there as hostess, starting tomorrow night. I mentioned you, Clay. He said that with the film festival and the high season coming up, the *She-She* is going to need another bartender. He told me to take you along to meet the manager if you were interested."

Cat and Clay accompanied Riley and Chauncey to the *She-She Club* on Wednesday night, arriving early, ten o'clock, and the club was empty. They met the manager, who explained to Cat what a hostess was supposed to do. It was evident to him very quickly that she had the talent and knew what to do instinctively. Clay was tried out assisting at the bar. Fortunately, one thing he had learned in the navy was how to make drinks, and at the end of the night he was hired for two hundred francs a week, plus tips.

Life became centered around the *She-She* and Haut-de-Cagnes after that. Cat and Clay worked at the club six nights a week. Riley and Chauncey performed four. They were part of a trio, along with a pickup French drummer who lived in Juan-les-Pins, and even though they could play guitars like they slept with them every night, Riley was only a so-so singer and a bigger name band commanded the stage on Fridays and Saturdays. The four of them drove back and forth to the club together most nights, thirty minutes each way, and it was close to five in the morning before they were able to flop into their beds. Clay slept until noon, usually, and then met Cat and Darcy and their two guitar playing friends at the Café St. Jacques for a long lazy mid-afternoon lunch; lots of wine, Cat and Riley toking some very fine grass. Except on Sundays. On Sundays Jean Pierre drove over from his base in Toulon and the four of them, minus Riley and Chauncey, drove further up in the mountains until they found a place with a view. They spread a blanket and picnicked, whiling away hours; Darcy painting, often using Cat as a model; Clay and Jean Pierre dozing in the sun, talking or reading. Jean Pierre's aloofness dissipated gradually, and he and Clay began to develop a healthy respect for each other.

Weeks passed. A mistral came and went. The sea and the beach began to warm and the first flock of vacationers started to appear. The Cannes Film Festival commenced in mid-May and the *She-She* became a wild and decadent place. It was not the most prestigious club in Cannes, but among a certain group it was considered one of the in places to go, and for the next ten days it was filled by a crowd numbering more than two hundred every night until closing time. It was a posh club, the dancing area encircled by a white stucco wall adorned with large oil paintings of tasteful nudes that hung over built-in, deep oval-shaped leather booths. The dance floor was marble. Mahogany boxes containing complimentary cigarettes were placed on each table. The *She-She* was expensive. Drinks were fifty francs each, with a two drink minimum. Clay soon discovered that with tips he could earn more than double his salary and be entertained as well by the late night jet setters who came to party and to be seen. Young women in backless dresses, low slung slacks, and see-through tops were there to show off their bodies to young men on the prowl in flashy blazers and open-collared shirts unbuttoned down to their waists. There were older jet setters, too, in from their yachts and villas, all tanned, some sleek and well preserved, but others amusing as they tried too hard to have fun, their flabby, perspiring bodies wasting away as they drank too much and the night got late, and the lights flashed on at four o'clock, stripping away their facades.

Just before the start of the film festival Jean Pierre brought Clay a letter he had received from Marianna, and in it she described what had happened after his escape. Robert had written a short article about it that appeared on the front page of the *Times*. Larry Smith had run some film on national news. The FBI had traced the sale of his Corvette to her, had come to her apartment in New York and questioned her. Taking no chance on a wiretap, Clay and Jean Pierre drove into Nice and Jean Pierre called her from a phone booth. He gave her the number and told her to go to a telephone booth to return the call. She phoned ten minutes later, and she and Clay talked. He told her about his tiny apartment in Cagnes, the new name he had assumed, his job at the *She-She*. She vowed to come and join him as soon as she graduated. A month had passed since then, and he had heard nothing from her.

Clay and Cat had off the last Sunday in May, and they went into Nice for dinner with Jean Pierre and Darcy. It was not late when they got back to Cagnes. Cat had been sniffing cocaine in the car and was even higher than usual. She insisted that they all come up to the apartment for coffee and a game of bridge. In the living room, they tossed some pillows on the floor around an old battered coffee table. Cat placed a card deck on the table, lit up her hash pipe, and passed it around. "I have an idea, she said. "Let's play strip bridge."

"Don't be ridiculous, Cat," Darcy said testily.

"Oh, come on Darse," Cat coaxed, "it's only a game."

Darcy inhaled on the pipe and shrugged. "Okay. Why not? How do you play?"

Cat explained the rules. A couple falling five hundred points behind had to strip to their underwear; at one thousand points, all the way. Darcy was paired with Jean Pierre and they were trounced in the first two games, down seven hundred points. They took off their jeans and sweaters. Jean Pierre smiled at Darcy, as if to say, 'sorry'. She tried to act nonchalant, but her face was growing red. She played the next hand without raising her eyes. Clay bid and made a slam, and now Darcy and Jean Pierre had to strip and play the next hand naked. They were all getting high now, and Cat was quick to tease. "Ooh-la. Would you look at that," she laughed, pointing at Jean Pierre's crotch where he was becoming stiff and flushed. Darcy kept her knees closed, but her nipples were budding like it was springtime. "Coffee should be ready by now. Let's take a break," Cat said as she stood up and strutted into the kitchen, wiggling her ass. She returned in a couple of minutes carrying a tray holding a coffee pot, cups, and an open bottle of white wine, having left her jeans and underpants behind in the kitchen. She bent over proudly and placed the tray on the table for all to imbibe, wearing nothing but a short, white see-through blouse. She sat down on a pillow next to Darcy and started fondling her breasts. "Let's have some fun," she said, half closing her eyes and puckering her lips.

"No thanks," Darcy said disgustedly, and she started moving away.

Cat motioned to Jean Pierre. "Come over here. I think my step-sister's horny as hell and needs some good loving." Jean Pierre slid over, put his arms around Darcy and gave her a gentle kiss. She surprised him by kissing him back aggressively. As he pulled her down across his lap to give her a long, deep kiss, Cat knelt down on the rug and wedged her face between Darcy's thighs. Darcy closed her eyes, tilted her head back, and started squirming. She spread her legs and Jean Pierre took over. She locked her legs around him.

"Now it's my turn," Cat said drunkenly, still on the rug on her knees, waggling her tongue. She motioned for Clay to come lie down. He felt more than just a small throb in his jeans from watching the action. He pulled the jeans off, slid under her and she went down on him, climbed on and fucked him until they both came in one giant, sweaty, spasmodic orgasm. Cat rolled off and fell asleep in seconds, breathing heavily beside him. He stumbled to his feet, walked into the kitchen and looked across the hallway into Darcy's bedroom. She and Jean Pierre were lying on the bedcovers, and he was stroking her head gently. Clay lurched up the stairway to his garret and collapsed and slept until noon the next day.

Clay was tending bar at the *She-She* on the eighth of June, and it was jammed with tourists when he was called to the telephone. It was three o'clock in the morning. "Let's talk fast!" Marianna said excitedly on the other end of the line. "I'm at the station in Lyon, and my train is pulling out soon."

"Marianna! I can't believe it. You're in France!" Clay said, full of surprise. "What about graduation?"

"That was three days ago. Listen. My train is due in Nice at eleven in the morning.. Can you meet me?"

"Get off in Antibes, the last stop before Nice. I'll be there. How are you?"

"Fine. Fine," she said hurriedly. "I have to go now. The train is leaving. I love you."

Clay was waiting on the platform for her at ten-thirty the next morning when Le Mistral chugged into the tiny station in Antibes. Marianna saw him through the window from the train. The sun was out and the day was bright. Clay was beaming. She opened her bag and made a few passes at her face with powder. She looked in a little mirror, freshened her lips with lipstick, and straightened her hat. It was a white, wide-brimmed felt hat she had bought in Paris just for the occasion. She stepped off the train carrying two small suitcases, walked briskly toward him, and shook his hand very businesslike. "You look good," she said. "All tan and healthy looking." She was pasty white by comparison.

She looked different, he thought. More serene and mature; much less spontaneous than the young girl so filled with the effervescence of a few months ago. "I feel good," he said. "The simple life here agrees with me. I hope you'll like it."

"I hope so too," she said, looking serious. "I've come prepared to live simply. This is all I have, and I spent all my money to get here. I've come to stay, though, if that's all right with you?"

His eyes crinkled and he laughed. "No commitments?"

Marianna pulled the wide-brimmed hat down over one eye and smiled out from under it. "No commitments!" she said as she leaned up and kissed him.

They went on a picnic the next weekend. Jean Pierre and Darcy and Cat and Riley came too. They packed a lunch and six bottles of wine in some rucksacks and started hiking up the road out of Cagnes. It was hot, hiking. The road was dusty and passing cars stirred it up. The sun was straight overhead, and the pine trees along the road cut off the breeze. The road came out of trees after awhile and way off they saw a steep bluff and a little waterfall and below it a stream in a clump of trees. They found a path and went across a meadow. The path crossed the stream and wound its way back around to the waterfall. Jean Pierre sat down and opened up his bag and took out a blanket and three bottles of wine. They had lunch and drank the wine and Clay lay down for a nap. Cat lay down beside him, sipping wine and smoking some weed, which was becoming a common habit with her. Darcy went off to the top of the hill with her drawing pad, and Jean Pierre trailed after her. They had been inseparable ever since the night of the bridge game. Riley had brought his guitar, and he started picking out some tunes and trying new words with them. Marianna listened to him for awhile, and then made some suggestions. In a half hour they were working seriously together. She made up lyrics and hummed them to a tune. Riley would pick it out on his guitar, she would make corrections, sing it, and then write it down. In the course of the afternoon she created five new songs, and Riley asked her if she would join his band. "We need a good singer. I'm the only one who can sing, and I'm not very good," Riley told her modestly.

Marianna and the band practiced for the next ten days at the *She-She* in the afternoons when it was empty. At the club she had access to an electric piano for her first time ever, a Fender Rhodes Suitcase 73 with a fifty watt power amp and four built-in speakers. She experimented with all its new tonal possibilities that allowed her to compose many new arrangements and dominate the rehearsals. She could sing in both French and English and the band members recognized her vocal and music superiority at once. They decided to rename the group and call it "Kira and the Band", and from that time on, Marianna's voice and her keyboard became the featured lead of the band. Riley thought her name was Kira, the name she had been using in Cagnes. She and Clay had decided the first day she arrived that an alias would be wise. Even though she already had legitimate American and Swiss passports in her real name, arrangements were made for another visit to the Corsican and the purchase of a fake French passport for her under the name of Kira Chastain. The band opened on a Tuesday at the *She-She* and was a huge success. By the first week in July it was drawing over-capacity crowds on week nights, and by the first of August *Kira and the Band* had taken over the weekends, with standing lines waiting to get into the club.

It was too good to last. Clay came back to the apartment after a trip into Nice one afternoon and found Marianna drunk and passed out on the bed. The room was a mess. Broken dishes and sheets and pillow cases were scattered about and the smell of vomit was putrefying the air. Darcy and Jean Pierre were there, looking tired and haggard. "What in the hell happened?" Clay asked.

"Cat told her about the bridge party," Jean Pierre said grimly.

"The bitch! What did she do that for?" Clay exploded.

"Marianna was trying to give her some advice and tell her she shouldn't hang around Cagnes all day drinking and smoking dope so much. Cat was stoned. She blew up and told her about how she had made it with you."

"God!"

"She took it badly, Clay," Darcy said hollowly. "I tried to talk to her, but she locked herself in the water closet and drank a whole bottle of whiskey. She's been throwing up for hours."

Clay spent the rest of the afternoon cleaning up the apartment, and when he left for the *She-She*, Marianna was still unconscious. She did not wake up until late the next morning. He made her some soup and she sipped it. She looked horrible. "Fella', it didn't mean a thing. Believe me. There was nothing to it," Clay started saying.

Marianna shook her head from side to side. "I'm over it," she said wanly. "We always said...no commitments. I can't blame you for doing it with someone else."

"It was nothing like it is with us, Marianna. We were all stoned. It just happened. It doesn't change the way I feel about you."

"I hated you, you know. My first reaction was to screw Jean Pierre to get back at you. Did he tell you that?"

"No." .

"You should thank him. He talked me out of it."

"I think you're taking it too hard."

"Maybe so. But things will never be the same between us again. You know that, don't you?"

"They're still the same with me."

She stared straight ahead. "Well, we'll see," she said softly. "I understand how Cindy Sue felt now. I may never be able to forgive you either, Clay."

The bridge party was not mentioned again. With August had come the annual onslaught of vacationers on their holiday. The days were balmy. The nights started to cool. There was a festival somewhere on the Cote every weekend. In early September, as the crowds were leaving, Jean Pierre chartered a yacht out of Antibes, a sixty-footer complete with a three man crew, and invited Clay and Marianna to join him and Darcy on a three day cruise. He was very mysterious about it. He invited Cat and Riley to come too. They left on Sunday morning and headed down the coast to St. Tropez. They anchored off Tahiti Plage at two o'clock and swam and sunbathed until dusk, and then motored around the point to the port and tied up at the seawall right across the street from the bars until Tuesday. They had cocktails out on deck and watched the evening crowd milling about the port. At ten o'clock they went ashore and walked to a restaurant perched on a rock at the entrance to the port and feasted on a fresh, poached salmon that Jean Pierre had pre-arranged and special ordered. Afterwards, they wandered the narrow streets of the tiny little town window shopping before returning to the yacht where they drank scotch and perrier and talked and laughed until four in the morning.

Jean Pierre rented a car the next day and drove them out to the beach, Plage de Pampelonne, a five mile stretch of white sand reachable only by driving down a dirt road through pine forests and vineyards. Clay and Marianna fell in love with the spot at once. A strong breeze was blowing, but the sea was a clear, beautiful blue. The air was salty and dry. It was not too hot, and the beach was not crowded. They spent the day at a little private plage that had mattresses and umbrellas, and like everyone else, they didn't wear a thing. It was calm and peaceful.

They had dinner in the cabin on the boat that night. The crew served them a bouillabaisse, and after dinner they had champagne and cognac. Afterwards Jean Pierre announced that he had something to say. "You may have wondered what this little excursion is all about," he said, as if he had something very secretive to tell them. "Very simply, I wanted all my non-French friends to see what St. Tropez is like in September."

"It's heaven," Marianna chimed in, and they all nodded.

"That wasn't the only reason I brought you here, though," Jean Pierre said smiling. "I have several announcements." He paused, and the five of them all waited. "First, my divorce was final last week." Everyone clapped and cheered. "No applause please," he continued. "It cost me one million francs. Second, I've just received orders transferring me to Berlin. I have to be there next week. That's why I wanted to spend these last few days with my dearest friends." Clay and Riley groaned, and Cat started to say something, but Jean Pierre held up his hand and stopped her. "And last but least," he said, "Darcy has something to say."

Darcy stood up and burst out laughing. "Jean Pierre, the crazy fool, has asked me to marry him! Even crazier, I've accepted! We're going to be married on the boat going back to Antibes tomorrow, and I'm leaving with him this weekend."

There was a rush of congratulations and then Marianna, half drunk, rose up and proposed a toast. "To Darcy and Jean Pierre, who have carved a niche in all our lives. And now that you rats are running out on us, we hope you will remember our friendship and how sweet and warm life was in Cagnes when you're freezing your asses off up in Berlin in the wintertime! We all shall anxiously await your return."

Jean Pierre and Darcy were married the next day and left on Thursday. That same night Marianna was sitting at the bar at the *She-She* talking to Clay during one of her breaks when Cat came up and handed her a small box with a note. Marianna glanced at the note. "Your singing enchants me. Could you join us for a drink?" the note said. The box contained a bracelet of opals and pearls.

Marianna handed the bracelet to Cat. "Please return it," she said crisply.

"Oh, I don't think you should. It's from Howie Nussbaum," Cat said. "Clay and I met him last spring at a party. He's very important."

Marianna looked at the short, bearded, balding man sitting at a long table next to the stage. "He looks like an old lech to me," she said disgustedly.

"He is. But why don't you talk to him just for fun. Tell him you're a friend of mine," Cat implored.

Marianna looked at Clay. He shrugged. She went over to the table for the five minutes remaining in her break, and then sang another forty minutes before she came back to the bar. "I gave him back his bracelet, but he's having a party in Monaco Sunday, and he wants the band to play. He would pay us well," she said. "You're both invited too. Want to go?"

Cat was ecstatic. "I've been to one of his parties. It'll be a blast!"

Marianna looked at Clay. "Sure, why not?" he grumbled. "We can see how the other half lives for a change."

They drove over to Monaco on Sunday afternoon, and when they saw Howie's compound, they were taken aback. It was like a castle as Cat had described, a large complex of white stucco buildings with orange tile roofs sprawled on rocks on the edge of a cliff overlooking a cove across a spit of land that separated the cove from the main harbor in Monaco. In addition to the main chateau built around a giant patio and kidney shaped pool, there was a wing of apartments used to house guests - Cat said Howie had told her he kept girls there all the time for entertaining; a small marina was at the foot of the cliff, and a helicopter pad was next to it. Three cabin cruisers were tied up at the dock and thirty people were already at poolside drinking bloody marys when the three of them were ushered onto the patio and introduced around. The women, all young and wearing string bikinis, outnumbered the men two to one. The men were older. In a matter of minutes Clay and Marianna were introduced to a Beirut banker, a Saudi prince, an Italian count, a finance minister from South America, and a movie producer showing off one of his young starlets. The starlet was only wearing bikini bottoms. She had a big chest and laughed a lot, and a photographer was busy following her around taking pictures.

They had not seen Nussbaum yet and were still being introduced when he barged up between Cat and Marianna, draped his hairy, suntan-oiled arms around them, and kissed each of them on the cheek. "The chanteuse and kitten! How're you doing kids?" Nussbaum jested in his usual ebullient manner.

Marianna slipped out from under his arm and turned toward Clay, and said very formally, "Mr. Nussbaum, I'd like you to meet my fiancé, Clay Anderson. I think the two of you two met once in La Gaude."

Nussbaum, who had not even noticed him until then, slapped Clay on the back and chortled loudly, "why sure! Clay Anderson, the American pilot! How've you been kid?"

"Just fine, Howie. How about you?"

"Great, kid! Just great. The market's up. So are sales. I see you've been doing all right too." Howie winked and nodded toward Marianna. They talked just a few moments before Howie noticed the arrival of more guests. He gave Cat a familiar pat on the behind, directed them inside to a place to change into swimsuits, and dashed off.

Marianna and Clay lounged around the pool until Riley and the band arrived. Marianna left to go change, and at six o'clock she and the band started to play. Howie walked up and stood next to Clay watching for a few minutes, then surprised him by asking him to come up to his office. They went inside and upstairs to a suite of offices, one to the left for two secretaries and phones and files; the middle one being Howie's inner sanctum, furnished with a thirty foot Persian rug, two Roche Bobois leather sofas, a thick glass coffee table, an immovable altar of a mahogany desk in front of a floor to ceiling window of stained glass separating built-in book shelves on one side from a wet bar on the other. A wall safe was built into the corner. Off to the right was a private conference room having a burnished cherry wood rectangular table seating eight. A door led from it to an outside balcony and steps down to a garden behind the chateau. Howie motioned for Clay to sit down on one of the sofas and offered to pour him a drink. He accepted a cognac. Howie offered him a cigar, and he declined. Howie lit one up and said, "I spoke with Kira and Riley a little while ago. You know I own the She-She Club so I know how great she's been doing there. I've offered her and her band a contract for the next year, but Kira's not too keen on it. She said I should ask you about it first. That's the main reason we're talking."

"Any other reason?"

"Could be. You know, I've liked you ever since I met you, Clay. I don't think bartending is in your future. I'd like to offer you a job with Utopia."

"I appreciate that, Howie," Clay said quickly and humbly, "but I don't think I'd be very good hustling mutual funds. I'm probably a much better bartender"

"I'm not talking about selling mutual funds. I want to hire you as a pilot. We just bought a new Lear Jet and I need two more pilots. I could pay you twelve thousand dollars a year to start."

"Are you serious? That's more than I was making in the navy."

"Aw, it's not that much. We'll have a fleet of four jets, and a helicopter. You'd be the tenth pilot. I think you'd like it."

"Just tell me when to start!"

"How about tomorrow?"

"Tomorrow sounds great!"

"Good. Then it's settled. You just go to Cote d'Azur tomorrow and find our chief pilot and have him start checking you out. I'll call him tonight."

"I can't believe this, Howie! I don't know how to thank you."

"It's my pleasure, kid. Before we go, though, I do want to talk to you about the proposition I had in mind for Kira and see what you think about it."

"Sure. What is it?"

"I own another club much larger than the *She-She*. It's in London. Things get a little slow at the *She-She* in the winter. It would be great if I could book Kira at my London club for a couple of months this winter. I'd have her back down here for the film festival and the summer season.

"What does Kira think?"

"She didn't want to discuss it just then. But I intend to talk to her later, and I'd like to be able to tell her I have your support. I know Riley wants to do it. The contract I would offer would make it well worth their while. When they're in London, I'd even pay a studio for them to record an album."

"I'd think she'd jump at it. I assure you I won't stand in her way. I just hope your flying job offer has nothing to do with it."

"Absolutely not," Howie assured him, and then he stood up to indicate that the conversation was finished. They went back to the pool.

Marianna was singing her last song. She finished and Howie went over to meet with her. They sat at a table alone and talked for a long time. Clay was at another table with Cat, and they had several drinks. After awhile, Marianna came over and joined them. "I guess Howie told you he offered me a job flying?" Clay said. "He told me he made you an offer too."

"Are you going to take it?" she asked hastily.

"Yeah. How about you?"

"No."

"No kidding. How come?"

"Because I'm going to be otherwise occupied this winter...like maybe having a baby." She smiled impishly and Clay sat back and looked at her and at the way she was looking at him. She had that nervous squirrel look she got whenever she was happy. "Don't worry," she said. "I don't expect you to marry me. I just thought I should tell you this time so I don't get slapped around again."

PART TWO

Whom the gods love die young no matter how long they live.

---E. Hubbard

VIII

෨

SIROCCO

The summer of 1970 was a harsh, dry summer on the Cote d'Azur. A burning sirocco - that peculiar quirk of nature created when strange wind currents lift waves of brutally hot gritty air out of the Sahara and carry them gently across the Mediterranean to blast the south coast of France with a dust-hazed, suffocating heat - had lasted for two weeks. Siroccos were not uncommon to the Cote. A severe one occurred every three or four years. But this particular sirocco was the longest, driest, hottest, and most severe in more than two decades. It drove the mosquitoes from the coast and up into the mountains and dried up the Var River to a trickle. The lush fields of lavender and carnations wilted, the cork oak leaves parched and turned brown, and the needles on the evergreen pines scorched and fell to the ground in huge brittle piles that ignited in the sun causing forest fires to erupt with such alarming frequency that they started filling the valleys with gray billowing smoke. Unable to rise and penetrate the hot hazy layer of air, the smoke clouds grew thicker as the days passed, blanketing the hillsides and giving the entire countryside the appearance that it had been blitzed by an aircraft attack from a thousand B-17 bombers.

On top of the highest peak overlooking the valley, the atmosphere was oppressive. The air was heavy, dry and still, and the walls and rooftops of the houses in the village were caked with an orangish dust so thick that it could be scooped up in handfuls. A raging fire on the mountainside had blocked the road leading down to the coast. The inhabitants of the village had been marooned on the mountain for three days.

On the patio of the most resplendent villa in the village a young couple was picking over the remains of their lunch. There were two empty bottles of wine on the table. They were drinking from a third, and they were having an argument. The young man sat hunched over the table, somber and subdued. Having just turned thirty, his tanned and weathered face was already starting to show the early signs of age. His face was still lean and taut, but he had not shaved in three days and his beard had a blondish salt and peppery look. Flecks of gray tipped the ends of his hair, especially behind his ears, and deep creases in his forehead spoiled the smoothness of his tan. It was his eyes that belied his age mostly, though. When they met hers they peered straight through her, dull-like, oozing with a tired and lifeless indifference.

She looked at him, her hand on the table, her glass raised, eyes smoldering. Still lithe and delicately beautiful, she, too, bore the marks of time. Tiny wrinkles around her eyes were starting to betray her. Underneath her fresh sunburn her complexion betrayed a sallow pallor, a result of too many late nights in smoky nightclubs and too many days pent up in lonely hotel rooms in faraway dreary cities. Standing upright, hands on her hips, Marianna Haizet screamed at him. "What the *hell* do you have to leave in the morning for?"

"What the *hell* do you care?" Clay Stoner snapped back at her.

"Because I've been gone for months! We haven't even had time to talk since I've been back!"

Without looking up, Clay poured a glass of wine and drank it down. "I told you," he said, "I have to fly Howie to Amsterdam tomorrow. Then to London. After that, who knows? We should be back in three or four days."

"Why don't you tell him to get someone else?"

"Because I'm Howie's chief pilot. And he pays me good money for flying him around. That's why."

"He owns you, you know that?"

"You're a fine one to talk. You don't think he owns you? That little party in London..."

"You'll never forgive me for that, will you?"

"I don't think so."

"I got over you and Cat."

"That was different. We didn't have children then."

She slammed her glass down on the table, spilling what was left of the wine. "I'm not putting up with this bullshit anymore!" she shouted at him, and she whirled and stalked across the patio to the edge that hung out over the cliff, rested her hands on the wall for a moment and calmed herself, and then came back to the table. "I explained it all to you before. Nothing happened in London," she said, trying to make him look at her. "I don't care if you believe me anymore, but...but I'm warning you, if you don't forget about it and stop making me miserable, I'm leaving you, and I'm not coming back."

"So leave," he said coldly. "We're not married. You know as well as I do the only reason we're still together is because of the twins."

"And if I leave, they're coming with me Clay. That's something you'd better not forget."

"Then do it, Marianna! I can forget you in a snap. All of you. Just like *that!*" he said with a click of his fingers. He stood up and left her sitting there and walked into the house. He returned in a short while with a full bottle of liquor, opened it, and poured it into a glass of ice and added a tumbler of water. The liquid turned a milky, yellowish color. She watched him drain half the glass in one long gulp. "Here, try it," he said. "It's Pernod. It's very good. It tastes like licorice."

"That's all it is with you, isn't it? Some new drinks. Some more *haps*. You're a drunk. Clay."

"So? You're a lousy fucking mother."

She started to slap him and he grabbed her wrist. She could not believe what he had said. Four years ago she would have hated him and attacked him and hit him. She knew him better now, and she calmed. She reached over and touched his hand. "You don't mean that," she said gently. "I...I know I've been away too much with the band, and that we've had our differences. But that doesn't mean we have to destroy everything. Doesn't it say something for us the way our relationship has persevered? There were good times. We've got Cassie and Cody, our little twin bears, and they're happy and healthy. Our life together hasn't been that bad." He just sat there, bleary-eyed, until she shook him. "*Goddamnit!* Will you look at me?"

"Maybe not bad," he said finally, "but is that good enough?"

"I...I know what you mean," she said haltingly. "Maybe it's not as intense with us as it used to be. But you can't expect a relationship to stay that way forever."

"I did. You used to," he said accusingly.

She stared deep into his eyes. There was something odd in them that troubled her - something tired and old and wise and sad. She reached over and touched his hand. "What's wrong, Clay?"

He sat there a moment, a little high and unable to look away. Then he answered her. "I'm not happy, Marianna."

She stood up, walked around the table, and placed her hand on his shoulder. "You shouldn't feel that way fella'," she said fondly. "Look around. We don't have it so bad here. Jean Pierre lets us rent this place for practically nothing. Every morning we can get up and breathe the air and look out and have the whole Riviera at our feet. And we finally have enough money to be able to enjoy it. Be realistic. I can think of a lot of men who'd be happy to trade places with you."

"Maybe so. But I'm tired of it all, Marianna. I admit it was exciting at first, being in this beautiful spot and flying to all kinds of different places, going to the parties and meeting interesting people. But I'm bored with that now. I guess as I get older I sense life starting to pass me by. You've become a big success. Me...I feel like I've sold out. I'm nothing but Howie's flunky."

"Everyone sells out some of the time. That's part of growing up," she said, and she laughed for an instant, trying to humor him, until she saw the look in his eyes. She saw them narrow and saw that she had said the wrong thing, and her mind started flooding with the desperate sense of a crumbling affair.

"You think I'm soused, don't you?" he said, looking at her drunkenly,

"I don't think you're very sober."

"Maybe I'm sober enough to know I'm wasting my life, Marianna. You don't know what I have to put up with flying for Howie."

"That's not fair, Clay. I know Howie can be disgusting at times, but he's been very kind to us. He's done a hell of a job promoting the band - getting us tours and record contracts. He promoted you to chief pilot before you were thirty. What do you think you can expect from him?"

"Howie's a scumbag, Marianna. And Utopia's a corrupt, slimy organization. If you only knew half the things I see flying him around. Things I'm not supposed to talk about. I need to get out before it's too late. I want to go home – and soon."

She stared at him in disbelief. "You're talking *crazy*, Clay. You'd end up in prison."

"They'd have to catch me first."

She started pacing frantically around the table and waving her arms. "You know, I'm beginning to think you're really dumb, fella'! You'd be a fool to throw away what we have here to take that kind of chance."

He looked up at her, his eyes a dim blur. "I know the worst could happen. But I want to go home, to Creekwood, and take Cassie and Cody with me. I want to walk down Main Street and show them off and shake everyone's hand, and go rabbit hunting with my dad, and skinny dipping again at the lake with my mom. She doesn't even know she's a grandmother, Marianna. I want her to have a chance to see her grandchildren...I just found out she has cancer."

"Oh, my God!" Marianna's abrasiveness wilted. She stopped her frantic pacing and walked over to him. "Why didn't you tell me?"

"I didn't know it myself until ten days ago," he said a little dazedly. "I've been meaning to tell you. I called my dad the last time I was in London, and he started crying on the phone? It was strange...I'd never heard him cry in all my life."

"Did he give you any idea - how bad?

"Maybe a year."

She leaned over and placed her arms around his neck, her enormous dark eyes gushing at him with a sad, devoted look. "Clay," I'm sorry," she said. "I didn't know. In fact, I think I'm beginning to understand a lot of things I didn't know before. Like why you've been so edgy since I've been back. Why you drink so much. Maybe even why you haven't been interested in sex. I understand how important it is for you to go see your mother. It's just that I'm so afraid you'd be arrested."

"I think my passport would get me back into the States safely," he said, raising a fist to muffle a hiccup,

"But then what?" she said quickly. "You're still a wanted fugitive. You'd have to hide out in the States for the rest of your life. That's no future. Surely you realize that?"

"Oh, I'm not so sure," he said, eyeing her defiantly. "Things are a lot different now than they were when I was court martialed, Marianna. Most of the country was in favor of the war then. They thought we would just go over there and win it in no time. Now they know they were suckered. Fifty thousand kids have fled to Canada to duck the draft. College campuses are erupting. Half the members of Congress are saying worse things about the war now than I ever did. Tet and Kent State, they changed a lot of things.

People aren't stupid. They were fooled for awhile, but they know now what a lie it's all been. Johnson was suckered. The generals lie about the body count. It's a total farce, and now, Nixon is just winding it down so he can get out gracefully and announce that we won. That way everybody's happy. Everyone who wanted us to win is happy, and everyone who wanted us to get out is happy. It's no skin off Nixon's ass if a few hundred thousand more people get killed in the process. He won't be accused of losing the war until after he's re-elected."

"Do you really believe that?" she said, becoming strangely quiet now. "No one could be that vile."

"*Do I believe it!*" he roared drunkenly. "You goddamn better believe I believe it! After we pull out Vietnam is going to collapse, and then everyone else will believe it too. That's when they'll know for sure just how much they were suckered."

"And so what if you're right?" Marianna asked him. "What good does that do you?"

"I don't know for sure. I've thought about it. I think there will be amnesty for the draft dodgers someday."

"You're not a draft dodger, though. You've already been convicted."

"If I turned myself in and appealed, I think I'd be acquitted. I can't believe anyone would want to send me to prison for what I said, knowing what they know now."

She eyed him squarely and shook her head. "You know, you're starting to sound like Don Quixote again. You thought you were so right they couldn't convict you in the first place. You saw how that turned out."

"I'm willing to take my chances."

"Well, at least we'll have a few days to think about it while you're gone. Maybe there's a smarter way." She pulled him closer to her and rested her head on his shoulder. "I love you, Clay Stoner, and you know why? Because there's a poet in your soul. Most people are blessed with being able to put up with things the way they are. You aren't able to do that, and that's already caused us a lot of grief. I'm sure it's going to cause us more...but I have a vow to make."

"What's that?"

"Wherever you go, I'm going with you."

Clay got up a little unsteadily. He ambled over to the edge of the terrace and looked out over the valley. The air was shimmering from the dry, furnace-hot heat of the sirocco. "It's hot, he said. "Fires are breaking out in the pines again. If we don't get some rain soon, this whole mountain may go up in smoke. I'm not even sure I'll be able to get down the road to the airport in the morning."

"That would be fantastic!" Marianna said, as she walked over beside him, slipped under his arm, and gave him a little squeeze around his waist. "We could spend the whole day in bed, just like we used to in Cagnes. Remember?" He looked down at her with a smile that told her that he loved her. "You do remember those days in Cagnes, don't you Clay; our squalid little flat; you tending bar and hustling your ass off for a lousy couple a hundred francs a week? We were happy then. Everything was so simple. Life was fun. I don't know how we let ourselves get so messed up. Or why things have to be so complicated. It seems so much has happened these past few years I can hardly remember how it all began."

He looked out over the valley again. Out ahead of him, as far as he could see, the grain fields were scorched and yellow. Below him the pine trees were smoldering and burning their way toward the range of mountains far off to his left. He looked toward the jutting peninsula of Antibes, only faintly visible in the haze, and he pointed beyond, toward Nice and the sea. "It began right out there," he said quietly. "Remember...I was low on gas and had to land? It'll be five years ago tomorrow - Bastille Day."

IX

༄

A LETTER TO LARA

On Bastille Day morning, twenty minutes after the sun poked its first rays of light over the ridge from the Italian side of the Maritime Alpes, Clay Stoner was up and about. Marianna was up too. She made coffee and they drank it on the second floor terrace, facing the sea. The morning was bright and clear. They could see all the way to Nice and make out the fishing boats just starting to get underway, heading out into the mist through the opening in the seawall that encircled the old port.

Clay was scheduled to meet Howie at the Cote d'Azur aerodrome at ten o'clock. He was leaving La Gaude early, though, so that he would be able to get down the mountain before the sun started rekindling the pine forests and a host of new fires erupted that would almost certainly block the road. He finished his coffee quickly, stuffed a few last minute things in his flight bag, and said goodbye to Marianna.

Angelo Tarallo was waiting for him next to the reflecting pool in the courtyard. "Bon giorno, signor," Angelo said, grinning and cheerful as usual. Angelo was an elderly Italian, small and dark and wiry with bushy eyebrows. Born in nearby Ventimiglia, he had married Genevieve, a French woman from La Gaude, and had moved to the village many years before. His forte was gardening; Genevieve's housework; and ever since they came to the village, the two of them had taken care of the Girard villa with a gentle, patrician-like pride. After exchanging brief greetings, Clay and Angelo meandered down the steep cobblestone lane through the center of the still sleeping village and out through the gate in the wall that surrounded it to the road along which the cars were kept parked and where Clay's new Alfa Romeo was sparkling in the dawn.

Angelo had washed and waxed it the night before especially for the trip. Marianna could see them from the terrace off her bedroom. She watched the Alfa start up and wind around the first bend and disappear in a dust cloud. She waited until the dust dissipated and the road was empty, and then, doing something that was seldom her custom, she went back to bed.

She was still mulling over their conversation of the night before. The thought of Clay going home had shocked her into thinking about some things for the first time now - things she had purposefully erased from her memory for years. She took off her robe and stared into the large, half-moon shaped mirror that covered most of the wall. She looked at it for a long time before making a momentous decision. She rose from the bed, stepped to the desk in front of the mirror, took up a pen, sat down, and commenced to write:

Dear Lara,

It seems strange calling you Lara, but when I visited your home in Creekwood at the end of 1965 you graciously asked me to call you by your first name, so I will. You may ask why I write now after so many years. The reason for my silence is that I have been living in France with Clay most of that time. We have carefully avoided corresponding from here lest our messages be intercepted by authorities who might have him arrested and extradited if they learned of his whereabouts. We decided also that if you did not know where we were, you could never be accused of aiding and abetting him as a fugitive. Now, because of a greater fear, I am daring to take a risk and throwing caution to the winds. Nevertheless, as a precaution after reading this letter, please destroy it.

Clay has just learned of your illness and wants very badly to go home to see you. But if he does, I am afraid he will be caught and arrested, and the life we have made here together ruined. I think I have a better idea. Could you and your husband come visit us here in France? I have a little money stashed away, so the cost of the trip would be my treat. I feel I owe you that since I am the one who has had the opportunity to be with your son these past few years, and not you. I would like to spend time with you and, more importantly, introduce you to your grandchildren. Yes! Clay and I are the parents of twins, three and one-half years old, a girl named Cassie and a boy named Cody. It is time they get to meet you.

This letter may be a bit longer than I intended because I have so many things to tell you about our lives. After Clay's court-martial he fled to a small village in the south of France called Haut-de-Cagnes where Vic Powers' widow, Darcy (who you may remember), and her step sister were living. He rented a garret in their apartment house and got a job tending bar in a club called the She-She in Cannes. I came to live with him in June of that year; twenty-three years old, just a dumb young coed who made a spur of the moment decision to trust my soul to him.

She pondered that decision. *I was only thinking about living one day at a time then, not what it would be like spending my life with a man who might be a fugitive forever. Oh, I knew there would be some tense moments - our relationship had been tense enough before I came here - but I never dreamed our life together would turn out the way it has. The simple fact is that Clay and I are not the same people anymore...Life is strange. I'm not sure I can sort out the past four years, really. I'm so numbed by it all. But I will never forget how it was with us in the beginning when Clay adored me, and the affair we were having was still beautiful.*

Through a fortuitous set of circumstances, within a month after arriving here I became the lead singer for a band playing at the She-She. I had obtained a false passport by then under the name Kira Chastain, and we called our group 'Kira and the Band'. The club was owned by Howard Nussbaum, who heads a worldwide financial conglomerate in Monaco called Utopia International. At the end of that summer he invited us to a party at his chateau, learned that Clay had flown in the navy, and offered him a job as a corporate pilot for Utopia. That same month Darcy

married my cousin, Jean Pierre, and moved with him to
Berlin, and Clay and I moved out of our squalid little third
floor garret and down to the much larger second floor
apartment that Darcy had vacated. It gave us two rooms
of our own and a living room, kitchen and bathroom that
we shared with Darcy's stepsister, who everyone calls Cat;
but life was still Spartan. By then I knew I was pregnant.
We had to buy a car. It was only an old, used Citroen 2CV,
very tiny with a wooden frame, but the down payment left
us penniless. We both worked our butts off for the next
four months trying to save some money to buy things for
the baby. Clay was the most junior co-pilot then, but whenever he came home he was all smiles, relaxed, happy to
be flying again. His job was to ferry Nussbaum's high pow-
ered sales managers around on their weekly junkets to
cities like London, Madrid, Rome, Athens, Cairo, Tel Aviv,
Beirut. He was gone from Monday to Friday, and since I
sang at the She-She on Fridays and Saturdays until three
in the morning, the only night of the week we had together
for awhile was Sunday.

*Those were fantastic times, though, each weekend like a honeymoon.
We used to wake up late, make love and lie in bed until noon, and Clay
would hold me very gently and we would talk...we don't do that much
anymore, but back then we talked about everything together.*

I quit singing at the She-She in early December. I was
starting to look and feel very pregnant by then, and Clay
wanted me to stay home. It was a dismal winter. Clay was
away most of the time, and it was rainy and lonely.

*Our friends from the summer had left as soon as the weather turned
cold, all except my dear, sweet Cat. She had always been a little too wild for
me, but that winter we became really close friends. She was like a doting
mother, almost as excited about my having a baby as I was. She insisted
that I get plenty of exercise, and we spent our afternoons together walking
about Haut-de-Cagnes, window shopping, perusing art galleries, sipping
tea at the café in the square. She did not want me to drink alcohol, so she*

stopped drinking around me. And she quit smoking in our apartment. She was there to drive me to the hospital when I went into labor, and she sat up with me all night through the pains.

The babies arrived in February. I was premature by more than a month, and Clay was off flying somewhere. I wasn't very brave, I guess. All I remember is that when the contractions came, I started screaming for a pill until the doctor came and gave me one that knocked me stupid. Luckily, I'm fairly wide-hipped. I managed to give birth to the twins - Cassie was breach - without any complications. Having twins was a complete surprise. They're beautiful children. Cody is a lanky, broad-shouldered, dark haired boy with enormous brown eyes, very serious. Cassie is totally different, petite, fair-haired and curly, with crystal clear blue eyes just like her father's, and mischievous as hell.

Legally, they're mine, I guess. Their father's name is recorded as unknown on their birth certificates. I hadn't had time to discuss it with Clay, and I was paranoid at the time that the FBI might still be trying to track him down, even through birth records. So I used my fake passport, and the twins were brought into this world with the last name of Chastain. When Clay came back from his business trip he agreed it was probably the smart thing to do. He said we could always change their names someday.

I had thought having a baby would be nice. Oh! What I didn't know! I had no idea how babies could change things. Those two little bears consumed me for awhile. The apartment was bitter cold, and with two cribs and the four of us, conditions were cramped, to say the least. I soon learned it was impossible to live without a washer and dryer. To this day I don't understand how you young mothers survived before those things were invented. They were our first big purchases, other than the 2CV, but with the car I felt we were buying some freedom. Spending money on a big, bulky material thing like a washing machine that you just couldn't pick up and move whenever you felt like

it was a new experience. The commitment was frightening. I didn't know how much until a few weeks later when
Nussbaum invited Clay and me to a party in Monaco. I
hadn't been out of Cagnes since Cody and Cassie were
born, and Nussbaum hadn't invited us to a party since I
quit singing at the She-She. Wanting to make a good im-
pression, I went out and bought, what for us, was an expensive evening gown, and on Saturday afternoon I spent
three hours getting my hair fixed, the first time I had been
to a hairdresser since I left the States. Clay and I were
literally walking out the door that night when we all of a
sudden realized that we had two kids asleep in the bedroom and that neither of us had thought about getting a
babysitter.

*That was when I really knew my life had changed - and Clay's life
as well. We weren't free anymore. We had the kind of commitments that
we'd always tried to avoid, and I wondered then about what impact that
was going to have on the relationship we had that had flourished so well
without them.*

Fortunately, our landlady was available on short notice
to stay with the twins, and Clay and I got to the party before dinner was served. Things might be different today if
we hadn't. Nussbaum asked me that night to come back
to work at the She-She, and I accepted.

*In fact, I jumped at his offer with all the shameful exuberance of a fe-
male bitch leaping out of her litter for a bone with her pups still clinging to
her teats. I wasn't ready then to be just a mother and a homebody. I got in
touch with the band from the She-She the next day. They were playing at
a club in London and were thrilled when I called them. They showed up in
Cagnes a month later. We had three days to rehearse before opening at the
She-She in early May, one week before the start of the Film Festival. Nussbaum was there to check us out, and he must have liked what he heard. At
the end of our first night he offered to double our pay if we would stay and
play through the end of summer. The guys agreed without hesitation, so I
said okay without thinking too much about it.*

I guess that's when I really started becoming a professional entertainer - and when life started becoming more complex. I was at the She-She five nights a week. Clay was gone. The twins stayed downstairs with the landlady every night until I got home. What little social life Clay and I did have revolved around the afternoon parties every other Sunday at Nussbaum's chateau.

That was where he entertained all his good customers on the Cote, and he liked having young attractive women around for them to rub elbows with. He invited us to all his weekend parties and, given our dependence on him, our attendance was practically mandatory. Cat was invited to all of them too. In a few short months I learned what it was like to be on the fringe of the jet set - how to parry a rich old leche's hint or promises of all the good things that could be in store for me in exchange for a few days, or a night, or even a few hours of my company. There were suggestions of lavish gifts, cruises in the Aegean, a private jet to Rio for the Carnival. Of course I snubbed them all to stay with Clay in the tender bliss of our modest little shared apartment in Cagnes. But I sort of liked going to the parties then. I met a lot of interesting people. So did Cat. For every proposition I turned down, she probably accepted two. I began seeing her less and less. She was seldom home. Cat went home to Washington for a month in July. When she returned, she surprised us and moved out. She just told us one night and was gone the next day. She moved in with Nussbaum in Monaco. I thought she was making a terrible mistake, but that was three years ago, and she's still there with him. She's pretty heavy into cocaine now, though, and I worry about her.

The rest of 1967 passed rather uneventfully. Cat moved out and Clay and I took over the rest of the apartment. It gave us the whole floor and some breathing room finally. In August Jean Pierre and Darcy were able to escape from Berlin and spend the month at his family's villa in La Gaude, a little village in the hills about eight miles north of Haut-de-Cagnes. We saw them almost every day when Clay was home.

Jean Pierre rented a sailboat, and we were able to get away for a weekend sail over to Corsica and back. Those were my first two whole nights away from Cody and Cassie, and as much as I loved them, it made me realize how much I missed my freedom. It was so tranquil and peaceful bobbing out there on the Mediterranean, sipping wine in the moonlight; but it frustrated me that I was not able to divorce myself and enjoy it more because of the nagging concern I had for the two squawky kids I had left to the care of our landlady.

Jean Pierre and Darcy packed off back to Berlin in early September, and Clay and I settled in for our second winter in the south of France. The band went back to England. The crowds at the She-She dwindled, and I sang there only occasionally on weekends with a couple of local pick-up bands.

In the spring I decided to go home for a visit. I had been in Europe for almost two years, never once having communicated with my parents. But the sting they had given me after I broke my engagement because of Clay was wearing off, and I wanted to see them and tell them about Cody and Cassie and try to patch things up. In late April - it was 1968 - I hired a woman to come stay with the twins and flew to New York. I landed at Kennedy on a damp Sunday morning and took a taxi straight to my brother's apartment on Morningside Heights.

I had stayed in touch with Robert through the exchange of a phone call about every six months or so. He knew that I was with Clay but didn't know that we had children. I was expecting to find him still asleep, but instead, his roommate told me he was with a group of students barricaded inside one of the main academic buildings on the Columbia campus. He had been there for almost a week, his roommate said, and he gave me a newspaper to read about it. The devastating Tet offensive had occurred in Vietnam only a couple of months earlier, the draft was at its peak, and students were starting to revolt. Columbia was in a crisis mode at the time. I left my luggage in Robert's apartment, went straight to the campus, and had little trouble finding the academic building my brother was occupying. I stayed with him and the students there for two days.

Robert was at the end of his junior year then - he now works for the New York Times - and in the two years I had been away he had become a mature and good-looking guy; quite a rogue actually, over six feet tall without an ounce of fat. He had the same angular jaw, sensual mouth and dark laughing eyes that I had so admired in him when he was younger. He was still the same old Robert...except he was now caught up in a cause. I was confronted by a strange new phenomena when I entered that building. All my life I had been a private person. But there I was thrown into an atmosphere of sharing and togetherness I had never known - and probably never will again. Half the students were young coeds in their teens look-ing eager and unhardened despite a lack of sleep, food, drink, and baths for most of a week. They shared the few blankets they had and slept on stone cold floors. They were not vandals or hard core radicals like some of the students in the other buildings. They only wanted peace, not war - and for the Columbia administration and faculty to side with them. Robert ex-plained to me their grievances - something about the ROTC, and a military contract with the University, and a gym. I never understood it all, and I did not know if they were right or not, but in my heart I knew that they were certainly not wrong. About one o'clock in the morning on my second night six hundred policemen appeared out of nowhere and surrounded the building. They were wearing helmets and were armed with teargas guns and wicked looking nightsticks. A police captain shouted through a bull-horn for us to come out and surrender, or else they would attack. We came out peacefully, to his probable surprise, and we were all herded into wait-ing paddy wagons. More than seven hundred students were hauled away that night, but before we departed that same captain started shouting at the crowd of onlookers to disperse. They were students from the dorms, a couple of thousand who had come out to the quadrangle just to watch. Most had been going to classes and did not support the occupation of the buildings. But when ordered to disperse, some of them started to jeer. The police, I know, had come anticipating a fight, and they had been spit at on campus for more than a month and had good reason to hold a grudge. But what happened next was sheer horror. The police went berserk and charged into the crowd of innocent bystanders swinging their sticks wildly, and they kept at it for ten minutes until the campus was cleared. No one was killed, but skulls were fractured, arms broken, eyes put out; nearly two hundred admitted to hospitals. The spectacle nauseated me, and that night a part of my soul was injected into the anti-war movement. Clay's court martial came flooding back to me. I thought about his words and what might have been a kind of foreboding when he said, "if this country is not strong enough to face up to a single, simple voice of dissent...without try-ing to persecute the dissenter...then God help us all". I feared then where all this divisiveness might lead. Would we end up fighting in the streets, brother against brother, father against son? I still do. That was all before

Kent State and it's still going on. This war - even though it's not called a
war, and that's a joke - has caused me so much grief.

Were it not for the war, I'm sure Clay and I would be married and
living a normal life now somewhere in the States. And I agonize over the
thought that Robert may be drafted and sent over there. Clay agonizes too.
It still bothers him that he lost so many friends over there...and that he
didn't go. But enough of that...

Robert and I were taken in a bus to the nearest precinct station, finger-
printed, booked and locked in a large cell with about fifty other students.
No one slept that night. The students started singing old Pete Seeger and
Joan Baez protest songs. I was so moved that I sat down in a corner and
in just a few minutes wrote one of my own. I showed it to Robert, and he
stood up and interrupted the others and asked me to sing it. I did, and everyone was polite and quiet. The first two verses I will never forget:

> "Why do we do it,
> Kill each other every day?
> We are all one people,
> Does it have to be this way?
> It is madness, it is insane,
> What else is there to say?
> As long as children are learning to kill...
> Instead of to play
>
> Why do we do it,
> Work ourselves to death every day?
> There more important things
> Than a job just for its pay.
> It's a mistake, too much pain,
> So leave that job, don't stay
> As long as children are learning to kill...
> Instead of to play."

We sang that song over and over that night until dawn came and some
of us were released. That was more than two years ago, and I never could
have imagined then that when I set it to music and recorded 'Why Do We
Do It?' this past spring that it would rocket to become a number one hit
throughout the States. But then, at that time, I didn't know a lot of things.

Robert telephoned our father at seven in the morning and told him what had happened and that I was in jail with him. We waited. At ten o'clock a lawyer came, posted bond, and we were allowed to go. I was hurt. I had expected my daddy to come rescue me, and he had sent his lawyer instead. That was the last day we would ever talk. Robert and I went to Chock Full-O-Nuts for coffee, and I called my father at his office. His voice snarled at me: "you vanish for two years and I hear nothing! Then when I do it's only because you need me to get you out of trouble!" He was as cold as a bucket of dry-ice. I begged him to forgive and forget, but nothing moved him. I told him about living in Europe with Clay and that we had two children - his grandchildren. He became enraged and told me to go back to my family - that I was not a part of his anymore. And then he hung up. He never asked about the twins, what their names were, or their age or sex or anything. I sat in Chock-Full-O-Nuts and cried for thirty minutes. Wailed was more like it. My father had put me through torture for the third time, and I decided right then there would never be a fourth.

My attempt to visit my parents did not work out well, to put it mildly. They refused to see me and broke my heart. Forever, I think. I doubt that I will ever see them again. Robert and I went back to his apartment. I packed and left for the airport and boarded the first flight to Paris. I felt ten years older when I arrived in Cagnes the next day...disillusioned and devastated. My band was back from England by then, with a new drummer from South Kensington, Tommy Mitchell, who was really quite good. We opened at the She-She a week later, just in time for the start of the Film Festival.

I was playing at the She-She during that summer of 1968 when Martin Luther King and Robert Kennedy were assassinated. If you remember, riots were taking place across the States: Detroit, Newark, Watts. They bothered Clay and me immensely, but they had much less impact on our life on the Cote than did the death of Jean Pierre's mother in July. Jean Pierre and Darcy came for the funeral and stayed through August. It was not one of our happiest times together. They were en route to Dakar, in Senegal (West Africa) for a two year assignment, and they were both miserable about it. The weekend before they left they invited us to La Gaude for dinner and asked if we would like to stay in their villa while they were gone. Our only cost would be wages for the housekeeper and gardener, about four thousand dollars a year, three times what Clay and I were paying in rent. We thought about it for all of thirty seconds before we accepted. So it was at the end of the summer that Clay, the twins, and I moved out of our little apartment in Haut-de-Cagnes and eight miles further up into the mountains to the villa in La Gaude. At last we found there the simple solitude and casual friendliness both of us cherished.

Within a few weeks we were able to stroll in the streets and shop in the stores and know everyone by first name. And they knew us, but only as Mr. and Mrs. Anderson; Clay and Kira. They assumed we were married. No one in the village knew about Utopia International, or that Clay was a pilot, or that I sang with a band, or even what was happening in Vietnam. La Gaude's contact with the outside world was practically non-existent, especially in the wintertime.

After Christmas that winter I joined the band in London for a six week engagement at Nussbaum's cavernous cabaret in Soho. It seats five hundred; a huge dance hall. Other than one forty-five minute show, we had nothing to do except play music for dancing three hours each night, and it was during that time that we melded together as a really fine band. I had bought an electric piano when Clay and I moved to La Gaude, and during my spare time while he was gone I started composing; writing lyrics, then working on melodies and chords to go with them.

My Juilliard background came into play as I learned the logic by which one note follows another, and how to lengthen a phrase or a chord pattern to blend lyrics and melody in unconventional ways. I brought the arrangements to Soho with me and passed them out to the band. We tried a new song at the dance hall each night, and by the second or third night we would have it down pat. As musicians, the band and I hit it off great. Riley, the lead guitarist, is as good as they come playing counter melody. And he's been together with Chauncey's rhythm bass so long now that they coalesce on stage as if they were fraternal twins. Tommy had already carved out his niche with us the prior summer at the She-She, but in Soho he proved that he was more than just a find, wowing the crowd by twirling his drumsticks two at a time without missing a beat. He could also sing, and he and Riley harmonized well as a background duo. Tommy is a year older than Clay and didn't come up via the normal path of a drummer. He speaks almost flawless French, his father having been an English banker in Paris where Tommy went to school for six years before entering the Sorbonne and studying music for two. That is where he took up drums and quit school when he was twenty one. He's a very cocky and attractive guy, tall enough, with long wavy hair in an Elvis style; sensual, dopey looking eyes. The girl groupies really dig him, and I know he's wanted to get in my pants since the first time we met. But he has a good heart, and as a drummer...well, he's got the beat, and he's helped the band broaden our scope. Our music isn't any single type - we blend many genres: rhythm and blues, country road-house rock, soulful folk and ballads. It's just our music, really. I often take a funky bluesy lead on the keyboard, Riley's guitar is held back and chorded, with the exception of a few tasteful frills, then Chauncey picks up the rhythm and Tommy blends in with his beat. Most of our songs try to tell a story, especially my ballads, and we're getting better all the time...but back to that first winter in London.

Nussbaum came up to see us play a couple of times. The week before I planned to go home to La Gaude he made us a proposition, offering to pay for the recording and distribution of an album if we'd sign a two year exclusive contract with him. The rest of the band wanted to sign right away, but Nussbaum and I haggled. In the end, after he agreed not to book me for more than six months a year, at least half of which had to be in the south of France, we signed a contract entitling him to twenty percent of our income in return for him paying all our expenses. I thought it was a good deal. The band agreed. My share of the cut was forty percent, and I thought I wouldn't be away from Clay and the twins any more than we could tolerate. I was excited.

I called Clay that night to tell him that I had to stay in London for awhile longer to record an album. His reply was curt and short. "I hope that makes you happy, fella'," he said, and then he hung up. In retrospect, I guess that was the beginning of the deterioration in our relationship.

The album was entitled very simply, *Kira and the Band*. Several of the songs on it had already been popular hits; love songs like Ray Charles' *Cry Me a River* and *I Can't Stop Loving You*, Carole King's *Will You Love Me Tomorrow*, Piaf's *Non, Je Ne Regrette Rien*. By then *Non* was one of my trademark songs (not that anyone could ever imitate Piaf). I sang it part in English, part in French, and the crowds all seemed to think it was great. The flip side of the album contained songs relating to the angst of youth: *Blowin' in the Wind, Where Have All the Flowers Gone*, and several originals composed by yours truly. One of them was released as a single, *Mad Generation*, a song about kids, parents, alcohol, benzedrine, and the war machine.

'Mad Generation' eventually made it to the top ten on the singles charts in Britain; top forty on Billboard. My share of the royalties were pretty good. I had the entire month of April off. Ten weeks had been the longest Clay and I had been separated in three years, and when I got back to La Gaude he seemed overjoyed to see me - at first. But after a few days he started making snide remarks about my lack of caring for Cassie and Cody. He insinuated that Genevieve was more a mother to them than I was...that son of a bitch! He never worried about the twins when they were babies. He was seldom home, and when he was he never lifted a finger to help. Not once did he ever change a diaper, or get up in the middle of the night. I was playing at the She-She five nights a week, but he never considered that. When Cody and Cassie were babies, they were all my problem. But now that they're three years old and I have Genevieve to take care of them, he accuses me of being a lousy mother. The hypocrite...We've fallen victim to a vicious circle of resentment. Clay gets me enraged, and I will lash back at him, and he'll start drinking. That's the way it's been ever since last year when I came home for April and then left again after the Film Festival for a five week tour in England to help promote our first album.

The Band and I were back in the south of France last summer for the height of tourist season. We were invited to play at the Juan les Pins Jazz Festival for three days, jamming on the same sacred stage in the pine grove made famous by Ray Charles, Count Basie and Ella Fitzgerald. We played at the She-She and at a cabaret in Monaco and a few other nearby places, so I was able to be at home with Cody and Cassie almost every day. But Clay started flying Utopia's new South American run last summer, long flights to Caracas, Rio, and Buenos Aires with ten day round trips and only four days on the Cote in between.

When he was home, the resentments flourished and only grew deeper. I didn't want it that way. I don't think Clay did either. It's just that we're both very explosive people. One night when I told him that Howie had scheduled the Band to perform at a music festival in Montreux for a week, he flew into a rage and threw one or our breakfast table chairs off the second floor balcony and watched it drop six hundred feet down into the valley...I've come to learn that Clay's a very sensitive and complex man. He can't stand anyone impinging on his freedom. Rules, laws, bureaucrats, petty nuisances - they all drive him berserk. But when it comes to someone he cares for, he's totally demanding and possessive.

I'm only now beginning to understand him. He didn't like the influence Howie had over me; but he doesn't like it now, either, since I've started becoming my own person. What really sticks in his craw, though, is the control he feels Howie has over him. Clay can't stand being subservient to anyone, and I know he feels that's what Howie is doing to him.

Nussbaum has become quite important since we went to work for him. Utopia is ten times as big as it was four years ago. It manages several billion dollars of assets and has thousands of salesmen. The newspapers say Nussbaum is worth more than a hundred million dollars. They also say he's wanted in the States for something. I don't know anything about it except that he doesn't go to the States anymore for fear of being arrested...It's ironic. Here I am. Integrity has always meant everything to me, and neither of the two people who have the most influence

over my life can set foot on American soil without the fear
of going to jail.

*Clay was ready to quit Utopia last fall. One night when he was drunk
he told me he felt like he was nothing more than a bus driver for the mafia.
He didn't explain, but I'm starting to worry about what he meant. Ever
since, flying has been nothing more than a job to him. He used to love it.
But for months, now, I've watched him come home from trips looking
burnt out and tired and head straight for the bar and start drinking and
just stare at the wall. I've watched the strength I so admired in him just
waste away. And I must admit, as it's eroded, I've started to lose some
respect for him....You know, young people all have illusions. Clay was
mine. But something's happened to him. When I first saw him changing, I
thought it was because he was jealous of my career and the fact that I was
making more money than he was. Now, I'm not so sure. Howie promoted
him to chief pilot last fall and doubled his salary. That seemed to perk him
up at first. He had the responsibility for scheduling six aircraft and managing fifteen pilots. I could tell the challenge excited him...The momentary
bliss lasted only three weeks. Howie had scheduled the band to be in London for eight straight weeks that winter, first to record an album, and then
to play at his club for a month. When Clay found out, he was furious. He
wanted me to refuse. I told him I couldn't because of my contract and that
it wouldn't be fair to the band. He started accusing me of being a lousy
mother again - and so it went until I left for London.*

    I was in London the first week in February cutting
my second album when Clay flew into Heathrow to drop
Nussbaum off. I went out to the airport to see him. The
weather was horrible - freezing rain. The taxi ride took two
hours, so we had just enough time for one coffee before
he had to leave to fly back to Nice. The ride back to my
hotel took another two hours, and when I arrived, I had
an invitation to a party in Nussbaum's suite. Quite frankly,
the party got out of hand. Everyone had too much to drink,
and I was on the verge of leaving when Clay walked in un-
expectedly. His aircraft had a maintenance problem and
he planned to spend the night with me. When he saw the
party scene he became infuriated. We had a violent con-

versation. He walked out, slamming the door, and didn't come back.

I had thought the four hour trip to the airport had been worth it. Clay kissed me sweetly and gently before we parted. The telephone was ringing back at the hotel when I walked into my room. It was Tommy Mitchell; his room was next door to mine. He said Howie wanted us to join him at a party in his suite. We took the elevator up to the penthouse and walked in just as he was finishing a small private dinner. Two foppish members of the British aristocracy and a wealthy, corpulent Arab were dining with him. Five minutes later two hookers arrived. They were dressed in fur coats, cashmere sweaters and costume jewelry, trying to look high class, but in a coarse sort of way. Within an hour none of us were sober. Howie, Tommy, one of the English lords and I were sitting on a sofa around a coffee table drinking champagne and laughing at one of Tommy's obscene jokes. Howie had his arm draped loosely around my shoulder. The second Englishman was on another sofa with one of the hookers. She had taken off her sweater and bra and had her hands in his pants, fondling him. The Arab and the other hooker were in the bedroom. Its door was open, and we could hear their muffled sounds. Then the doorbell rang. I thought it was room service bringing up another bottle of champagne that Howie had ordered. Instead, it was Clay. Tommy opened the door, and Clay looked across the room at me, his face turning crimson, and then ash white. He mumbled something about his plane having a broken alternator and not being able to get it repaired until morning. Right then the Arab walked out of the bedroom with his hooker half naked. Clay muttered some apology for intruding and then walked out and slammed the door. I chased after him all the way down to the lobby and caught him on his way out. Right in front of the doorman he told me, "go fuck yourself". Then he got in a taxi and left.

That was more than five months ago, and things have not been right with us since. Nor have we seen each other much. I was in La Gaude for a few days in March, but we argued constantly until I had to return to London to rehearse for a tour of the States to promote my second album. It was a collection of anti-war songs entitled, 'Kira: On Love and War'. Every song on it was an original written

by me. The big hit, of course, was *Why Do We Do It*, but I didn't know how big at the time.

We rehearsed for ten days. Basically, I had been a night club, cabaret and dance hall type singer until then. In clubs I'd learned to pace myself, talk a lot with the audience, create settings, and then just sing the way I felt. I knew this tour would be different, playing twenty one-night stands, each up on a stage in a large auditorium or arena where you lose the intimacy. We were almost unheard of in the States and were only going to be performing for the first thirty minutes of each concert to warm up the crowd before the real big-name entertainers came on stage - an enormous challenge. I always try to extend the range of what I do. I knew by then that I had a voice, but for the first time I had to consider things other than just my music and singing: the way I moved my body, what I was doing with my arms and legs, facial expressions. It was a new experience for me, but after the rehearsals, I was confident that the band and I would put on a darned good show.

The band and I were in New York during the first week in May, staying overnight at the Drake Hotel after having completed two thirty minute performances at the Fillmore East in front of an audience of more than three thousand when Robert arrived at my room, wild eyed. He asked me to turn on the television and the late night news. The news, of course, was Kent State.

That afternoon a crudely disciplined assortment of national guardsmen had been sent in to halt a student protest at the small college campus in Ohio. Robert and I sat down on the floor and stared at the television screen as the catastrophic story unfolded. We watched for what seemed like hours as films were replayed over and over showing the troops marching up to a position on top of a grassy knoll - kneeling - taking careful aim - then blasting away into a crowd of students. The President had called them bums, Robert told me. Never have I seen such gut wrenching emotion spill out of a picture tube. I cried. So did Robert. We watched interviews with government officials, most of them callous assholes who kept mouthing justifications for the slaughter, seeming to say that the students got what was coming to them. I was sick and numb. Robert was shaking with rage. He just didn't understand, he said, moaning, how any human being with a speck of brains could have sent those greenhorn guardsmen onto a campus with loaded rifles.

Two nights later the band and I were playing to a packed house of four thousand at the New Haven Arena. The crowd was in an anti-war mood, and before we were half way through our set, they started shouting for us to play *Why Do We Do It*. The record had been out only two weeks, and I didn't even know they had heard of it. We played it, and when we finished the crowd roared for encores.

Hit songs are often lucky, I guess. I think we were lucky. Our album hit the streets a week before Kent State and struck a chord that captured the mood of the time.

Four Yale professors came backstage after the concert. They were part of a group organizing a peace demonstration in Washington on Saturday, a program that would include speeches and music about war and peace throughout the day. They asked us to come and perform. We huddled for a minute and decided we would do it, despite our scheduled concert at Ohio State University on that night. We telephoned the agent in New York who had booked the tour and told him to charter a plane at our expense from Washington Saturday evening that would get us to Columbus in time for the show.

That's how I ended up at four o'clock on the second Saturday afternoon in May going on stage in front of the Washington Monument to perform before a milling throng of a hundred thousand disparate people who came to protest the war that day.

I faltered a moment at the microphone, unnerved by so many people sitting impatiently on the grass waiting for us to entertain them. They had been listening to speeches for two hours and were getting restless. But they cheered as we were introduced, and that calmed me. I started singing my half-English, half-French version of 'Non, Je Ne Regrette Rien', and the crowd quieted down. But when I began the next song, 'Why Do We Do It', the crowd stood up roaring, and at the end of the first verse a group of thousands interrupted us, pointing their middle fingers at the White House and screaming "fuck you, Agnew!" They stopped after about thirty seconds, but after the next verse, the wild scene was repeated - as it was several more times again for the next ten minutes until the crowd wore itself out, finally. There was little else to be done after that, except to say, "thank you", and slip away quickly as possible to catch our plane for Columbus.

Things began happening after that. Our agent in New York called us the next day and said that his telephone was ringing off the wall. Orders for our album were rolling in from across the country and we were in demand everywhere. We were scheduled to be back in France in a week to play at the She-She during the Film Festival, but Howie cancelled those plans and had our agent book us for six more weeks in the States. And so we stayed and did another twenty five performances - this time getting paid three times as much per night compared to what we were paid for the first twenty. We played Las Vegas for a week. I was on a couple of television talk shows. Our last performance was on the fourth of July at the Illinois State Fair.

The flight home was long. Eighteen hours to be exact. I left Chicago on the afternoon of the fifth. My plane out of Kennedy was two hours late, so I missed my connection in Paris and had a four hour layover before the next flight to Nice. I dozed most of the way, just grateful to be going home and having the rest of the month off to recover. I had been gone ten weeks and had done forty five performances in twenty two states. I was wasted. I still am.

My homecoming was a giant letdown. Clay was away on a trip. Angelo met me at the airport and drove me to La Gaude. I learned that Cody had a broken arm. He had fallen out of a tree. Clay came home the next day and acted as if Cody's arm had been all my fault...I don't blame him,

I guess. I really haven't been much of a mother these past seven or eight months.

Or a lover...I don't know whose fault that is, though. I've been home for a week now, and Clay hasn't touched me once. But then, I haven't encouraged him as much as I know how, either. And I'll be damned if I'm going to take the initiative! If he wants me he's going to have to show it first...I did want him so much last night, though, after he told me about his mother. I tried to signal him in my own way. Instead, he got drunk. That's really became a problem with him. I don't know what to do about it.

That's when he told me about you and about wanting to go home now. And that's when I decided to write this letter. For safety's sake, I will forward it to you through Robert. Please let him know if you will come. I pray that you do.

Love,

Marianna

X

🐚

UTOPIA

One mile out of La Gaude Clay skirted the Alfa around a wooden barrier the forest rangers had placed in the middle of the road. The road looked clear, and he and Angelo continued on down. The road ran parallel to a stream. Off to the left, below them and stretching as far toward Italy as one could see was the burned out pine plain. Behind them were the mountains, the west side of their slopes still dim in the early morning shadow. The road dipped sharply to cross the stream and then it continued winding, rising occasionally, but always descending toward the coast. Angelo was nervous, and he wanted to talk. "Signor Clay must be joyeux now that Madame Kira is home, no?" Angelo said as he squinted his eyes and peered down the road. Angelo often mixed his French, English and Italian together, especially when he was nervous.

"Certainly, I'm happy," Clay said as he drove fast, the wind blowing through his hair.

"You sure, signor? Genevieve say you don't act like it."

Clay looked at Angelo. Angelo was looking straight ahead. "What else does Genevieve say?" Clay asked curiously.

"That you been snapping at her and the bambinos lately...and that you drink too much. Something wrong, Signor Clay?"

Clay looked at Angelo again and saw his bushy eyebrows knitted together in a frown. He laughed and shook his head and shouted over the sound of the wind. "Nothing's wrong Angelo. What makes you think that?"

"I don't know, signor. Just Genevieve don't think you and Madame Kira are very happy anymore. That makes us unhappy too."

Ahead was a sign with a picture of an S-turn. The woods were smoldering and billowing smoke now, making it difficult to see more than a few yards ahead. Clay slowed, and not unwisely. Around the first turn a burning tree had fallen across the road. He braked hard, stopping inches short of crashing into it. He and Angelo got out of the car. The tree was heavy, but with twenty minutes of pushing and sweating, they were able to move it enough for the Alfa to get by. They continued going down, around more curves and through deep dust and hazy smoke until they reached the coast. As the road flattened, Angelo relaxed and smiled for the first time since leaving La Gaude. Ten minutes later they drove into the oval, palm tree lined driveway at the Cote d'Azur aerodrome. Clay drove around to the Utopia hangar, parked in front and opened the trunk. He took out his bags and handed the car keys to Angelo. "I'll see you in three days. You be careful going home now."

"Oh, I will signor," Angelo assured him. "I'll wait until the forest rangers go up, and then I will follow them. I will be very safe." They both looked at the Alfa for a moment, all covered with powdery red dust now. Then Clay patted the old man on the shoulder and hurried inside.

Clay's co-pilot was waiting for him in the operations room. They went over the flight plan: an hour and a half to Amsterdam, thirty minutes on the ground there, then forty-five minutes direct to London. They were flying the Jet Star, which was sort of unusual. The Jet Star was the queen of Utopia's fleet, a large four engine aircraft that could carry nine passengers in luxurious comfort non-stop for three thousand miles. The interior was trimmed in mahogany, the seats all leather. Suede sofas in the rear of the cabin formed a lounge that could be converted into a mini-bedroom. The Jet Star was normally flown on the long haul, cross Atlantic runs. For short trips, though, the Jet Star was very uneconomical fuel wise. Utopia usually only used it when it was needed to carry a large number of passengers. This trip was a short one, and Clay was puzzled. Howie had said he wanted it. But according to the flight plan, they were picking up only two passengers in Amsterdam.

Howie showed up right at ten-thirty. Cat was with him, decked out and looking foxy in a pair of large, black-rimmed sunglasses and a tight white satin jump suit open at the neck. Clay took their bags and helped them aboard. They were airborne six minutes later and in another nine minutes were leveled off at twenty-six thousand feet. Clay turned the aircraft over to the co-pilot then, and went back to the cabin to perform one of the many corporate pilot chores that he found so odious. Howie and Cat were lounging on the sofa, squeezing each other, as Clay stepped into the cabin. "Does anyone need anything?" he asked very discreetly.

Howie sat up. "How about a martini on the rocks?"

Clay unlatched the bar compartment, tossed a handful of ice cubes into a plastic cup, filled it with gin, doused in a little dry vermouth and walked back to the rear of the cabin and handed it to Howie. "What about you?" he said to Cat.

"Can you fix a tequila sour?" Cat cooed playfully.

Clay went back to the bar, opened a package of whiskey sour mix, poured the contents into a glass of ice and filled it with tequila. "Anything else?" he asked when the task was completed.

Howie patted the seat right across from him. "Sit down for awhile, kid. I've been wanting to talk to you." Clay sat down, bristling at the *kid*, but not showing it. "We haven't talked for a long time," Howie went on. "Your nose has been out of joint ever since you saw Kira in my room in London, hasn't it?"

"What Kira does is her business. We're not married, you know."

"Yeah, sure. Don't bullshit me. You may not be married, but you're living together and raising two kids. Not much difference. That's why I wanted to explain about that night. I just invited Kira and Tommy up to give the party a little class and talk some business details. I am their manager, after all. Nothing happened, Clay. So you don't have any bitch with either of us."

"That's what she said. So let's consider the subject closed."

"Good. Now we can talk about what's really on my mind. We're picking up H.B. Nicholson in Amsterdam. Ever heard of him?"

"Sure. Very important businessman."

"Much more than that. He's one of the richest and most powerful businessmen on the planet. He tries to keep his profile as low as possible, but the media all knows about his gigantic oil and real estate interests and everyone knows that his HBN Aviation is one of the largest defense contractors in the world. What they don't know is that he owns eighty percent of Utopia."

Clay's eyes widened slightly. "That is news. Everyone I know thinks you own it, Howie."

"That's what Nicholson wants everyone to think. I needed cash and sold control to him about five years ago. The deal's been great for both of us. You've seen how Utopia's grown."

"I know. But I've never understood how it all worked."

"Well, I still own twenty per cent, and I'm the nominee share-holder for a Gibraltar company that owns the other eighty, which is secretly owned by Nicholson, of course. Gibraltar doesn't tax anything, I don't pay taxes in Monaco, and the taxes there on Utopia's management company are next to nothing. We do have three Utopia funds registered in Monaco, but the management company is small and doesn't really get involved in picking or choosing investments. Our forte, particularly mine, is recruiting salesmen, and finding super salesmen to recruit other salesman. Utopia has thousands spread across Europe who charge big, fat commissions – as much as ten per cent – for bringing in customer money, frequently money from the type of person who doesn't want too much attention paid to where it came from. The customer gets a share certificate in one of our funds, we collect his money, pay the salesman a fraction of the commission and then buy into other funds around the world - including the States - who do all the investment work for us.. We don't even send out customers' statements. Utopia's fund share values are computed daily and published in major newspapers all over the world, so a customer can know exactly what his account is worth at any point in time without having to worry about getting statements in the mail that might end up in the wrong hands. All we do is rake off the commission spread and deduct an annual fee. Utopia's really just a big fund of funds."

"I didn't think Utopia was allowed to sell its funds in the States."

"It's not. But it can make investments there. That's what makes it a great front for Nicholson. It gives him the perfect vehicle for making deals; getting control of companies by mingling some Utopia Fund cash with his own to make investments outside the probing eyes of the government, particularly the SEC and the IRS." Howie winked. "Pretty neat, huh?"

"Sounds a little shady to me."

"Oh horseshit, boy! That's the way the world works. Whatta you think the Swiss banks have been doing the last fifty years? The Swiss act so prim and pure and honest. But do you know what? If it weren't for all the hot money stashed away in their secret bank accounts, the economy of that whole god-damned country would go down the drain so fast the suction would make your ears pop. Utopia's no different."

"Why are you telling me all this, Howie?"

"Because I trust you, kid. You and Kira are very special to me... but it's more than that. I didn't make you chief pilot for nothin'.

Quite frankly, I'd like to see you get more involved in the business. You've been seeing and hearing a lot of things flying me around. Just like now. Besides the two of us only three other people know what I just told you, and you're the only person at Utopia who'll know about my meeting with Nicholson today. I need someone who's smart like you that I can rely on. I assume I can trust you, can't I kid?"

"Certainly," Clay said, and he kept his eyes steady as he said it.

"Good. Because starting tonight, I'm going to show you what makes Utopia tick."

"What happens tonight?"

"Utopia's sponsoring a party in London at the Berkeley Hotel. I won't be there until late, so I want you to escort Cat. It just so happens that her father, David Asquith, is hosting it for us. But he's going to be quite busy."

"This is getting complicated," Clay said, confused. "What does Cat's father have to do with a party for Utopia?"

"He's been representing Nicholson in his government dealings for years. Represents Utopia now, too - working on our little SEC problem. He's flying in a handpicked entourage from the States for tonight, everyone of whom is important to Nicholson or Utopia. We wantta show them a good time."

"Why do you think I was invited to come along?" Cat squeaked proudly.

Clay looked at his watch. They were twenty minutes out of Amsterdam. He broke off the conversation and went back to the cockpit. They had to circle around Schipol and land to the south and then taxi two miles back up to the north side of the field to the private aircraft terminal, so they were five minutes behind flight plan when they arrived. As soon as Clay shut down the two turbines on the left side of the Jet Star, a black Mercedes pulled out of the shadow of the terminal and started heading toward the aircraft. Clay unstrapped, leaving the two starboard engines still idling, and hurried down the steps to meet it. A muscular looking man, medium height, solid jaw, dark hair, dressed in a grey suit and wearing dark sunglasses stepped out of the Mercedes and held open the door. A tall, gaunt man with slicked down black hair emerged. He was about sixty years old, Clay guessed. He was wearing a dark blazer, but no tie, and he had on sunglasses too, so that Clay could not see his eyes, only that the skin underneath them was pock-marked and pallid. Nicholson glided stiffly past Clay and handed him a briefcase without as much as a nod. His associate handed Clay a suitcase and, as his left ankle twisted at a near ninety-degree angle causing an awkward limp, he followed Nicholson up the steps to board the aircraft. As he did, his suit coat blew back in the wind, and Clay could not help but notice the revolver strapped in a holster under his arm.

Ten minutes later the Jet Star was in the air again, heading out over the North Sea and the English Channel. Clay stayed in the cockpit during the short flight, delegating the cocktail serving chores to his co-pilot. He never really got to see Nicholson. When they taxied up to the terminal at Heathrow another limousine was waiting, and Howie and Nicholson and the obvious bodyguard were off the plane and into it before Clay finished completing the post flight checklist. Half an hour later he and Cat were in a taxi and on their way to the Berkeley, a quiet, sumptuously indulgent hotel tucked down a side street off Knightsbridge, overlooking Hyde Park. They checked into their rooms at four o'clock and had two hours to rest before the cocktail reception.

At six o'clock Clay took the elevator up to Howie's suite on the top floor. Cat was almost ready. She had changed into a long blue dress accented with only a single strand of pearls. She looked very elegant. They took the elevator down to the mezzanine to the Berkeley's largest private reception area, a large wood-paneled room outfitted with an oak bar, numerous old, comfortable looking chairs and sofas, and three lavish round serving tables piled high with shrimp, canapés and caviar. The room had an eighteen foot high ceiling supporting several chandeliers. Halfway to the ceiling was a semicircular balcony, an oval stairway leading up to it, off of which were two smaller private meeting rooms. Perhaps a dozen people were there ahead of them when they arrived, most congregated near the bar. Cat's father greeted them at once and introduced them around, and Clay quickly understood how Asquith had gained his reputation as a mover and shaker. He was midfifties, sophisticated, glib and cool, with wavy grey hair and a faint trace of an educated Boston accent. He dominated the conversations with subtle name dropping and little risqué jokes. In the next few minutes the reception room started filling with guests, and Clay and Cat were busy meeting people - important people - and trying to remember names. They met several Washington lawyers and New York bankers, two members of the House of Representatives, a ranking member of the Senate Armed Services Committee; and their wives. They bumped into two union officials who Clay had met before. They were with a couple of young, sexy looking English bimbos and unabashedly boasted how Asquith had arranged the dates. Clay remembered the officials from the airport in Nassau when they had turned over two suitcases each containing eight thousand one hundred dollar bills to one of his passengers, a courier for Utopia, before he flew the cash back for deposit in Monaco. The two managed a Teamsters Union pension fund, he knew, and Clay had always assumed the cash was an undercover payoff for shady pension fund loans made to the Mafia. He wondered if any more suitcases were being delivered at the Berkeley tonight.

Howie arrived about six-thirty and ushered Cat and Clay along with him as he worked the room, collaring guests one by one and preaching the Utopia mantra. He kept at it non-stop until Asquith approached and interrupted him, introducing a newly arrived guest, a recently appointed SEC Commissioner, a short, neat little man with sandy hair and small dainty hands who smiled nervously. Howie immediately looped his arm over the Commissioner's shoulders and signaled to Clay. "Take Cat and get her another drink. The Commissioner and I wantta talk."

Clay and Cat made themselves scarce. They were standing by an hors d'oeuvre table helping themselves to caviar when Nicholson arrived, wearing a tuxedo and red vest, a floppy red handkerchief dangling from his breast pocket. Asquith met him at once and ushered him through the crowd, numbering about seventy now, and straight toward the Senator from the Armed Services Committee. Clay watched the two men meet, shake hands and smile, and as they did he watched Nicholson's eyes slowly take the Senator's measure. Nicholson wasn't wearing his sunglasses now. His eye sockets were dark and deeply hollowed - eyes like Auschwitz eyes, Clay thought, the kind of eyes that greeted passengers getting off the trains with smiles before sending them to the showers. In less than a minute Nicholson and the Senator walked over and up the stairs to the balcony above the reception area and into one of the private rooms off it. They shut the door. Clay looked around. There was an odor in the air. He couldn't see it, but he could detect the pungent smell.

Cat obtained another drink offered by an affable waiter, and they walked over next to a pillar in the corner. "What the hell are we doing here, Cat?" Clay asked her. "Do you really enjoy all this bullshit?"

"Oh Clay, don't be so provincial. This is big time!" Cat said as she raised her glass and bumped into another waiter, causing her drink to spill. As the embarrassed young man rushed to help her sop up the stain on her dress, Clay surveyed the room. People were still arriving, and it was very crowded now.

"Jeezus!" he gasped all of a sudden.

"What's the matter?" Cat said, as she looked at him and saw the color go out of his face.

Clay stared at a man at the bar. The man's back was to him, but every now and then he turned his head and Clay could get a good view of his profile. He was wearing a dark blue suit, not a uniform, but there was no mistaking him. Clay grabbed Cat by the arm and started steering her through the crowd and away from the bar. "What's the matter?" Cat asked again.

"There's a man at the bar," Clay said with a deep breath. "It's Admiral Martin, the guy who had me court martialed!"

Cat did a slow double-take. "Are you sure?" she asked, clutching Clay's wrists.

"Could I ever forget. It's time I get the hell out of here, Cat."

"Let's go up to my room," she said, still grasping his wrists. They started toward the exit hallway, but at the same time they saw David Asquith taking the Admiral in tow, moving across the room in front of them. They stopped, turned away and waited. A few seconds later the Senator emerged from the room on the balcony and descended the stairs rapidly. He nodded to Asquith and the Admiral as he passed. Then Clay saw Asquith pat the Admiral on his shoulder and Martin trotted up the stairs very unobtrusively, entering the same room the Senator had just left.

"This is getting too interesting," Clay said to Cat. "Let's stay." He steered her back to the hors d'oeuvre table. A waiter came by with glasses of champagne on a tray, and they each grabbed one. Clay's mind was clicking away. Martin, he knew, and much to his chagrin, had been promoted to Vice Admiral since the court martial. Clay didn't know what Martin's job was now, but he did know that he was observing a highly clandestine meeting, obviously pre-arranged, between a very high ranking military officer and the head of the largest defense contractor in the world. It had to mean something. Just then he felt a tap on his shoulder and turned around. Staring him in the face, of all people, was *Cindy Sue!*

"Clay! I don't believe it. My first night in Europe, and I bump into you!"

"Cindy Sue! What are you doing here?" Clay said, dumbfounded.

"Tim got a complimentary invitation from this Utopia outfit. Three free nights at the Savoy, if you can believe that. But after that we're taking off for two weeks on a tour of the continent. I'm finally going to see Europe, Clay. We're gonna visit eight countries!"

"Why how nice," Cat interjected with a sarcasm only she could manage. "You'll have almost two whole days to see each one."

"Where is Tim now?" Clay asked.

"He's off somewhere talking to a Mr. Asquith. That's who arranged the invitation for us."

Before they could talk further, the concierge came to the middle of the room and commanded everyone's attention. A row of limousines were lined up outside the hotel waiting to take the guests to the theatre, and the concierge announced it was time to leave. "Well, I guess I'd better go find Tim," Cindy Sue said as she stared over the crowd. "He has a meeting in the morning with the man who owns Utopia, a Mr. Nussbaum. They have some important banking business to discuss. But if you're still here after that, why don't we try to get together?"

"Who in the hell was that?" Cat asked as Cindy Sue pushed her way toward the door.

"Would you believe my ex-wife," Clay said, shaking his head, still in a state of disbelief.

The reception room started thinning out quickly. Clay watched as Admiral Martin emerged from the room on the balcony and go down the stairs and out the exit. He took Cat by the arm and walked her over to Howie. As they neared him, Asquith barged up, looking anxious, and Clay heard him ask, "what do you think about the Commissioner?"

"For the right price, he'll deal," Howie muttered quietly. Asquith shrugged, as if to say he'd known it all the time.

Asquith left with the crowd, but Howie stayed. "I can't stand theatre," he remarked drunkenly as he lifted the last flute of champagne off one of the waiter's trays. "The kitten and I are going out to dinner. Hang around tomorrow, Clay. I'll call you. I may want you to fly to Switzerland." He took Cat by the arm and brushed past

Clay toward the stairs. Nicholson was just coming down. "How did it go?" Clay heard Howie say.

"Excellent. Very excellent," Nicholson said, and Clay saw that Auschwitz smile again. "I think it's been a very profitable evening for both of us." Clay eased away and took the elevator up to his room. He lay in bed for a long time, thinking.

What had been going down tonight? The bankers and lawyers were undoubtedly there because they had many wealthy clients who they could advise on how to funnel money into Utopia's off-shore accounts - for fees, of course. The Teamsters officials were probably just very good customers who could be counted on regularly to siphon large amounts out of the pension funds into private investment accounts at Utopia. Clay knew that HBN Aviation was in a fight to the death competing for a defense department contract award for the next generation of navy fighter aircraft. That could certainly explain the presence of a Senator from the Armed Services Committee that would ultimately decide the award. Martin's role he could not fathom yet, but a man like Nicholson would not be meeting with an Admiral unless he was after something. The SEC Commissioner was new, from a different political party than the one he replaced and now one of the three out of five votes Utopia needed to be approved to market its funds in the States, which, if it could be arranged, would be a gigantic coup. For the four years Clay had been flying for Utopia, he had not ever been allowed to fly any Utopia aircraft into the States because of a warrant initiated by the SEC that would have enabled the aircraft to be seized by Customs. Most everyone he had met tonight had some good reason to be there - except Tim Collins. Tim was a big fish in Creekwood, but Creekwood was surely too small a pond for Utopia's concern. *Why had Tim been there?* Clay fell asleep still pondering.

Howie telephoned Clay early the next afternoon and invited him up to his suite. "Where's Cat?" Clay asked as he sat down around the coffee table with Howie.

"Out shopping at Harrod's. That goddamn broad must think I'm made out of money. But forget about her. I want you to fly to Zurich in the morning and open a few bank accounts for some of our new customers."

Clay frowned. "I don't know much about Swiss bank accounts."

"Well, if you're gonna be involved in the business, it's about time you learned. It's not very complicated." He pushed a pile of manila envelopes across the table. "All you have to do is take these and fly to Zurich. They contain all the necessary instructions. Take a taxi to the Union Credit Bank. Here's the address. It's on a side street just east off the Bahnhofstrasse. Utopia owns it. Ask for Ernst Biderman, our manager. He'll be expecting you before noon and will take care of the rest. You should be able to finish everything and be back here by late afternoon. I'll have a courier meet you at Heathrow to pick up the documents. Cat will be there too. I want you to fly her back to Nice tomorrow night. I'll be staying here. In fact, I'm going to the States for a few days."

"No kidding!" Clay was surprised. "I thought there was an arrest warrant out for you in the States."

"Aw, that was nothing. It's just that the SEC banned Utopia from soliciting investors in the States unless I let them see our records. I couldn't do that. It would've been the end of Utopia. So, a couple of years ago they subpoenaed me to testify before the Commission. I didn't show up, so I was held in contempt or something. It's no big deal. Asquith was able to get the charge dropped, and we got everything else worked out with the Commissioner last night. By next month we should be able to able to start selling in the States - and this time legitimately."

"Where does the Swiss bank come in?"

"As you'll find out, it's not much of a bank. We just use it as a conduit to add an extra layer of security. Let me explain. Let's call it part of your education. Some of our customers are more important than others. From time to time they get money from somewhere that they don't want anyone to know about, or where it came from, or where it's going. They want individual private banking services handled securely and discretely. You follow me?"

"Sort of," Clay said, wary now.

"You see, even though we won't give the SEC any of our records or account files, Monaco could always grab them. And some of our *extra-special* account holders don't want to take any chances. That's why we have a Swiss bank." Howie pulled out a pen and started sketching boxes and arrows on a notepad. "First, we set up a secret numbered bank account for those extra-special guys at Union Credit. Usually they're opened with just a token deposit. Clean money. Taxes paid on it. We call them VIP accounts. The deposit then goes into a trust account that Union Credit opens and transfers under *its* name to Utopia's management company in Monaco, such as Union Credit VIP Account Z25. That's the only record kept in Switzerland –

that initial deposit. The next step - and an important one - Union Credit signs over to the customer a power of attorney, in bearer form, authorizing whomever has the power in his possession to operate the Z25 account at Utopia anyway he wants. He can make deposits, withdrawals, transfers, give us instructions to make specific investments for him, or whatever. Of course, we encourage him to invest most of his money in our funds. For instance, say he wanted to invest a million dollars in Utopia Fund without anyone knowing it. He deposits the cash with us in his designated Z25 Union Credit trust account in Monaco. You've hauled enough of our couriers around to know how the cash gets there. We then issue shares of Utopia Fund in the name of Union Credit for the benefit of the Z25 trust account. It's an ingenious system. Preserves complete anonymity. It's legal and as secure as you can get. If Monaco ever cracked down and wanted to get into Utopia's books, the VIP accounts would all be in Union Credit's name. We don't have very many of these type of accounts, and most of them represent big dollars unless they are a favor we do for someone in exchange for a quid pro quo, such as the SEC Commissioner. No one can ever connect the identity of the accounts with the transactions taking place and the balances they contain unless they get access to the statements at Utopia and the dossiers at Union Credit at the same time." Howie chuckled. "That's because I keep a duplicate set of the VIP statements locked up in my office out at the chateau, so if Switzerland or Monaco got a hold of just one set, I could get the account numbers switched at the other location so fast that they could never be connected."

"Is that what I'm doing tomorrow, opening some secret accounts for those *extra-special* VIP customers?"

"Whatta you think?" Howie grinned. "You saw who was here last night."

Clay took off early the next morning and was in Zurich by eleven o'clock. A taxi deposited him at Union Credit thirty minutes later. The bank was located on a narrow side street about six blocks from the Paderplatz, and it looked nothing like a bank; more like a nondescript four story townhouse. Clay entered the foyer, crossed to the elevator and pressed the button for the third floor upon which a single set of double doors awaited him. Next to the doors, above a doorbell, was a small golden nameplate that said simply: Union Credit Bank Ag. Clay pressed the buzzer, and in a few seconds the door was opened by a receptionist - bleached blonde - awesome chest - a gum chewer. He stepped inside and announced, "Clay Anderson to see Herr Biderman." He glanced about as he waited. The entire operation occupied only three rooms and a reception area. The door to the room off to his left was closed, but its upper half was glass and through it he could see that it was a very large room that housed a bookkeeping department; three clerks, files and their desks. Behind the receptionist's desk was a conference room that had a long table covered with a green cloth, and to his right, Biderman's office. That was all. Five employees.

Ernst Biderman emerged from his office wearing a ludicrous smile. "Ah, Mr. Anderson," he said very formally as he extended his hand. "We've been expecting you. Come right this way." Biderman was surprisingly young for a Swiss bank manager, but his mannerisms were older than his age. He was very prim, the kind of person who always looked as if he should be wearing a tie. His handshake was limp, and he had a habitually nervous smile that caused one side of his pencil thin mustache to curl up and give his face a strange lop-sided look. With as much pomp as he could muster, he escorted Clay into the conference room and introduced him to one of the most important functionaries of the Swiss banking system - the counselor at law. The counselor was typical Swiss, quietly serious and perfunctory; no time for small talk. He asked for the envelopes. There were seven in all, each containing a passport, a London bank cashier's check for ten thousand dollars payable to Union Credit, and a signed power of attorney authorizing the counselor to act as agent in the opening of an account. Very methodically, the counselor signed seven documents that Biderman placed before him attesting to his powers to open the accounts. He next executed a series of trust agreements that directed the bank to open seven new accounts and transfer the deposits to private investment trust accounts at Utopia in Monaco, such accounts to be held in Union Credit's name, as agent. Biderman then filled out and signed authorization forms in duplicate for each new account, assigned each of them a number and a code, xeroxed copies of the passports and placed the paperwork for each in a separate dossier. Next he called in his secretary, handed her the dossiers, told her to deposit the checks and to telecopy the authorization forms to Utopia, along with a wire transfer of seventy thousand dollars for the seven new trust accounts. With that task completed, he handed the passports and copies of the new account authorizations over to the counselor, and said expansively, "now, let's have lunch while we wait for a reply. The telecopies will take six minutes a page."

They went down the street for a simple lunch, if one can have a simple lunch in Switzerland. Still, they were finished and back at the bank within an hour. A telex from Monaco was on Biderman's desk. It confirmed receipt of the deposits and listed the account numbers established in Union Credit's name for each. Biderman wrote each of the account numbers down on separate forms that were in a stack on his desk, hastily scribbled his signature on the bottom of each one and handed them to the counselor. "Here are the bank's powers of attorney for your clients," he said amiably. "They can do whatever they want with their accounts at Utopia now."

The counselor took the powers, the passports and deposit receipts, collated them, and handed them to Clay to place back in the original seven envelopes. Then he ceremoniously announced that the transactions were complete. Before the three men finished shaking hands, the receptionist with the big boobs walked in and informed Clay that a taxi was waiting. She walked him down to the street, held open the taxi's door, and handed the driver a voucher covering the cost of the ride to the airport. "What a system," Clay whispered to himself as the taxi pulled away from the curb.

The Jet Star landed at Heathrow at four o'clock, and Cat and one of Howie's couriers were waiting as it taxied up to the terminal. Clay turned the envelopes over to the courier, a quiet, shifty-eyed fellow, and the courier promptly left. By five o'clock the Jet Star was in the air again, heading for Nice. Clay leveled it off at twenty-seven thousand feet, turned the aircraft over to his co-pilot and went back to the cabin. "If you want a drink you can get your own this time," he told Cat pointedly. He poured himself a coke and sat down beside her. "How are things going now with you and Howie?" he asked.

"He keeps me in style. We go to lots of parties. But I must admit that after three years he is getting to be a bore."

"Why don't you move out?"

"And do what? Go home? I tried *that* three years ago, as you know. Didn't work."

"What does your father think about you living over here with Howie?"

"My father! The great David Asquith! What a laugh. I introduced him to Howie. He doesn't care. Never did. In fact, he's probably the main reason I'm here."

"How's that?"

"He and my mother had a miserable life together. He cheated on her. And he never paid any attention to me...until one summer I came home from boarding school and he sexually abused me."

"Your father!"

"Yes. My father very much liked stroking a fourteen year old and teaching her how to make him feel good by fondling him too."

"What an asshole." Clay was incensed.

"Fortunately, he and my mother divorced later that year and I didn't have to live with him anymore. It was quite a coincidence that he ended up marrying Darcy's mother a few years later. I warned Darcy to be careful of him. As I got older he invited me to some of his parties, mainly to help entertain his clients. The parties were fun. I guess that's the only thing I know how to do. Entertain men." As she said it, a seductive stench creeped into her voice. She was wearing a short mini-skirt and a blouse at least two sizes too small. It was stretched so tight it looked like the buttons were ready to pop. She was intimately familiar with the interior of the Jet Star. She reached over and flipped a switch. The sofa started sliding down flat, and a metal screen dropped from the ceiling to the floor, enclosing them in a snug little cocoon in the rear of the cabin. "There. That's much more comfortable," she said as she leaned back against a pillow and stretched out sensuously so that Clay could see up her skirt. "I've heard about something called the 'mile-high club'. Any chance you'd like to indoctrinate me as a member?" She asked the question with a coy little grin.

"Knock it off, Cat."

"Oh, come on. Howie won't mind. He knows I've fooled around."

"Not with me."

"If I remember, there was one night in Cagnes?"

"That was before the twins, Cat. History. I'm a devoted, faithful father now – no different than a husband."

"What makes you think Marianna's so faithful? She's on the road with Tommy Mitchell all the time, and I know he has the hots for her. "

"Which shows Tommy has good taste," Clay said, becoming irritated.

Cat sat up and raised one knee and rested her chin on it so that her crotch was in plain view. "I'd think you'd get bored with just one woman, especially one who's away all the time."

Clay felt a stirring, and for a few seconds he was tempted. Cagnes wasn't so long ago that he couldn't remember. But then he thought about the drunk Marianna had thrown...how hurt she had been...the twins. "Cover up, Cat," he said softly. "You're my friend. And Marianna's friend. Let's keep it that way." He flipped the switch to raise the metal partition.

"Okay. Sorry. Just testing you," Cat said with a playful pout. She reached into her purse, pulled out a gold case and extracted a neatly rolled and wrapped cigarette. She offered it to Clay. "Want a toke? Best grass I ever had."

"No thanks. And you ought to lay off that stuff."

"You'll never guess where it came from."

"No. I wouldn't."

"You're ex-wife's husband. Expensive case. Good grass. He gave it to Howie as a gift. He's a new customer. Howie thinks your Mr. Collins is just another drug dealing, tax dodging, money launderer. And he's met enough of them to know."

Clay turned and headed toward the cockpit, not saying a word, leaving Cat alone, smoking and looking despondent. Nor did he say much to his co-pilot during the last hour into Nice. His mind was still at Union Credit. He had been at the table and able to watch the details of most of the transactions, and though he could not read the names, he had been able to catch glimpses of the faces on the passports. One he did not recognize. A second he did not know but was certain he had seen the face at the party at the Berkeley. Another was a picture of a man in a white navy uniform with lots of gold braid and three stars on his shoulders. Admiral Martin, for sure. There was also no doubting the faces of the Senator and the SEC Commissioner. Then there was the image of Tim Collins that had astonished him. He could hardly conceal his stare until the next passport photo astounded him even more. It had been almost a dozen years, time enough for appearances to change, but the last photo looked to him very much like that of Terry Malone!

Angelo met Clay at the airport, and they drove up to La Gaude in the Alfa together. It was dark, but the air was clear. It had rained while he was gone, and the forest fires had subsided for the time. Marianna had a tiny blaze going in the old stone fireplace when he arrived. The children were asleep. She gave him an espresso, and they lay down on some pillows on the floor in front of the fire. It was pleasant in the room. The windows were open, letting in a cool night breeze. The fire was warm, but not too warm. It gave the room a nice pine smell. Clay touched Marianna's hand, and she looked at him with her squirrel-like look, the one he had not seen in a long time, and then she said, "So how was London? Good trip?"

"Terrible trip. Howie is a criminal, Marianna. Big time."

She jumped. What do you mean?" she said, and she sat up abruptly.

"Just what I said. On this last trip I finally learned all about it first hand."

"Well...don't just lie there like a dummy. Tell me."

"Neither of us is blind, Marianna. We've both known that Utopia's not the most lily white institution in the world; that it's always been haven for hot money looking for a safe place to hide."

"So? Are Swiss banks any different?"

"That's what Howie said. But Swiss banks don't have salesmen out combing the world with quite the same fervor that Utopia does soliciting the crooked money - or sending pilots like me to transport it so that it can be laundered safely through Utopia's network. Utopia's evil, Marianna, a cobweb of trusts and joint ventures and banks and asset management firms - all designed to dodge taxes and move money around in a way that it can never be traced. If you knew how many times I've picked up couriers with suitcases full of cash, it would blow your mind. I hate myself for it...I'll never understand why I've stayed."

She nestled against him, trying to soothe him. "Clay, listen, all that may make Howie a bad person. But has he broken any laws?"

"He tells me he hasn't, but he's lying. And now he's getting me involved. I spent this morning opening secret bank accounts in Zurich. You'd never guess for whom?" He told her about his trip for the next half hour, about Howie and Nicholson being in business together; the party in London; Zurich; the secret numbered accounts he had witnessed being opened - the Senator - the SEC Commissioner - Admiral Martin . He did not mention Tim Collins or Terry Malone.

When he finished, Marianna put her arm around him and dug her nails into the back of his neck. "You need to get out. Clay. Now!"

He lit a cigarette and took a long, slow drag before he said anything. "That's not so easy," he said finally. "If I walk out now Utopia will just go on, spreading its evil, continuing to corrupt. I can't tolerate that, knowing that I was a part of it for so long. Something has to be done about it."

"You're talking crazy again, Clay."

"Maybe," he said coldly. "Things are very confusing right now. My brain says get the hell out of Utopia as fast as I can. My conscience says I have to go home and see my mother - and soon, no matter what the risk. But deep down, something says stay - stay and get some proof - put Howie and Nicholson out of business... and Admiral Martin and all the rest of the extra-special secret account holders, whoever they are." For a moment his eyes shined dangerously. Then his voice cracked. "Right now I don't know what to do, Marianna. I'm all mixed up."

Marianna started rubbing the back of his neck. "Clay, about your mother, there's something I haven't told you... "

He tensed. *"What?"* he said, looking as if he had heard a shot.

"No, it's nothing like that. She's all right now. I wrote her a letter the day you left telling her everything about us and invited her to La Gaude. Today, I decided couldn't wait for an answer, so I went into Nice and called her. I told her about Cassie and Cody and she almost cried she was so happy." Clay stared at her blankly as she ran on. "We should have told them sooner. They're going to Texas for a few weeks in September. Your mother is going to be taking some treatments there, and she says the doctors are very hopeful. I asked her to come see us before she goes."

"What did Dad think about that?"

"I didn't ask him. I just went to American Express and bought them two airline tickets to Paris and mailed them. He won't let her come without him. And you know what she said? ...Wild horses couldn't keep her away."

Clay reached over and hugged her, and then kissed her on the eyelids. "You're a good woman, Marianna Haizet," he said with a tenderness he had not displayed in months.

She kissed him back. "If you really mean that, then let's have a bottle of champagne. I've had one on ice all day just waiting for you to get home." She went into the kitchen. The fire had gone down. Clay added a couple of sticks of driftwood and stirred it. He blew on it awhile and started it blazing again. Marianna came back with the bottle and two glasses, and they lay down on their backs in front of the fire and talked. They talked about many things. They finished the champagne and then had a scotch. About one o'clock in the morning, Marianna sat up. "Clay?"

"Hmm..."

"What about making a deal?"

"What do you mean?" he said, rolling over.

"You know a lot of things. Maybe if you told the FBI what you know, you could make a deal. Get a pardon or something"

Clay pushed himself up and started pacing back and forth. She could see his wheels turning. "What time is it in the States?" he asked anxiously.

"About seven in the morning."

He walked over to the telephone and dialed the long distance operator.

"Who are you calling?"

"Robert. I'm going to ask him to try to arrange a meeting."

"A meeting...with whom?"

"Randy Whitney. He's one guy who believed in me. And he works for the Justice Department now, in the Criminal Division for the Attorney General."

XI

༄

TOWER IN THE SKY

Sometimes, but not often, a rain comes to the South of France in late July. This year one came for three days. It fell gently and soaked in, and with it a light wind swirled down the Var River Valley, picking up dust and dissipating the suffocating red haze. When the rain ended the sirocco had vanished...just gone in the same mysterious manner it had arrived. The hills turned to a soft green overnight, the soil in the valley breathed and became fertile again, and the smell of jasmine filled the air. The only traces of the oppressive days in July were the grain fields that had withered and turned brown during the sirocco, the dried up cracks in the land, and the burned out timberlines that tracked their way in a speckled fashion across the plain and through the foothills all the way to the base of the mountains. But the countryside was hardy and resilient. The valley land was deep and rich. The fields were already starting to reawaken and blend into a hue of gold and red and saffron. In the winter the rains would come, the cracks in the ground would close and the powdery ash on the timber would wash away. In the spring warmth would flood the hills and the earth would burst into bloom. The land along the coast would break forth in bougainvillea and roses, the valley would be carpeted in grass and carnations, and in the uplands, on the hillsides underneath the cork oaks and umbrella pines, fields of fragrant lavender would flourish - and the sirocco of 1970 would be all but forgotten.

August came, and with it days that were bright and clear, skies that were cloudless. The mountains stood up against the sky in the north and the east. The sun was warm, but not too warm. The night breezes off the Mediterranean caressed the coast and gave the air a refreshing, tangy taste of mint. August was the month of idyllic weather, and the French all knew it. It had always been that way. It was the month half the country closed up shop and went on holiday - and in sports cars, trucks, and sedans hauling campers and trailers and sailboats behind, or on motorcycles and mopeds, some hitchhiking with backpacks - they formed in caravans and all headed south for the Cote.

On the second of August Jean Pierre and Darcy arrived in La Gaude to stay for a month. Their two years in Senegal had not changed them much. They both looked dark and tan and healthy. Jean Pierre still wore his hair cropped to the nub in military fashion. Darcy was still soft and warm, and very much on the way to becoming a settled-in mother of a four and a half year old beautiful young daughter, Jacqueline, who had Darcy's coloring and dark curls and mimicked her father when she walked, strutting in his military fashion. Jean Pierre was settled-in too. In fact, if there was any noticeable change in them, it was that they were both content now, content in a married, family sense that Marinna and Clay still had not achieved. And they were happy. They were moving to Paris in September. Jean Pierre had been promoted to major and transferred to a post in Versailles. He had paid his dues, and the hard life was over for them now.

Two days after Jean Pierre and Darcy moved in, Marianna and Clay flew to Paris. Their Air France flight landed at Orly at eleven o'clock on a sunny Friday morning, the same time that Bill and Lara Stoner's flight from New York was scheduled to arrive. They went straight to the international terminal and waited anxiously in a crowd outside the customs area. Clay saw her then, and his face flooded with relief. He thought maybe she would be different, but his mother was still as beautiful as he remembered her, scintillating, looking more like a woman in her thirties than the forty nine years that she was. She was pale and looked tired, but other than that he saw little change in her - except for one eyelid that drooped ever so slightly. His dad, though, had the appearance of a shell of a man. His face was drawn. His eyes were lowered and they darted about nervously, unsmiling, as he shuffled through the crowd loaded down with baggage, looking out of place. Clay was finally able to see in person the effect of the strain he had been going through.

"Mrs. Stoner! Over here!" Marianna called out to them. Lara Stoner's eyes sparkled suddenly, and she actually ran to meet them.

She threw her arms around Clay and hugged and kissed him. She turned to Marianna and reached out and clutched one of her hands in the two of hers. "Thank you so much for asking us to come," she said as she blinked back a tiny, joyful tear.

Lara could not sit still, and she bubbled with a childlike exuberance on the taxi ride in from the airport. She kept looking and pointing at things with all the excitement of a young schoolgirl and asking Marianna questions. Clay had reserved two rooms at the Plaza Athenee, and as soon as they checked in, Lara was eager to go out and start seeing the sights. Bill Stoner groaned. He was too tired, he said. Marianna and Clay took his cue, and they insisted that they all go to their rooms and nap for awhile.

They went out in the early evening to Maxim's for dinner. Maxim's made Bill Stoner uncomfortable. Not just because it was the first time he had ever been to such a fancy restaurant. That would make many men uncomfortable. No. Bill Stoner was the type of man who could go to Maxim's a hundred times and never feel comfortable with the white gloved maitre d's and waiters hovering about, menus in French, the pompous flare of the wine steward opening a bottle, flaming crepes suzette prepared at the table. Clay was aware of that; but he also knew that his mother would adore it. And she did. She even had a brandy alexander after dinner and got tipsy. Afterwards they went to the Lido for the early show and ordered a bottle of champagne. The semi-nude dancers made Bill Stoner just as uncomfortable as the waiters at Maxim's. In the Ozarks men did not take their women to those kinds of places, and when Lara insisted on staying to see the late show, he started to protest. She would hear none of it, and she got her way. It was after three in the morning when they arrived back at the hotel and retired to their rooms. Marianna and Clay were unable to sleep right away. They made love slowly, peacefully until the grey of dawn started creeping through their window. Marianna's head was on his chest and he was stroking her back as she stared out the window. "Do you think we should have sided with your father and insisted that she leave earlier?" she asked wistfully.

"No," he said in a soft voice. "She was happy tonight. She's dreamed all her life about going to Europe. Now that she's here, we're going to see that she enjoys it. And we're going to treat her just like nothing is wrong."

Marianna leaned her head back and closed her eyes. "She's an amazing woman, Clay. She has such a zest for life."

They toured Paris the next day, with Marianna serving as guide: the Eiffel Tower, lunch in an outdoor cafe on the Champs d'Elysee, the Louvre, Notre Dame. Marianna hailed a taxi afterwards and directed it to drive up the Boulevard des Capucines toward the Opera. In front of the Olympia Music Hall, she halted the driver. They exited the taxi and she led them inside. The hall was not very modern or elegant, but it was steeped in tradition. "I just wanted you all to see it," Marianna said impishly as they stood in the dim light looking at the stage and the ornaments on the ceiling. "Piaf gave her last concert here. I haven't told anyone yet, but I'm giving a concert up there on that stage in December."

Clay was surprised, and he could see that his parents were even more so. He started to explain about Marianna's singing career, but his mother cut him off. "Marianna wrote me all about it," she said. "And since I received her letter I've read everything I could find in the States about Kira Chastain. I bought her two albums and I've listened to them a dozen times. So has Bill. We think she's fantastic. Our only regret is that we've never been able to see her perform."

That evening they taxied to the Place St. Germain-des-Pres and found themselves a ringside seat at the Cafe Deux Magots, a noted second home of the expatriate writers of the twenties. They ordered wine and watched the street scenes, artists sketching portraits on the sidewalk, strolling musicians passing hats among the crowd for contributions, apache dancers performing in the street and then scurrying after coins tossed to them by the crowd. They left and dined early at a small nearby bistro on the Rue Jacob, unpretentious and much more to Bill Stoner's liking. He even ordered scampi instead of his usual steak and remarked that it was very good - and Marianna saw him starting to smile a little.

They checked out early on Sunday and drove out to Orly for their flight to Nice. They landed shortly after noon. Angelo was there with Jean Pierre's five-liter Citroen to meet them. They all packed into the car and headed toward Cagnes, and through it, and up the road into the hills. When they reached La Gaude, Angelo stayed behind at the car to tend to the suitcases as Marianna and Clay led his parents up the narrow cobblestone street to the villa. At the gate, Marianna said, "this is where Clay and I live." She unlatched the gate and ushered them into the courtyard.

Lara Stoner's eyes widened and fluttered in disbelief. "You live here! Why it's like a fairy tale! I've never seen such a beautiful place!" she gasped, truly overcome.

"Close your eyes," Marianna said, taking her by the arm and guiding her around the reflecting pool and through the courtyard ahead of the two men. She turned her head and looked at Clay and saw him nod. Then she said proudly, "Open." In front of them were Cassie and Cody, staring shyly. Three and one-half years old now, they were not used to visitors at the villa. Marianna and Clay, for the family's safety and protection, had kept them carefully sequestered. Cody was the first to utter a word. He walked formally toward Lara, held up his hand to touch hers, and in an almost worldly manner said, "I've heard about you. You are my grandmother. I'm so happy to meet you." Cassie ran and hugged Lara around the waist.

For the rest of August the courtyard at La Gaude echoed with the sounds of children and laughter. In her typical take-charge manner, Lara Stoner monopolized the children, and by the end of the first week Cassie and Cody and Jacqueline were all three calling her "Nanny." They would run to her whenever there was a fight to arbitrate, or cuts to be tended or tears to be dried. She read to them, told them stories, taught them new games, spoiled them, helped mold their little characters as she passed on to them how different her life had been growing up on a farm in the Ozarks. Marianna was overjoyed. She had August off, the first one in five years that she did not have to sing at the She-She. Her only scheduled engagement was a three hour concert on stage in the garden next to the Place Massena in Nice the third weekend of the month. The Band flew in from London to join her, and Clay took his parents to see her perform. It was almost as much a new experience for him as it was for them. He had not seen her sing in more than nine months - and she had changed. Her voice was richer now, projecting an intense feeling. She sang her French love songs in a voice that hovered between earthiness and eeriness and her ballads in a voice that was honest, urgent and loving. And when the band broke out in a driving, bluesy American guitar rhythm, she cut loose on the piano with a rich, warm vocal style and a bouncy, boogie-woogie New Orleans beat. Bill and Lara were enraptured, and Clay sat there too awed to speak. He had a hard time believing that this was the woman he had lived with for four years - the mother of his children.

Clay took the next two weeks off as the end of summer approached. Marianna and Darcy got up early in the mornings and went shopping in the village. They would come back with fresh

baked bread and croissants, juicy melons, and sausages and flowers, and then prepare a lavish breakfast for the rest of the household. They ate late - all together, including the children and Angelo
and Genevieve - around a large stone table on the second floor terrace underneath a large red awning that allowed them to look out
over the valley without being blinded by the sun. Sometimes they
stayed at La Gaude the entire day, just basking in the warm bluest
of blue air, the three women lying out on the upstairs patio, sunbathing and talking. Sometimes Darcy dabbled at painting; Marianna worked on new songs. Clay and Jean Pierre spent hours in
the courtyard with Bill Stoner, drinking beer and teaching him how
to play boules. On other days then went on excursions; to Haut-
de-Cagnes to show Bill and Lara the tiny apartment where they
had lived for two years; to lunch at the Cafe St. Jacque, spending
an afternoon just "hanging around," drinking wine under the oak
tree and watching the people in the square. They drove up into
the mountains to Grasse to visit the perfumeries, and to Monaco to
tour the palace and casino. Most days, though, they sojourned to
the Yacht Club in Antibes. Marianna bought Lara a bikini and she
wore it the first day. Bill was rattled. When she stepped out of her
skirt and he saw her, he turned crimson and did not know what to
say. In Creekwood she would have been a scandal. He had never
seen or heard of anyone in Creekwood wearing a bikini...but the
Cote was not Creekwood, and he held his tongue. He was not a
worldly man, but he could see that he need not be embarrassed.
She was just as natural as Marianna and Darcy. Her curves were not
quite as sharp and her flesh was more womanly. Still, in the eyes of
many men, she was every bit as alluring. And as the days passed
she grew younger, her tan deepened into a lush golden bronze, and
she did not look ill anymore.

The sad part was that it all had to end. On her last night in
La Gaude they all dressed for dinner. At seven o'clock they gathered outside in the courtyard: Clay and Marianna, Lara and Bill,
Jean Pierre and Darcy, Cassie, Cody, and Jacqueline. Angelo served
them wine and pate and caviar. Genevieve had been in the kitchen
all afternoon preparing a bouillabaisse. Jean Pierre was telling a
long story about some of his exploits with the Foreign Legion in
Africa when Lara reached over and touched Clay's hand. She nodded toward the door into the den, and they both quietly slipped
away.

In the den, with the door closed, Lara spoke. "Son, I had to talk to you before I leave. It may be a long time before I see you again. There are things I want you to know." Clay sat down. His mother's illness had not been mentioned the entire month. He wondered if she was going to talk about it now. To his relief, she continued down a different track. "You are my only child," she said, staring at him, one hand pulling at her cheek. "There's a reason for that. I almost died when I had you and could never have another. I guess that's why you're so special to me. When you got accepted to Annapolis, I was so proud. I thought it was your ticket out of the Ozarks, on to bigger things. That's why I may have seemed dismayed when you came home that Christmas with Marianna. Don't get me wrong - I liked her. But you have to realize son, that mothers can be very possessive. I didn't think you knew what you were doing. I thought you might still be in love with Cindy Sue and that Marianna was just a young girl you were infatuated with because she was different. I know better now. Marianna is different, but I think she's right for you. She's the kind of girl - woman now- that I very much would like to have as a daughter-in-law."

Genevieve called before Clay could say anything. Dinner was ready. Everyone gathered in the main dining room and stayed for three hours, stuffing themselves with salad and bouillabaisse and bread and wine. For dessert, Genevieve served a grand marnier soufflé. It was after midnight by the time they finished, and not even the incessant chirping of the cicadas disturbed anyone's sleep on Lara and Bill Stoner's last night in La Gaude.

Clay and Marianna drove his parents down to the airport very early the next morning to catch the Air France flight bound for Paris and New York. The farewell was brief. Clay looked at his mother now, as she kissed Marianna goodbye, laughing and looking tan and healthy, the way he wanted to remember her. The sun and the sea and the mountain air had worked a miracle, he thought...and hoped. He and Marianna stayed at the airport watching through the glass until the flight was in the air. Then they drove slowly back to La Gaude, slowly and aimlessly with Clay's mind up in the sky on the Air France flight with them. He did not see a single tree or flower or lilac bush the entire way.

Jean Pierre and Darcy left by car for Paris on the following Monday. A week later Clay was on a commercial flight to Paris, but not to see them. He was going to Paris to meet with Randolph James Whitney.

Since July Clay and Whitney had communicated several times, not directly, but by passing messages through Robert. Whitney was aware that Clay had some information that he thought was sensitive and would be valuable to the Justice Department. He also knew that Clay was living in Europe somewhere and would not come to Washington. He suggested meeting in Paris in September. He was attending an Interpol conference at the Intercontinental Hotel.

Clay was at Orly by mid-morning. He telephoned Whitney as soon as he landed and arranged to meet for lunch at the Cafe du Soir, a well known establishment near the Opera. At one o'clock Clay was waiting in a taxi parked across the street about a half block from the cafe. He saw Whitney arrive and enter. Clay pointed him out to the taxi driver and handed the driver a hundred franc note to deliver a message telling Whitney that plans had changed; that he was to go with the driver. As soon as the cabbie left, heading for the cafe, Clay scribbled out another note saying, "*meet me at the Cafe Bretagne. The taxi driver knows the way.*" He taped the note to the steering wheel, slid out, crossed the street and ducked down an alley. He saw Whitney and the cabbie come out, read the note, and drive away. He waited and watched another two minutes until he was convinced no one was following them, and then he hailed another taxi and instructed its driver to take him to the Bretagne, a quiet little bistro over on the Left Bank near the Invalides. Whitney was already there, seated at a table and perusing a menu when Clay walked in and sat down quietly beside him. "I'm sorry I had to lead you around this way," Clay started to apologize. Whitney cut him off.

"You're call last month...I regret it's taken us so long to meet, but the Justice Department doesn't just jump on a plane and fly across the ocean because someone wants to talk. For you I made an exception. I gather you don't think I'm a man of my word when I promised this meeting would be in total confidence!" Whitney said testily.

"Randy, Randy," Clay said, forcing a smile. "You work for the law. I'm an outlaw. I can't be too careful."

Whitney looked away and did not smile. He removed a pipe and fine leather grained tobacco pouch from his pocket, poured some of the tobacco into the pipe bowl, packed it down very meticulously, lit it, and took three strong puffs. He looked at Clay again and said coldly, professionally, "We both know what your status is.

So I want you to know before we go any further that you will get no special favors from me."

"I'm not here to ask favors."

"Good - because you won't get any, Clay. I stuck my neck out once for you. I was going to appeal your sentence and fight it all the way. Then you skipped out and made me look like a horse's ass."

"I'm sorry," Clay said softly. "But you said yourself that it was a kangaroo court; that I'd be locked up for months before my case could be reviewed. You shouldn't blame me too much if I decided to skip."

"Well, you made a mistake. I could have won that appeal, Clay. If I tried now, you wouldn't have a chance. Best I could do for you now is a plea and a year. So let's hear your story. "

"You might change your mind after you hear what I have to tell you. "

"I doubt it very seriously. But go ahead. Let's hear it. I've got an hour."

Clay hesitated, looking at Whitney, a brusque, successful hardened lawyer now, a much different person than the impressionable young man who had defended him less than five years ago. For a few seconds he thought about dismissing the entire idea, about just putting down his menu and stalking out into the sunshine and catching a plane back to Nice and forgetting the meeting with Whitney ever happened. Maybe the world deserves Utopia, he thought. Instead, he said, "I'm on to something, Randy. I don't know where it leads, but I think it reaches high up in Washington. It involves tax evasion and money laundering for sure. Political corruption. Probable bribery. I'm short on proof, but I know some names. I'll give them to you if you'll try to help me."

"So what else is new," Whitney said cynically. "I get names all the time, Clay. I'd probably be the richest man in the world if I had a dollar for every crook the Justice Department knows about but doesn't have enough evidence to prosecute. Unless you can come up with some specifics - hard evidence - we're both wasting our time."

"Have you ever heard of David Asquith?"

There was a perceptible tic in Whitney's left cheek. "Asquith? Sure, I've heard of him. He's the senior partner of Asquith, Armstrong, and Teasdale. Very important law firm in Washington, and he's one of the most important lobbyists in town. He's a good friend of my boss's boss, the Attorney General – and he's a rain-maker when it comes to raising campaign funds for the President."

"He's also H. B. Nicholson's lawyer."

"That's right," Whitney said, taking serious notice now.

"Have you ever heard of Utopia International?"

Whitney's eyebrows arched. "Certainly. Howard Nussbaum's organization based down in Monaco. I'm part of a task force that's been investigating it. How did you know?" He leaned forward, interested.

"I *didn't* know. But it's not Howie Nussbaum's organization, Randy. Nicholson owns control of it. It's a front for many of his business dealings. And that's not all. I'm sure the Teamsters' pension fund managers use it as a primary conduit for laundering their kickbacks from the mob. And I have good reasons for believing that some other important people in Washington are involved. Asquith's the go-between."

Whitney's eyes squinted, and he started puffing on his pipe in a rapid, spasmodic manner. "How did you learn all of this? Do you know it took us nine months of hard investigating just to find out what you know?"

"I can't tell you that. The important thing is that I do know, Randy."

"Well, you'll have to do better than that, Clay. You haven't told us anything we aren't onto already."

"Okay. I know that our old friend Admiral Martin opened a numbered bank account with Utopia in Switzerland in late July. I know that he met secretly with Nicholson the night before he opened it, and Asquith arranged the meeting. I also know that the same night he met with Martin, Nicholson had a highly clandestine meeting with a quite well known Senator – a ranking member of the Armed Services Committee." Whitney's pipe dropped out of his mouth, and he knocked over his drink. Clay went on. "I also know that Asquith arranged a meeting between Nussbaum and the new SEC commissioner; again, the same night. Three weeks later the Commission lifted its ban on Utopia from selling mutual funds in the States. Nussbaum arranged for the Senator and the Commissioner to open secret Swiss bank accounts also. So there. That's three names and some specifics. They're probably only the tip of the iceberg."

"How do you know all this?"

"Because I helped open the accounts," Clay said matter-of-factly.

Whitney was still mopping up his spilled drink. He glanced about nervously, and then whispered, "Clay, what you're saying is dynamite! The entire task force at Justice was flabbergasted when the SEC dropped its ban on Utopia. We thought we had all the evidence we needed to indict for money laundering and promoting tax evasion. We were all ready to prosecute when the Attorney General told us to drop the case. We never did understand why."

"What about him?"

"Who?"

"The Attorney General. Do you trust him?"

Clay saw Whitney's eyes narrow and stare blankly for a moment, then widen again. "Sure, I trust him. Even if he is one of Asquith's best friends."

"Then why are you so uptight?"

"The Martin - Senator - Nicholson connection. It's too much of a coincidence. You may not know about it, but HBN Aviation has been competing for a giant defense contract to build a new multipurpose fighter, one that can be used by both the air force and the navy. The Defense Department and the air force favored another manufacturer's design. Well....last month the Armed Services Committee turned them down and sided with the navy's recommendation. The entire six billion dollar contract was awarded to HBN. Guess who was in charge of the navy's evaluation program?"

"Admiral Martin?"

"You guessed it."

Clay leaned back in his chair, lit a cigarette, inhaled and sighed. He had known it. He knew there had to be a connection. He relaxed and smiled inwardly, all the way down to his toes. "So what do you think now?" he said. "Do we have a basis for working together?"

"We certainly do, Clay. I don't know how you get all your information, but you've given me enough leads to go back to Washington and start a hell of an investigation. I'll have to get some other departments involved, so it may take longer than you'd like. A few months, probably. But I'll see that it gets done, no matter who's toes get stepped on. If we can make a case, we'd want you to testify, of course. If that happens, there's a good chance we could arrange to get your court martial sentence taken care of. I can't promise, but I'll try."

"What can I do to help in the meantime?"

"Just keep your eyes open. We'll need more evidence. If you come up with anything else, call me. Let me give you my phone number." Whitney took a business card out of his wallet, wrote his home phone number on the back, and handed it to Clay. "Now, how can I get in touch with you?" he said quickly.

"Randy, I trust you completely," Clay said as sincerely as he knew how. "But I don't trust Washington. For the time being let's just stay in touch through Robert. He knows how to reach me if something's important."

"Robert. You know that kid's making a name for himself as a reporter for the New York Times. Your court martial may have established his career. His sister helped you escape, didn't she?"

"No comment."

"Okay. Have it your way," Whitney smiled for the first time as they both stood up. "It was good to see you again, Clay. I mean it."

They walked out of the dim restaurant into the bright sunlight together, and each summoned a taxi. Clay's took him to Orly, and he was home in La Gaude with Marianna in time for dinner.

A month passed, and with it the end of summer. September eased into October, the tourists went home, autumn came to the Cote, and the nights became sweater weather. The flowers and lush green hillsides faded into the background, the breeze picked up, the sea changed color from blue-green to grey, sailboats were hoisted up into dry dock, the beach deserted. Marianna was scheduled to leave for six weeks at the beginning of November, going first to London to meet the band and cut an album, followed by a concert tour timed for the release of the album; seventeen performances, one every other day in seventeen major European cities: London, Dublin, Manchester, Antwerp, Amsterdam, Copenhagen, Zurich and many others before ending on the fifteenth of December at the Olympia in Paris. She told Clay about a proposal Howie had made. Howie suggested that it would be a good idea for her to rest up before the tour, get away and totally unwind. He owned a small villa in Menorca and offered to let her use it for the rest of the month and take Clay with her. Clay was against the idea at first, not desiring any more association with Howie than was required, but Marianna prevailed. "We haven't really had any free time alone for what seems like ages, "she said. "And it comes with a sailboat." So, in mid-October, leaving the twins behind with Angelo and Genevieve, they took off for Menorca.

If one takes off from Nice and flies southeast on a heading of two hundred and twenty degrees for three hundred and thirty miles, and the wind does not drift him off course, he will pass over the island of Menorca, Isla del Amor, it is sometimes called by the natives, a twenty-five mile long, ten mile wide isolated speck in the sea. For its size, Menorca is an island of many contrasts. The people speak an old style Spanish, but with a strong French and Arab accent. Most of the island is a low, rolling limestone tableland garnished with hills and ravines and dozens of small beaches on sandy coves, or calas, as the Menorcans call them. There is a softness to that part of the landscape, a neat rural network of stone fences separating country villages and whitewashed farm houses that have wrought iron windows and water catchments on their roofs. But the north coast is different; wild, rocky, dark green with vegetation, and steep cliffs punctuated by gorges where the sea pounds in wintertime. Winter is short, but often accompanied by the Tremontana, a gale-like wind out of the north strong enough to cause the trees and bushes on the coast to all bend southward and give the area an abandoned, rebellious look. The north coast notwithstanding, Menorca is a quiet little island, especially in the off season. It had no scheduled air service from France. To get there one had to fly to the neighboring island of Mallorca, and take the daily ferry, or some other type of boat - or charter a plane.

Clay had decided to go by seaplane. He and Marianna were at the Nice aerodrome by nine o'clock on Sunday morning. Clay had rented a single-engine Otter, outfitted with pontoons, and his young French co-pilot was going to fly them to Menorca and ferry the plane back to Nice. The morning was bright and the weather clear, but Marianna was frightened. And not just because of the implications of the conversation between Clay and Whitney. The long flight over open water in a single engine aircraft made her nervous. After take-off Clay climbed in the back seat with her and tried to comfort her. "Listen," he said, his voice muffled by the steady chug of the six hundred horsepower engine, "I want you to stop worrying. The Utopia thing will work itself out somehow." He managed a smile, meant to reassure her.

She snuggled up to him and buried her face in his chest, and whispered. "Make me a promise, fella'. Let's just make love and not even mention Utopia for the next ten days."

He pulled her tight against him. "You know, you haven't called me fella' in a long time," he said, and he took a playful nip at her boobs.

They spotted Menorca about noon and flew along the rugged north coast until they saw the Bay of Fournelles, a deep water lagoon, their landmark, a three mile long glazed body of water almost completely enclosed by a maze of high reefs and shoals that protected it from the wind. They flew over the lagoon, and on the leeward side they saw three white sandy coves carved into the cliffs, each two hundred yards wide and harboring a large house cuddled in the rocks on the side of the cliff. The pilot banked the sturdy Otter into a very gentle one hundred and eighty degree turn, and they came down and landed softly in the lagoon with hardly a splash. They taxied in toward the middle cove, one protected by a jumble of huge rocks on each side that partially closed its mouth and cut the cove off from the rest of the lagoon. The Otter taxied through the narrow opening in the rocks and toward an old stone quay that jutted out from the beach. Two Menorcans were standing on the end of the quay, an old man and his son. They were waving their arms. The Otter taxied up to within ten yards of them, and then Clay opened the back door and threw them a rope and the pilot cut the engine. The Menorcans hauled the aircraft next to the quay, Clay handed them the luggage, and he and Marianna disembarked. They waved to the pilot and started walking down the quay. By the time they reached the foot of the cliff the aircraft had taxied through the breakwater and was making its takeoff run down the long narrow stretch of the lagoon. They stopped and watched it lift off and dip its wing to the right and set course toward Nice, and then they followed the Menorcans up a hundred stone steps, half way up the hillside to the house.

The next ten days were a precious time. Marianna and Clay found the solitude they both cherished. The house was a veritable retreat; split-level, snug and cozy, with two fireplaces and a huge master bedroom; a pinewood deck that jutted out over the water. The other two houses on the lagoon were vacant. The caretaker and his wife and son lived on a farm a mile away, and they only came by once every three days to change linen and check to see what was needed from the store. It was four miles to the nearest village and a restaurant. The aloneness was total - no work to be done, no children, no newspapers, no telephones. And the weather was good. The days were warm and sunny. The nights were crisp, but not too cold. Marianna and Clay wore sweaters in the morning. But by afternoon they were able to scamper naked in the surf and bronze their butts on the beach in the sun, out of the wind behind the shelter of the rocks. On the second day they walked the entire length of the lagoon exploring and searching for shells, feeling pleasant in the light breeze with the cool sand squishing between their toes. On their way back they stopped and skipped flat stones across the water for an hour.

"Remember when we first met and you said you just wanted to find an island and be a beach bum the rest of your life?" Marianna said as she hurled a stone that skipped seven times before nose diving to the bottom of the lagoon. "At the time I thought it was a joke. Now I'm not so sure. It's so peaceful here; so far away from everything ugly...nothing to do but love each other. I wish life could be this way forever."

Clay grabbed her hand and started running into the water, leading her and leaping the waves, and when they reached waist deep level, he squatted down until his shoulders were submerged and pulled her to him. She floated her legs around him, and they kissed, tasting of salt water. "You know, it could be like this forever," he said very seriously. "We could go back to La Gaude and get Cassie and Cody and come back here and just stay. We should have brought them with us."

She unwrapped her legs and stood up, hands on her hips. "Be realistic, Clay," she said as she looked at him like a doting, scolding mother. "We can't live the rest of our life here."

"Why not?

She frowned. "It's just not practical, that's why."

Clay shrugged. "You're right I guess," he said as he splashed water in her face and laughed. "It gets too cold here in the wintertime anyway."

On the third day they went sailing, and he asked her something that had been nagging him for many months. "Have you ever made love with Tommy Mitchell?"

She looked at him curiously, and then laughed. "Well, well! Aren't we becoming the nosy one. Whatever gave you that idea," she said teasingly.

"I've seen the way he looks at you. And I've seen you dance with him at parties. You dance well together. Too well, like you must have practiced quite a few times."

She snuggled up and formed a pouting oval with her lips. "Oh, don't tell me Clay Stoner is jealous. Whatever happened to the old *no commitments?*" She laughed again and tickled him under the arm.

"*No commitments* is ancient history," he said sternly, accusingly.

She looked at him seriously then, and didn't say anything for awhile. She had to admit that she and Tommy had been thrown together in quite a few compromising situations while on the road, and that he *was* attractive. And she had come close to making it with him in London one night last winter, a night that she had been really down on Clay not long after the episode in Howie's suite. She and Clay had been talking on the phone long distance and gotten into an argument. He hung up on her and she went next door to Tommy's room seeking some solace. They smoked some good dope and drank wine for awhile, and then Tommy started caressing her and she was right on the verge of thinking the hell with Clay and lying down with Tommy. But he had fondled her too long and given her time to think. If he had manhandled her more, she didn't know what would have happened. But she might have...She looked at Clay, glaring at her, waiting for an answer. "Nothing has happened between Tommy Mitchell and me," she said without a blink. "We go out together sometimes. But he's never touched me." She saw him break into a relieved smile, and she knew she had been right to fib a little. There was no reason to muck up the basic truth with a description of what might have been. The only fact that mattered was that she had never slept with anyone else since she had met Clay, and that is the way the score is kept. She had never broken the faith. Clay had not been that true.

Clay steered the sailboat, a thirty-six foot sloop, into a cove just around the point from the entrance to the bay. He dropped anchor about a hundred yards offshore, near a tiny, rocky island in the middle of the cove, started up the diesel and backed the boat down until the anchor dug into the bottom. The water was chilly, so they decided not to swim. They had each brought a book, and they read most of the afternoon. Clay went to the bow and lay down on a mattress and started reading Catch 22. He was reading it for the second time. Marianna stayed in the cockpit. She was reading The Prophet, by Kahlil Gibran.

Late in the afternoon she started humming to herself and singing the same tunes over and over, each time changing the words slightly. She disturbed Clay's concentration. He was curious, and he went back to the cockpit and sat down beside her and asked her what she was doing.

"I've lifted some words from Gibran and I'm trying to put them to music," she said wistfully. "Listen and tell me if you don't think this is beautiful." She sang softly. Her voice cracked with emotion.

> *"It was but yesterday we met in a dream.*
> *You sang to me in my aloneness,*
> *And I of your longings built a tower in the sky.*
> *Now our sleep has fled, our dream is over.*
> *It is no longer dawn and we must part.*
> *Farewell to you and the youth I spent with you,*
> *And if we should meet in another dream,*
> *And you sing to me a deeper song,*
> *We shall build another tower in the sky."*

"I agree with you. That certainly is beautiful," Clay said when she finished.

She rested her head on his shoulder and stared out to sea. "Yes, it is beautiful," she said after a long pause. "But it's sad too. I've been sitting here for an hour trying to put the words to music...I keep thinking that I didn't read this today just by chance. I feel it's trying to tell me something. Forewarn perhaps. I feel...I don't know how to describe it...but I feel afraid. We've spent our own youth together in a dream, Clay. I can't cope with the thought of it ever being over...for us to part...or to get old...or die. I have this scary premonition that something bad is going to happen."

Clay leaned over and kissed her on the nose; then her eyelids. She smiled at him. He patted her on the head. "You're crazy," he said; and then he got up and went to the stern of the boat and hauled up the anchor. Marianna helped him hoist sail. They tacked out to sea, and then tacked one more time around the point on a course that took them straight into the cove and the quay at the villa.

They drove into town on Saturday night, a tiny hamlet called Fournelles that was occupied at most by four hundred residents - if one counted the cats, dogs, pigs, chicken and sheep. They motored in on the Vespa that came with the house, on a dark night on a dirt road that was rutted the entire way. They went to the only restaurant in town and ordered paella. The restaurant was in an old stone house, and it resembled a cellar - or cave. The tables, eight of them in all, were wooden and hand carved, as were the chairs. About fifteen people were having dinner, all local Menorcans who knew each other, so Clay and Marianna's entrance was conspicuous. The waitress, young and barefooted and looking virginal in a white, lacy, flowing Catalonian skirt asked them in Spanish if they wanted the seventy peseta paella. Marianna cut Clay off before he could speak. "Esta nuestro lune de miel...our honeymoon," she blurted. Nos gustaria tener una paella grande por doscientos pesetos y el mejor vino de la casa." Marianna's Spanish was Castilian, not the Catalan of the Menorcans, and the young waitress was confused. She went to the kitchen, and in very short order the owner of the establishment was at their table. He wanted to make sure there was no mistake, he said, and when Marianna assured him that they did, indeed, want a two-hundred peseta paella and the best wine in the house, the owner broke into a wide grin and promised that he was going to serve them the grandest paella in the history of Fournelles. And he did. Or at least they thought he did. They were served a heaping bowl of saffron cooked rice, crowned with prawns, shrimp and squid, slivers of lobster, mussels, clams, chicken, spicy garlic sausage, fresh green peas, red mullet garnished with pimentos, and two fine bottles of wine. They feasted for two hours, and about midnight, as they were finishing with an espresso, the owner brought out three bottles of iced-down champagne, compliments of the house. One bottle he popped open for Clay and Marianna, the others he poured for the remaining diners. The Menorcans all raised their glasses.

Lune de miel...honeymoon!" they toasted, grinning, their eyes dancing suggestively. A young flamenco guitarist started strumming a guitar in the corner, chording slowly at first. But as everyone finished eating he started putting words to his music, and he was good, like a young Jose Feliciano. The Menorcans began to sing along with him, Catalonian songs, and Marianna could not resist the urge to join them. Even Clay, who carried a tune worse than a honking goose, chimed in for awhile. They sang in unison for more than an hour, and couples took turns dancing in a tiny area next to the guitarist, whirling and stamping their feet, clapping hands, and snapping their fingers with rhythm. Marianna sang a duet with the guitarist. The Menorcans clamored for her to continue, and she did, until finally, at two-thirty in the morning, it was time for the restaurant to close.

The ride back to the house on the Vespa was not a sober one, but somehow Marianna and Clay managed it. Two more nights they scootered into Fournelles to have dinner and sing and dance with their newly made friends. They spent the days alone, savoring every moment. They were depressed when Saturday came and they had to leave. They packed in silence and were on the quay for almost an hour, waiting, before they heard the roar of the Otter coming down the lagoon to spirit them away. Once they were in the air they both curled up and slept all the way to Nice.

XII

GOING HOME

Another month passed, temperatures along the Cote cooled into the fifties and the beaches depopulated. Marianna and the Band were off on tour in the north of Europe, Copenhagen or someplace, and Clay had still heard nothing from Whitney. On a damp, cloudy Sunday afternoon, he decided to call him. He drove into Nice and placed the call from a telephone booth.

"Clay. It's good to hear from you," Whitney said cheerfully as he came on the line.

"What's happening?" Clay asked.

"A lot," Whitney said, and his voice changed suddenly to one of caution. "I can't discuss too much on the phone, so don't call me here anymore, but I'm sure you were right, Clay. Payoffs in all three cases. But we can't prove it yet. We wanted to wiretap Nicholson to see how involved he may have been personally in the jet fighter shenanigans, but the Attorney General vetoed it. I'm convinced he's in Nicholson's back pocket too, and it could go even higher than that. I've put some undercover agents on the case, trying to nail down the money trails, but I doubt if the Swiss will be very cooperative. It may take awhile. How about you? Anything new on your end?"

"Nothing too important. I've been keeping a diary. Dates. Places. I have some more names. Mostly small time tax evaders. No big fish, though."

"Good. Keep at it. We'll go after the little fish sooner or later. But right now we want the big ones. I'll be in touch with you through Robert when we need you - when it's time to come out of the closet. Hopefully, it won't be too long."

Clay felt good when he hung up - frustrated, some, because he wanted things to move faster - but good, because he felt confident that Whitney was making progress. The Justice Department cast a wide net. Meanwhile, he would wait and bide his time.

Clay flew almost every day for the next two weeks. - fifteen cities in twelve days. The trips were mostly routine. Howie was busy making his semi-annual visits to the European sales offices. Clay was home for a weekend in mid-December, though, and on Saturday he invited Genevieve and Angelo to dinner. He spent the entire afternoon preparing it himself; sautéed shrimp, poached salmon, a caramel custard. After dinner he invited Angelo and Genevieve into the den for liquors and coffee. He turned on the television and let Cassie and Cody stay up to watch. At nine o'clock he switched channels, and in less than a minute *Kira and the Band* were on the screen, airing live from their concert at the Olympia Music Hall. Genevieve was awestruck, recognizing at once the Kira she thought she knew and for the first time realizing she was a performer. She sat on the edge of her chair and kept shaking her head and saying "c'est fantastique! Madame Kira est fantastique!" Cassie and Cody were thrilled, and they pointed excitedly at the screen and giggled and shouted at the start of each new song, "ooh-la! Mommy! Mommy!" Angelo said nothing. He just sat quietly, smiling, and nodding his head and tapping his foot in time with the music. Toward the end of the hour Marianna sang her French-English version of *Non, Je Ne Regrette Rien* and Clay thought the concert was over. Instead, Marianna picked up the microphone and walked to the edge of the stage. The camera zoomed in on her, and her face covered the screen. Clay could see that she was strained with fatigue. She started talking to the audience.

"This is a new song the Band and I just recorded last month. It's already been released in the States, so I hope you like it. It's about a love that's very special to me. I call the song...'Tower in the Sky'."

She sang with her eyes closed and with an intensity that caused the audience to hush. Her voice was pure and clear, slender, but determined; haunted. When she finished there was a stillness for a moment, a quiet electricity in the air that only emanates from a special performance, and then the audience stood and started whistling and cheering and shouting "bravo" for the next two minutes until the show went off the air. Clay shivered. He stood and switched off the television set and turned to the children. "Well...that's your mommy, kids. I hope you never forget her." His voice was choked.

Clay waited an hour, and then on a hunch, he telephoned Jean Pierre's apartment in Paris. Darcy answered. The connection was poor, and he could hardly hear her, but in seconds she had Marianna on the line. "I just walked in as the phone was ringing. How did you like Tower?" she said, gasping as if she were out of breath.

"It was magnificent. So were you. I thought you would be out celebrating."

"The single of *Tower* is selling in the States like there's no tomorrow! We have to go back...," she went on excitedly, as if she hadn't heard him, and her voice started fading.

"Goddamn French phones," Clay muttered. "You have to speak up," he said very loudly. "I can't hear you!"

"I said we have to go back to London tomorrow to finish the album!" she shouted.

"When are you coming home?"

"...day."

"When?"

"Thursday! Will you be home?"

"Yeah. And I have a surprise proposition for you," he said as a burst of static came over the line."

"*A what?*"

"A proposition," he shouted.

"Fantastic...I'm exhausted. One more thing..."

"I think it's time we got married!" he interrupted, shouting again"

"I can't hear you!"

"*I said I want to marry you!*" he practically yelled.

She burst out laughing. "What for?"

"Because I *love* you."

"That's a *commitment!*" she yelped.

"I know. But...ready...make..."

He was fading out badly now, and Marianna could only hear every other word. "I can't hear you anymore," she said loudly. "I'll see you Thursday, fella'. We'll talk about it then."

They hung up. They each had five days to think about it. But it was very late on Thursday when Marianna returned home to La Gaude. She was too tired to discuss it, and they went to bed early.

A ringing telephone awakened Clay early the next morning. The call was from Cat, and she spoke rapidly in a jittery, nervous voice. She asked him to meet her at noon at the flower market near the port in the old section of Nice. He puzzled over the call as he drove into the city to meet her. She had sounded strange. He hoped that nothing was wrong with her. He was not going to be able to stay long because he was meeting Howie at the airport at two o'clock for a quick flight to Barcelona. He was at the market on time. After ten minutes and no sign of Cat, he started browsing among the vendor's stands. He stopped and purchased a bouquet of carnations from an old Provencal woman who looked particularly poor and lonely. He was loitering by her stand, admiring the flowers, and he did not recognize Cat at first when she sidled up to him. Her hair was pulled back under a scarf, and she had on a raincoat and a large pair of broad-rimmed sunglasses that shielded her eyes. She took him by the arm, and they started walking. "I thought you should know," she whispered, "Howie has learned from my father that someone from the Justice Department has been snooping around and trying to prove that Utopia bribed the SEC. He's also trying to get the Swiss banking authorities to verify the names of several Americans who he claims have accounts at the Union Credit Bank."

"So...why are you telling me this?" Clay asked innocently.

"Because I was with Howie and one of the SEC commissioners in our suite in London the day after Utopia's party, and Howie did bribe him. He says I'm the only person who could know. He doesn't know about you."

"What are you talking about?"

"Don't take me for a fool, Clay. You saw Howie talking to the Commissioner at the party. You heard Howie tell my father that the Commissioner would deal."

"You're mistaken, Cat. I was pretty drunk that night. You may have heard something. But I don't remember a thing."

Cat stopped walking and turned to face him. "Clay, let's not mince words. I've always managed to take care of myself without meddling in anyone else's affairs. But you and Marianna are the only friends I have. I'm telling you this because if you are involved, you had better be careful. Howie's not fooling around." She reached up and removed her sunglasses slowly. The sight was nauseating. Her right eye was swollen shut; the socket and area around it converged into one giant purple and black hematoma.

"Howie did *that?*" Clay said, engulfed by a wave of revulsion.

"That's right," Cat nodded. "He would have killed me if I hadn't been able to convince him that I didn't know anything. He's deadly serious about this. And scared. I heard him on the phone yesterday with my father and Nicholson. They were talking about getting rid of whoever is pushing this investigation. They were even discussing *murder*, if necessary, Clay."

"Clay jumped. "Did they mention any names?" he asked, trying to look outwardly calm.

"Yes. Someone named Whitney. He works for the Attorney General, I think."

"Howie discussed Whitney with your father and Nicholson?" Clay felt his body go limp and his mind start to panic.

"Yes. Two days ago."

"Cat, thanks for telling me this. I have to go right away. I'm flying to Barcelona in an hour. But please. Do me a favor."

"I'll try," she said hesitantly.

"Get out, Cat! Get out now before it's too late."

She looked at him, but not with the taunting, teasing, laughing eyes that were her normal self. She only had one eye to look at him with now, and it was not laughing. "Get out! Get out where?" she said woefully. "Who's ever going to become seriously interested in a twenty-eight year old druggie who's already fucked up her entire life?"

Clay left Cat standing in the flower market and ran to his car. He drove six blocks to the Hotel Negresco, double parked in front, and raced inside to the telephone booths. It was seven o'clock in the morning in Washington. He placed an overseas call to Whitney's residence. There was no answer. He tried the office number and got the same result. He paced around the lobby one time, and then he went to the booth and called Robert in New York. It was a very sleepy voice intimating hangover that answered. "Robert, you have to get in touch with Whitney," Clay said hurriedly. "Tell him I said his life is in danger."

"What are you talking about?" Robert squawked, shocked wide awake now.

"There's no time to explain! I'm on my way to the airport. You have to locate him and tell him that I said the bad guys are on to him and are out to get him. He'll know what I mean. Call me in La Gaude tonight and let me know if you reached him." Clay ignored Robert's request for more details. He hung up and drove immediately to the airport. He was late, and Howie was already there, smoking a cigar and pacing about anxiously. Clay ran through his pre-flight check-list in half the normal time, and by so doing he was able to have them in the air two minutes ahead of schedule.

The flight to Barcelona took less than an hour. Howie was only going for a short meeting, and they were on the ground less than three hours. They were back in Nice by seven o'clock. A limousine was waiting to pick up Howie, and as soon as it left Clay turned the post flight duties over to his co-pilot, fetched his Alfa, and sped toward La Gaude. He raced up the winding mountain road in less than twenty minutes, parked, and jogged up the cobblestone lane to the villa. Marianna met him as soon as he stepped through the gate into the courtyard. "Robert called an hour ago. Whitney is dead," she said, trembling.

"No!"

"His car went off the road into the Potomac last night, and he drowned. The police are calling it an accident. But Robert said you were afraid something was going to happen - that you called him a few hours ago, before they even found the car, and that you told him to warn Whitney." Marianna's face was a mask of horror. Clay put his arm around her and steered her into the house and sat her down before he told her about the conversation with Cat. When he finished, she looked at him, her face flickering with a faint trace of hope. "Couldn't the wreck have been a coincidence?" she said plaintively. Clay shook his head, and she clutched his arm. "Then we have to get away!" she cried. "I knew Howie was a lecherous slob. You told me was a crook. But I never thought he was a murderer! He'd do the same thing to you that he did to Whitney."

"Yes. He certainly would," Clay said grimly, "but I've known that all along."

"You've known! And you dragged us into it!" she sputtered in a rage. "Did you think about me or the children at all?"

"I did."

"That's great! We're packing and moving out of here now!

"No. We're staying here just as if nothing has happened, Marianna. If we leave now, Howie will know for sure that I tipped off Whitney. And I don't know where we would go right now. The one lesson I have learned is that I can't rely on anyone else to take on the responsibility for dealing with Howie and Nicholson and the rest of the scumbags. It's too dangerous. Somehow, I'm going to have to figure out another way. I owe Whitney that much. Meanwhile, tomorrow is Christmas Eve, and we have a party at Howie's coming up the week after that."

On Christmas Eve, after arranging all of Cody and Cassie's toys in a neat circle around the tree, Marianna and Clay opened a second bottle of Chateau Neuf-de-Pape and flopped down on pillows on the stone floor in front of the fireplace. Marianna gazed dully at the flickering fire. Clay saw a look of youthful anguish - the same lost look she had the summer they first met - that day on the bench in the rain in the park in downtown Nice, the day she had told him about trying to commit suicide.

"Do you think Cody and Cassie will like their Christmas?" Marianna blurted out all of a sudden.

"Certainly. What's the matter, fella'? Don't you think we got them enough?" Clay said sensitively, and he watched her eyes.

"I hope you're right," she sighed, avoiding his stare. "It's just that I feel really rotten tonight. I feel like I haven't been a very good mother all these years. I've been away from the twins too much. I think they consider Genevieve to be more a mother to them than me."

"You're so wrong, Marianna. If you could see how excited they get when I tell them you're coming home, you wouldn't think that for a minute."

She shrugged. "That's only because they know I always bring them presents," she said, still staring into the fire, as if mesmerized by its crackling, orangish flame. Her glass was empty and Clay poured some more wine. "You know," she said, "we're not poor anymore, Clay. I haven't told you, but I should make more than a half million dollars this year from my cut of the road tours and the royalties coming in from the *On Love and War* album."

Clay let out a low whistle. "You're making me feel like a kept man. That's pretty good."

"I know. And Howie tells me that the way *Tower* is selling I ought to make more than that next year just from royalties even if I don't work a single day."

"So why don't you take a sabbatical from clubbing and touring for awhile?"

"That's what I wanted to talk to you about," she said, turning to face him and looking very solemn. I feel like I've been running on a treadmill ever since the twins were born, Clay. This last year on the road was too much. I was worn out before this last tour. Now

Howie is scheduling the same routine for next year. He's booked the band in London starting the second week in January, and is already scheduling a tour in the States for next summer. I don't want to go."

"You're under contract to him until May."

"I know. But I can't do it anymore, Clay...the one night stands, the noisy crowds, the late nights and traveling...the thrill's all gone. And we don't need the money. So why don't we just quit and pack up and go someplace else? Please..."

"Oh, sure. Where?"

"I don't know!" she cried. "Anywhere! Just get away from Howie and Utopia, Clay! Don't you understand? I'm petrified. I can't get Whitney out of my mind. I can't stay here and work for Howie anymore. Not another day."

"Yes, you can," Clay admonished her. "You're leaving for London in two weeks. You can survive it here until then, and for a few performances afterwards. If things work out the way I plan, the odds are you won't ever have to come back."

She calmed down and looked at him soberly. "What kind of plan?"

"Stealing Utopia's secret account records."

"You're insane!" Marianna erupted incredulously. "Why don't you just rob Fort Knox while you're at it! Do you know what will happen if you get caught?"

"I don't intend to get caught. I was thinking about this even before Whitney was killed. Howie keeps a copy of the VIP Union Credit investment accounts and their codes in his office out at his chateau. The matching records that tie the codes together with names are at the Union Credit Bank in Zurich. When I was there I saw exactly where they're kept - in an old file cabinet in a room that wasn't even locked at the time. I intend to talk to Cat at Howie's party. I'm sure she could get into Howie's safe and make a copy of the statements sometime when he's not around. If so, I think I could get the dossiers at Union Credit. I'd have to coordinate the timing with Cat and plan a simultaneous visit to Zurich. The secretary there knows me. If somehow I could get Biderman out of the office for awhile, she would let me in. I think I could pull it off. Afterwards, we could all meet up at Jean Pierre's in Paris."

Clay was talking fast, and Marianna just sat there quietly for awhile, mesmerized, looking at him and shaking her head. When he paused, she interrupted. "First, what makes you think Cat will go along with all of this?" she said quietly, maintaining her composure.

"She will. She wants to get away from Howie as much as you do." Clay managed a smile, wanting to reassure her. "She has to."

"How can you be so sure? Have you thought about what a deadly game you're asking her to play, Clay? And us? Four years ago I would have thought I had no right to tell you what to do. But now I do. If you don't care about what happens to us, you should at least care about what happens to the twins. Have you even thought about what you're going to do once you get the records - if you do?"

"Yes. We're going home, fella'. And we'll turn everything over to the news media. I can't trust working through the government anymore. We've seen how that didn't work. Nicholson and Asquith have too many ties. Utopia has to be publicly exposed - the facts printed in every newspaper and broadcast on every television in the whole goddamned country. It's the only sure way to see that something gets done – that it all doesn't just get covered up and die."

"And what if no one cares?"

"What do you mean?"

"I mean what happens if you take this risk, and then go around telling everyone how corrupt Utopia is and telling them that Howie and Nicholson and Admiral Martin and Senator what's-his-name and the SEC Commissioner are crooks...*and no one gives a good goddamn!* Don't you understand, Clay? You're taking on the system! People don't care! If they did, something would have been done about it long ago."

"People care, Marianna. Whitney cared. He was trying to do something about it."

"Yeah. And he's dead."

"That's right. And that's why I have to follow through on this. You know, I told Whitney that I thought Martin and the Senator and the SEC Commissioner were just the tip of the iceberg. The last time I talked to him he told me I was right - that the corruption went much higher. Just let your imagination wander, Marianna. How high do you think he was talking about?"

"Maybe all the way," she said, very subdued.

"It's possible. And if I get the books, and expose the evidence, maybe the world will have a chance to know."

"And what if they still don't care, Clay?" she said again. "What happens then? We would have to keep hiding forever?"

He didn't answer. He lit a cigarette and looked at her. "Let's drop it," he said frowning.

Christmas passed uneventfully. It rained, a steady drizzle that spread a chill throughout the house. Clay spent the day assembling the toys they had bought for Cassie and Cody and listening to their complaints because he could not assemble them fast enough. Marianna and Genevieve went to church, the first time Marianna had been to church since Clay could remember. They stayed home the next four days. Utopia's planes were not flying, and Clay only had to go to the airport once to work out schedules for the coming week. As the thirtieth of December approached, though, he and Marianna started becoming anxious. They were invited to a dinner party at Howie's chateau and intended to discuss Clay's plan with Cat that night. They worried about what her reaction might be. At four-thirty in the afternoon on the thirtieth the telephone rang. Marianna answered it. "It's for you," she said to Clay. "It sounds like long distance."

Clay took the receiver. His father was on the phone. His voice was that of a broken man. "Clay...son, I thought you ought to know," Bill Stoner said. "Your mother has taken a sudden turn for the worse. She's dying. She only has a few days."

Clay felt as if he had just been karate-chopped in the back of the neck. "Where are you?" he said, rubbing his eyes.

"In Creekwood. I brought your mother home yesterday. I've taken her to all the best hospitals. They all say the same thing. There's no hope." Clay heard his father's voice choke and start to cry. "She's in such terrible pain, son. She asks for you. She wants to see you."

Clay shuddered. His hands grew cold. His head stated to ache. He winced and closed his eyes - and for a moment he saw his mother. They were fishing for channel cat at the lake...she was skinny dipping in Possum Hollow...he was listening to her recite to him from her books. He agonized and gulped for breath. After what seemed like a minute, but in truth only a few seconds, he said, "Dad, I'm coming home. I'll be there as soon as I can." And then they hung up. There was nothing else to say.

Clay walked out of the room, up the stairs and out onto the terrace. It was grey and a wind was blowing, and it was chilly on the terrace. He stood there a full five minutes looking down at the Var valley, then into the mist hanging over the coast and toward the mountains in the north, all snow-capped and covered with clouds. He could feel tears in his eyes. This is the last time, he thought. I may never stand here and look out over this valley again. He shook himself and regained his composure. Then he started thinking about what he had to do next. His mind was a jumble. He hurried down the stairs and confronted Marianna in the living room. "Start packing," he said excitedly, spouting orders. "You're taking the bears on the next plane for Paris. Go to Jean Pierre and Darcy's and stay there until I get in touch with you."

She had known something was wrong as soon as Clay had picked up the phone. Now she was frightened. "What are you talking about? What's the matter, Clay?" she queried him desperately.

"My mother's dying. I'm going to Howie's party tonight and somehow get those account records - then to Zurich in the morning - and from there straight to Creekwood. I want you and the kids out of it. I'll send for you when I think it's safe."

"No!" she cried out in terror.

"Goddamnit! Can't you see this is no time to argue? Now do as I say!" He hurried to the telephone and started making calls. He rang Air France first and booked Marianna and the twins on the seven o'clock flight to Paris. Next he called the Utopia hangar at the airport and scheduled for the Lear Jet to be gassed and pre-flighted and ready to fly out that night. Then he telephoned Jean Pierre's apartment in Paris. A baby sitter answered and informed him in very broken English that Jean Pierre and Darcy were skiing in Megeve and would not be home until the next day. Bursting with frustration, he placed a call to Robert in New York. He let the phone ring twelve times and there was no answer. "Damn!" he exclaimed, and he swung his fist in the air. "Nothing's going right."

"That's because you're behaving irrationally," Marianna said, calm and collected now. "You realize that don't you? You were going to plan everything so carefully. Now all of a sudden you're changing everything."

"I'll work it out! Don't worry!" he shouted at her defiantly. She could tell he was frantic.

"I guess there is no way I can talk you out of it, is there?"

"No!"

"How do you plan to go about it?"

He looked at her - challenging him - and he sat down in a chair, shaking his head and muttering, "I don't know, fella'...I just don't know."

"Then I'm calling Genevieve," she said very softly. "I'm going with you to the party. Angelo and Genevieve can meet us later at the airport with the twins."

"Like hell!"

"Shut up!" she lambasted him. "You don't know whether you're coming or going right now, Clay. You need me. And I just may have an idea that will work."

Less than three hours after Bill Stoner's phone call, Marianna and Clay were in the Alfa driving the back roads up through St. Jeannet, across the Var River and into the mountains of the Alpes Maritime. They had just spent two hours racing about, packing in a frenzy. They had left the twins with Genevieve and Angelo. Marianna had explained to them that Clay's mother was dying, and that she and Clay had to go to the States right away. But first they had to go to Howie's party, she said. The poor old couple was bewildered. Marianna asked them to bring the twins and their luggage to the Utopia hangar at midnight, and to wait in the parking lot until she and Clay arrived. Angelo and Genevieve agreed, of course, but they knew something was seriously wrong. They saw the many bags that had been packed and sensed that Clay and Marianna were not intending to return anytime soon. And then Clay really shocked them. "If we don't show up at the airport before dawn," he instructed them, "I want you to be on the first flight to Paris in the morning and take the twins to Jean Pierre and Darcy's." He gave them money for tickets. Angelo and Genevieve just nodded, dazedly, too stunned to ask them any questions before they left for the party.

A few miles after crossing the Var River they intercepted the Grand Corniche, the winding, twisting road that would take them on a descent for the last several kilometers into Monaco. Clay and Marianna were still arguing about her idea, and at the top of a crest he pulled over to a parking area on the side of the road to argue some more. She had proposed a plan that was simple, but brazen. They had both attended enough of Howie's soirees to know that he always kept his upstairs bedroom and office doors locked whenever guests were in the house. They also knew that he usually carried the keys around with him. Marianna was willing to bet, she said, that he also would be carrying the key to the safe in his office where the secret account records were kept. And sooner or later during the evening Howie would get drunk, as he usually did. When that happened she would proposition him, and ask him to give her the keys so she could slip off unnoticed to wait for him in the bedroom. She would leave the keys for Clay in the bathroom next to Howie's bedroom. As soon as Clay got everything he wanted out of Howie's office he was to walk along the hallway corridor, talking loudly as if he were looking for her. She would use that as an excuse to break things off with Howie and insist on going back downstairs to the party. Clay did not like the plan at all, and he told her so. He lowered the top on the Alfa, and for several minutes they sat in the car on the side of the road looking down at the dark sea, and argued snappishly about her idea. In the end, though, Marianna forced him to admit that he had no better plan. "Then that settles it," she said finally.

"How can you tolerate the thought of Howie touching you?" Clay said, as he felt himself giving in to her logic and hating himself for it.

"Because I know how important this is to you."

"It's not that important."

"Yes it is. Please don't worry about it, Clay. I can handle Howie. He's all bluster in public. But he's gentle as a lamb when you get him alone."

"How do you know?"

"Cat told me. She says he's a real pussycat in the bedroom."

Clay wiped his hand over his face, not saying anything for awhile. He was agonizing inside. This woman he loved so much was ready and determined to risk everything for him. And he was going to let her do it. He looked at her at last and said, "all right. You win. But I'm telling you, Marianna, if you're not out of Howie's bedroom within two minutes after you hear me calling your name, I'm coming in and...I'll kill him if I have to." He wrenched on the ignition. The Alfa's engine roared to life, and they accelerated out of the parking spot and on down the Grand Corniche into Monaco and to Howie's soiree.

The soiree was a loud, noisy affair. There were at least seventy guests. Cat was conspicuously absent. Not feeling well; hurt her eye, Howie said. Dinner was served buffet style about nine o'clock and as the guests fanned out to the various tables a three piece combo started playing old tunes from the forties and fifties. Marianna maneuvered herself very skillfully and wound up at a round table for six and in a seat next to Howie. During the dinner she was subtly provocative. When someone teased Howie about having a penchant for younger women, she was quick to say how she had always been attracted to older men. She eyed Howie when she said it, and smiled. He started flirting with her then, and she kept nudging him and giving him suggestive looks until, by dessert time, he felt confident enough to place his hand high on her thigh and start rubbing it gently. She opened her legs and reached down and took his hand and moved it up firmly between them and let him feel for a minute. Then she took his hand away and reached over under the table and gave his crotch a playful squeeze. Howie's eyes widened. His mouth opened and he grinned at her. But before he could say anything, she pushed away from the table and sashayed briskly toward the bar. She bided her time. Howie attempted to approach her twice, but each time she teasingly fended him off. Sometime after midnight, he approached her a third time. By then, as she had anticipated, he was slobbering drunk. To make sure, she asked him to escort her to the bar and order cognacs. The bartender gave them each a double shot. "Do you know that you've always turned me on," Howie slurred huskily, and he sidled up to her and gave her a squeeze.

"You've sure never done much about it," Marianna murmured as she rolled her tongue sensuously back and forth over her upper lip.

"Why don't we go up to my room and make up for some lost time?" Howie gestured toward the stairs.

"What about Cat?"

"What about Clay?"

"He's a big boy," she said as she lifted an open champagne bottle from the bar. "I'll take this and go up alone so Clay doesn't see us together. Give me a few minutes."

"Sh-hure, honey. But the bedroom's locked. You'll need these." Howie handed her a key ring containing a half dozen keys. She winked at him, and then, concealing her nervousness, she walked away and up the stairs to his bedroom. She unlocked the door before stepping quickly down the hall to a bathroom and placing her purse containing the keys underneath the sink. In seconds she was back out and into Howie's bedroom with the door locked. She poured two large glasses of champagne. Into one she emptied the contents from three sleeping pill capsules. Then she waited.

Three minutes later Howie knocked at the door, and as soon as she let him in, he made a grab for her. "Easy baby," she cajoled him. "Let's have a drink first."

Howie would hear none of it. "I didn't come up here for champagne, sweetheart," he said roughly. He pressed against her with his sweaty, flabby body and kissed her. His breath was reeking.

She pushed him away gently. "Howie, not now. Not tonight. We've both had too much to drink. Some other time when we can relax and enjoy it." She sounded very genuine.

"What are you? *Some kind of tease?*"

"I'm sorry. You just got me carried away for awhile. Have some champagne and let's just talk."

She handed him a glass and he gulped most of it down. "I don't wanna talk," he said gruffly. "If you don't wanna get it on, let's go back to the party."

Marianna jumped. This man is a killer, she thought. I can't let him leave now, not until Clay is out of his office. Her instincts took over. She reached down and unzipped his pants. "Come lie down. I'll do you," she said in a commanding voice. She led him to the bed and sat beside him on the edge, fondling his puny cock until it hardened. But he was drunk, and not able to come easily. He started thrashing about and talking dirty. "The next time we're together it won't be like this," he said, breathing hard, his brow sweaty. "We'll do it dog style and you'll love it. You'll see." The mere thought sickened her, but she humored him, and when he asked her to move her hands faster, she did. She handed him the rest of his glass of champagne and started whispering to him, encouraging him to drink, and get it over.

An eternity seemed to pass before she heard Clay's voice in the corridor. He knocked on the bathroom door next to the bedroom. "Kira! Are you in there? It's time to go home," he said loudly enough for Howie to hear.

Marianna stopped massaging and whispered anxiously. "It's Clay! I have to go before he finds us! I'll go outside on the balcony and down the steps in back so he won't see me." She started to rise from the bed, and Howie grabbed both her wrists.

"Finish it," he hissed in a dangerous tone. "Suck me off."

"Kira! Are you up here?" she heard Clay call again.

"I...I can't," she stammered.

Howie twisted her wrists roughly. "Finish it, goddamnit!" he said in a manner threatening enough to convince her that she was not going to be able to get away without satisfying him. She was scared now. Clay had the door key. In another minute he might barge in the room and cause a disastrous confrontation. Howie had bodyguards downstairs. Again, she did what she had to do. She lowered her head and gave Howie two or three quick, hard, deep sucks, and then started jerking him rapidly until he grunted and the warm, sticky stuff trickled in her hand.

"I have to go now," she said softly. Howie didn't answer. He was out. His mouth was open and he was snoring in a drunken stupor. She got up and slipped quickly out of the room. Clay was standing at the top of the stairs like a lonely sentinel, holding a giant briefcase and glaring at her. She ran to him, took the keys, went back to the bedroom, stepped inside quietly, and placed the keys on the lamp table. Howie never moved. Two minutes later she and Clay were in the Alfa racing toward the Grand Corniche. Her body was drenched in a nervous sweat. But as it dried in the wind, she calmed, and the sweeping feeling of adrenalin and nausea that had caused her to think she was going to be sick started to ebb.

"Did it go all right?" Clay asked, looking over at her anxiously.

"Certainly!" she snapped. "I told you it would, didn't I?"

"Did Howie try to make a pass at you?"

"Sure. He tried, and I handled it. Okay? So what about you? Did you find what you wanted?"

"I think so!" he said very excitedly. "I won't know for sure until I study it. But I think it's going to be dynamite, Marianna! I have lots of statements with codes and account numbers, transaction histories. All I need now is to match the numbers with names."

"That's good," she sighed. She leaned back to relax and let the wind blow in her face. She felt unclean. But she was hopeful that her sacrifice had been worth it.

They made the drive to Cote d'Azur in half an hour. The aerodrome was cloaked in haze, dark and empty. They drove around to the west side of the main terminal building and saw Angelo and Genevieve parked in the Citroen out by the Utopia hangar. Clay switched off the headlights and drove toward them. Behind them he could see the silhouette of the sleek Lear jet, all gassed and poised and ready for him to fly Marianna and the twins safely away. Angelo and Genevieve saw them coming and were standing next to the Citroen when they pulled up. No one said much. The twins were sound asleep. Angelo helped Clay load the suitcases on the aircraft and carry the children aboard and strap them into their seats. The four of them gathered outside beside the plane then. "Au revoir," Genevieve said, and she said it in a way that told them all that this was really goodbye.

"Au revoir. Et merci" Marianna said, and her voice cracked. Then she and Clay turned and hurried aboard the aircraft and pulled shut the door.

Clay took off without filing a flight plan. Nor did he communicate with anyone on the radio for the next hour. Ten minutes before they landed at Le Bourget, he called and requested an approach clearance and for a taxi to meet the plane. It was after three o'clock in the morning when they landed. A taxi was waiting. Marianna and Clay helped the sleepy, tottering twins down the three short steps of the Lear and into the car, and then Marianna walked over and hugged Clay tightly. "Take care, fella'," she murmured.

He kissed her on the eyelids. "I'll call you tomorrow when I change planes in London," was the last thing he said before the taxi pulled away. He walked into the small operations building next to the hangar. The one attendant was half asleep. Clay roused him and told him he would be staying three days. He plunked down a deposit and left instructions for the Lear to be parked in a hangar until he was ready to leave. Task accomplished, he sauntered out the door into the clear, frosty night and walked three hundred yards to the hotel across the road from the main terminal building and took a room. He needed some sleep. He was going to have a long day ahead. Hopefully, he thought, Howie would not find the Lear for awhile. If so, he would find the contents of the pilot's flight bag scattered all over the cockpit floor.

Clay was aboard the eight o'clock flight for Zurich. Three hours of sleep had refreshed him. He felt alert now and ready to tackle Ernst Biderman and the Union Credit Bank. After clearing customs in Zurich, he checked his briefcase into a locker at the airport, confident that Utopia's records were locked away safely until he returned. He kept with him the pilot's valise he had emptied in the Lear. It was a damp, grey and forlorn day, and in the half-hour taxi ride from the airport he started reassessing his plan. He was going to be downtown before eleven o'clock. Howie would probably still be asleep, or at least not mobile yet. But maybe not! The more time that passed the stronger the chance of Howie discovering the records missing from his safe and realizing that Marianna had to be involved. He could no longer afford to wait until Biderman went out for his typical one o'clock lunch, knowing that Howie would call him first thing. Clay saw little choice. He was going to have to try to bluff his way past Herr Ernst Biderman.

The taxi dropped Clay off at a small hotel two blocks down the street from the bank. He hurried inside and placed a long distance call to the Utopia hangar in Nice. A young, French Algerian girl who worked in the office and kept track of the aircraft schedules answered. "Cherie, any calls?" Clay asked her, as if he were at home and just calling in to check up on operations.

"Non, monsieur."

"Everything okay?"

"Oui, monsieur. Except for the Lear. It took off last night without a flight plan, and I don't know its destination or when it's scheduled to return

"Mr. Nussbaum took it to London," Clay said. "He didn't say where he would be, but if anyone calls, tell them that he's scheduled back at six o'clock tonight."

"Oui, monsieur."

Clay hung up and walked up the street to the Union Credit Bank. The building housing the bank was as innocuous looking as he remembered it. He exited the elevator on the third floor, noticing that the carpet was starting to show signs of wear, and rang the buzzer. The gum chewing blond opened the door promptly and recognized him right away. She announced Clay's presence to Biderman over the intercom and, momentarily, the prim little banker walked out of his office, looking puzzled. "Mr. Anderson! This is a pleasant surprise. Come in! Come in!" he said smiling, as he ushered Clay into his office and shut the door. He waited for Clay to sit down, and he offered him a cigar. "Now, what good fortune brings you here?" he asked stiffly.

"Howie sent me to pick up the VIP dossiers. He wants to go over them in Monaco this weekend. He said for me to tell you that he'd have them back to you before noon on Monday."

Biderman drew back and stiffened even more than usual. "That's highly irregular, isn't it?" he said, laughing nervously. "Is something wrong?"

"I dunno," Clay shrugged. "I'm sure Howie has his reasons."

"Well...that could be a problem." Biderman stammered. "Do you mind if I ask if you have any written authorization?"

"No. I don't have a thing," Clay said brashly. "Howie just called me last night before he took off for London and told me to hustle up here first thing this morning and get the stuff. That's all."

Biderman looked perplexed. "This is a bit unusual," he said cautiously. I'm under strict orders from Howie not to let anyone see our records except him. I hope you don't mind if I try to call him? I just want to protect myself, of course."

"Not at all," Clay said. "You can check operations at the hangar in Nice. If anyone knows how to get in touch with him, they should." Clay waited, watching anxiously while Biderman made the call. Less than half an hour had elapsed since he had phoned the hangar. What was the chance Howie might have called in the interim? There was always the chance, he thought. *And, if so...*

Biderman hung up, looking worried. The young French Algerian girl had just confirmed to him that Howie was in London, whereabouts unknown, and was not due back until six o'clock. "I don't know what to do now," Biderman groaned, looking confused and shaking his head. "I would have thought Howie would have called me. Maybe I should telephone Sam and see if he'll authorize me to give you the books." Sam was Utopia's chief financial officer.

"If you do, it's your ass!" Clay said boldly, his eyes glinting. "The reason Howie didn't call you is because H. B. Nicholson thinks there are some irregularities in some of the accounts. He's meeting Howie in Monaco tonight, and the two of them want to go over the dossiers without anyone in the organization having a chance to mess with them in the meantime. That includes Sam, because Nicholson thinks he could be part of the problem."

Biderman gasped. "You...you know about Nicholson? I didn't think anyone in the organization was even supposed to mention his name."

"Well, I just did," Clay said, bluffing like crazy. "And it's going to be my ass, too, if I don't meet them tonight with the files. So come on, Ernst. Just get them for me, and let me be on my way."

Biderman was wavering now. "Well I...I guess that should be all right. Utopia does own the bank." he said hesitantly, and then his mustache twitched two or three times and he conceded. "Listen, I'm sorry to make such a fuss, Clay. I hope you understand. It's just that I'm responsible for all these records. There are some things in them that would be very embarrassing if they fell into the wrong hands."

"I understand," Clay said, giving Biderman a kind pat on the shoulder. "If it will make you feel better, Ernst, I'll have Howie call you as soon as I see him tonight and confirm that everything's okay."

Biderman smiled, looking as if a great weight had been lifted from him. "Oh, I would appreciate that," he said with a sigh. He promptly signaled his secretary to come in and bring him the VIP dossiers. In a matter of minutes, Clay had filled his valise. He reassured Biderman one more time, and then he walked calmly out the door and down the creaky stairs. At the street he ambled around the corner, dropped the façade and quickly broke out laughing. He laughed until the tension released in a rush and tears came into his eyes.

He hustled to locate a taxi and arrived at the airport just as he had planned, a scant fifteen minutes before Swiss Air's one o'clock flight to London. He retrieved his briefcase from the locker and hurried to purchase a ticket. For the first time in a long time, he used his real passport. When Biderman and Howie learned what had happened, if they checked the Zurich airport they were not going to find Clay Anderson's name on any passenger manifest. Clay Stoner's, yes. But not Clay Anderson. It was Clay Stoner who was going home.

Clay had to change planes and layover in London for an hour and a half. As soon as he landed he telephoned Jean Pierre's apartment. The baby sitter answered. "Kira Chastain, please," Clay said anxiously.

"Madame's not here," the woman replied in a fluttering, high-pitched voice. "She came very early this morning and left the children. She is gone now."

"Gone! Where?" Clay half-shouted.

"To Missouri. If you are Monsieur Stoner, she said for me to tell you that the children are in safe hands, and that she will meet you in Creekwood."

"Damn!" Clay thundered in the phone booth as he slammed down the receiver. He was exasperated for a moment, but his anger cooled quickly. Deep down, he was pleased. He had time for one more call. He telephoned Robert in New York. Clay was going to be pressed for time in New York. Just one hour to clear customs and taxi over to LaGuardia to make his connection. He asked Robert to meet him at Kennedy. He had a story for him, Clay said. They could talk about it on the ride between airports.

As it turned out, Clay need not have been concerned about having to rush between airports. On Friday, the thirty-first of December, New York was hit with its first major snowstorm of the winter. Large, crispy dry flakes started floating down about ten-thirty in the morning, the same time that Clay was boarding a Pan Am 707 at London's Heathrow Airport. By five o'clock, when he arrived at

Kennedy, seven inches had already fallen, and the gentle dry flakes had long since given way to stinging missiles of sleet whipping horizontally through the air. The international arrivals terminal was its usual bedlam, so it was a stroke of good luck when Clay was able to find Robert quickly. The drive to La Guardia, though, was a different matter. The first task was to find a taxi, no simple undertaking in a snowstorm on New Year's Eve with a hundred passengers waiting ahead of them. They were lucky again. Robert spied a taxi dropping off a passenger away from the crowd. He and Clay ran for it. The driver wanted to go home. Fifty dollars changed his mind and persuaded him to brave the sleet and slush and Friday night holiday traffic and chauffeur them to La Guardia. The twelve mile drive took more than an hour, giving Clay and Robert ample time to talk. Robert was curious about Clay and his sister. "I've only seen her twice since your court martial, he said. "The last time was this spring when she was touring the States with her band and going by the name of Kira Chastain. I have all three of her albums. I don't know if you know it, but the latest one, 'Tower in the Sky', has become a smash hit here. Our parents don't have a clue where she is or that she's become a famous singer, and she hasn't told me much about her whereabouts or her life. I do know, though, that she's been living most of it in Europe with you. Somewhere near Nice, I think. I figured that out from the phone number you gave me." He said it more in the form of a question than a statement.

"We've kept our lives as private as possible for reasons I'm sure you understand," Clay said reflectively, pulling at his ear. "We've been together ever since she graduated from Juilliard. We also have two children. Twins. A boy and a girl. They will be four years old in February."

'That's fantastic!" Robert exclaimed, truly pleased "And what about you? What have you been doing all this while?"

"I'll fill you in some other time," Clay said hastily. "At the moment your sister and I are in a very dangerous situation. We need your help."

"I'll do anything you ask," Robert said solemnly.. "One thing I know - despite what my parents think - is that you've been good for my sister. She loves you. And I've seen her grow up so much since she met you.

"You've grown up quite a bit yourself," Clay said pointedly.

Robert chortled. "If you mean because I have a job as a reporter for the New York Times, don't let that fool you," he said half-serious, half-joking. "I'm the same as always. I still smoke pot and wear my hair long. I go to work in jeans. Never wear a tie. It's a fun job. I'm free. I can sort of make my own hours."

"Free enough to take off for a few days and work on a story?"

"Depends on the story."

"This is not just any story, Robert. Trust me. It could be front page for weeks. Worth a Pulitzer Prize maybe. You wouldn't believe it if I told you."

"Try me."

"I can't just yet. You're safer not knowing. People have already died because they knew too much."

"You mean Whitney."

Clay nodded. "I'm sure of it."

"I think so too," Robert said quickly. "I knew something was suspicious when you had Marianna call me to warn him. I poked around down in Washington. They did an autopsy on Whitney. He would have died from an overdose of heroin if he hadn't drowned first. He was probably unconscious when his car hit the water. The police think he was driving stoned, and that's why they called it an accident. But I checked. Whitney didn't do drugs."

"That's why I said it's dangerous if you know too much. Another thing - your sister doesn't know I'm talking to you. She'd be very upset if she knew I was getting you involved."

"You can't get me involved unless I want to get involved. What do you want me to do?"

"Call your chief editor tonight and get him on a plane down to Creekwood as soon as you can – like tomorrow."

"Call him tonight! On New Year's Eve and get my ass fired! No thanks!" Robert squawked. "There's no way I can get him to go to Creekwood without even knowing what the story is about, Clay."

Clay squinted and stared straight ahead. "I'm afraid that's what I'm asking you to do," he said flatly. "I can't risk a leak, Robert. I want to get the New York Times and CBS News to come down to Creekwood. We can hole up at my grandfather's cabin for a couple of days. I have all the evidence right here in my briefcases. I'll let you and them go over it...verify it. Then I want the story released simultaneously and immediately to the entire country. Once it's public, it can't be covered up. That's the only way to make sure no one else gets killed. So whoever comes down has to have the authority to release the story without any further approval. Understand?"

"Even...even if I can get my boss to come," Robert said shakily, "how will you ever get CBS there? Don't you think it would be easier to do this here in New York?"

Clay turned and looked at Robert. "My mother's dying," he said grimly. "I have to be with her in Creekwood, so I want you to get CBS down there, too. You know Larry Smith. He's national network now. Call him. Tell him he has to come."

"What do I tell him if he says no?" Robert said, flustered.

"I don't care what you tell him! I don't care how you do it. Just get him there! I'm counting on you, Robert. Be a hero."

They were at La Guardia now. Clay left Robert in the taxi at the curb, muttering to himself, and rushed inside to check on flights. Fortunately, his scheduled flight to St. Louis had been delayed and was not leaving for another thirty minutes. He had time to ring Petey Monroe's number, startling the young girl from an answering service who picked up the phone. Clay told her that his name was Clay Anderson and that he would be arriving in St. Louis in three hours. He wanted to charter a plane and have it waiting there for him to fly to Creekwood. He promised to pay triple the standard fare. He hung up with the girl saying that she would do her best to locate Petey, but making no promises.

He was the last person aboard the St. Louis flight. The aircraft was nearly empty. He had three seats to himself. He was exhausted, and he slept most of the way. He was awakened by the pilot announcing over the cabin speaker that the weather in St. Louis was below minimums for landing and that they were going to have to hold.

Clay was drained. It had been a harrowing day. First, the flight to Zurich and the big bluff at Union Credit. Then the trip to London, a change of planes, seven hours to Kennedy, the taxi ride to La Guardia. Now, here he was, twenty hours after leaving Paris, orbiting in a holding pattern over St. Louis and struggling to keep from being lulled back to sleep by the gentle turns of the Boeing 727 as it droned round and round through the freezing rain. For the first time he felt a twinge of fear. His father's phone call had forced him to act before he was ready. Howie was probably already looking for him - Howie *and* Nicholson. He wondered how they would go about it; how safe he would be in Creekwood. *Ah, Creekwood!* He could be there in an hour if the ceiling would lift enough for the pilot to land, and if Petey was waiting for him with his King Air. Those were two big ifs. It was a bad night out. A night not fit for ducks, his mother used to say. He leaned his head back and closed his eyes, listening to the sound of the rain drumming on the fuse-lage of the 727 as it sliced through the night...and remembering: the cypress swamp; the woods and hills; the winding creeks; the lake. He was like the salmon, he thought - during a run. Each year they fought their way in from the sea and upstream against the rapids, many dying in the process, just so they could return to their birth-place in the inland rivers when the time came to spawn. For the first time in five years, he was really going home.

XIII

∽

SLIM SPARKS IS DEAD

The sound of engine power eased as the 727 commenced its descent into St. Louis. The aircraft ballooned upward as its flaps were lowered, and the movement jolted Clay awake. The aircraft started bouncing around. Power was added, reduced, and added again, and then, with a thump, the 727 was on the ground. In a very short time it was parked in front of the terminal. Clay was the first passenger off, dashing down the steps into a freezing rain whipping across the concrete. He ran the fifty feet to the terminal, drenched by the time he reached the door, and headed straight to a bank of telephones where he dialed the charter flight desk. It was a waste of time, he knew. Petey was not going to be waiting for him; not at nine o'clock on New Year's Eve in this kind of weather. Still, he had to check. He was already contemplating his next step - renting a car and striking out down the winding road in the ice on a drive that would most likely take him the rest of the night - when the dispatcher at the flight desk came on the line and told him that, yes, there was a King Air from Creekwood parked outside waiting for a passenger.

A short taxi ride took him from the main terminal to the small hangar on the opposite side of the field where he found the King Air's pilot asleep in the lounge. Clay shook him and asked, "where's Petey?"

The pilot sat up, blinking awake. "Petey's at a New Year's Eve party tonight. I do most of his charter flyin' now," the pilot said. "Petey's too busy flyin' cargo." The pilot was very young.

"And you flew up here tonight all by yourself in this stuff?" Clay asked, surprised.

"Uh-huh. Petey said it was triple rate."

"Well...I don't know if it's your guts or lack of brains, but whichever, let's go." Outside, a glycol truck was standing by, and within fifteen minutes it had the King Air hosed down and de-iced, and they were on their way. The flight was rough. The King Air bounced all over the sky, through sleet, thunderstorms, and lightning. But the gods were with them. The ceiling at Creekwood lifted to five hundred feet just as they arrived overhead, and they were able to home a needle in on the radio station and descend beneath the overcast. Once landed, Clay unstrapped, and darted out of the King Air before its propellers stopped turning. He helped tie down and secure the aircraft in less than a minute, and then, in the young pilot's pick-up truck, they sped off toward town - and the old nursing home that served as a hospital.

He was not prepared for the shock of seeing his mother. She looked skeletal, her face yellow, her hair thinned out. Worst of all for him was her head. No longer the shapely oval he remembered, it was skinny and long and caved in now, looking almost as if it had been squeezed and flattened inside a waffle iron. The sight devastated him, and he felt the last vestiges of his youth start to drain away. Bill Stoner and Marianna were sitting on the edge of her bed. "Hello, Dad," he said. No answer. "When did you get here?" he asked Marianna.

"About three hours ago," she whispered. "I beat the bad weather out of St. Louis, rented a car and drove down. She's been asleep ever since I arrived."

As if she heard them, Lara Stoner started stirring and opened her eyes. Her eyes were glazed at first. Mercifully, she was drugged and in that terminal stage of semi-existence when life is sustained only by bottles of dripping glucose and vast arrays of tubes poked into arms and noses and mouths. Lara saw him then, and her eyes sparkled with a glint of recognition. She struggled pitifully to sit up. Clay embraced her, and kissed her on the cheek. She smelled of decay. "I knew you would come," she said in a raspish whisper. "I tried to make myself pretty. But I guess I fell asleep and got mussed up." She fumbled for her hairbrush and mirror and started swiping clumsily at her hair.

"Oh come on, Mom. You're still as pretty as ever, and you know it," Clay said, admiring her valiant effort to maintain her dignity.

"No, I'm not. I didn't want you to see me this way, son." She touched his hand and said very softly, "do you know...they even make me wear diapers."

"Oh, pooh! You look fine, Lara" Marianna said, brimming with cheerfulness. "You just need to get all the rest you can so you can get out of this place and go home."

Lara Stoner looked at her indulgently, knowing the truth but playing the role. "You're right, Marianna. And when I do get out of here the first thing I'm going to do is go see your darling little 'uns again...take 'em some presents. I'll spoil them to death if you let me." And so it went. Clay knew his mother was too smart to be fooled by all the phony pablum everyone was dishing out. But she went along with it. He wanted to have a real conversation with her...to tell her how he wished he could be a child again...how he wished they could go back and do all the things they used to do together. Instead, they made small talk: the weather, the pearl necklace his dad had given her for Christmas, whether or not the Cardinals would win the pennant in 1971. After awhile, she dozed off into another heavy, drug-induced sleep. Marianna, Clay and his father went out in the corridor to talk.

Bill Stoner saw that the two of them were exhausted. He had been exhausted enough himself the last few months to recognize the look when he saw it. He insisted that they go home. "I'll stay with her tonight," he said wearily. "She won't wake up again before morning." He ushered them to the top of the stairs on the second floor, and then he turned and shuffled off quietly down the darkened corridor toward Lara's room.

Outside, as they approached Marianna's rental car, a silver grey, Chevrolet Impala, Clay stopped and put his arm around her. "I'm too keyed up to sleep," he said. "It's only midnight. Let's go to the dance at the club. The party will still be going strong and it'll do me good to see some of my old friends; especially to see Slim Sparks again." Marianna kissed him softly on the cheek and, without saying a word, she hopped behind the wheel of the Impala and started the engine.

The New Year's Eve dance at the Country Club had always been the highlight of the Creekwood Christmas season, the one event each year where Clay could expect to see all his friends in the course of a single evening. He had not been back to the club for more than five years, though, and as soon as he and Marianna walked into the foyer, he sensed a change. The club was decorated differently now. The old, white stucco walls had been painted a bright pink and adorned with outlandish modern paintings; the once simple tile floor was covered with a deep, light blue pile carpet; the lights were dimmer; and instead of a coat rack in the foyer, there was now a cloak room with an attendant checking coats. But it was when he led Marianna into the ballroom that the change he had sensed became real. Up on the stage, in the exact spot where Slim Sparks and his band had provided the New Year's Eve entertainment ever since he could remember, a heavy metal band from Paducah was playing acid rock with a beat that was deafening and monotonous. Clay stood motionless at the door in disbelief. He peered through the smoky haze in search of a familiar face, thinking that at any moment one would appear and greet him with a shout of recognition. A minute passed, and Marianna tugged at his sleeve. "We might as well try dancing to this stuff," she said resignedly. She took him by the hand, and they plunged into the crowd. They danced one number, and after it was over, someone tapped Clay on the shoulder. He whirled, expecting to see one of his old friends. Instead, he was confronted by a man of about fifty years old he had never seen before.

"Say. Aren't you Clay Stoner?" the man said as he tilted up a half pint of whiskey in a brown bag and took a swig and grinned.

"I don't know. Am I?" Clay said warily, remembering all of a sudden that he was still a fugitive from the law.

"Sure you are! You played halfback for Creekwood back in fifty-eight. Remember the Porterville game?" the man said, his eyes gleaming.

"Sort of," Clay said, still a bit wary. "As I recall, it was a very close game. Both teams were undefeated at the time. Creekwood won."

"That's right! Thirteen to seven! And you intercepted three passes. Ran one for a back for a touchdown. Caught another in the last minute in the end zone that saved the game."

Clay started to smile. "Well, you certainly have a better memory than I do," he said, as amazed as he was flattered that a man he never knew still remembered such details of a high school football game that had taken place so many years ago.

"My memory should be pretty good," the man said, bleary-eyed and wistful looking now. "You see, I was Porterville's coach. That was the best team I ever had."

Marianna dug her nails into Clay's arm, edging him toward the dance floor and away from the drunken man. "Well, you gave us a helluva fight," Clay said politely as they turned aside.

The coach stepped in front of them. "You know," he said, "we never should've thrown that ball in the last minute. We could've run it in and beaten you guys." Clay laughed and tried to step around him, but the coach moved to block his way. "You may not realize it," he said, looking sweaty and pathetic and sad, "but that was the worst day of my life...If it weren't for you, we could've gone undefeated. And then you went out and lost your very next game to Flat River. "

"Quite frankly, we don't much care!" Marianna burst out all of a sudden. "Is that all you can think to talk about on New Year's Eve, some old high school football game that's nothing but ancient history now? Is that all your life is about - football?" she ranted. Clay had never seen her like this before.

The man was shaken, and he stuttered as he attempted to answer. "Uh, no. I don't coach anymore. I...I'm in sales now," he said meekly. "Mattresses out of Memphis. I'm just up visiting for the holidays."

"Well, it was nice to meet you," Marianna demurred. "Hope sales are going well." Grabbing Clay's arm, she brushed past the coach out onto the dance floor. "Is that guy for real?" she whispered once they were dancing, still fuming.

"He meant no harm," Clay replied, trying to calm her down. "You just don't understand the people around here." After the next number he steered her over to the bar and slapped a five dollar bill on the counter. "One scotch and soda and one gin and tonic, please," he said, scarcely noticing the skinny, clumsy bartender who mixed the drinks. The bartender looked like a mole that had just crawled out of a hole.

"Hey, Clay. Here you are. Betcha don't remember me," the mole said, grinning stupidly as he plopped the drinks on the counter. Clay looked at him. The face was a distant memory. He tried to recall...to think. But he could not come up with the name...He was tired. "It's Rat! Don't you remember me? Ole Rat!"

"Rat! Of course! How are you?" Clay blurted out, starting to smile as a wave of recognition enveloped him. Rat had been the football team's equipment manager; the water boy, the gawky, semi-literate kid who had taped ankles, handed out towels and mopped the dressing room floor. He saw Rat's long toothy grin, fangs that protruded out over his lips, and wondered how he ever could have forgotten.

"It's really good seein' y'gin, Clay. How long yuh home fur?" Rat said, full of exuberance.

"I dunno. Just a few days I reckon," he replied, slipping back into his old Ozark lingo.

"Sorry to hear that. What yuh 'doin' now, anyway? Still in the Navy?"

"No. No, I'm not," Clay said, fidgeting, surprised to learn that there was someone in Creekwood who had not heard about his court martial. "I've been out of the Navy for a long time now." Marianna nudged him. "Oh, excuse me. Rat, this is Marianna Haizet. Marianna, this is my old friend..." Clay paused, realizing suddenly that he had never known Rat's real name. Wavering his finger up and down, pointing at Rat for a moment, he said finally, "Marianna, this is my old friend Rat."

Rat stared at Marianna and gulped. She was wearing a black, tight fitting suede jump suit with a low cut neckline that showed off the soft bronze tan that still lingered from Menorca. "How do you do," she said politely, offering her hand.

"Hi. Ah...ah kin tell. Yore not from around here, are yuh?" Rat stuttered.

"No...I'm afraid not, but Clay has told me so much about Creekwood that I feel like I am," Marianna said, knowing it was the right thing to say.

Rat beamed and clasped her hand. "Did...did he tell you about our football team?" he said, with excitement in his eyes.

"No. Does Creekwood have a football team?" she said unflinching, smiling, her eyes wide-eyed and innocent looking as Rat let her hand go limp.

Rat's mouth dropped. The grin wiped off his face, and he looked crushed. Clay hastened to slap him on the back. "She's just kidding, Rat. Marianna's from Europe, and they don't know much about football over there...So what'cha been up to?"

"Bartendin' some. Here and down at the Driftwood. But farmin' mostly. Sharecroppin' sixty acres south of town for Terry Malone. Doin' real good, too."

"Malone! Is he back in town?"

"Oh, yeah. Came back 'bout three years ago and teamed up with Tim Collins. Makin' it real big. Fact is, he's helpin' us *all* make it. He's right over there if you wanna talk to him."

Clay turned to look. Standing at the far end of the bar, wearing an expensive tuxedo and sleek red vest in sharp contrast to the rest of the crowd, was Terry Malone. Clay would have recognized him anywhere, lean, hard and erect, ordering drinks with the same aplomb he had always shown when standing in the pocket threading needles with his passes. Clay dragged Marianna toward him. The other bartender handed Terry two drinks, and he started to walk away. Clay tapped him on the shoulder. "Hey, Malone!" he said excitedly.

Terry turned and looked at him and blinked. "Why I'll be damn! Clay Stoner. How are you?" he said flippantly.

"Fine. You?" Clay burbled.

"Can't complain. Have you moved back here?"

"No. I'm just home to see my mother."

"Oh, yeah. I heard. Sorry."

"I can't believe you're back, man! And farming! If that doesn't take the cake!"

"It keeps me out of trouble." He gave Clay a wicked smile. "Actually, farmin's goin' good - real good, if I don't say so myself."

"That's great, Terry. The last time I was home I heard farming was on its ass."

"Yeah, I know. I guess I hit it just right."

Clay punched Terry playfully in the chest and changed the subject. "Say! Where's Slim? I thought for sure he'd be playing tonight."

"Slim's lost it," Terry said nonchalantly. "The kids are bored with him. Too old and out of touch, I guess. I hear he's really gone downhill...just sits out at the farm, drinkin' all day."

Clay winced. For the second time this night he was witnessing one of life's little crumbles. First his mother. Now Slim. Slim had said that this would happen some day...that he would be just as good as dead when it did. *Is that what it's all about - getting old and dying - no one to care about you anymore?* He shook his head to clear his eyes and then remembered Marianna. "Hey fella', I haven't introduced you," he said, looking embarrassed. "This is my old buddy, Terry Malone. Terry, Marianna Haizet."

Marianna had been taking in the conversation, and she did not like the impertinent attitude Terry was displaying. She nodded. "Clay's told me a great deal about you," she said formally, as friendly as she could pretend to be.

Terry eyed her slowly up and down. "Not bad," he smirked." Where ya' from sweetheart?"

"Around," she shrugged. "France at the moment."

"Well ain't that somethin' else," Terry teased. "I must have taught ole Clay here pretty good. You're a real looker honey, ya' know that? Ever fool around?"

"No I don't, and my name *ain't* honey," Marianna said with rapier-like quickness, "and I can't imagine that you could ever have taught Clay anything."

"Well la-di-dah. Ain't you the quick-witted one?" Terry said as he leaned over, peering into her eyes, tapping his finger gently on the end of her nose.

"Or maybe you're just the slow-witted one," she quipped back, brushing his finger away.

"Hey, listen babe. Don't think just because you're from France that you're such hot shit around here."

"Oh, I don't," she said with her feigned, wide-eyed innocent look again. "I just hope you don't think *you're* hot shit because you *are* from here. Cold, is more like it."

Terry turned red, and tiny blood vessels started popping up underneath the skin on his forehead. Clay had seen him like this before when he lost his temper, and he stepped between them. "Hey, easy, you two. Easy," he said.

"Easy, my ass!" Terry erupted. "I don't have to put up with this fancy broad talking down to me like that, Stoner! You may not know it, but I'm somebody around here now."

"Listen. No harm done. Let's forget it. Okay?"

"Sure. Okay," Terry said, still seething. "I'll be up the lounge with Mona Faye if you wantta get together for a drink later."

"Mona Faye?"

"Yeah. Kay and I got divorced a long time ago. But ole Mona Faye still does it like a rabbit. Pretty good, too." Terry tilted up and downed one of his drinks, slammed the glass on the counter, and then shoved his way roughly into the crowd.

Clay turned to Marianna. "What did you start that for?" he said testily.

"Start it! I didn't start anything! I just can't believe that's the great Terry Malone you told me about - your best friend growing up - mister cool! He's nothing but a *jerk!*"

Clay wrapped his arm around Marianna's waist and walked her over to a table that was cluttered with half filled glasses, soggy napkins, and an empty whiskey bottle in a paper sack. They finished their drinks and made their way out of the ballroom, through the foyer, and up the short flight of stairs to the smoke-filled lounge.

Judy Collins saw them as soon as they walked into the room, and her raucous voice cut through the haze like gunfire. "Hey, Stoner! Over here!" she shrieked. She stood up, a tower in her high heels, and rushed toward them. She gave Clay a bear hug and a smothering kiss that plastered lipstick on both cheeks. "It's been such a long time!" she squealed. "Here! Let me look at you." As they stepped back, Clay could see that the years had not been kind. Although her warm smile and classic features were still there, Judy now carried a few too many extra pounds on her five foot ten frame. She turned to Marianna. "And I remember you," she said, pointing a finger and cocking her head. "Slim's Place. The night Chuck Stanback and Patsy Foster were killed." She hesitated and sighed for a moment. "That was a horrible night we don't want to think about anymore," she said then, and she draped her arms around Clay and Marianna and led them over to the longest table in the lounge, one right next to the fireplace. Donald Joe Baker was at the head of the table, sitting between Petey Monroe and Bobby Lee Crawford. Donald Joe was telling a joke, and they were laughing. He heaved his large carcass out of his chair when Judy approached and reached out to shake Clay's hand. "You may not have heard, but I'm a Baker now," Judy said. "Donald Joe and I are married."

Clay froze a second. "The two of you got married! When the hell did that happen?" he said with a surprised laugh to conceal his letdown.

Donald Joe spoke up hastily. "'Bout three years ago. Judy was gittin' to be an ole maid. Someboduh had to make an honest woman out of her. And ah wasn't gettin' any younger. Marriage of convenience yuh might say," Donald Joe chortled in his deep southern drawl.

And from the looks of them, they hadn't done anything but drink and eat ever since, Clay thought. Donald Joe was heftier than ever. How could Judy Collins, winner of every beauty contest she ever entered, have done it? She had the talent and the looks - the personality - family money. She could have gotten out of Creekwood, gone somewhere and done something.

"Remember my brother, Tim?" Judy said to Marianna. Tim Collins was sitting at the other end of the table, looking mean and drunk. He nodded at Clay and Marianna. Cindy Sue was sitting next to him, and Clay shut his eyes when he saw her. The dark eyes, the full pouting lips, the olive skin - they were all still a part of her. But she was starting to show the onset of a double chin and was wearing so much gaudy jewelry that she looked like she should be featured as a rhinestone cowgirl in a television commercial.

Terry was with Mona Faye, sitting at the far side of the table next to the wall. He had his hand up her dress, and she was loving it, giggling and nibbling at his ear. They hardly noticed as Marianna and Clay sat down across from them, Marianna next to Cindy Sue and Clay next to her brother, Bobby Lee. "We ain't seen you in a coon's age, Stoner. When'd y'all get in?" Petey Monroe asked them.

"Just tonight. Your pilot flew me down from St. Louis."

"Well I'll be goddamned! I should've known it was some dang fool like you up there who'd wantta fly tonight."

"I was sure surprised to find that kid at the airport instead of you. How's the crop dustin' business goin'?"

"Don't have time for that much anymore," Petey said smugly. "There's been a lotta changes around here, Clay. I've got six planes now. Keep 'em flyin' day and night. Haulin' freight mostly. Spend most of my time managin' now."

Clay observed that Petey, Terry, Donald Joe and Tim were all wearing tuxes, and Bobby Lee his full dress army officer uniform, the only five men in the club dressed so formally. "Business must be pretty good," he said.

"Yeah, it has been," Petey said, taking a gulp of his beer. "Terry and Tim and I've been doin' all right the past couple of years."

"Would you believe that dumb sonavabitch Petey's a millionaire!" Donald Joe laughed. "When we were both freshmen at Arkansas State, he flunked out first semestah. That's how dumb the sonavabitch was. Even ah made it through Arkansas State. Now he's the big biznessman, and ah'm still a gopher workin' for my dad down at the grain company."

"Havin' a little luck's better than bein' smart," Petey said, a cocky swagger in his voice.

Clay saw Marianna's eyes raise to the ceiling. She leaned over against him and muttered under her breath, "Jesus Christ! What is this bullshit?"

Clay turned to Bobby Lee, who had surprised him by his quietness when they had sat down. A shiny set of captain's bars rested on his shoulders and a cluster of medals draped over his chest. "Hey, Bobby Lee," Clay said, "where'd you get all the brass?"

"Nam. Two tours. Sixty-six and sixty-eight," Bobby Lee said with uncharacteristic abruptness.

"And still in one piece. That's great. What are you up to now?"

"Teaching ROTC...down at Ole Miss."

"*ROTC!* No kidding!" Clay said, laughing.

Bobby Lee shrugged. "Keeps me busy."

"What about you, Clay?" Tim Collins interjected from his end of the table in a nasty tone. "Last thing we heard about you was your court martial. We heard you deserted."

There was a silence around the table, and it hung there for a few seconds like the eerie stillness that precedes the onset of a tornado. Then Marianna spoke up, very self-composed. "The court martial was just an elaborate ruse so Clay could go underground. He's doing some highly secret work overseas for the government - something he's not at liberty to talk about." Marianna had rehearsed this story well before leaving La Gaude.

Cindy Sue took the cue. "I wanted to ask you about that when I saw you in London last summer," she said to Clay. "What happened to you after that cocktail party?"

"I had to leave. Sorry. I had to take care of some business in Switzerland the next day"

"What kind of business?" Tim asked abruptly, eyes glinting. He exchanged a wary glance with Terry.

Marianna elbowed Clay and quickly changed the subject. "Hey! Lighten up everybody! No talking business tonight. It's New Year's Eve! Time to be happy!" She directed everyone's attention back to Cindy Sue. "So, how did you like Europe, Cindy Sue?"

Tim answered for her. "Once you've seen it you can have it as far as we're concerned." He looked at Cindy Sue and smiled; she smiled back, nodding in agreement. He asked Marianna: "Do you still live in New York? I think that's where you were living the last time you were here."

"No," Marianna said. "I moved to Europe several years ago."

"Smart move," Tim blared out. "I don't see how anybody could stand living in that city with all the niggers, and spics and jews."

"I don't need to listen to any of your racist crap, Tim," Marianna said, eyeing him with disgust.

Donald Joe intervened, like a big playful bear trying to inject some humor into the situation. "Listen, honey," he said laughing. "We're not racists around heah. But we do know enuff to call a spade a spade when we see one."

"That's not funny," Marianna bristled.

"God!" Bobby Lee groaned. "You sound just like one of those pinko liberals from the New York Times."

"My brother works for the Times. It may be liberal, but at least it tries to get its facts right."

"Facts my ass!" Bobby Lee boiled over. He had been listening quietly throughout the conversations, but now he became virulent. "If the Times had told the truth about Nam, we would've won the war by now! But they've been lying for years! Same with the rest of the media. That's because they're all run by a bunch of communists!

"You think Cronkite's a communist?" Marianna responded, incredulous.

"Probably. Did you see the big to-do he made over Kent State?"

Marianna was beside herself. "Don't you think Kent State warranted a big to-do? It's not everyday that the national guard marches onto a college campus and guns down unarmed students!"

Terry Malone, who had been devoting all his attention to Mona Faye's body, suddenly swung his arm around, knocking over three drinks in the process, and bellowed out drunkenly, "those goddam draft dodging students got exactly what they asked for!" Whiskey slopped all over the table and splattered Mona Faye and Cindy Sue. Everyone jumped up to wipe off the mess. When the commotion died down and they were seated again, Bobby Lee asked Marianna a question so that they all could hear.

"You don't really think the National Guard shot those students, do you?" He said it with a queer look in his eye.

Marianna thought he was joking. "Well...yeah. I sort of do," she said, muffling a laugh. "I sat there watching it on television. I saw the Guard march up a hill and turn and kneel...take aim. Then I saw an officer swing his arm downward and the troops start blasting away and some dead kids were on the ground after it was over. At least that's what it looked like to me."

"Well, you're wrong. The Guard didn't shoot those students. Chinese communists did!" Bobby Lee announced with an air of conviction, sitting erect, arms folded across his chest. "We have proof! The students weren't even shot with the same kind of bullets the Guard was using."

"Oh come off it, Bobby Lee," Clay interrupted, also thinking it was a joke and that Bobby Lee was just goading Marianna. "What are you talking about - we have proof? You're nothing but a goddamn piss-ant army captain. A ROTC instructor for Christ's sake! If that kind of information had filtered down to your level and there was any truth to it, it would have been all over the news before now."

"You *see! See! That's what I mean!*" Bobby Lee screamed wildly as he stood up and pounded his fist on the table. "The media is all run by communists! That's why you haven't heard anything about it!"

Clay was speechless. He saw the raving, maniacal look in Bobby Lee's eyes, and he knew it was no joke now. He stood up. "You're badly mistaken, Bobby Lee," he said quietly, coldly. "You're simply...fucking...crazy."

Terry jumped up, waving his fist at Clay. "You know, you sound like one of them," he said, squinting his eyes in a weird, threatening way. "How do we know you're really undercover and not some goddamn left wing deserter like the papers said?"

Judy grabbed Terry's wrist and pulled his fist down. "That's enough, Terry. Don't you realize Clay's mother is dying?"

"If he thinks he's gonna get some sympathy from me because of his mother, he's got another think comin'!" Terry sneered.

Clay snapped. He threw his drink in Terry's face, and Terry jumped forward, lunging at him, knocking over a chair. They were separated by the table, and before they could reach each other Donald Joe had Clay in a bear hug, and Judy and Petey each had hold of one of Terry's arms. Marianna grabbed Clay's hand. "Let's get out of here," she insisted, and she dragged him away from the table before anything else could happen.

"They're crazy! They're fucking crazy!" Clay cried out once they were out of the lounge.

"Cool it, Clay," Marianna said soothingly.

"Cool it!" he ranted. "Do you realize that lunatic Bobby Lee could be a general someday? Just the thought scares me to death!" He was still steaming when they reached the ballroom. "I just don't understand it," he muttered as they danced to a slow song. "Bobby Lee and Terry were my best friends. Judy's tossed it all away and married good ole Donald Joe. The girl I was once in love with is married to that ratshit, Tim. How did it happen? How could they all have changed so?"

Marianna kissed him on the eyelids. "Maybe you're the one who's different. Tonight I learned that this town is in its own little world, Clay. Only you've outgrown it...and *they* know it...and they don't like it."

The band started playing *Good Night Sweetheart* and people started to leave. At the end of the song, Marianna and Clay went back to the lounge. The long table was empty. Everyone was gone except Donald Joe and Judy. Donald Joe was slumped at the bar. Judy was trying to coax him to go home, but Donald Joe was hearing none of it. He was drinking a rusty nail and insisted on ordering Clay one too. Donald Joe looked despondent, and he wanted to talk. "Ah'm sick and tard of it, Clay," he mumbled.

"Tired of what?" Clay asked as he sat down beside him and accepted the rusty nail.

"Mah dad. He's gonna lose the family land. We haven't had a profit on a crop in seven years, and he won't let me do a thing about it. Just keeps me workin' down at the grain company - and for what? Nothin'."

"I thought farming had been good," Clay said. "Terry Malone said he was doing great."

"Terry and Tim are. But that's because they ain't growin' cotton." Donald Joe looked around to make sure they were alone. Marianna had gone off to a booth with Judy. "If yuh can keep yore mouth shut, I'll tell yuh a few things."

"I can keep my mouth shut," Clay said.

Donald Joe gulped down another rusty nail, then stared straight across the counter at the liquor bottles stacked against the wall and started talking. "Yuh know, Tim took ovah the bank and all the Collins land 'bout five years ago when his old man died. What yuh don't know - two years later he was 'bout bankrupt. He was losin' his ass tryin' to grow cotton, and so was ever'one else his bank was loanin' money to. The bank was 'bout to go under...Then Terry Malone came to town. He rented some of the Collins' land and started growin' pot. Tim saw the money in it, and he and Terry went partners. They bought or leased up most all the land around here 'cept ours, and they got half the town sharecroppin' for 'em."

"Half the town's growing weed?"

"Just about. And Tim and Terry asked mah Dad to join up with 'em. Sort of like a syndicate. We rent our land to Terry. He farms it; handles the sales through his contacts, whoever they are. Petey takes care of flyin' the stuff out. Tim handles the money. Launders it through his bank. Profits go into a Swiss bank account and we share fifty-fifty. No risk to us...'cept Dad won't do it."

"Knowing your Dad, I'm surprised he hasn't turned them in."

"He could never do that to Old Man Collins' son. Dad and the Old Man were best friends for fifty years." A telephone on the bar started ringing, interrupting their conversation. Donald Joe picked it up. "Hullo," he said drunkenly. "Who?" He handed the receiver to Clay. "It's for you. Long distance." Donald Joe acted so nonchalant that Clay was sure it was another of his jokes. No one could be calling him long distance who knew he was at the Creekwood Country Club. He refused to accept the phone. "No. Ah'm serious. It's fur you," Donald Joe insisted. He tottered and almost fell off his barstool as he shoved the receiver into Clay's hand.

Clay took it, fully expecting Donald Joe to burst out with one of his giant horse laughs as soon as he learned who was on the line. Probably some wife looking for her husband, he thought. He picked up the receiver and heard a faint feminine voice on the other end of the line, "Clay, is that you?"

"Darcy? How in the world did you find us?" Clay blurted out, astounded.

"Just a guess," came her muffled, crackling voice. "We're just home from Megeve. I tried calling your father's house a few minutes ago, but got no answer. Then I remembered how you used to talk about the New Year's Eve party at the Country Club, so I decided to give it a try. I can't believe I got you."

"Neither can I. Pretty amazing, isn't it?" Clay said, starting to feel the effects of his rusty nails now.

"It sure is. So tell me. How's the party? Is Slim Sparks still as great as ever?"

"Slim Sparks is dead, Darcy."

"Oh, no! That's terrible. I'm so sorry, Clay."

"It was bound to happen...as a matter of fact, they're all dead."

"What are you talking about? Who's all dead, Clay?"

"Slim'n all the rest...Chuck, Vic, Sammy...all my friends. They're just dead, Darcy. Dead and gone and buried."

"You sound drunk, Clay Stoner!"

"Yep - that I am. You'd be too if all your friends were dead."

Marianna walked over and jerked the phone away from him. "Darse, Clay's stoned," she said. "Don't pay any attention to him. Slim Sparks isn't dead. He's just not here tonight." She started speaking French then. Clay tried to watch her face and listen, but her words and the lounge were all starting to become a blur to him. In less than a minute Marianna picked up the phone and carried it to the end of the bar so that no one could overhear the conversation.

She huddled there for five minutes and hung up shortly after Judy had managed to coax Donald Joe to leave. It was three o'clock. Ten in the morning in the Paris they had left more than twenty-four hours ago, and Marianna and Clay were wasted. Clay was also very drunk. She helped him outside to the Impala, demanded the keys and climbed behind the wheel.

They did not talk on the ride home. Clay was too out of it to talk. In the driveway, after she shut off the ignition, Marianna turned and jostled him awake. "I also spoke with Cat on the phone tonight," she said. "Cat's with Darcy in Paris. She's beat up pretty badly, Clay."

"What do you mean...beat up?" he said, sitting upright and sobering all of a sudden.

"Just that. Howie knocked her around quite a bit, trying to find out if she knew anything. She says she'll be all right in a couple of days, though. A tooth knocked out, but nothing broken. But she's terrified. She ran away and left everything she had at Howie's place. She's been driving all night. Just got to Paris about an hour ago."

"Did she tell you what happened?" Clay asked, wide awake now.

"Enough. They're after us, Clay. Howie's talked to Nicholson. He's already sent his bodyguards up to La Gaude looking for us. Cat says they'll stop at nothing to find us."

"She didn't tell them our real names?"

"No."

Clay shook his head from side to side. "Cat's a true friend. Did she say how Cody and Cody are doing?"

"They're fine for now – but what about later, Clay?"

"I don't know about later," he said, fighting off the urge to go to sleep on her shoulder. "It's been a long day, fella'. We're both bushed. Let's go to bed and talk about it tomorrow."

She leaned over and kissed his eyelids, and then they got out of the Impala and zig-zagged wearily into the house and to bed.

The telephone awakened Marianna at nine in the morning. It rang four times as she lay in bed, trying to decide if it were part of her dream or not. She rolled over and saw Clay still sleeping, motionless as a stone. She knew then the telephone was not a dream; she scrambled out of bed and rushed to answer it. Robert was on the line, talking rapidly. He would be in Creekwood with his editor by late afternoon, he said. When he started mumbling about how Larry Smith was on the west coast and could not make it until the next day, Marianna became totally confused. She could not comprehend what he was talking about. She asked him to hold and roused Clay, who woke up with a terrible headache. He rolled out of bed with no clothes on and stumbled to the phone. After listening to Robert for two minutes, he hung up and placed a call to Petey Monroe. He made arrangements with Petey for one of his planes to pick up three passengers in St. Louis the next day at two o'clock..

"What's that all about?" Marianna asked after he finished his conversations.

"Robert's coming this afternoon. He's bringing his editor with him. Larry Smith will be here tomorrow." Clay was so abrupt that she did not press him any further. All she could discern was that the news media was en route to Creekwood.

They dressed quickly and drove to the hospital. Bill Stoner was sitting in a chair by Lara's bedside, asleep and snoring. He awakened when they walked in. He looked exhausted. He needed a shave. His eyes were hollow and red, his face splotchy. The look of a broken man, Marianna thought. She had never seen the effects of the slow, tortuous suffering of a lingering death before, and for the first time, the extent of the strain Bill Stoner had been under all these months registered on her. She felt guilty - not for any specific reason - just guilty because of all the time Clay had spent with her in the past five years away from his mother. Bill Stoner pulled himself wearily out of his chair. "She had a very bad night. Call me if there's any change. I'll be back this afternoon," he said as he put on his old grey hat and shuffled dazedly out of the room.

An hour later Lara Stoner began breathing heavily. She started gurgling and became steadily worse as fluid accumulated in her lungs and she struggled to breathe. Marianna ran out of the room and down the corridor, searching for a doctor. She found one coming out of another patient's room, grabbed him, and ushered him back down the corridor to Lara Stoner's room. As they entered, Clay screamed. "My mother's *dying*, goddamnit! You have to do something." He physically shoved the doctor toward her bed. The doctor called for a nurse and asked Clay and Marianna to go to the waiting room. He shut the door and Marianna and Clay turned and walked away, each unable to bear knowing what might happen next.

It seemed like hours passed. In reality it was only forty-five minutes before the doctor walked into the waiting room. "She's sleeping peacefully now," he said in a kind, but somber, voice. "I had to stab a needle in her chest and drain off the excess fluid. That's the second time this week. I can't promise you that she'll make it through this time." *The sad truth.* Nothing could be done about it, and Clay knew that now. Shoving the doctor some more was not going to help. *How can they stand it, he thought? Doctors - working every day with dying people.*

Bill Stoner returned in mid-afternoon. A short while later Lara stirred and opened her eyes. Clay sat next to her, and she stared at him, blinking vacantly as if surprised to see him. It took her several seconds to assimilate the surroundings, and as she did, she broke into a warm, serene smile, one that seemed to flood with joy as she recognized she was alive. Clay stared at her, and the way she looked, and he wanted to cry. He had thought he would never hear her voice again. They started talking about the distant past - the winter they spent together when he was five on the island off the coast of Florida; his first baseball game when he was ten and he was hit in the stomach by a pitch, doubled up on the ground, and she came running out of the stands to see if he was all right and help him to first base; the times she had let him play hooky so they could go fishing together at the lake; the night she had sneaked him out of Annapolis under a blanket in the back seat of her car, and then back in again, just so they could go to her motel and stay up all night talking. They laughed. And Bill Stoner laughed. The joy lasted twenty minutes. Then the pain came cascading back and in a matter of seconds she was transformed into a pitiful, whining creature again. "*God, no more!* I can't stand it. Give me a shot. Please give me a shot!" she started begging, screaming.

Marianna summoned a nurse who injected the pain killing solution Lara was craving, and soon she was oblivious to the world. Clay gazed down at her, drifting off. Her eyes were part open and her pupils had disappeared behind her sagging lids. Two glazed, yellowish orbs stared at him. Seeing her this way tortured him. This is obscene, he thought. No one as beautiful as she should have to endure this kind of humiliating, disgusting suffering any longer... He no longer hoped. He knew her body was beyond saving. He was ready for her to die now as quickly and painlessly as possible. The thought numbed him. He had never, ever imagined anything so cruel - standing in a hospital room praying for his mother to die.

After telling Bill Stoner they would be back to relieve him at ten o'clock that night, Marianna and Clay went downstairs to the waiting room. Marianna was shocked to see Robert there, pacing back and forth, puffing on one of his Old Gold filters. With him was his editor, Ian MacInnis, a tall genteel man, late fifties, with wavy, silvery hair and a faint trace of an English accent. Clay could see that Robert was tense. MacInnis did not crack a smile. The eight hour trip on New Year's Day, four of it down backwoods roads into the Ozarks in their rental car, had him obviously disgruntled. He was stiff and crisp until Marianna walked up to him, batted her eyes, smiled, and introduced herself only as Robert's sister. "We're going to a cabin up in the woods," she explained "You can hole up and work there. Around here you would attract too much attention."

Minutes later the four of them were in the two rental cars, heading up into the hills. By the time they reached the five mile gravel road which led into the lake from Hays Ridge, it was getting dark. The road was a rough drive through dense woods until they reached the main lodge a half mile from the cabin. A thin wisp of smoke curled from the lodge's chimney. Three cars were parked in front. Duck hunters, Clay thought. No one else comes here in winter; an ideal spot for sequestering Robert and MacInnis. The final quarter mile into the cabin was covered with fresh snow, and with no tracks to guide them, it was impossible to avoid the rocks and potholes; they were all relieved to make it without mishap. Clay retrieved the door key from underneath a rock on the window ledge, unlocked the door and escorted them inside. No one had been to the cabin since September, so it was cold, dank and musty. Clay lit a small fire, then went outside in search for more wood while Robert and MacInnis unloaded their typewriters and suitcases. Marianna, Robert, and MacInnis were still in their coats, huddled by the fireplace warming their hands when Clay returned. MacInnis stood up, hands on his hips. "Given that I've let you drag me all the way out here to this god-forsaken place on a New Year's weekend, could you now please tell me what this is all about?" he said gruffly.

"Sure. Government corruption at the very highest levels. Bribes. Money laundering. Probably murder," Clay said almost casually. "I think you'll find it interesting enough to make it worth your while."

"Well, I hope so! Otherwise your young friend here is going to have some explaining to do," MacInnis said, staring coldly at Robert.

Clay ignored the bluster. "My main question is whether or not you'll have the final say to print this story if you think it warrants it - which it will?" he asked MacInnis pointedly. "Or will you have to go through some formal approval process?"

MacInnis looked insulted. "I've been with the Times for thirty years," he snapped. "The paper knows how important my reputation is. I do my own editing and it prints what I write, without question."

With that reassurance, Clay launched into a recap of events: his court martial and escape; his career as a pilot with Utopia; the dozens of couriers with suitcases full of money he had flown in and out of Europe over the years; the Nicholson-Utopia connection; the party in London, the Senator, the SEC Commissioner, Admiral Martin, the secret numbered accounts he had opened in Switzerland; his meeting with Whitney and the unusual circumstances surrounding Whitney's death; the theft of Utopia's records. Robert and MacInnis scribbled notes rapidly, too astonished to interrupt. "I haven't had time to really analyze the records," Clay said finally. "But I did get a chance to skim through them flying across the Atlantic. There are some names there that will blow your mind." Clay got up and went outside to Mariannas's car, returning momentarily with a suitcase. He set it on the dining table and flipped it open. "Here," he said. "This should be all the proof you need. Take your time and study it. I'm going back to Creekwood for the night. Marianna will stay here with you. There's coffee and soup and stuff in the cupboard. I'll bring some food out tomorrow."

Robert and MacInnis were busy dissecting the Utopia books when Clay left for Creekwood. He drove straight to the hospital. His father was alone in the waiting room when he arrived, slumped in a chair and staring blindly at the opposite wall. He stood up when he saw Clay, walked over and put a hand on his shoulder. He said simply, "your mother died about an hour ago." Clay felt a rush of emotion - and then nothing. The news did not devastate him as much as he thought it would. He only felt weary and numb now. He looked at his father. There was anguish in his face, but Clay also thought he saw there a trace of relief. His dad had done everything possible to save her. He had sold his business and spent months traveling with her from one hospital to another in search of the possible miracle cure. His life's savings had been wiped out. He was in debt. He had never stopped searching, though, as long as there was hope. For the last two weeks he had been at her bedside twenty hours a day, having to just sit there, watching her consumed with pain. That pain was gone now. The agony was over. What happened to Lara Stoner from now on was meaningless as far as Bill Stoner was concerned. For him, the funeral would only be a show for other people's sake. Clay felt the same way. His mother was just a body now, a carcass to be dumped in a hole in the ground. He preferred to remember her when she was alive, the lovely, living creature she was. Not a body.

"I suppose we have to make some funeral arrangements," Clay said quietly.

"I've already called Thornton's," his father said. "They're up in the room with her now. I'm meeting Dave Thornton at the funeral parlor at eleven in the morning."

Clay and his father slept late. They were met at the funeral parlor at eleven o'clock by Thornton's young son and promptly escorted downstairs into a room filled with caskets. In a few minutes Dave Thornton appeared, dressed impeccably, a white carnation in his lapel. His hair was slicked back; his eyes were heavy and his face was long, trained over many years to show the proper look of bereavement. He steered Bill Stoner to a gleaming six-thousand dollar casket and began describing its attributes. Clay's skin crawled. He was steeled enough to recognize what was happening. "Of course, the service is all included in the price," Clay heard him say. Clay left the two of them talking, walked away, and browsed among the lower priced caskets until he found a much less expensive one that appeared perfectly suitable.

"Hey, Dad! Here is one I like," he called out.

Thornton rushed over to inspect it. "Yes. That's certainly a nice one," he sniffed. "But it comes without the fiberglass liner and the ninety-nine year guarantee. I'm sure you would want Lara to have the one with the liner, wouldn't you, Bill?"

"But I like this one. Its color is more like Mom," Clay persisted. He noted Thornton's jaw tighten and wrinkle as he grit his teeth. They discussed the relative merits of the caskets back and forth for five minutes. Eventually, Bill Stoner chose the model and color Clay had selected, but with a liner that added a thousand dollars to the price. Clay knew it was a rip-off, but in the frame of mind his dad was in he also knew the damage could have been much worse. Even though he was almost broke, Bill Stoner was in no mood to quibble over money. Once satisfied, he cut Dave Thornton off, and hastily scribbled out a check, ending the distasteful transaction. Then he took Clay by the arm and led him silently out of the parlor.

Marianna was at the house when they returned. Her eyes were red. "When you didn't show up at the cabin this morning, I decided to borrow Robert's car and drive in. I was afraid this might have happened. I'm sorry fella'...truly sorry," she said, and she gave him a short hug.

The house was mobbed with a growing crowd of friends and neighbors arriving with casseroles, baked beans, and pies, all wanting to help and offer condolences. Bill Stoner wanted no part of it and went into his bedroom and locked the door, leaving Clay and Marianna to listen to the many expressions of sympathy. At three o'clock they managed to slip away and each drive one of the rental cars out to Petey Monroe's airstrip. The strip was deserted and still. A house trailer served as Petey's base of operations. Clay got out and checked it. The door was locked. He walked over to Marianna's car and climbed in the front seat, and they watched the sky. It was grey and overcast. Five minutes passed before they heard the drone of the King Air from somewhere in the clouds. It soon was on the ground, belching smoke as it taxied up to the house trailer. Larry Smith jumped out, followed quickly by his camera crew. As Clay and Marianna watched from the car, Smith paced back and forth excitedly, waving his arms. Clay heard him shout at Petey. "Where in the hell are we? Where is Robert Haizet? He said he'd be waiting for us when we arrived."

Clay got out of the car and walked out to the plane. "Robert sent me to pick you up," he said as he approached Smith from the rear.

Smith whirled and looked at him. "Who in the hell are you?" He squinted and peered at Clay for several long seconds. "I think I remember you," he said hesitantly, stroking his chin. "Clay Stoner, right? I covered your court martial in Norfolk four or five years ago."

"That's right," Clay said, as his eyes met Smith's, also remembering.

The five of them loaded the two cars quickly and piled in. Smith rode in the Impala with Clay and Marianna. His two man crew with their camera and audio equipment followed in Robert's car. Clay introduced Smith to Marianna. "Haizet! Of course! Robert's sister!" Smith exclaimed. I should have known. You were at the court martial too."

"That's right. I was the girl friend...the speed freak whose testimony helped convict him," she said, smiling insipidly.

Larry Smith started looking at her strangely then. After they had gone a few miles he leaned back and said, "you know, it's funny, but your face...I'd swear I've seen you somewhere recently - much more recently than the court martial."

"Does the name Kira Chastain ring a bell?" Clay interjected from behind the wheel.

Smith's head jerked. "Son-of-a-gun!" he said, snapping his fingers. "The Washington Monument. The Kent State protest last spring. That was you, wasn't it?"

"Mm-hmm," Marianna said, nodding shyly.

"Well I'll be damn! This is getting more interesting by the minute. I have your latest album, 'Tower in the Sky'. What in the world are you doing all the way down here in the sticks?"

"This is Clay's home town. His mother died last night. I came to be with him."

"Oh...," Smith said.

Her response cast a pall over the car, and they were quiet for the next few miles. But once they were on the gravel road leading out of Hays Ridge, Smith's curiosity got the better of him. "After you ran away, where did you go?" he asked Clay point-blank.

"Europe. I've been flying for Utopia International for the last four years. Corporate pilot."

'Utopia, huh?" Smith said, raising his eyes. "Does that have anything to do with why I'm here?"

"Could be," Clay said as they reached the turnoff onto the rutted road that led to the cabin.

MacInnis and Robert had a roaring fire going when the five of them entered the cabin. MacInnis was sitting at the dining table banging away at his typewriter. Next to him was a half empty bottle of scotch. Robert's typewriter was on the oak-grained coffee table. He was leaning over it, pecking away and puffing on a cigarette. The ashtray on the table was piled high with Old Gold Filter butts. Clay walked over to the refrigerator and took out four beers, popped one open, and handed the others to Smith and his crew. They sat down at the dining table and Clay started telling his story, reciting the sequence of events just as he had done for Robert and MacInnis the night before. When he discussed Whitney, Smith started to frown, and when he finished, Smith looked at MacInnis.

"Well, what about it Ian? Do we have a story here or not?"

MacInnis opened his mouth, but no words came out. He sat there, somewhere in that never-never land between a six cup of coffee high and half-bottle of scotch low, his eyes glazed, hands shaking. He responded, finally, his voice trembling with emotion. "More than that," he said. "I've been over and over it all day. I walked down to the lodge three times and called our news desk in New York to check out the details...They check. The proof is all here. Four senators and seven congressmen have secret accounts at Utopia...two cabinet officers...an SEC Commissioner...a half dozen admirals and generals! Those are just the big fish. The list goes on and on containing your run of the mill tax dodgers and money launderers."

"Holy shit!" Larry Smith whistled.

"There's more!" Robert burst out, his eyes radiating. "The dates of some of the account transactions are also very interesting. For instance, Admiral Martin - you remember him, the Admiral who convened Clay's court martial. Well, through a secret Swiss bank account, he and a top ranking senator on the Armed Services Committee each had an account opened with Utopia about two weeks before HBN Aviation won the huge and highly controversial navy fighter contract last summer. The records show that the day the contract was awarded five hundred thousand dollars was transferred into each of those Utopia accounts!"

"Some coincidence," Smith muttered.

"The SEC Commissioner...same thing happened. Two days after the SEC lifted its ban on Utopia - zap! Five hundred thousand dollars transferred into an account for him. And that's not all," Robert said as he reached over, picked up his beer, and took a long gulp. "Clay may have missed one of the biggest payoffs of all. He never told us about any possible Supreme Court connection. But the account evidence shows that a certain Supremes's wife has a secret million dollar account at Utopia! It just so happened that her husband was the swing vote in the five-to-four decision last summer that overturned on appeal an anti-trust decision that would have cost HBN Aviation *a half-billion dollars.*"

"Jeezus Christ!" Smith exploded, and he stood up. "God bless America. When a half-billion dollars is at stake, you can buy anything, I guess. Even the Supreme Court!" He shoved his hands in his pockets and started pacing back and forth between the dining table and the fireplace with his head bent down. "What else?" he said, as he ran one hand through his hair.

"There's the White House connection," MacInnis said quietly. Smith's head whipped up and around. "I can find no direct evidence that the President's involved," MacInnis went on, "but everyone who touches him seems to be - two of his most recent appointments, his favorite cabinet officers, some of his closest friends. He's either blind and stupid...or, God forbid, a part of it."

Smith stopped pacing. The sardonic sense of humor he displayed on the evening news every night was gone from his face now. He stumbled around in a circle with his arms raised toward the ceiling, barking out orders and behaving in much the same fashion as an eccentric movie director on a production set. "This story is dynamite!" he exclaimed. "I want to run it tomorrow night as a special! Right after the evening news. I know that scoops you, Ian, but this story deserves prime time television first. You'll still be able to hit the street before dawn the next morning with all the in-depth nitty gritty that no other paper will have. Fair enough?"

"Do I have a choice?" MacInnis groused.

"Super!" Smith bubbled, clapping his hands. "Then let's get on with it. There's a lotta work to do. I'll start on a script right now. We can do some filming here tonight and drive to St. Louis first thing in the morning. One of my guys can go down to the lodge to phone and charter a jet to be waiting for us there. Clay, I want you and Marianna with me on TV tomorrow night when I bust this story. We can finish filming it on the way."

"My mother's funeral starts at eleven in the morning. I'm not leaving until it's over," Clay said in such a way that he left no room for argument.

Smith groaned and slapped his forehead. "Damn! Okay. We'll try to film it all right here then. Ian, I'll plan to do a brief introduction. Then I want Clay to tell his story, just as he did earlier, straight and simple and to the point. Then I'll interview you, Ian, in a Q & A format, and let you present all the evidence you and Robert have uncovered in the books. That'll give it the Times stamp of credibility that you will be publishing the next morning. Okay?"

"Fine," MacInnis nodded.

"After that, I want to turn this into a human interest story. Personalize it, you know. Run some footage of this cabin, and get some film of Marianna and Clay. Play up the love story between them; how they fled the country; how they've been living all these years in exile. It's a powerful message about what the war's done to the youth of this country. Before we leave in the morning we can go down to the lake and get some shots of them along the shore - walking in the woods and that kind of stuff. I'd like to dub in a couple of Marianna's songs for the background. I don't suppose we have any of her records out here?"

"I brought one of her cassette tapes with me from New York," Robert replied.

"Fantastic!" Smith shouted. "Then let's go to work."

Marianna and Clay departed for Creekwood at six o'clock, leaving behind them the clackety-clack of typewriters reverberating off the walls of the little log cabin in the clearing in the woods. They arrived at the funeral parlor at six thirty. A crowd had already gathered. Clay walked over toward the casket, stopped ten feet away from it, and gazed at his mother. She was laid out fine, he thought. Thornton had done a handsome job and deserved to be proud, for whatever that was worth. But he did not want to go any closer. He stood there for a minute, waiting for his mind to clear, and then he went to the head of the receiving line and took his place beside his father. The line was long, and it moved slowly. The family network had done its usual amazing job of passing the word. The Stoner side of the family was few in numbers. But Lara's family included scores of cousins, aunts, uncles and nieces scattered across the hills of the Ozarks for more than a hundred miles. They were seldom seen except when they congregated for weddings and funerals - particularly funerals. And because Lara was one of their favorites, they had all come to Creekwood. Clay stood with his father politely acknowledging their sympathies for half an hour. Then he saw Cindy Sue maneuvering her way around the line toward him. His thoughts flashed back to New Year's Eve. It seemed so long ago now. Had he ever really loved her? Surely once, he knew. It's funny how things change.

Cindy Sue edged up to him and whispered in his ear. "You're wanted on the phone."

"Who is it?" he whispered back.

"I don't know. He wouldn't tell me, but he says it's urgent," she said, looking helpless. "But before you talk to whoever it is, Clay, I want you to know something. I overheard Tim making a call yesterday to the Mr. Asquith who invited us to the party in London. Tim told Mr. Asquith that you were here in Creekwood; that you were at the party in London and he thought you knew about the connection between some of the people there and Utopia's business in

Switzerland. Tim was very upset and asked Asquith what could be done about it and was told not to worry. Asquith said something about getting in touch with H.B." Cindy Sue ushered him over to a private sitting room off the parlor and handed him the phone.

"Hello," he said quietly.

"Clay, it's Rat!" a hushed voice said from the other end of the line. "I thought I should warn yuh. I'm down at the Driftwood, and I just overheard Malone and Tim Collins talkin' with four guys at the bar who said they heard that yuh was in town and they was lookin' for yuh. Serious lookin' guys. I don't know where they're from, but they were all wearin' suits. Terry told 'em they could prob'ly find yuh at the fun'ral parlor. They're leavin' here right now."

Clay took a long time to answer. "Thanks, Rat," he said, remaining outwardly calm.

"Jest thought yuh should know. Don't tell no one I told yuh," Rat said nervously. And then he hung up.

Clay let out a long, deep breath and turned to Cindy Sue. "Would you do me a favor?" he said calmly.. "Go find my Dad and Marianna and ask them to come in here a minute." Cindy Sue knew him well enough to know something was wrong. She nodded and hurried out of the room. In less than two minutes she was back with Marianna and Bill Stoner.

"What's the matter son? People out there are waiting to talk to you."

"Dad, they're many things you don't know, but Marianna and I could be in great danger if we stay here any longer. Some strangers were down at the Driftwood asking about us, so we have to leave now. We're going up to the cabin for the night."

Bill Stoner sat down and slumped back in a chair. "You know son, I know the government still wants you, but you can't be on the run forever," he said with a worried look. "Maybe it's time you turned yourself in."

Marianna interrupted. "Mr. Stoner, we need to explain some things to you in private," she said anxiously. Cindy Sue took the cue and left. Marianna then plunged hurriedly into a disjointed explanation. She told Bill Stoner about the television crew out at the cabin, the show that was going to be aired on national TV the next night exposing evidence that she and Clay had provided of high level government corruption, evidence so serious that people were looking for them and willing to kill them to stop it.

"That's why I can't afford to turn myself in right now," Clay said when she finished.

Bill Stoner shook his head from side to side. "Well...I never have been able to change your stubborn mind much. But I still think it'd be better to turn this over to somebody like the FBI and let them handle it."

"I've already tried the Justice Department, Dad. It didn't work. The lawyer in charge of the investigation was murdered. Case dropped. The only way to make sure this doesn't get covered up again, the only way for the country to find out what's going on, is the way we're doing it."

Bill Stoner's eyes reddened. "I'm...I'm sorry." he said, bowing his head and staring at the floor. "I'm just worried about you and Marianna....I hope you know what you're doing, son."

Clay reached out and placed his hand on his dad's shoulder. "See you tomorrow at the funeral," he said gently.

His dad looked up, tears in his eyes. "You're still comin?"

"You know I am." Clay took Marianna by the hand then and led her quickly out the back door of the parlor to the Impala in Thornton's parking lot.

The drive to the cabin was slow and hazardous. A light sleet had begun falling and a thin glaze of ice was coating the road. At the Hays Ridge turn-off Marianna interrupted what had been twenty minutes of total silence. "It's unfair, isn't it? she said morosely.

"What's unfair?"

"Life - how much your mother wanted to live it - how young and beautiful she was. That's what's so unfair...that someone like her has to die when there are so many other people to whom life is less important."

Clay took his eyes off the road and closed them for a second. "I'd rather not talk about it right now," he said, and he started taking deep breaths to help fight off a deepening sense of despair..

They drove another five miles in silence, and then she asked him, "do you think you'll be safe at the funeral tomorrow?"

"I don't know"

"Do you think we should go then?"

"I have to go. But I've decided one thing. You're not going."

She sat straight up and burst out laughing. "Oh, you're funny! Very funny. You don't think I've come this far to let you go without me, do you?"

"If it risked leaving Cody and Cody without a mother...yes. They're more important than the funeral, Marianna. If the FBI has tracked me here, you could be arrested as an accomplice. And if we're arrested, Howie and Nicholson will learn about it. After what happened to Whitney, I'm not sure we'd be safe, even in jail. So I forbid you to go."

Forbid. A word no one except her father had ever said to her. She did not say anything. She looked at him and she could tell by the look on his face that he was deadly serious. She slid away from him, across the seat and against the door, her mind in disarray. She huddled up and started to cry softly. He was right, she knew. Her first duty was to the twins. She shook her head. "You know," she said at last, "everything you ever wanted me to do, I did. Are you sure you don't want me to come?"

"I'm sure," he said.

They were startled when they walked into the cabin. Its main room was rigged with camera lights giving it the look of a movie studio and the flames in the fireplace made the lights seem to flicker. Everyone was working. Robert was lying on the sofa, scribbling on a yellow pad of paper with at least twenty wadded up pages lying on the floor beside him. MacInnis was pounding the typewriter at the dining table with bank dossiers and account statements scattered all about. Smith and his crew were in the bedroom with the lights off. They were editing and splicing a film clip they had shot while Marianna and Clay were gone. When they saw Marianna and Clay come in, they stopped, poured themselves a drink, and sat down in front of the fireplace. Marianna told them about the warning Clay had received from Rat about the strangers in town. Larry Smith's reaction was swift and intense. "I think we should haul ass out of here right now!" he exclaimed in a strident tone of voice. "We need you on that program tomorrow night. Not locked up in jail somewhere."

Clay reminded Larry that he was staying for the funeral no matter what, when, all of a sudden, his pilot trained ears heard the faint sound of a car engine sputter and die, and the funeral quickly became the farthest thing from his mind. Concealing his alarm, he stood up casually and strode over to the gun rack, unlocked it, and took out his dad's two Browning semi-automatic twelve gauge shotguns. He inserted several shells in each gun, double zero magnums, and then he turned and faced the group. "Someone's outside," he whispered, pressing his index finger to his lips. Six faces turned ash white in a split second. "Turn down the lights and act like everything is normal. Robert, take this," he said as he flipped Robert one of the guns. "Take Marianna and go hide in the bedroom." MacInnis started to protest. "Just keep calm," Clay said. "You're hunters and you rented this place. You're just down here on a hunting trip." He switched off the overhead lights. Thirty seconds later they heard a knock at the door.

"Hullo! Sheriff Hawkins here...Clay! I know you're in there, old buddy. So open up and let me in."

Clay nodded to Larry Smith, and then he stepped into the bunkroom behind the door. Gingerly, Smith opened the cabin door, and Hogjaw Hawkins swaggered in, scowling, his revolver still holstered. He looked around the room, and his jowls started to quiver. "Whar's Stoner?" he growled.

"Who? I don't know what you're talking about," Larry Smith said, talking fast, sounding very east-coastish. "We're just down here on a hunting trip - renting this place for the weekend."

"Hunters!" Hogjaw bellowed, as he thrust his giant jaw into Smith's face and caused him to stagger backwards three steps. "Don't give me that horse puckey! I just talked to Cindy Sue Collins at the funeral parlor, and she told me Stoner was on the way up here. And there's a rented Impala parked outside. Engine's still warm. Now whar is he? Clay! You can come on out now!"

Clay's mind was a scramble. Was Hogjaw alone? Or did he bring others along with him? He might as well find out sooner rather than later, he thought. He stepped out into the main room. "Anyone with you, Hogjaw?" he said as he leveled the Browning semi-automatic at Hogjaw's hulking waistline.

Hogjaw started to stutter. "N-n-nobody. N-now you listen here, Clay. You put that gun down. Ah've gotta take yuh in, and ah-ah don't want no trouble."

"Take me in for what?"

"Tim Collins called me before I talked to Cindy Sue. He told me you were in town and that he'd checked with the FBI about you. He told me they said you were still wanted and that they'd be comin' here tomorra to pick yuh up. He said it was mah duty to try to find yuh and hold yuh 'til they git here."

"And you're here all by yourself to do that? You sure they're not already here and waiting outside?"

"Nope. This is just between me and yuh tonight, Clay. Gotta take yuh in. So come on."

Clay looked at him real hard and decided he believed the old cuss. Hogjaw was too dumb to fool him with an answer to the same question twice. He lowered the shot gun. "Hogjaw, let me introduce you to everyone," he said as he walked over, placed an arm around one of Hogjaw's massive shoulders and guided him toward the sofa. "This is Ian MacInnis, who you may have never heard of, but he's a famous journalist, two-time Pulitzer prize winner and a senior managing editor of the New York Times. And this here is Larry Smith, CBS's Washington correspondent. You probably have seen him on the national news." Marianna had slipped quietly out of the bedroom by then. She walked over and handed Hogjaw a cup of coffee and smiled. "I don't know how much you're into music," Clay said, "but this is Kira Chastain, lead singer of 'Kira and the Band.'"

Hogjaw's mouth gaped open at least six inches, and he started stuttering again. "Ah-ah've seen both y'all on teevee. Wh-what are y'all doin' here in Creekwood?" he managed to say.

"Let's sit down and I'll tell you all about it," Clay said warmly. They sat down, and with a flair of dramatics, Clay launched into his story. "Hogjaw, you've stumbled into something that even the FBI doesn't know about. We'll let you in on a top secret...my court martial and escape...it was all faked so I could go underground and counterspy for the CIA. All of us here...we're all working with the CIA now."

Hogjaw's huge tongue hung dog-like from the corner of his mouth. "Well, ah'll be damn! The CIA!"

"That's right," Clay said. "And right now we need your help. I'm supposed to make contact with a KGB agent at my mother's funeral tomorrow. You've gotta hold the FBI off until after that. It's a national security thing, and if the FBI comes crashing into the middle of it, all the CIA's effort will go down the drain."

Hogjaw frowned and his eyebrows knitted together. His mind wheels were spinning. "Got any 'dentification?" he mumbled after a moment.

Larry Smith, having recovered from his initial surprise, picked up on Clay's charade and was the first to react. He flipped his business card on the table. "None of us carry CIA identification. Too dangerous. But here's my telephone number in Washington. Call it anytime. The office will verify I'm on a CIA mission." Hogjaw relaxed. He had one more cup of coffee, hoisted himself from his chair, slapped on his white stetson, shook hands all around, and told Clay he would see him at the funeral. After telling everyone "you can count on me," he sauntered out of the cabin, swaggering proudly with the satisfaction that he, Hogjaw Hawkins, sheriff of Creekwood County, was now sharing one of the nation's innermost secrets with the CIA.

XIV

⌇

SEASHELLS

The seven of them stood looking at each other without moving. For two minutes the only sound in the cabin was that of the fire crackling, and then they heard Hogjaw's car engine turn over and its rumble fade away down the trail."

"Jeezus! That was close!" Smith blurted out as the woods once again became silent. He turned to his crew. "One of you guys hike down to the lodge right now and call the office. Make sure we have someone there to confirm our story if that bozo calls. And don't think we're home free," he warned the rest of them, having already made the transition from Hogjaw to business at hand. "We still have the FBI problem, Clay. What if they do show up at the funeral tomorrow? I'm not very confident I'd trust your friend, Hogjaw, to be able to hold them off. I think you're crazy if you go."

Clay shrugged. "I have to," he said, stone faced.

Smith became very upset. "What about you, Marianna? You're coming with me, aren't you?"

"I'm sorry. I'm not leaving Clay."

Smith's face flushed in frustration. "Damn!" he shouted, and he pounded his fist on the table.

Robert chimed in with a suggestion. "Your charter plane is not scheduled to leave St. Louis until two tomorrow," he said to Smith. "The funeral will be over by twelve-thirty. If Clay can get that Petey fellow to fly us up right after the funeral, we can all make it."

"I can't risk it," Smith said emphatically. "It's supposed to snow tomorrow."

"All right, then," Robert said. "Since Marianna is not going to the funeral, I'll stay here with her and drive her out to the airstrip.

If Clay doesn't show up by one o'clock, we'll assume he's been arrested and take off without him. We can be in St. Louis by two."

"I don't like it," Marianna said. "I'm not sure I trust that Petey."

Smith intervened. "I'll call Petey about the charter and tell him it's for me, the same guy he flew down this afternoon. "Robert, you park on the blacktop outside the gate to the airstrip until Clay gets there. That way Petey won't know who his customers are until you're all ready to go. I'll promise him a big bonus for getting to St. Louis on time."

"That sounds like a reasonable plan to me," Clay said. "I hope you agree, Marianna."

She hesitated, looked into some steely eyes, and said, "Do I have a choice? Okay."

Smith relaxed. "Great! Now let's get to work." His cameramen doused the lights and started running the tape Smith had filmed earlier. Marianna and Clay sat down on the sofa and watched. The film began with Smith standing in front of the stone fireplace. In the background they could see a fire burning and the mounted head of the ten-point buck over the mantle. Smith's delivery was poignant.

"People of America," he began, "this is Larry Smith reporting to you from a remote cabin on a lake down in the wilderness of the Missouri Ozarks near a small town called Creekwood. This story is going to describe to you - the American public - one of the most disturbing stories this journalist has witnessed in more than twenty-five years of covering the news - a story beyond belief - a story about pervasive corruption that exists in the highest levels of our government. Telling it in his own words is quite an unusual young man, a product of the Ozarks, the son of a garage mechanic, an Annapolis graduate, a navy pilot, a young man whose beautiful mother, still in her forties, was buried in Creekwood today. I first met this man about five years ago when I covered his court mar- tial - an event that resulted in him becoming the first officer in this country to be convicted and sentenced to prison because he refused to drop bombs on Vietnam and stood up against what he consid- ered to be, in his own words, 'a stupid war'. In these past two days, under most unusual circumstances, our paths have crossed again. And during this very short time I feel I've gotten to know him. In a few moments you will learn how, after fleeing this country to avoid incarceration, he stumbled upon evidence that indicts the very system that convicted him. His name is Clay Stoner, and he is not your common criminal. By tomorrow I expect his name will be well known...But this is not just the story of Clay Stoner. Or just another tale of petty corruption. It is much more than that. It is also a story about a young man and a woman whose love for each other and this country has caused them to come back to it now after five years in exile, and yes, risk their freedom to reveal what you are about to hear tonight. The woman is Marianna Haizet, and this is every bit as much her story as it is Clay Stoner's. She is the mother of their two children and becoming quite a noted personality in her own right. I know the name Marianna Haizet means nothing to most of you. But for those of you who have heard of Kira Chastain of 'Kira and the Band', whose recording of 'Tower in the Sky' is at this very moment the number one selling record in America, that Kira is a stage name. In reality, Kira is Marianna Haizet. So at this time, people of America, allow me to introduce you to Clay Stoner and Marianna Haizet - or Kira, if you prefer."

Smith flipped on the lights. "Well, what do you think?" he asked anxiously.

"I never saw anyone sling so much bullshit in my life," Marianna said, and Smith broke into a smile.

"It must have sounded good, then," he beamed. "That makes one reel that's a wrap. So come on. We've got a long night ahead."

For the next two hours Smith and his crew worked with Clay and Marianna. They filmed Clay three times sitting at a table in front of the fireplace narrating the chain of events that had led to his decision to abscond with Utopia's books and records and, because of Whitney's death, go public with them instead of turning them over to the government. Marianna sat beside him, adding a few words of her own, and each time the narrative ended she stood up, and as the camera zoomed in on her face, she walked over to the gun rack and started lip-synching the words of *Tower in the Sky* while Smith's audio man played the tape in the background. Smith was satisfied, finally, and at two o'clock Marianna and Clay tottered off to the bedroom and collapsed, exhausted, into the cabin's only double bed.

Clay fell asleep instantly, a habit developed during his years as a pilot, even though he knew he might be arrested at the funeral, and despite the noise in the main room where Smith and Robert and MacInnis were busy rearranging things, typing and editing, and working on the next day's script. He had learned long before that there was no point fretting about something out of his control and that a good night's sleep was the best way to prepare for a day ahead that might be harrowing. The effect on Marianna was just the opposite. She tossed fitfully for hours, nervous and frightened. Tomorrow she and Clay would emerge from the underground. It would mark the end of their life together as they had known it, she knew. They were going on national television and taking on the system. One slight misstep, one miscalculation, and the system and all its power would destroy them, just gobble them up and spit them out like black chaws of tobacco. She was convinced of that. She looked at Clay's face, shadowed in the light from underneath the door, the way his mouth went, the curve of his cheekbones, the way his hair grew around his ear and on his neck, and she marveled at the way he was able to sleep so peacefully. She nodded off, finally, and fell asleep with her hand on his chest.

Clay awakened with the first glimmer of dawn. Marianna's side of the bed was empty, and the enticing smell of bacon frying permeated the cabin air. He slipped into a pair of jeans and a white turtleneck and walked into the main room of the cabin. He was the last one up. MacInnis and Smith and his crew were sitting at the dining table, looking sleepy, quietly drinking coffee. Marianna was at the stove, brewing another pot and scrambling some eggs. Robert was helping. "That goddamn Impala Marianna rented has a flat," Robert grumbled. "Just a nail, but the spare's flat too."

Clay sat down at the table, and Marianna poured him a cup of coffee. "We want to start the shooting early," Smith grunted. "I'd like us to be on our way to St. Louis before ten o'clock. It looks like it's going to snow soon." Marianna looked out the window. The morning was grey and misty, the temperature hovering around freezing. Perfect weather, she thought, for lying indoors in front of a fire.

They finished breakfast hurriedly and went outside. Like most of the other cabins around, the Stoner family cabin was perched on a steep hill that rose up two hundred feet from the edge of the lake. That was the kind of lake it was. No flat ground along the shore, just hills that rose straight up. The boathouse was also on top of the hill, a few yards in back of and below the cabin. Leading out of it was a little train track that carried people and boats on a dolly - much in the same fashion as a San Francisco cable car - up and down the hill very slowly between the boathouse and the dock. For the next hour Smith and his crew shot footage of Marianna and Clay in the outdoors; riding down the hill huddled together on the dolly, the two of them dressed identically in jeans, white turtlenecks, and two of Clay's old brown leather flying jackets with the fur collars turned up; walking through the woods holding hands; skipping rocks on the lake; sitting on the boat dock, knees tucked under their chins, their arms wrapped around their ankles, laughing and talking; and finally, a shot of Marianna lying down with her head in Clay's lap, looking up at him lovingly, the audioman adding a few bars of *Tower* in the background. "All right, that's the final wrap," Smith announced. The filming was finished at nine-thirty. Smith's crew started packing their gear on the dolly. When they were ready to leave, Smith walked over to Marianna and Clay. For the first time since he had arrived in Creekwood he was not his usual cocky self. Marianna could see it in his face. He was genuinely concerned. He tugged on his ear and fidgeted, and then he lowered his eyes and said, "sure you don't want to come with us?"

Marianna placed both of her hands on his shoulders and leaned into him and kissed his cheek. "We'll see you in St. Louis", she said very tenderly. "Not later than two." Smith didn't say anything more. He looked at her for a moment, and then at Clay before he turned and walked over to the dolly and climbed aboard. MacInnis was next. He shook Clay's hand and hugged Marianna, and then joined Smith and his crew. Robert accompanied them, on his way into Hays Ridge to be dropped off at the Texaco Station to get the flat tire repaired. Marianna and Clay stood on the dock, watching and waving as the dolly jolted its way up the track. Robert kept waving back at them until the dolly disappeared under the trees and out of sight.

Marianna and Clay sat down on the dock, leaning against each other, and stared out across the lake. The lake was quiet and still now, looming cold and harsh-looking out of the mist. It was very different from the lake Clay had known so well, the one of summer and bright lazy days when the distant hum of motorboats, the splattering flap of fish jumping, and the occasional sounds of music and laughter could be heard from the cabins on the tops of the hills. "Someday..." he started to say and stopped.

Marianna nestled up against him, warming away the morning chill. "Look over there," she said, pointing toward the east side of the lake. Clay looked, and his eyes searched the shoreline. He saw nothing but grey clouds and trees. "You know," she said at last, "if you looked just above those trees, and if you could see through the clouds, I'll bet just on the other side of those hills you could see a sunrise...Still friends forever?" she asked impishly. He smiled and nodded and draped his arm around her, and they both sat there on the dock, staring across the lake into the grey cloud of mist that shrouded the top of the tree line. She nudged him after awhile. "Robert won't be back with the tire for at least an hour. Let's go make out," she said softly, lovingly.

They climbed aboard the dolly and gazed out at the lake and did not say anything as it lurched slowly up the hill. The cabin was cold as ice. The fire was out, and Clay started another. Marianna was already under the covers when he strode into the bedroom. He switched the lights off, undressed, and slid in beside her. In the darkness he found her and kissed her, and she felt the texture of his lips. She was in a mellow mood and not prepared for the way he swarmed over her then with a flurry of kisses. And until she reached the early stages of orgasm and every thought whisked suddenly from her mind, she kept thinking how this was like the old days, the first few times with Clay when they had made love in such a desperate way...as if each time might be the last.

Clay eased out of bed at eleven o'clock. He put on his only black suit and packed his suitcase. Marianna was still lying in the bed, naked, covered only with a sheet despite the frost in the air. He knelt down beside the bed and kissed her once again lightly on each eyelid. "Here are the keys to the Impala. The service station guy should have Robert back with the tire soon. I'll see you at Petey's before one o'clock."

She stroked his cheek. "Take care fella'," she said with a contented, sexually satisfied, warm loving look.

He walked quickly to the door and outside into the clearing. He looked back at the cabin. It looked small and deserted - three rooms of stone and logs that blended into the woods. As soon as Marianna left it would stay locked up again until springtime. He wondered if his dad would come up here even then. He turned and started walking down the road to the lodge. One of the owner's sons, his old fishing buddy, would be there he knew, and would drive him into town.

The drive took half an hour. The lodge owner's son dropped Clay off behind the chapel just a few minutes before eleven. He entered unobtrusively through a side door and was ushered to a special pew to the left of the altar. His father was already there. Clay looked around for a minute before he sat down, and he saw that the chapel was jammed with people. Thornton had opened up the balcony, and it was full, and downstairs at least fifty people were standing in the entranceway behind the pews. He stood there for awhile with mixed emotions. The view of everyone who had turned out to show their respect for his mother flooded him with a great sense of feeling. But what was that feeling? He had learned New Year's Eve that he was a stranger in Creekwood now, as alien to it as Muslims are to Jews. This was not his town anymore. Still, all these people had come to the funeral, and there was something to say for that. *Who was going to show up when he died?*

At a respectable five minutes after eleven, the minister started the eulogy. He was a Southern Baptist minister, and he began in the same manner as most eulogies. He cited numerous examples of Lara's performance in the role of beloved wife and devoted mother. He mentioned the bereaved husband, the grief-stricken son, the town full of her friends whose lives would always be missing something now that she was gone. And then he talked about how she had faced up to her death with a courage that could only have been made possible by God. Clay's skin started squirming. What is this bullshit, he thought? Does this guy have any idea what my mother went through before she died? He was becoming agitated until he looked around. He saw tears gleaming from a hundred pairs of eyes, and he quivered. He bit his lip to stem his own tears and turned back around to concentrate on the minister. And the man redeemed himself then. He announced that he was going to read a final passage that he had specially prepared for Lara Stoner, and when he recited it, his eloquence made all the rest of the ritual seem inconsequential. "We shall be stricken by Lara Stoner's memory sometimes," the minister orated with a majestic wave of his hand, "and the old affections shall rush back on us as vivid as the time when she was our daily talk, when her presence gladdened our eyes and her voice thrilled our ears. Death is but a parting only as this life is concerned. A passion like Lara Stoner comes to an end and is carried off in a coffin. She drops out of our lives one way or another, and the earth clods close over her and we see her no more. But as all of us here today know, Lara Stoner has been a part of our souls...and she is eternal."

The entire ceremony lasted less than thirty minutes. When it was over, Clay stood up to embrace his father. In the middle of the embrace the side door opened suddenly, and he flinched. He turned, fully expecting to see FBI agents walking in with handcuffs to take him away. Instead, it was the pallbearers, friends of his father's. They proceeded to the altar and in less than a minute hoisted the coffin out through the door to the hearse waiting in the driveway. Clay and his father were ushered out right after them and into a limousine behind the hearse, and in almost no-time, the procession was underway. Directly in front of the hearse, leading the procession, was Hogjaw Hawkins, dutifully dedicated and proud in his new sheriff's car with its red light rotating. At least eighty automobiles and a scattering of pick-up trucks with their lights all shining started meandering their way out of town. Their destination was the Stoner family plot, three hundred square feet in the Creekwood cemetery where Bill Stoner's parents and grandparents already lay buried. And as the procession began, the snow that had been threatening all morning started to fall. The flakes came down crisp and gentle at first. But they were large, and they began rapidly covering the ground, and by the time the procession reached the cemetery, the snow had become a horizontal deluge. A small, awning-like tent had been erected over the gravesite. There was room for fifteen metal folding chairs under it; not nearly enough room to shelter the crowd that had gathered. Most of them stood out in the elements, getting soaked, and as a result, the graveside ceremony was brief. As soon as the coffin was lowered and the end of the rite signaled by the minister's familiar 'ashes to ashes and dust to dust', the crowd started to scatter. Only a group of about thirty close family and friends remained under the tent to offer Clay and his dad their last condolences. One was Lara's older cousin, a dirt farmer from southern Arkansas who had gotten up at four o'clock in the morning and driven three hundred miles just to be there one hour for the funeral. He was leaving to drive straight back now. Clay had never met him, but he was the mourner who touched him most. He was still thinking about the man - the humble way he had come up to say how much he had cared about Lara - when he felt a tug at his sleeve. He turned to look and saw Rat staring at him. Rat's clothes were soaked and his hair was plastered down. "Oh... hi, Rat. Thanks for coming," Clay said warmly.

Rat shook his head vigorously from side to side like a dog does when it's wet. "Y'know those guys I told yuh 'bout last night?" he gulped and whispered excitedly, blinking the water out of his eyes. "Two of 'em are right over there!" Clay looked in the direction Rat nodded. Thirty yards away, partially sheltered under a large oak tree, two strangers wearing dark hats and long black raincoats were standing with their hands in their pockets, watching as if they were waiting for the crowd under the awning to disband. Clay's eyes glinted. The good old FBI, he thought, handling things with class, waiting for the funeral to break up before they busted him. Clay's eyes glinted again, and something in his brain ticked. He stared hard at the two men for a few seconds. The man on the right stepped out from behind the oak tree then, his left ankle twisting with an awkward limp. Clay felt a shiver. He had seen that man before. Where was it? *Amsterdam*...Nicholson's bodyguard!

Clay pushed his way through the crowd to his father and grasped both his shoulders. "I'm sorry, dad, but I'm going to have to leave again right now. I'll try to explain later." Without waiting for an answer, he started walking with a group of departing mourners toward the gate leading out of the cemetery. He tried to appear natural. But when he glanced over his shoulder, the two men were walking fast, even the one with limp, gaining on him, and when their eyes met, all pretenses were dropped. Clay saw Hogjaw Hawkins standing in the middle of the highway just outside the gate, directing traffic. His patrol car was parked behind him, engine running and blocking one lane as a long line of traffic waited to exit the cemetery. Clay wondered for a brief moment how Hogjaw might do stacked up against two professional hit men. The thought was ludicrous. He started running toward Hogjaw's car. "Come on Hogjaw!" he shouted. Hogjaw turned and looked at him in a queer sort of way as Clay ran past and motioned toward the patrol car. "Come on! It's the KGB! They're trying to kill me!" Clay shouted again as he ran and leaped in the driver's side of the car. He pulled forward ten feet and waited for Hogjaw to lumber in the passenger side, and then he spun gravel and swiftly accelerated away. As he did, he looked over his shoulder. The two gunmen were running in the opposite direction. They were running toward a dark blue Oldsmobile.

Clay hit eighty miles an hour heading out of town, and after he turned onto the blacktop, Dogtrot Road, he upped it to a hundred. The Oldsmobile was nowhere in sight but Clay guessed they would head straight for the airstrip as soon as they got their car free of the cemetery traffic. He explained that fact to Hogjaw, and Hogjaw never questioned him. He just got that grim, stupid look of determination on his face like he used to get in the football huddle before each play. He reached down and removed the riot gun from its case on the inside of the right front door, cocked it open, and inserted two double-zero magnums. He sat there, rigid, with the gun across his lap as they turned off the road and sped through the gate to Petey's house trailer. The King Air was parked on the taxi apron and looked ready to go. No one was in sight. Clay honked. In a few seconds Petey and Terry Malone stepped out of the trailer with beers in their hands, walked a few steps toward the car and stopped. "Come on in and have a beer!" Petey shouted, waving his arm.

"No time!" Clay shouted back. "Where are the other passengers?"

"Not here yet! Come on in!"

"That goddamned flat tire," Clay muttered as Hogjaw opened his door and stepped out of the patrol car. Clay backed it up - and he saw the silver-grey Impala then, jutting out from behind the trailer. What had Rat said...*four of them.* He had only seen two at the cemetery! "Hogjaw! Get back!" he screamed frantically.

Hogjaw crouched over and turned just as two heavy-set men came charging out the front door of Petey's trailer blazing away with Uzi automatic sub-machine guns. The air exploded and window glass shattered in a thousand pieces. Petey and Terry were cut down in an instant, and Hogjaw flew backwards against the side of the patrol car. A split second later Clay felt a burning stab as a slug ripped through the flesh of his arm. He slid down below the dashboard and stared at Hogjaw. Hogjaw was lying half in and half out of the car. His shirt was ripped with holes and a sweat was already popping out on his forehead. He tugged his revolver out of his holster and handed it to Clay. A brief look passed between them, and then, as if on cue, they both rose firing just as the machine gunners charged up to the car. Hogjaw caught the one on his side with both blasts of the riot gun from ten feet. It blew the brains out the back of his head. Clay threw open the door on his side and rolled out onto the ground, catching the other gunman by surprise. The gunman got his burst off first, but he was shooting on the run and missed. Clay took careful aim and plugged him with two well placed shots in the gut, and the gunman went down with his Uzi still firing, blasting holes in the ground. Clay scrambled to his feet and ran forward and shot him twice in the head to make sure he was dead. He stumbled back to the car and collapsed to his knees in a puddle of red snow beside Hogjaw. Marianna and Robert burst out of the trailer then, and came running. She threw her arms around Clay, sobbing hysterically, and when she squeezed him, the pain in his arm nearly blacked him out. He shook her off. "Help Hogjaw," he moaned.

They tried to comfort Hogjaw. He was still alive. But from the way he was urinating and excreting out of control, Clay knew his life span was limited to a matter of minutes. They hovered over him, and Hogjaw began to mumble. "We showed 'em, didn't we ole buddy," he groaned. "KGB'll learn they can't fuck...they can't fuck with Creekwood, huh?" He forced a puny grin that quickly faded. "Stoner ole buddy...ole buddy..." His eyes closed and his head collapsed to one side. Clay looked around. Petey was obviously dead, but Terry was crawling toward them on the ground. Both his legs were shattered, but his upper body looked intact.

"Why'd you do it Terry?" Clay screamed.

"I'm sorry man," Terry groaned. "Tim Collins said they were FBI. I didn't know they wanted to kill you until your friend Marianna showed up. They got the drop on us. Intended to kill us all. No witnesses that way. I guess...I guess I just screwed up and fumbled the ole ball one last time." He coughed and faded into unconsciousness. Clay felt for a pulse. There was none.

"Car's coming!" Marianna shouted suddenly.

Clay looked down Dogtrot Road and saw the blue Oldsmobile racing toward the airstrip. "That's the other two! Quick! To the plane!" he yelled.

They ran for the King Air and scrambled aboard. Clay eased himself gingerly into the pilot's seat and fumbled with the controls, cursing each unfamiliar switch and knob until he figured out how to get the engines started. He had them purring in a matter of seconds and they started taxiing just as the Oldsmobile drove through the front gate. Clay taxied as fast as he dared, and without slowing to check the magnetos or wait for the cylinder head and oil temperatures to warm, he swung the aircraft onto the runway and rammed the throttle all the way forward. The Oldsmobile pulled alongside at the same instant. Clay heard the crack-crack of Uzis again, and the zing of a slug whizzing through the cockpit as the King Air gained speed and started pulling away. At ninety knots he hauled the plane off the ground and into a whirling snow. Seconds later it was enveloped in a solid blanket of white. Clay glued his eyes on the instrument panel and relied on instincts honed from thousands of hours in the air to fight off the searing pain in his left arm that caused the gauges in front of him to become a blur. As the King Air passed through five hundred feet, he turned on the automatic direction finder and set the aircraft on a heading toward

St. Louis. He leaned back then, wincing in pain, and turned toward Marianna who was in the front seat beside him.

Her head was tilted at a jagged angle, and her mouth was wrenched open, trembling in agony. "I'm hit," she moaned softly, and she slumped over in his lap. He glanced down and saw a spreading red stain under her armpit where a bullet had punctured her chest.

"Oh God!" he cried out, and tears started instantly flooding his eyes. He felt his head swimming. The wound looked bad. He tried to lift her head up. As he did, he sensed an engine shudder. He glanced up to see an oil pressure gauge falling rapidly to zero. He looked out at the starboard engine. It was laced with bullet holes, and oil was pumping out of it like spray from a split in a garden hose. "Help Marianna! She's been hit!" he cried out to Robert in the back. He called on his instincts again. He had to forget about Marianna and fight the controls until he had the engine shut down and feathered and the plane trimmed to maintain a reasonable semblance of level flight. The next forty-five minutes were chaos. Marianna lay with her head in his lap, her wound spurting blood while Clay wrestled one-handed with the plane. Robert took off his jacket and shirt and stuffed the shirt under her arm to try to plug the bleeding. It stemmed it very little.

She started drifting from one delirium to another. In one of her conscious moments she made a feeble attempt at humor. "You must say one thing, Clay Stoner," she said with her squirrel-look smile, "it sure has been tense." She coughed as she said it. Blood gurgled out of her mouth and down her chin. Her eyes closed, and she went out again.

Clay had his hands full. He radioed St. Louis Approach Control and requested a straight-in radar vectored approach.

"Aircraft calling St. Louis Approach, be advised that St. Louis is below minimums for landing," a controller's voice replied calmly and professionally.

"Then I'm declaring an emergency! Now give me an approach," Clay yelled back at him.

"I'm sorry. We do not have you on flight plan, and I repeat, the St. Louis airport is closed. I can give you a clearance to Chicago."

"Listen you idiot!" Clay screamed into the mike. "I said this is an emergency! I've got one engine out. I've been shot. I've have a passenger dying in my lap. Now you better clear the goddamn runway because I'm *comin' in* whether you like it or not!"

The controller jolted into action. "Roger. Understand emergency," he replied. "Switch to one-twenty-six decimal-two and contact radar for a final approach into runway two-niner now...And good luck, sir."

Clay switched to the final approach frequency and looked down at Marianna. He took his good arm off the controls for a moment and stroked her hair. Her forehead was hot, and he could feel her shaking. "We're gonna make it fella'. Hang in. We're gonna make it," he said, shaking her roughly.

She looked up at him and smiled weakly. "Let's don't start lying to each other now," she said, and she rolled her head from side to side.

He was unable to answer her. The final controller began spouting instructions over the radio just then, and as he lowered the landing gear the aircraft hit a wall of turbulence. Clay began fighting for their lives. The ceiling was zero. The crosswind component was thirty knots. He started sweating and talking to himself. He was going to land this sucker on one engine with one arm no matter what. At four hundred feet he felt a tug at his sleeve and heard Marianna whisper, "we always said no commitments, remember? But now I'm asking for one. Take...care of...Cassie and Cody for me...will ya' fella'?" He was too busy to look at her. The King Air popped out of the overcast less than five seconds before its wheels touched the runway, and as it rolled out, Clay felt a surge of relief. He glanced down at Marianna. She was snuggled in his lap, looking peaceful... innocent...still; the same way she had looked that day asleep in the car with the Norwegians - that day they had hitchhiked in the rain to Nice together. He taxied rapidly to the terminal and cut the engine.

An ambulance was waiting. Within two minutes they were in it, racing toward a hospital. A paramedic rode with them in the back. He felt Marianna's pulse, pounded on her chest, blew in her mouth, lifted her eyelids. After five minutes he turned to Clay and said, "I think she's gone."

The words crested and smashed down on him like a tidal wave. He closed his eyes and started to cry out. He wanted to scream, to swing out and smash something. Instead, as the initial wave subsided the world went blank; and he slumped over sideways and passed out.

He heard the faint sound of a door opening and someone stirring in the room. He opened his eyes and looked into a haze. He saw Robert walking toward him and a nurse walk out of the room and close the door. He was in a hospital. He could tell by the smell.

"How do you feel?" Robert said quietly.

"All right...I think."

"You lost a lot of blood and went into shock. But it's just a flesh wound. The doctors say you'll be all right by tomorrow."

"Marianna's dead, isn't she?"

"Yes."

Clay took a long deep breath and shuddered. "I'm sorry Robert. It's my fault for getting her involved."

"You couldn't have stopped her." Robert said, and his voice cracked.

"Yes I could. She told me it was stupid."

"Don't say that. Please, don't say that, Clay. Smith and MacInnis should be in New York by now. The story will be all over the country in a little while. Marianna wanted that as much as you did."

Clay looked at Robert and saw a mixture of pain and hope in his eyes. "What time is it?" he said.

"Six o'clock. You've been out almost four hours."

"That's seven o'clock in New York. Turn on the television. The program should be on soon."

Robert reached over and flicked on the television. It came on in the middle of a skin cream commercial. At the end of the commercial a message flashed on the screen, and a voice from the station announced the interruption of normal programming because of an upcoming special broadcast. The message faded out, and Larry Smith appeared. He was standing in front of the cabin's stone fireplace underneath the buck's head over the mantle. It was the first tape he had filmed last night, and Clay watched and listened to every word as it began. "People of America, this is Larry Smith reporting from a remote cabin on a lake down in the wilderness of the Missouri Ozarks near a small town called Creekwood..."

Clay lay his head back on his pillow and stared bleakly at the ceiling, not listening anymore. Why did I do it, he thought? Marianna said we couldn't change the system. She was right, and it all seems so unimportant now. People don't care about knowing what's wrong. They prefer believing in lies if lies are what make them feel good. Sort of like religion. Like Creekwood. People don't want to hear about other people's problems. They don't give a damn really. When it gets right down to it, people are really only out for themselves.

Clay heard Smith's tape reaching the end of his introduction, and his interest perked again. He rolled over to watch as Smith said, "at this time people of America, allow me to introduce you to Clay Stoner and Marianna Haizet – or Kira, if you prefer." Clay sat up, waiting anxiously for Marianna's face to come on the screen. Instead, there was no more tape, just Larry Smith sitting behind a desk in CBS's New York studio, live, looking as if he had just witnessed an execution. Smith started talking, not in his usual rich, smooth baritone, but in a voice that was strident, broken, and out of control. "You have just watched one small reel of a film made last night in Creekwood, Missouri," he said emotionally. "The story we intended to broadcast next on this program is so epic in proportion that seven people were gunned down just a few hours ago for the sole purpose of preventing its release. Six of them are dead. One of those is Marianna Haizet. She died from a gunshot wound about three o'clock eastern standard time this afternoon in...in an ambulance on her way...on her way to a hospital in St. Louis." Smith's voice was choking. His eyes had grown red and glossed over. He continued, struggling with every word. "Clay Stoner has survived. He's in a hospital in St. Louis, now, where I left him about three hours ago. The doctors say he will live. I...I know Clay would want this program to go on. I'm sure he's watching, waiting for all of you to learn what he knows. But Clay...Clay...the rest of the story cannot be told tonight." Smith looked straight at the camera. Tears were rolling down his cheeks. He wiped them away and the anguish in his voice was evident to everyone watching as he composed himself. "Ladies and gentlemen," he said, "an hour ago my camera crew and I, along with Ian MacInnis of the New York Times, were met by the FBI when we landed at Teterboro Airport. Only God knows how they knew we were going to be there. They seized most of our film, but we managed to sneak two small reels past them, one of which you just saw. All of our documents and records, however...all of the evidence necessary to prove the story we were going to broadcast to you tonight, was confiscated by the FBI. At the same time we were served with a restraining order from a federal judge that prohibits us - temporarily, we hope - from publicly broadcasting or publishing anything relating to the accusations contained in this story. CBS wants you to know, as does the Times, that this has never happened in the history of this network, or the paper, and that we will do everything in our power to bring this story to you sometime in the future. But we have no choice tonight except to cut

this program short. I would like to end it with a few minutes of a
second short reel of film we shot this morning that my cameraman
slipped through Teterboro in a fishing tackle box. Since it contains
no evidence or accusations pertaining to anyone, our lawyers do
not feel that it violates the restraining order. So Clay, if you are listening - and Marianna, wherever you are - God bless."

The next voice Clay heard was Marianna singing *Tower in the
Sky*. He looked dazedly at the television. She was lying in his arms
on the boat dock, the words of her song echoing softly in the background. He watched, benumbed, and when he heard her cool voice
sing "*farewell to you and the youth I spent with you,*" he shuddered and
fell back on the bed. Robert came over and sat down next to him,
crying.

What now, he thought? Life goes on. But what's it all about.
First you live. Then you die - with little justification as to who goes
first, or how. Chuck was snuffed out in his prime, along with Patsy
Foster. Jimmer. Vic and Sammy. Whitney. Hogjaw. Petey, Terry...
For all practical purposes, even Slim Sparks. And my mother. She
was too young to deserve it...Now Marianna. When she died, I died
too...except life will go on. He lifted himself out of bed, his left
arm heavily bandaged, and walked slowly to the closet. He started
dressing. Robert looked at him queerly. "What do you think you're
doing?" he asked.

"I'm leaving. Tell your parents I'm sorry, Robert. Tell them I
loved Marianna more than life. I hope that means something to
them. But it's not safe for me here. Not as long as the Nicholsons
and Nussbaums and the Tim Collins' are still out there. Maybe
Smith and MacInnis will prevail and put them and their ilk out of
business. I hope so, but that's no longer my affair. Right now, it's
down the back stairs. Goodbye my friend...and my almost brother-
in-law."

Robert smiled weakly. "Where will you go?" he asked, still, devastated by the death of his sister and not fully comprehending what
was happening.

"To get Cassie and Cody." And then, he thought, I'm going to
take them far, far away where no one knows us, where no one will
ever find us. To an island...one with pink powdery sand and palm
trees and coconuts and air that tastes of salt and a sun that always
shines. And we will spend our days together collecting seashells...
and I'll never, ever, go home again.